THE
CHALET
Series

THE TOYMAKER

authorHOUSE®

AuthorHouse™
1663 Liberty Drive
Bloomington, IN 47403
www.authorhouse.com
Phone: 1 (800) 839-8640

Published by AuthorHouse 08/14/2017

ISBN: 978-1-5462-0388-9 (sc)
ISBN: 978-1-5462-0389-6 (e)

DEDICATIONS

I want to thank two of my best friends and Published Authors and Mentors, Clare Seven and Jack Manick for pushing and sometimes dragging me across the finish line. With out them, I don't think I could have done it.

Writers Note

Even thou all characters, events and the Chalet were developed in my mind, I would take the odds that with the rich and famous in the world, they may just have a place to have fun in much like the Chalet.

WARNING

Do not attempt any of the play or procedures in the stories.

THE DOCTOR'S TOYS

I t was just before 9 am as the Rolls Royce Limousine pulled into the private air plane parking area at the Dresden airport. Across the tarmac many large Boing and Airbus passenger plane from all over Germany and Europe were landing and departing. So many people traveling thought this area.

Peter got out of the driver's seat and went to the rear guest compartment to check on the refreshments for the soon to arrive passengers. Peter found the morning snacks of crackers, cheese, and finger sandwiches, cavalier and to quench the thirst, a bottle of wine from the Chalet. It was a good vintage but the best was waiting the passengers for their two week stay at the Chalet. Peter finished the checks of snacks and proceeded to take a rag from the trunk and wipe down the exterior of the Limo.

Peter had been the Private driver of the Chalet for over 40 years. He was an older man in his later 60s. A quiet man except when asked questions by the many private visitors to the Chalet. Even thou he was a short man, just 5 foot 4 inches, he was a sharp man. The years in the army taught him to be a careful dresser, always making sure his uniform was crisp with straight creases. He had seen many things and heard many conversations form the passengers he would transport to Chalet.

Today's group was a group of four surgeons, two from Berlin, one from Great Britain and one from Ireland. Four female doctors, all surgeons and top in their fields. Two of them were general surgeons, one was a plastic surgeon and the forth was an OBGYN All but the OBGYN had been to the Chalet at least four times. This was the first time for her. For the chance to come and stay for two, two week vacations a year, they happily paid the sum of $250,000 per year. The many entertainment items made the price worth it.

Peter was listening to the arrival traffic on the radio in the front of the limo. He heard the call signs for the private jet carrying the doctors. They were on final approach and should be at the gate within minutes. Peter readied the luggage cart for the bags each was bring with them.

The plane taxied to the arrival gate and shut down its engines. When the wine of the turban fans of the engines came to a halt, the passenger door opened and the steward stood in the door. The portable stairs unfolded from the belly of the plane and the railings were set. Peter proceeded to the luggage hole door as the crew from the gate opened the hatch and filled the cart with bags of many sizes and colors. The crew placed the bags carefully on the cart and wheeled it to the rear of the Rolls and loaded them.

Peter made his way to the bottom of the stairs and motioned to the steward to have the women deplane. First off was Elsa. She was a brunette in her late 40s, well built with 36DD breasts, and 5 foot 9 inches tall. Next to come was Gertrude, blond, mid 40s, 5 foot 8 inches with 38D. Rosland was the third woman to come down the stairway. She had dark brown hair, mid 40s, 5 foot 9 inches and 36D breasts. Rosland was the plastic surgeon of the four. The forth female passenger was Helma. She had striking long black hair, early 40s at 5 foot 6 inches. She was the OBGYN surgeon. This was her first time to visit the chalet and was a little nervous at first.

Peter escorted the woman to the rear door of the limo. One by one they entered and were seated. Peter made sure they were comfortable and that they had access to the snack bar and the bottle of wine. The women began to snack on the crackers and cheese, with just a little caviar on the side.

Peter went to the trunk and made sure the bags were placed inside, closed the lid and seated him self in the driver's seat. He turned to the open window between the women and himself and greeted them and told them to enjoy the hour and a half trip through the country side.

He also remained the four of the rules list and that they should refresh themselves with them. He than pushed a button on the instrument panel and the window shut. This let the women talk freely and more free to talk about what they were there to enjoy.

The limo exited the airport and began the journey to the Chalet. As the miles sped by, Peter remembered the thousands of time he had brought guests up the winding roads. The Chalet was situated in the lower western part of the Sachem area of Germany. From time to time, Peter would use the microphone to point out the scenic parts of the trip. The green valley with the many different animals grazing to the streams with the wooden bridges they would travel over. The air turned a little colder as they began to gain altitude toward the Chalet.

A little over an hour and a half had passed when Peter announced that the Chalet was now in view on the top of the mountain. It was situated in the many larger mountains of this area. Many of them had snow showing even thou it was still only August. Helma was ah struck at the first sighting of the Chalet. So high up and wow was it a great sight. Another ten minutes had passed as the Limo pulled up to the fenced in area with the carded gate.

Peter opened his window and inserted his key card. This did three things. First it announced that they had arrived, second it opened the gate and third it let the tram car operator to ready the tram car for the visitors. Peter pulled up to the tram house and stopped the car. He again got on the microphone and reminded the woman that past this point and until they reached their secured rooms, that they were not to discuss why they were there.

Peter went to the rear door and opened it. He helped the women out of the Limo and told them he would drive to the rear of the Chalet and deliver their luggage to their rooms. The women walked to where the tram operator was standing and entered the tram car for the ride to the top of the mountain and the main entrance of the Chalet. Peter drove around the outer fence to the rear of the Chalet to place the luggage on the elevator to the living area.

The ride up to the main entrance was aw inspiring. The women just looked at each other and talked of the mountains on all sides and the view of rocky cliffs, and tall pine trees. Below were the vast fields of grapes with the many workers trimming and picking the fruit. This area of Germany was known for its great wine and champagne.

Helma just couldn't keep from being overcome by the story book picturesque view. The others had seen it several times before and were dreaming of the upcoming two weeks. The trip took maybe tens minutes in total as the tram pulled into the dock at the main entrance of the Chalet.

The door opened onto a marble terrace with a marble arch. Standing under the arch was Wolfgang, the Manager of the Chalet. He was an older Gentleman in his late 60s. A man of 5 foot 6 inches tall and was extremely loyal with the owner but very strict with the staff. He had been the Manager for over 30 years and had outstanding reputation for providing both a great vacation as well as privacy of the guests.

Wolfgang walked over to the four women and welcomed them and kissed each of their hands. We have been expecting you and everything is as you requested. I will take you to your rooms so you can freshen up after your long trips.

Your luggage has been placed in your rooms and unpacked. I know that three of you have been here prior so I know you should be able to navigate the many floors and relaxation areas. As for you, Helma, I will be around in an hour to collect you for the grand tour of our chalet.

As for your toys, I believe that they should be in house in two or three days. A reminder, you are to keep to yourselves what your visit is about. The four of them strolled to the glass front elevator. Wolfgang inserted his key card into the slot and the doors opened.

Helma, the elevator will only come back to the main entrance with care of a senior staff member. This keeps guests from leaving prior to their two weeks of fun and relaxation. You have been assigned to room number six on the first floor. Wolfgang inserted his master key card into the lock on the door.

It opened into a master living and lounge area. There were several couches covered in suede and trimmed in shiny black leather. A wine cooler and small, well stocked bar sat against the back wall. A large refrigerator sat next to the wine cooler. It was already well stocked with snacks and prior requested treats for the group to indulge in.

4

Four individual bedrooms doors, two on each side of the room, and a keycard was in an envelope on the large oaken dresser. On each door was the name in gold foil lettering of the individual who was to occupy the room. As in the past, your key card will allow you access to all the public areas and recreation areas of the Chalet.

Wolfgang wished the women a pleasant vacation and told them if they needed anything, to just call the front desk and a senior representative would assist with their needs. As normal, you will need to read and sign the rules/contact which I will pickup when I return in an hour to show Helma the building and grounds. A last thought, your toys should be arriving within two or three days. Please enjoy your stay. Wolfgang departed the room, closing the door behind him.

The four women looked at each other and decided to look over and sign the contract/rules sheet prior to getting comfortable. Helma looked at the others and picked up the paper work. She began reading the rules and looked at the others for guidance. Elsa spoke up and informed her that all guests had to sign it.

Other than the normal things like conduct on the grounds and recreations area, you can not talk to anyone other than us whom we should meet tomorrow about the "TOYS". You will find the clause at the end stating that you will be kept and become the new Toy for another group if you violate them.

All four signed the last sheet and inserted them into the large envelope setting on the coffee table in the middle of the room. Finishing this, each took out their key card and entered their individual bed and living quarters. The rooms were as breath taking as the ride up. Each had a king size bed against the rear wall. The bed was made up with silken sheets and a pile of king size pillows at the head of the bed.

To one side was an oaken set of drawers and a free standing cabinet which held their hanging clothes. Against the other wall was the bath and shower room. A six foot long cabinet with double sink and five foot high mirror hung above. A china toilet with oaken seats sat next to a tall cabinet which contained stacks of fine towels. On the other wall housed a five foot by five foot sunken tube with gold plated water faucets.

A five foot shower was next to the tub. To complete the room was a two person steam cabinet to relax in after a busy day or night. The three woman which had been there before decided to take a bath to relax and than an hour nap. Helma took a quick shower and dressed in a relaxing summer outfit to await Wolfgang's return.

A knock on the door indicate Wolfgang's return. Helma answered the door and was again greeted with a kiss on the hand. He indicated that she should bring her key and follow him around the Chalet. He started by giving her some of the history of the Chalet.

It was originally constructed by a King of the area in the early 1600s as his rest and relaxation area and summer castle. In the early 1800s, it was turned into a winery. After the war, the owner, Carl Schmidt bought it from the Government and converted it to its present palace. You will get to meet him at some point in you stay.

There are six levels above the two large floors which contain the winery/press room and the Play area. These areas will be shown to you by either Ilsa or Frieda. They are in charge of the play room and the TOYS. You will be given a guided tour of the lower areas in the morning after your breakfast.

You are housed on the first level and your key card will only access to this level of living area. If you wish to spend time with any of the other guests, they must first let the front desk know and than you may proceed to their room.

We have arrived at the fifth floor. The doors opened onto a huge area. One side housed the dining room. Their stood an assortment of two, four, eight and twelve chair tables each with a silk table cloth. Meals are served at eight in the morning, noon and supper at six. If you get hungry between meals or are involved in our many recreations, a snack bar is open 24 hours a day for your convince.

You will just need to show your key card for admittance. The other side of the floor consisted of chairs and couches for sitting and enjoying the sights surrounding the Chalet. A dance area completed the area with rich wooden floors and a full bar for your many preferences in beverages.

Let's go to the top or sixth floor. Wolfgang and Helma re-entered the elevator and proceeded to the top of the Chalet. They stepped off the elevator and Helma took a deep breath. What she saw was so breath taking; she had to take a step back to take it in.

From the top, she could see all the surrounding grounds. Where to start was the first question she had. Wolfgang pointed to the farthest corner and they walked the many yards to the parapet surrounding the top. First was the chair lift to take skiers to the top of the next mountain. In the winter, we have one of the most challenging ski slops in Germany. We have some of the best packed power for fast down hill skiing.

To the left are our three tennis courts. Each has a clay base to exchange shots. We get some of the best tennis players come here to either relax from tournaments of to rehab from injuries. To the far left is the Olympic size swimming pool. There are two different sides to the pool. The left is for the beginners and ranges from three and half feet to over eight, the twenty five meters and the right side is for racing. If starts a seven feet and goes to twelve feet with diving boards. If you want to scuba swim or strap on a tank, just ask and a session will be arranged for you use.

Looking back on the top of the sixth floor, we have cabana tables for sitting with a good drink or a light snack. The small building at the near end by the elevator has beach towels, sun screen and beverages. There are areas which have fine white beach sand to lie in as well as lounge chairs. These are co-ed areas and you may also do nude sum bathing, but no adult activities are allowed. If you hook up, you must use either yours or their rooms. If you have any other questions, again, just ask any of our many personnel. I will escort you back to your room now so you can join your friends.

Wolfgang escorted Helma back to her room and made sure her key card preformed correctly. Roseland was sitting on one of the glorious couches to the side of the room. She told Helma to get a glass of wine from the cooler and join her. Helma did so and sat next to her. It did not take long for the two girls to hug and kiss. As it turned out, all four of the women were Bi and enjoyed the close company of a mature, beautiful woman. Hands were now sliding to and fro over the soft white flesh of each other.

They were slowly stopping to explore the others many female assets. Within ten minutes there was a pile of clothes in the center of the room and both were naked. They kissed and lightly sucked on each others pink nipples. What a wonderful feeling they had. The activity moved into one of the rooms and onto the king size bed. Their embraces were as active as a pair of teenagers. It didn't take long before they were locked in a sixty-nine position taking in each others tender lips and enjoying the juices of love.

Late afternoon was approaching so the women agreed to shower and change into some formal clothing for dinner and dancing. They proceeded to the elevator and Gertrude slipped her key card into the lock, they entered and she pressed the fifth floor button. They arrived and all were set back with the beauty of the evening sun coming into the room.

They went into the dining area and were seated at a four chair table. Their waiter came over to the table. Ladies, would you like to start with some house wine before ordering? They all shook their heads and a bottle with four glasses was brought over. This is tonight menu from which you should be able to find a true delight to feast from.

They picked up their menu and began the task of selecting a culinary delight. Elsa went first. I will have the Rib eye stake, medium done, scalped potatoes with a light cheddar cheese sauce and tender snow peas. Gertrude was next. I will have the northern ocean tuna, lightly browned, mixed, buttered vegetables, and a chief salad. Roseland started as soon as Gertrude was finished. I will have the sea food platter. A mix of jumbo fried shrimp, fried white fish and steamed oysters, and a fresh fruit salad to finish.

Helma was just so excited with all that happened. I will have a one pound hamburger with a thick piece of cheddar cheese melted over the top. Also a large order of golden French fries lightly dusted with grated Swiss cheese. The other three just looked at her and with a shi, told the waiter they would order dessert later. He departed and the women did some light talking. It took a good half hour but the entries were exactly as ordered. Even the cheeseburger and fries were great.

They started to eat and did more light talking. They were going over plans for the next day when the waiter returned with the house specialty, a flaming rum cake with red cherries around the rim. He cut four slices and placed them on dessert plates. Each woman slowly tasted the cake and commenced to clean their plate. The remainder of the cake was placed in a box, for later in their room. The four finished the evening talking and dancing with those in the large social area. By midnight, the group retired to their room for a lot of cuddling and fun with each other.

The Toys

The small used car rumbled down the side roads in the area south of Dresden. Daniel Jones was trying to get away from the little town he had been employed. He had gotten in an argument with his boss and was fired that afternoon. Daniel was a good book keeper but his work was slowly going down beyond an acceptable rate. Over the last few months his interests had turned from giving his 100% to that of working out at the gym and female company. I know that if I get away from my past life that I can get myself on track again. At 40 years old, I can make myself better.

The journey was taking him into the lower hills and the afternoon was getting cooler. I am getting hungry and need to find lodging for the night. A road side sign alerted him that he was within 25 miles of a hostel for the night. His savings were slowly being eaten up in fuel costs and until he could get a new job, he would have to stay at lower cost places.

The outer edge of the town was now in site. He slowed his speed to the posted limit. Up ahead, he saw a younger woman sitting on a suit case by the side of the road. She had her head in her hands and seemed to be crying. As Daniel slowed and pulled up next to her, he could see and hear her crying out loud.

He took that the woman was most likely in her late 30s, but was showing like she was 50. As Daniel slowed to a stop just ahead of her, she stood up and she was a well built blond of 5 foot 6 inches. The other thing he noticed was her breasts which popped out to a 38DD. This was the part that impressed him the most. Not knowing why, he walked up to her and asked what was wrong.

Hello, my name Daniel Jones and can I help you? She raised her head, slowed her crying and answered that she was Carla Adams. Carla went on to state that she had broken up with her boy friend and was running away from life. We had a fight two nights ago and he told me to get out and never come back. I was so sick and bummed out that I even thought about just stepping out in front of a large truck along the highway to end it all. I could not even do this to myself. Carla started to cry and talk to herself as she stood there.

I stepped over to her and placed my arm around her shoulder and place her head on my chest. I understand how bad things are and I want to help you. We both sat down on the grassy area by the side of the road and talked. I told her of my story of being a jerk and getting myself fired from a great job.

Carla began by stating she was a waitress at a small diner. She did alright, but her X-boyfriend had started rumors of the happenings between them. This brought about the argument and than the owner fired her for insulting one of his friends at the diner. The owner did not even give her what she was owed for the weeks work. This left me broke and homeless.

Carla, I want to help as much as I can. Please let me buy us supper and we can share a room for the night. Carla stopped and thought for a minute. She knew that she had no money and was at a loss. She kind of knew that she would most likely have to give herself to him in trade for a ride, a meal and a dry bed for the night.

I know he is a well built man of 5 foot 10 inches tall. He was a handsome man and would be ok in bed. She turned to him and said she would accept his offer for the night and maybe ride with him during his trip. Daniel picked up her bag and placed it into the trunk. He opened the passenger door and helped here into the car. He reentered the car and they drove off toward town.

On the outskirts of the town, Daniel saw a sign for a slightly rundown hostel. He pulled up to the main entrance and entered to register for the evening. The desk clerk greeted the two of them and asked how long they would need the room. Daniel told the clerk that they had just met and only one night would be needed. The clerk had Daniel fill out the registration card and told them what a night would cost. Daniel produced the correct amount and was given their room number and key.

The clerk directed them to drive around the rear as the room was part of the back ring of rooms. He also told them of the in house restaurant and a discount was given for those staying over night. He even informed them of the outside rest area by their room and they should join them for some wine later. Daniel took the key and he and Carla got back into the car to drive around the back to their room.

The desk clerk knew he had found a gold mine with Daniel and Carla. He had secretly taken their picture during the registration process. He took the cards and went to the fax machine and transmitted both their pictures and registration cards to the Chalet. It turns out that this plus many other hostels in the area were feeders of men and women to the Chalet.

A short time later, a personnel message from Carl Schmidt, owner of the Chalet was received. There were a number of questions to be responded to. Were they married, were their families to come looking for them and what kind of physical condition were they in? The clerk wrote his answer back to Carl with his answers. The couple was both singles, in good health and had no families or children to tend with. They had no forwarding addresses and both seemed homeless.

Some time passed when the phone rang in the hostel office. Ilsa from the Chalet called in response to the couple and started to talk to the desk clerk. She told him that she and Frieda would be there within several hours and they would collect the couple for transport. You are to follow the normal expectations for the transaction. The clerk answered that he would attend to the necessary tasks and that by midnight, the couple would be ready.

Daniel and Carla pulled up and parked in the designated space for the room they were assigned. Daniel opened the door and escorted her into the room. It was clean with a queen size bed. They were both very tired and decided to settle into a warm bath and get ready for supper. One by one, they both got naked and drew a hot bath. They started to act like teenagers and both sat in the tub and wash each others backs and moved to a lot of touching and kissing.

Time passed and it approached supper. The two walked to the restaurant within the hostel. They were greeted by the waitress and seated in a dark corner. Daniel pulled out the chair for Carla and she was seated. He proceeded to the opposite side of the table and was seated. They were handed a menu and looked over it.

Daniel turned to the waitress and asked what she recommended. She replied that the house special which consisted of a generous portion of pasta, a brat and a tomato sauce over it was the special. Daniel looked at Carla and they shook their heads to take the special. This dinner for two comes with a bottle of wine which I will bring while you wait for the dinner. The wine was delivered and both started their first glass. During this time, the desk clerk waited his chance and added a special sprinkling of sex enhancement drug to the pasta sauce.

Their dishes were delivered to the table and both ate slowly. There was much small talk during dinner. As the sex enhancement drug took effect, the talk drifted to going back to the room and bed down for the night.

The dinner was now finished and both left the dining room in route to the room. It only took a few minutes to arrive and enter the room. The first thing they found was a bottle of wine sitting on the night stand with a note complements of management. Even thou both of them were normally light drinkers, the spiked dinner encouraged them to open the bottle and start drinking.

As soon as Daniel closed the door and drew the drapes, they stripped off their clothes and dove into bed. Daniel started by running his hands over her and she was grabbing his cock. A few licks on his cock brought him to get between her legs and lick her pussy lips. She returned the favor by taking in his cock in her mouth. The action went on for several minutes till she spread her legs and he began inserting his cock. They went on for several minutes until the knock out drops in the bottle of wine took hold.

As dark set in and it was determined both were out cold, Ilsa and Frieda entered the room to check on their status. Confirming their sleep, Frieda went to the truck and removed a large laundry cart. She rolled it over to the room entrance and pushed it in. The two women lifted Daniel first and placed him into the cart. Carla was next to find her place in the cart. Several dirty sheets and a blanket were placed over them. The knock out drug would keep them out for a half a day.

The desk clerk made his way to the room and greeted the women. They said that this is exactly as described and the deal was made. For his part, the clerk was given the car keys and an envelope containing the agreed amount of money. The Desk clerk was responsible for disposing the car, which he would repaint and title, and to make the luggage and other personnel belongings go away. This was the standard for producing people for the Chalet to use. From this point, no evidence of the Daniel and Carla could be found that they had ever been there.

Ilsa and Frieda climbed into the truck to start the two hour trip back to the Chalet. There was no hurry to return as long as they were in house by dawn. The roads curved back and forth till finally the mountain with the Chalet was insight. They approached the front gate and Ilsa inserted her key card.

They followed the road around the base until a doorway in the lowest area was in view. The truck was backed up, the lift gate unfolded and the laundry cart brought out on it and lowered to the ground. Frieda pushed the cart to the door, inserted her key card and entered.

This was both the entrance for the grape pressing room and also up to the TOY room. The cart was pushed up the steep hallway. She passed several door and stopped at the farthest one from the entrance. Again the key card was used to gain entrance. The massive wooden door was the rear entrance to both the TOY room and to the holding area.

She opened the holding room door to expose the many sets of chains and rings in the walls. In a cabinet in the corner were many sets of shackles and collars. All were rust and coated with human waste and some blood. These were used to secure the "TOYS" that were to be used for play. There were also sets of clean, sparkling stainless shackles and collars for the use of the Play Acting Slaves.

Frieda rolled the cart to the far corner of the dungeon style prison and dumped the two unconscious bodies to the floor. They rolled onto the floor and the sheets were repacked into the cart and it was rolled out. Ilsa entered the cell and she and Frieda went to work.

First the two were separated and place with their heads to the far wall. A set of rusty collars were placed around the necks and than attached to a large iron ring in the wall. The chain was just long enough for them to get to a feeding bowl on the floor. Next to come a set of wrist shackles. They were connect by a short chain and than the chains were attached to a ring in the floor. This allowed just enough movement to allow them to stretch a little without being able to touch their lower bodies or each other.

The final set of cuffs was placed on their ankles. A short chain was drawn out from the ankles to the second ring in the floor. This would not give them much room to move around on the floor. They were satisfied that the pair would be as uncomfortable as possible and very scared when they came to. The lights were turned off and Ilsa and Frieda departed for some well deserved wine and bed time. Their day started early and the four doctors would be given their tour and the rules gone over.

The Tour

Time came fast as the night of partying with each other came to a close and they drifted off to sleep. A chime in each of their rooms rang at 7 in the morning came far too early for the four. One by one they rolled out of bed and took hot showers. The leftovers from love making with each other left a crusty film on them. As they finished and dressed, each one emerged from their room and settled in the common room. Conversations ran the gambit from what the day would bring to wondering how the cool water of pool was going to feel in the afternoon.

They had an appointment with Ilsa and Frieda at ten to prep for the TOY room. Helma spoke up first and asked about what happens if Carl Schmidt was to show up and talk to her. Ilsa spoke first and described him as an older man in his late 60s. He came from an old wealthy family and that is why he could set up the Chalet. It is rumored that he has possible ties to the KGB or even the old Nazi Party. None of the guests know, only Wolfgang knew for sure.

It is also rumored that he brought Ilsa and Frieda from the KGB Enforcer section. Gertrude chimed in and said that none of this should ever be talked about again. Remember, the penalty for screwing up is to be held and become a TOY for a future guest. Helma immediately shut up and not a word was spoken again until breakfast. With that, they went up to level five for breakfast.

They took their place at a breakfast table and than proceeded to the buffet line. They took their plates and looked at the twelve foot line of items. Menu items of eggs in many forms, bacon, sausage, potatoes, pancakes and so many choices of fruit, what to try. They each chose small portions of many items. The cooking staff for the Chalet was one of the best in southern Germany. Each took their plates to the table and they found a pitcher of fresh coffee and one of hot tea. If desired, hot chocolate was also available.

Wolfgang walked over to their table and asked if everyone was happy. They all complimented the food and service. He reminded them that they had an appointment in the TOY room at 10; you do not want to be late. They finished their choices and at 9:45, got up and proceeded to elevator to the TOY room. They waited to be taken down to access the area in the second lowest level of the chalet.

Having been there on four prior trips, Elsa led the way. As they inserted one of their cards into the key slot beside the massive oaken door, an over head light came on indicating they could enter. Ilsa and Frieda came to the door and invited them in. At first, the lights were low and it was dead quiet. They were led to the costume room. The door opened and it was filled with hundreds of choices.

Frieda asked if the three that had been their before would like the same outfits or would they like to change. Elsa and Gertrude insisted on the leather ones they had last time. Roseland took Helma over to the many racks to explore.

Elsa and Gratitude took their outfits and headed to the dressing

15

area. Helma was excited to see theirs and was waiting near the dressing area door. They made their entrance and Helma was over whelmed. Each was wearing heavy, shiny black leather corsets all laced up in the back. Knee high black leather boots with lacing from toe to knee.

A set of black leather opera gloves and a black leather eye mask with embedded diamond like decorations around their eyes. To complete the costume, a black leather riding crop was hanging from a silken sash. Roseland decided on a riding outfit. She dressed in a skin tight set of breaches, Shiny black leather belt and a silken shirt with a puffy collar.

Helma went thru the racks and picked out one and put it back, than another. I guess being new; I am having a hard time to choose. She picked out her favorite uniform, a set of dark purple scrubs with surgeon's hat and a face mask. Her comments were she wanted to feel comfortable in play. Ilsa reminded her that she could change her mind if she wished.

The group was usher from the room and taken down another corridor. This corridor went past several large oaken doors and ended at the TOY holding room. Frieda went ahead to check on the wake status of the TOYS. She returned and told Ilsa that the both of them were still out from the night before. Ilsa turned to the four doctors and said that they would be able to get an advanced look at the TOYS prior to them being taken to the Toy Room tomorrow.

They all entered the cell and they stopped in amazement. This was the first time that they were able to see the TOYS before the fun began. Ilsa turned and said not to touch them and keep their voices low. We do not want them awake quite this early in the day. We will get them up later with a hose with ice cold water and explain their situation and how it was going to work.

I know that three of you have been in the Toy room and have played before. Helma, do you fully understand what is going to happen tomorrow? Helma answered that she had been totally briefed and understood that any doctor oath was out the window and that I will be inflecting much pain and even death in the up coming four days. Ilsa confirmed her answer and said that she and Frieda would go over the rules and fun tools with her later that afternoon. At that point, all heard stirring from both Daniel and Carla, so all withdrew from the holding cell.

Over the next hour or so, the four doctors went over the use of the whips and floggers on practice dummies. Helma had to be worked with as the first try got her tied up with her own whip and even had it land on her lower leg with a painful thud. The proper holding of the handle and where and how to aim brought her to the point she could land the tip within a four inch circle. She was so surprise and over come with joy with herself she took several more swings.

The group moved to the tools area where the many instruments were laid out. The tools ranged anywhere from the medical tools they used everyday in their practices. A vast assortment of speeders, forceps, speculums and scalpels adorned white towels. Catheter's, surgeons gloves and needles ranging from 24 gaga and up to ¼ inch to 1 ½ inch in length and syringes rounded out the medical section. Other items ranged from anal plugs, Habanero peppers, forty grit sand paper, and a pin prick parachute for Daniel, and two fucking machine. A great variety of brushes ranging from stiff scrub to steel bristle parts cleaning, candles, cattle prods, which was demonstrated on Helma's ass so she had an idea of its potential, hand cracked army telephone with many electrodes and a high wattage hair dryer.

Frieda turned to them and reminded them that all they had to do was ask and if a tool was available, it would be provided. There was a section of tool for the third and four days of play. Helma went over and picked up and played with several pieces to get the feel of them. She than turned and asked if she could get one or two of the anal plugs as she was fascinated with them and wanted to try them later in the room on herself.

Frieda handed her a Ziploc bag with several sizes of plugs and a tube of surgical water based lube so she could play with them that evening. Roseland chimed in and said she would enjoy showing her how they worked and would even join in with a double headed dildo to pass the evening. This item was provided and Frieda stated that these were often request play items to take to their rooms. I will see that they are delivered to your room in a doctor's bag so the other guests did not know what they were.

Both women thanked her for that. The final task for the day was the selection of the table for holding the TOYS down during play the first day. Elsa and Gertrude selected a butcher block table. The table had a top of 12 inches wide and three feet long. A small platform protruded from the end to strap the head down and prevent movement. This would hold Daniel down well while they played.

Roseland and Helma went over to a wall of surgical operating room tables. They each jumped up on the tables and talked over the pluses and minuses. Being a GYN Doctor, Helma suggested that they use the DRE Milano OB20 OB/GYN Procedure Chair.

Helma told Roseland that she has seen many woman squirm and thrush while delivering problem children and the chair didn't even move. She stated that Carla's legs could be strapped tightly into the leg holders and spread wide for access. With the decisions made for the tools for the first day, each woman was given a copy of the rules.

The rules were simple and covered all four days of play. Each day was broken into what could be done to the TOYS and the type of play and pain that could be imposed. The main idea was to get at least three days of play and if the forth day came about without the TOYS dying first, all the better.

The two jailers, Ilsa and Freda were there to provide technical advice and any additional tools requested. They were not to join in or play with the TOYS, except for the use of a cattle prod and being able to grab soar parts to get them to move.

The total session of between four and six hours a day would be recorded so they could be able to see the fun for the day but not to be taken away from the Chalet. In addition to the six woman and two TOYS, The owner, Carl Schmidt may drop by to see how all was going. His background in the information gathering services made him yearn to get back. He was authorized to ask questions and suggest better ways of play.

The days were broken down as follows;

Day one: The session was to last around four hours. The main goal was to make them as uncomfortable as possible, using the brushes, clamps, sandpaper and other tools. The work was to concentrate on the tender sexual parts and other openings. Only the head was exempted from harm. The TOY was to be able to walk back to their cell for overnight holding.

Day two: This session was to be in two parts and locations. The first part was in the Play room. Each TOY was to be strapped down to the wooden blocks with full access to their sexual areas. Again, the areas were to be caused as much pain as possible. The tenderizing process was to be continued until just the lightest touch would bring screams of pain. At this point, each doctor would put on strapons with varying sizes and lengths of dildos. No surgical lube was to be used during insertion. This was to get them ready for the next day.

The final part of this first location was to be completed with the liberal use of paddles, whips, riding crops and leather floggers. The four women would take turns going around using their item on the TOYS back, bottoms and the back of the legs. The idea was to bring them to an extremely tender area and bring up as many welts for the next day as possible. When maybe two or three hours had passed, the TOYS would be un-strapped and all would be moved to the lower level to the grape crushing room. They would be attached to the grinding station and whipped to get them to make the stones crush the grapes for wine.

Day Three: The TOYS would be placed on the wooden benches, face down at first. Using what ever means you desire, you are to work on the many welts. They are to be opened, the skin pulled back some and the exposed areas scrubbed in salt, pepper or pickle and lemon juice. This should take maybe two hours.

To finish off day three, the slow expansion of their rectal opening by use of the use of the medieval pear of agony. The stretching of the opening can take as long as you wish. To complete the day, fucking machines with many sizes of plugs are to be used without any lube. Any stimulus as peppers, salt or other item may be used on the plug as it goes in and out. After several hours of this, they will be placed back in their cell.

Day four: Day four is up to you. Remember at the end of what ever length of time will be the end of the TOYS visit. It doesn't matter if they die or not by the end, they will be taken away for disposal of their bodies. You may do or use any of the tools which you have seen plus a chest full of other more torturous tools.

By signing this form that you understand the rules, you are bound to abide by them. Also, telling anyone else about these will make you the next TOY to be used.

The four each signed the form. All except Helma were taken back to the room to rest before dinner. Helma requested a little more hands on explanation of the tools and procedures. Frieda took her back to the tool room and allowed her to pickup, feel and try each item she wanted to.

She walked over to the crank telephone and asked how it was to be used and how it felt. Frieda told her to strip her clothes off and place herself on the OBGYN table. Helma took her position on the table and Frieda placed leather straps around her legs, spreading them apart. Her arms were also strapped to the table. She asked Helma if she wanted a blindfold and gag or wanted to go without. She wanted to be gagged, but not blindfolded. I want to be able to see what you are using so I can get it right the first time.

Frieda turned to her after completing the tasks of binding and in a soft voice suggested that she may be a little submissive or even a little bit of a pain lover. A wave of excitement grew on her face as Frieda brought over two copper wire bundles. Each was around one inch in diameter and six inches long.

The first electrode was slowly place up her rectum until it met resistance. The second was very slowly worked into her pussy. The many coils of wire that made up the electro rubbed all the sided of her female tunnel. Care was made to make sure it rubbed against her clit for maximum effect.

Frieda than made the electrical connections and brought the telephone up to Helma's face. Are you ready for the experience of your life? Helma shook her head and prepared for the sensation to come. Frieda slowly turned the crank causing a small charge to enter and flow between her two holes. Helma tensed a little and jumped some. Frieda placed the telephone down and gently stroked Helma face and breasts.

Did you like your first taste of the toys? It took a few seconds but a hardy yes was done by a shake of her head. So you like the pain? Again, a hardy shake of her head for her answer yes. Would you like me to continue to turn the crank and let you try a higher charge to flow? Even from the gagged mouth, Frieda heard Helma pled for the adventure to continue.

The phone was again held up so Helma could see it. Frieda's hand took hold of the crank and gave it a good two to three turns. Helma's twisted and pulled, tugging against the bonds; she again pleaded for more and make it more intense. The play went on for several more cranks until Helma's white cream overflowed from around the electrode within her.

Frieda saw the enjoyment coming from her and said, slave, I am going to give you some more pain to let you experience the fun you give to the TOY tomorrow. Frieda picked up a pair of Japanese clover clamps. One at a time, she began to cup and rubs each of the breasts causing them to get hard and the nipple to stiffen. A nipple was now placed between her thumb and fore finger and rubbed back and forth.

The nipple began to harden and she placed a clover clamp down to the base of the nipple and she slowly let the clamp close. The pain set in instantly, and the other nipple was also pinched by a clamp. A small piece of twine was drawn thru a pulley in the ceiling above the bench. The string was attached to each of the clamps and a five pound weight at the downward end.

As the slack was removed and allowed to take effect, moans were heard from Helma. The weight was slowly pushed causing more pressure to be applied to the nipple. A slow moan came from the gagged soul.

Frieda again picked up the telephone and she cranked it. Slow, little movements caused the electric to bite into her and as that wore on; she would just crank it for all it was worth. Helma again began to thrash her head and body around but never asked for relief or to stop. By this time, there was a continuous flow of white fluid coming from her pussy. Somewhere an hour had gone by and Frieda stopped the play.

She removed the clover clamps and the electrodes from their holes. Oh so slowly, the bonds were released and the gag removed. Helma sat up and the two of them embraced each other. Helma, in a shallow voice talked and thanked her for the wonderful experience. Frieda just continued to caress her shoulders and petting the large breast. So what did you think of being a slave to me? I just don't know how to thank you for the joy. Frieda, can I please get down between you legs and pleasure you to thank you?

A gentle squeeze on her breasts and an approving look gave way to a great end to the day. As Helma got dressed to return to the room, Frieda requested to have supper with her. She approved and a time of seven was approved. Helma returned to her room. The time till seven would take forever. A long bubble bath and some wine to relax made the time pass.

The group was all getting ready for supper. Elsa seated herself next to Helma and placed her arm around her. Roseland and Gertrude sat across from them. Elsa turned and asked Helma what took so long for her to return to the room after the briefing? She replied that they went over many of the tools and their uses. Frieda also gave me a little insight into tomorrow. We had a wonderful afternoon after you left.

Roseland went to the pool and we went and played tennis. The recreations provided are the highest quality I have ever played at. You should try the ski area on our next visit. The powder on the downhill slopes is so fast.

Being the senior in the room, Elsa turned to the others and asked if they wanted to talk about what was to happen tomorrow. Helma was the only one to ask the big question. Did or does it still bother any of you about the fact that we will be ending life every so slowly? Gertrude started by saying to start it makes you think, but remember why you signed up for this.

We all need release from the day to day of playing GOD with those we tend to. I know it sounds strange, but how many times did we all wonder why we saved a life that just shouldn't be saved. We have found this outlet for our tensions a way to recharge our lives.

For instance, how many babies did you deliver from crack mothers that were so badly deformed or when Roseland performs face surgery for the tenth time on a rich bitch that just can't get the seventh or eighth face or nose job the Hollywood stars have.

We all have our reasons and remember, it is too late to pull out now without being placed on the table for the next session with someone else to work on you. You will be fine, just take your cues from us and you will do fine. If the screaming and begging gets too much for you, you can get ear plugs, but I think it adds so much. For the most part, these are losers with no families or any life to speak of.

They will never be missed and after the first day, you will have the desire to get into it more. Let's get ready for supper and some personnel fun with the toys in the doctor's bag they had delivered and you asked for. I want to try some of them on you. Let's get on the elevator and go up to the dining room.

They stepped into the dining area and headed to a table for four. As they started thru the menu, Frieda stepped to the table. She said hello and than requested that Helma join her in the private room to eat. Helma rose and excused herself. She walked slightly behind Frieda till they disappeared into a side room.

Frieda started by saying that this was an honor to dine with senior staff. Please have a seat and select you meal. Hilda wasn't sure of how to be with her after the journey into submission from earlier that afternoon. As we sit here this evening, we are just friends.

What you experienced this afternoon happens too many that come here for what you are about to do tomorrow. I have seen the hardest souls find an inner need to submit as well as be in charge as you will be. The reason I wanted to talk to you this evening is that we have many different packages than the one you purchased. They range anywhere from group play, relaxing play and even a slave package. If you are interested, I will have Wolfgang go over the slave package with you. It is much cheaper and is only a week in length. I will tell you that all this niceness and frills are in no way part of the package.

You will live as the two you saw this afternoon in the dungeon cell. You will go thru "hell" for that week. You will both suffer and serve Ilsa and me, much the way the TOYS of tomorrow, but without and damage to you body.

You will be at our will and go thru things that you have never thought of before. Having seen how you were at our private session this afternoon, I think you respond and enjoy it. I can guarantee that you go away both spent beyond and happier and more relaxed than any time in your life.

I want you to remember that when you return to you group, this conversion we just had is not for their ears. Just say that I wanted to help you relax for the upcoming day. Helma responded she would keep it to herself and they ordered their meal. The two had idle talk while eating and when finished, she rejoined her group on the dance floor for some fun times. Frieda just went back to work.

Both Frieda and Ilsa joined each other and headed for the TOY room level. On the elevator down to the dungeon cells, Ilsa asked why the private meal with Helma? I found that she had a slave side this afternoon and wanted to do some recruiting. Remember, Wolfgang always wants us to find more business for the Chalet. If she takes up the offer, I know we will have much fun with her and can she lick a mean cunt.

The elevator arrived at the level and they exited. They inserted one of the Key cards and the thick oaken door opened. They walked down the corridor to the dungeon cell area. They entered the area where the two new TOYS were chained. Frieda flipped the switch on and startled the prisoners chained to the floor.

They found them just waking from the knock out drug that had been laced in their wine. Little by little, they came around and started trying to figure what had happened and where they were. Well, it is about time you came around. My name is Ilsa and this is Frieda. As you are about to figure out, you are in a very bad situation. We are your jailers for the next few days.

Before you start yelling, the walls are over three foot thick rock and the doors are three inch thick oak, so yell as loud as you want, no one will hear you and you will only bring on disciplinary actions that you will not like. There are a few rules for your stay. Number One is that there is no way to escape. Many have tried and as you can see, the chains are very thick.

Each evening, you will be given a hosing down with cold water. You will not be given any towels or clothes. For the next days, you will be totally naked. You will be feed and given water at night only. A time limit of ten minutes is all you will have to eat and drink. This is the only meal for the day. If you give us a hard time during feeding, we will pull out cattle prods and we know where to stick them to get your attention.

Your day will start around ten in the morning and you will be moved to the play room. There are four females that will be working on you each day. They will not introduce themselves to you and it is not necessary that you know who they are. During their play with you, you can and are encouraged to scream and beg, none of which will persuade them to be kind or stop.

Are there any questions? Daniel spoke up and demanded to know why they were there? Well Daniel, let's just say that you were in the wrong place at the wrong time and for your tone of questioning, Ilsa stuck the cattle prod under his balls and pushed the button several time.

The shock came hard and hit him like someone kicked him in the balls. Carla, do you want to try the same thing or not? Carla just started to cry and beg for mercy. Sorry, you're not getting any from us. Frieda produced two bowels of water and set them on the floor just in range of the collar and chain. She than went to the cabinet and took out two cans of dog food.

She opened them and dumped the contents in the bowels. The smell was sickening, but who cares. She set the bowels down next to the water and told them to start eating. Carla took small bites, but Daniel said he was not going to eat it. Again the cattle prod was place on the tip of his cock this time and the juice let flow. Daniel jumped as far as his chains would allow.

Now are you going to eat or not? Daniel shook his head yes and started to push his face in the bowel. You have eight minutes left and remember you will not get fed again till this time tomorrow. At the ten minute mark, the bowels were removed and the high pressure water hose produced.

Ilsa attacked them from all angles with the ice cold water. She used the spray head to direct the water down into the sex areas and rectal areas. The cleaning done, she wound up the hose again and the turned out the lights and closed and locked the door to the cells area. Ilsa and Frieda departed the play area and headed up to their quarters for the night.

The darkness and quiet left Daniel and Carla very scared. Carla was crying and they both tired to comfort each other the best they could. Daniel, why are we here? Did we do something wrong? Daniel answered that he didn't know and hopped it would be explained in the morning. Do you think they will hurt us or even worse, kill us? I just don't know. They both got as close as their chains would allow and tried to drift off to sleep.

The Night Before

The group of four danced till around ten and decided to return to the room. They entered the elevator and went down to the first floor. They exited it and headed to the room. They entered the room and Elsa turned to the others and suggested they returned to their room and get naked. Each headed for their bedroom and it didn't take long for them to return to the common area.

Gertrude started to lay out the toys from the doctor's bag. Each also brought in many different toys from their own luggage. Several large beach size towels were laid out on the floor and pillows gathered from around the room. Elsa spoke up first. This will most likely be the last evening for several that we will have the time to enjoy each other. Those of you that are on a return trip will attest to the fact that playing with the TOYS can be as draining as a good round of surgery. Do we want to pair off or start with a group session?

All four moved to the center of the room and started to hug and cuddle together. Hands started to caress the many curves of each other. Hands found the wet little pussy lips and the ample breast and nipple flesh. Good, wet kisses were falling on each other and they were soon fully involved.

Roseland and Helma were now locked in a tight embrace, rubbing breasts and nipples together. Elsa and Gertrude decided to assume the "69" position and were licking and sucking wet and sloppy pussy lips. By the time an hour had passed, the four had switched partners and positions many times.

Since it was your idea Helma, you will go first. Gertrude and Roseland gently laid her back and spread the legs wide. Elsa took one of the medium size anal plugs out of the bag. She temped Helma by running it in front of her ever growing eye. I am betting that you have never tried one of these up your ass before.

Helma shook her head no and was told it was like nothing she had experienced before. Elsa uncapped the surgical lube and spread it thickly on the plug. She moved down between her wide spread legs and just let the tip rest on the little rose bud. Just relax and it won't hurt, at least too much.

The tip was pushed in and out maybe ½ an inch. Helma was moaning by now and begged for more to enter her. With a twisting motion, the plug began its entry into her very tight hole. The plug bottomed out and a cry of joy escaped her mouth. The tension on her legs was released and each of them took turns twisting and removing and reinserting it again and again.

Helma's body racked with excitement, the white juices flowed from her womanhood and sweat dripped all over body. The plug was removed and the process repeated on the remaining three. It was approaching midnight and all four know it would be a short night. A wake up call was set for 7 and they would need to prepare for the mornings fun.

Time to play with the TOYS

Day One

The 7 o'clock hour arrived and the four women woke. Each was still drifting on a cloud from the play of the night before. Each found themselves still naked and in need of a hot bath. Elsa hurried the women along and dressed for a simple breakfast in the dining room. Having found their table, they went to the buffet line and filled their plates, returned to their table and quietly ate and had coffee. The time was spent with small chit chat, mostly about what they were going to do that evening. They returned to their rooms to relax as they didn't have to be in the dressing room until around eleven as the play session didn't start until noon.

As for the TOYS, Ilsa and Freda were busy tending to their needs. It took some time to get them ready for the day's play. Ilsa opened the door and they entered. Frieda turned on the light and found the TOYS in a kind of sleep.

Good morning TOYS. Are you ready for a day in the play room? Daniel turned and started to cuss and beg for information. This action brought the cattle play into action again. He shut up quickly. In a quiet voice, Carla turned to the pair and asked what they had done to be in this position and what was to be done to them? Ilsa stepped forward and simply answered that they were the guest of the Chalet and were to be the play "TOYS" of four wonderful women.

They would only be here for four days and at the end would be taken away. Time for your shower and I suggest that you cooperate as the ice cold water allows the cattle prod to bit much worse than when they were dry. Frieda started with Daniel. The stream of water was run over his body and concentrated on his cock and balls. Next came Carla's turn. She tried to turn herself into a ball towards Frieda. For her effort, she got a swift kick in the ass and the prod in her pussy.

She instantly relaxed and opened her legs as much as possible. You see how much easier it is when you follow the rules. You will receive a bowl of water, but no food until later this afternoon. They each sipped and licked the bowels dry. We will return in a little while to prepare you for your first trip to the play room. The pair turned to the door, shut the light out and closed the door.

Ilsa and Frieda turned their attention to the preparation of the Play room. The entered the area and started by securing the wooden butcher block table and the OBGYN table in place. Next to come were the two instrument tables. They placed them on the outer side of the tables.

The women had done this so many times that it was kind of automatic. A dark blue medical type drape was placed on the table tops to present a place for the tools to be used. Only one ten foot long table would be need the first day. First came the electric items. A blue handled high shock value cattle prod with the safety in place. A ten foot in length set of leads was attached. At the ends were a set of alligator clamps to attach to either skin or the other items.

Next to come were assortments of insertable copper probes. Some were thin wire and others were thicker bundles of wire. The left end of the table received a variety of both extremely stiff scrub brushes combined with several stainless steel and brass bristled parts cleaning brushes.

An insertable penis gag, two different size anal plugs, a pinprick parachute and a needle block, 2 inches by four inches with twelve holes drill part way thru and each hole filled with thin 24 gage by ¾ inch long syringe needles. The center portion contained the rest of the tools.

This section contained common miniature vice grips pliers and a set of furrier's horse nippers. Two sets of spiked truss plates, used to join sections of wood and forty grit sand paper. Two different models of vaginal speculums in four different sizes for use in spreading the virginal cannel or the anal opening. A screw twitch used for the keeping open a horse's mouth which can also be used to crush a set of balls or grab onto the tong.

A pair of long bill alligator clamps used to inflect prolonged pain and also provide a point of attachment for electric shock. An assortment of operating room tool which were chosen by the doctors including clamps, forceps, and tissue tweezers with sharp teeth and forceps with pointed ends.

To round out the table was a plastic bear claw with its six sharp fingers. Normally this is used to impale meat at a butcher shop and move it around. The points are not sharp enough to rip into the flesh, but will make you think they could. This item will be replaced for day three with one with stainless steel scalpel blades in the ends to shred flesh. A drape was used to cover the table until both the TOYS and the doctors were in place.

The time was approaching eleven in the morning. Ilsa and Frieda returned to the cell block to transport the "TOYS" to the play room. The door was opened and the light turned on. Carla was huddled in a ball and Daniel just laid out flat. Both were scared of what was to come.

Ilsa stepped up to them and began to inform them of their choices. The first choice was to accept having an IV inserted into their arm to allow knock out potion to enter or second choice is to endure a beating and still have the IV inserted. Carla was the first to agree to not put up a fuss. Frieda took out an IV setup. She cleaned the lower arm with alcohol and inserted the needle set. The tubing set was hooked to an IV Bag contain a drug called Versed.

The lock on the tubing set was opened and within seconds, Carla was totally out and limps. Seeing that Carla was still breathing, Daniel decided he would cooperate and allow the IV to be placed.

With both "TOYS" now out and not giving any trouble, two patient transport gurneys were brought in, the chains removed, but leaving the shackles and collar left on and the bodies loaded on them. As long as the drug was being infused, they would be out of reality and limp making it easier to place on their tables and strapped down. They moved down the hall to the play room.

The trip took only a few minutes. Carla went first and was wheeled next to the OBGYN table. She was lifted onto the table. She was positioned assuring that her pussy was fully exposed. Next came her legs. They were placed over the leg holders and strapped down. A two inch wide belt was fitted around her waist at the belly button line. A second belt was place just below and under her breasts.

Both arms were drawn down and strapped to the side of the table. A penis gage was fitted in place and her head had two belts place to keep her head from moving. One went around her throat and the second around her head to keep her from both trashing and also so she cold not turn it to watch what was happening to both her and Daniel.

Daniel came next. He was placed on to the wooden butcher block table. His ass was placed so that his cock and balls and rectum extended just past the edge of the table. Next came the same two belts as Carla had to secure her torso. A small head rest was extended from the end of the table, he had a penis gage inserted and his head was secured with the two straps as Carla. His arms and legs were drawn tightly down along the sides of the butcher block table and secured to iron rings at its base. He could struggle as much as he wanted, but there would be very little movement.

At this point, Ilsa and Frieda stood back and inspected their work. Pleased that neither of the "TOYS" could get loose, they slowed the drug drip to the point it stopped. They removed the IVs and waited for them to regain consciousness.

The swimming feeling in their heads started to clear. They tried to both ask questions and scream as to what their situation was. Ilsa stepped up between the two and informed them of their situation. You are here as play toys for four doctors. Today will be the first of the four days I told you about. When you leave here today, the both of you will be in great pain in your crouch and breast areas.

Today will be the easiest one of the four days of play. The gags will stay in place until your four players decide they need to come out. I will tell you that if they tell you to do something, you had better do it. They have many ways at their disposal to make your life oh so much more painful.

When they finish today, you will be taken back to your cells and re-chained to the floor and wall. You will than be fed and watered. At no time will you be allowed to touch yourself or each other to bring any relief form the day's play. You are allowed to scream and cry during play. Relax and wait for their arrival. Ilsa and Fried left the play room and turned down the lights. For the two, time would pass so slowly until play started.

Elsa turned to the other three and said time is up and we need to move to the play room. They walked toward the play room singe file. Remember, three of us have been in there before and know what to expect. Helma don't worry how it will work, just watch Roseland to start with.

You will get into the rhythm and will enjoy yourself. One by one they entered the play room and stood between Daniel and Carla. Daniel looked straight toward the ceiling and Carla just started to cry. Both of them were very scared and had no idea of what was to happen to them or why.

Elsa and Gertrude stepped over to Daniel and Roseland and Helma stepped to Carla. Let us start with physicals of each one. Elsa ran her hands from the feet up toward the crouch. Gertrude started at the head and run her hands around the face, looking around the gag as best she could and checked the teeth. He has several missing, plus a crown. The neck felt firm and as did the shoulders. No cervical or clavicle problems. Now following the outline of each rib, all were intact.

Elsa continued to work up. Next to the groin to his cock and balls, lifting the sack and placing heavy pressure on each of his balls. She placed her hand around each and gave it a hard squeeze. Daniel let out a loud scream and relaxed as she released one and than grabbed the other.

This time she squeezed it harder. His cock came to full attention. Elsa placed her hand around it and started to milk it. When she got it to full erect, she took her hand and gave it a nasty whack. Now tears ran down Daniels's cheeks as did a loud crying scream. She turned to Gertrude and said that it seems to work well for now. Gertrude finished her inspection and found a scar on his lower left stomach area. Guess you had your appendix out, I'm guessing in your teens. I think he is in good condition for our play.

Now it is your turn to inspect Carla. Roseland, being the plastic surgeon, started at the head. She ran her fingers around the forehead and down to the chin. Finding all to be original, she went down to the breasts. She lifted each breast to look under for any sign of sutures. No beast work for this one. Now standing to one side of her, she took a nipple between her thumb and finger, crushed and twisted it till screaming started. Carla tried to pull herself loose, but the straps held tight. Good reaction to pain.

She has a nice set of breasts and nipples to play with. I have finished the inspection of my end, now it is time for you to practice your trade. Helma sat on the rolling stool and got between Carla's legs. For now, she is spread enough, but will have to be split further when we start. Wow girl, your have nicely shaped and large labia with many folds and layers of skin. Wish mine were as nice as yours.

Helma worked the skin of the labia between her fingers and pulled them apart till they felt like they would tear off. Screams of pain and fear came from Carla's gagged mouth. Helma turned to Roseland and asked her to hand her a Collins speculum, large size.

The lips were separated and the speculum inserted as far as she could shove it. Slowly she began to turn the screw to separate the two halves to open the vagina to it widest. The pressure and pain drove Carla to try to buck free, but without any success. I can see she is no virgin, but has not given birth. Without a test, I can't determine if she is pregnant. Area is a nice, tender pink and ready for fun.

With both inspections complete, Helma turned and suggested that they both have a catheter inserted and Urine drained. Make sure that you use the largest you can get into the pee holes. Take your time and make it go slow and cork screw them in. Make it hurt as much as possible.

The other three were pleased that she got into the game as fast as she did. Helma selected the one she wanted and started it down the pee tube. The trip down was slow without any lube. The pain was only starting and was maddening, and the twisting again had Carla coming off the bench. When the bladder was reached, the steady stream of warm yellow fluid spirited out into the collection cup. A full cup and a half was gotten.

Daniel was next. This was Gertrude's specialty in the OR. She milked the shaft to get it good and stiff. When she was satisfied, she started the tip down the long shaft. As with Carla, the lack of lube made it tough and painful to insert. The constant pressure along with the twisting got it deep into the bladder. Daniel only produced a cup of urine. He must have pissed during the night. Elsa turned and said that neither of them would become dehydrated as this pee would be fed back into them at a later time. A quick examination of the rectum found no material to worry about coming out anytime soon.

The examinations now finished, it was time to start the tenderizing process for the rest of the fours hours of play today. They flipped a coin to see which of the "TOYS" was to be started on first as it was more fun to hear each scream one at a time. Congratulations Daniel, you won and will be the first to receive your fun.

I believe we will start with some of the very stiff scrub brushes. Gratitude grabbed the ball sack and pulled it as tight as she could back over the cock and up toward stomach. Elsa took the triangular shaped brush and placed the tip at the base of the sack. She drew it so slowly up toward the cock, making sure each and every bristle made contact. Daniel let out some screams, not earth scattering.

Let's try this again. She repositioned the brush, placed as much pressure on the bristles and very slowly dragged it back up. This time, she lifted the brush and pushed it from top to bottom over the balls, one at a time. He is starting to like this so let's try another heavy duty square brush.

She repeated the procedure again and again several time. Daniels ball sack was starting to turn red and hurt when touched. As before, this was done maybe ten more times before changing to a stainless steel parts cleaning brush. Several quick flicks from bottom to top brought intense cries. Gertrude let the sack go and went to the table to select her tool.

She selected a steel wire brush with several rows of one inch long bristles. Would you do me the honor of pulling his sack up and back and Elsa did it. I am going to work around the rim of the ass hole. She flicked the sharp points around the sphincter.

The little tight area quivered and even a little drop of blood appeared. No problem, let's see if I can get more blood to start. After a dozen more passes, many drops were slowly dripping from the area. I think we need to stop the red so she reached for the container of salt and rubbed it over the area. The salt turned red and stopped the flow. It did on the other hand bring cries and tears to Daniel.

Let Daniel have a few minutes to himself and it's time for Carla to start her fun. Helma looked a Roseland and said this is my specialty area. With the speculum still in place, she took a pair of tissue tweezers and began to grab thin pieces of skin within Carla.

With the catheter removed, the rim of the pee hole presented a good target. I will start taking little nips at the flesh. The ends of the tweezers had tiny little interlocking teeth. She got hold of the skin and pulled and twisted at the same time. She took maybe six tries to get totally around and hole. Let us say we move down toward the clit. Let me have the Clemetson Uterine Forceps.

Roseland handed her the forceps. I am going to grab onto the skin here at the hood. She closed the serrated round ends and closed them tight on the tender skin. Carla let out a scream that shook the room. Knowing that she got a tender point, Helma both twisted and pulled on the tool. She pulled it almost till it tore it loose and backed off. She repeated the process a dozen times. I think it is time to return to Daniel, but first, I want a five pound weight to dangle from the forceps handles. She attached the weight and let it drop slowly, than let it finish by falling the last two inches. It almost made Carla pass out.

Daniels's eyes were as wide as silver dollars as he waited for the next thing to happen to him. Gertrude picked up the forty grit sand paper and than milked his cock till it was up and stiff. Let's see if I can polish the tip for you. Several times across the head and Daniel had his hands clinched in pain. How about along the sides? Do you think he will enjoy this as much? Elsa shook her head and said lets try. Gertrude ran the paper back and forth till it was red and very raw. Just a light touch on it sent him into spasms.

Elsa reached for the Schroeder Vasellum Forceps, the ones with the wonderful sharp points on each side of the tips. I don't know where to start, but this looks like a good place. Elsa took the cock in her hands and placed the tips on each side of the tip. Slowly the tips were closed and the points closed on and into the tender flesh. The more I squeeze, the better it will feel for you.

She closed them till they caught very tight and began to pull his cock away from him, twisting all the way. Small droplets of blood appeared and again screams came from his dry throat.

That was fun for me Daniel. Wonder how it will feel as I place one of your balls in-between the nice sharp points? Daniel began to plead for mercy as she placed his left ball between the points. Daniel you must speak up if you wish for me to hear. Elsa knew full well that there was no way she could understand, but took a good guess. The points closed in on the ball and caught the sack well. Again a small amount of blood ran down the wooden block he was strapped to. After pulling and twisting, Elsa let up the pressure and clamped them to his right ball. She got the same effect as she pulled and twisted.

When she tired, the forceps were removed. We must do something about all the blood coming from your cock and balls. Gertrude took a towel and poured some 70 % medical alcohols into the cup section she made. Let me clean that up for you Daniel.

Daniels hand waived and tried to tear loose from the bonds. That's good and now we can place a good crusting of salt on the wounds. As the salt started to work on his cock and balls, not only did his hands wave, his hands clinch, but his feet also waved. The pain was very intense.

I want to see them both have fun with their breasts and nipples. Let us both start to use the sand paper on the nipples and breasts. Stroke after stroke on the tender breast and nipple flesh started a new round of panic and screams. For some reason, Carla did a little better with the pain, but come to it eventually.

I think a pair of the rugged alligator clips on the nipples should add to the fun. They pinched up the nipples, took them in their thumb and finger and pulled them up toward the ceiling. When they were extended as far as they could get them, the clamps were placed at the base of the nipples.

The nipples were released and than they pushed the sharp clamps together, working the points into the tender flesh. Begging and plea's for mercy streamed from each of their gagged mouths. Let's place a string around each clamp and we can attach them to the rope and pulleys coming from the ceiling. The rope was brought down and attached to the string. Now let us place some weight on the ends of the rope, maybe five pounds each.

Gertrude looked at Elsa and commented that since Carla had the clamp on her hood that it should also be equally fun to have something like this for Daniel to have fun also. Gertrude picked up the pin point parachute and placed it around his ball sack.

The points immediately caused pain from the already damaged sack. A rope from the pulley above his balls was brought down and attached to the parachute. A five pound weight was attached and let drop. The ball sack with parachute jumped upward and sent him into spasms.

They all stood back to check out their handiwork. Roseland commented that she felt it was time to get some pleasure from the two of them. The other three agreed that they need some relief and to empty their urine.

They stepped to the head of the block and chair and un-strapped the heads and told them here is how it is going to work. Each one of us is going to stand over your head and place our womanhood tightly onto your mouth. You will give us the best oral sex that you have ever done. When you have satisfied each of us to our standards, you will than take in all our urine without spilling a drop. You will give top service to each of us and than maybe we will start all over again.

To make sure that you do a great job, we will be giving you encouragement. Helma and Elsa went to the tables and picked up several pieces of copper wire. One set of wires were a big bundle of wound wire. His was roughly shoved into the rectum while Daniel got one down his cock and secured. Carla had her wire bundle inserted into the love cannel.

Both the ends were connected to the old style crank Army telephone. Let us show you what you will receive if you stop sucking or bite any of us. Helma and Elsa took the handles of the cranks and gave it a twist. Daniel and Carla screamed and pleaded that they would do the best job they ever had done. Even though Carla that had never tasted pussy before said she would do an outstanding job.

One by one they each mounted a head and lowered their womanhood down onto a waiting tongue and mouth. Elsa said as she sat down, I forgot to tell you that we will control your breathing as we sit. This brought fear from Daniel and Carla. They each started licking and sucking to their best. The process went on until each of the women had come to orgasm and relived their pee into the mouths of the two.

There were only a few times that it was necessary to shock them to get a better job done. Looking at the clock, Roseland noted that as they finished their second time through, it was a little over the four hour time limit for the first day.

The Women dismounted from the two and started to remove the clamps and parachute from Daniel and Carla. Both were barely able to talk and lay limp. Ilsa and Frieda commended the women for such a good job and told them they would finish for the day. The Woman departed the play room, went to the dressing area and changed back into their casual clothing. They proceeded to their rooms for baths and a sauna until it was time for supper.

Ilsa and Frieda started with Carla. They started by releasing her feet and legs, than the straps around her belly and than her hands. Once she was released, the chains for her wrist and ankle shackles were attached and than she was transported back to the cell and locked into the iron rings.

Daniels turn came next and the shackles were chained again. He was led to the cell and also re-chained to the iron rings. Now that they were ready for a long night, Ilsa stood before them and told them that this was most likely the easiest day they would have.

The food and water bowls were placed and they were told to eat. They both looked like they didn't want to eat until Ilsa grabbed Daniel's balls and twisted. Frieda just had to grab a tender nipple to accomplish the same thing. Very good you two, we will be back in ten minutes and you had better have finished your food and water or we will get out the cattle prods.

Daniel and Carla eagerly dug into the dog food and drank the water. With as much pain as they were in, they at least could control not getting the prod. Frieda returned and removed the empty bowls. You two had better get as much sleep as you can as tomorrow will be much worse. She turned around and turned out the light. Both the "TOYS" drifted off to sleep as fast as their aching bodies would let them.

Day Two

Dinner of the night before had been scheduled as a formal event. Great amounts of superb food and wine was served. A live band performed and dancing went on till around ten. They than returned and got naked and laid around cuddling each other and fell asleep on the pillows and cushions in the living room.

When the 7 am chimes went off they again went to either baths or showers to wake up. After dressing casually and having breakfast at the buffet, they went to the dressing room to get ready for the days play. They all agreed to dress in the riding outfits of a nice blouse and breaches with knee high shiny black leather boots.

Ilsa and Frieda went about their chores of setting the toy room up for the days play. The room was cleaned the night before and pressure washed. Two different tables were brought in and bolted to the floor. These benches were much smaller than day one. Each had a top of two feet long by one foot wide. The two tables of instruments were set between them as the day before.

Two additional tables were at the foot of the benches. These tables contained a vast number of striking items. Two different riding crops, two leather poppers with one inch wide by eight inch long heavy leather tails, both a bamboo and a plastic coated steel core canes, two leather slappers, two bull whips, one four and one six foot in length, two long paddles, one leather with split tails and metal buttons and one nylon with ten sharp pointed studs, a heavy leather flogger with two foot tails with split tips and to finish a canvas hog slapper used to control hogs up the chutes into the truck.

Ilsa and Frieda proceeded to the cell to bring the two TOYS to the play room. Frieda walked in the cell first and turned on the lights. Daniel and Carla were lying there as quietly as possible to avoid pain from the day before. Time has come to wake up and get ready for the days play, bringing Carla to beg for compassion and not hurt her today.

This fell on deft ears and she had her chains released from the floor. A leash was attached to her collar and she was told to start crawling to the play room. She was helped to start by Frieda grabbing her womanhood and squeezing.

Carla let out a scream and started to crawl as Frieda led her by the leash. Ilsa brought up the rear with the cattle prod in her hand. As they entered the play room, Carla got a look at the tables of tools and whips and tried to stop in her tracks. A quick shock in her rectum and she did as told.

She stood at the base of the block and lay face down on the small top. Frieda started by securing her body with the wide belts making sure her pussy was an inch or two off the end and her head extending off the top. Her arms were pulled straight down and attached to the base of the wooden block.

Now came the legs for securing. Each was pulled forward toward the front of the base and secured to the iron rings in front making sure there was no wiggle room. Frieda now ran her gloved hand between the pussy lips and brought about a soft crying response. They finished by making sure that each breast was dangling down the side of the block.

Fine, now that she is secure, let's get Daniel. Daniel was shivering in a ball in the cell. You know what will happen if you don' cooperate and he laid out straight. His chains were taken from their iron rings and a leash attached to his collar.

Now start crawling and as they entered the room, he also balked some and Ilsa grabbed his soar balls and twisted. He did as he was told and was secured as Carla to his block. His cock and ball hung off the end as was his head off the other end.

The Four entered the toy room and walked to the head of the blocks. Elsa and Gertrude stood in front of Daniel and Roseland and Helma Stood in front of Carla. Each of the two women grabbed the hair of the ones they were going to work on.

The heads were jerked up toward the ceiling and each of the women spit into the mouths and faces of the TOYS. Ilsa spoke and told them that the first half of today's session would be a continuation of yesterday. If you thought that you were in pain before, you are to be given a stiffer dose today. Prepare yourselves as we are going to start the first half of today's fun.

Each team went to their tables and selected an assortment of brushes. A stiff one was used to start on Daniel's balls. It was slowly drawn from his ass hole, over his balls and than down his cock. Carla had her Labia spread and the brush slowly drawn deeply down into the wide opening of her womanhood.

These actions continued as many as ten times for each. Each draw brought begging, crying and screaming. Now let's apply the wire brushes the same way. These brushes were about an inch wide by four inches long. Daniel's started from just behind his ass hole and ended at the base of his balls. From there the draws encompassed both his balls, top to bottom and side to side. Gertrude started to milk his cock to get it hard.

The Wire brush was now brought around the base of his cock and all sides received heavy brushing turning the areas beet red with small droplets of blood. Over and over again this went on and he had screamed himself horse. An alcohol soaked rag was applied and than the area packed with salt. Carla didn't make out much better.

This time Helma and Roseland traded places in holding the labia open. Roseland took the blush and inserted it into the womanhood and started on one side, slowly bringing the brush from deep inside her to the outer lip areas. Carla whipped her head from side to side, screaming and begging intensely for mercy. Mercy was not to come. The dragging of the brush continued with the other side.

The tissue became very inflamed and painful. We must not forget the outside of the lips. Gertrude took a set of forceps and grabbed the edge of the lip and extended it outward. This time the brush was drawn from outer edge to the skin of her crouch and a zigzag motion was used. Some blood was drawn, but would be dealt with after at least five more reputations were completed. The area was almost blood red and dripping.

Helma decided to clean the area and dumped the entire bottle of alcohol into Carla's vagina. Carla tore at all her bonds but without any luck. A towel used to dry out the area and salt applied. Carla passed out at this point. This was not allowed so Roseland inserted the two points of the cattle prod up into the vagina and let loose with an extended shock. This action brought Carla back to reality and she knew where she was and what had happened.

Now for some real pain girls as they went to the tables and picked up a pair of truss mending plates. The plates were used to join pieces of wood together. Each plate was two inches by four inches and had thirty pair of quarter inch long sharp points on the. Girls, I will show you how they are used on Daniel.

Elsa started by placing one plate behind his balls and than the other one on the opposite side to the first. She placed her hands on the ends and squeezed the plates together. The points embedded themselves into the soft flesh. Pressure was slowly applied and the plates were slowly slid side to side increasing the pain. Daniel screamed as he had not prior and bucked his head side to side.

Elsa varied the pressure from end to end over a period of several minutes. As pressure was released, sixty little holes appeared as the plates were removed. With much enthusiasm, Gertrude took he plates and applied them to his cock. Daniel was no less comfortable as pressure was applied.

She than wiggled the plates from side to side. It took everything he had to stay conscious, but he did it. He did not want the cattle prod visiting any part of him. Elsa and Gertrude took turns working on his cock and balls.

It was Carla's turn to experience the plates. Since she didn't have a cock and balls, the plates were slid down the inside of the labia and the other placed on the outside. The pressure was applied slowly and the rubbing action was started. It didn't take long for the effects to start. The grinding acting brought tears and crying. The plates were traded to the other side and repeated many times.

Elsa looked at the clock and remarked that it was time to start on the strapons action. Each woman steeped to the table and retrieved their harness and placed it on themselves. Each of us should select the dildo of our own choice. We need to stretch their ass holes as wide as possible for tomorrow's fun.

Elsa selected one, two inches in diameter and ten inches long.

Gertrude picked up one that was only nine inches long, but two and a half in diameter. Roseland took the three inch in diameter and ten inches in length. Finally, Helma said she felt nasty today and picked up the one with half inch long stiff plastic spikes around the two inch shaft. Remember, there is not to be any lube used, and you can gage your own rate to be inserted.

We will work on each of them, one at a time and work on to the next. The screams started as the first one went in on the reluctant openings. Each woman had their own way to inflect as much pain as possible and stretch the tender passages. Each woman took five minutes at a time and moved to the next opening. During the times where they were not inserting their weapon, the stepped to the top of the bench, grabbed the head of the TOY and forced the bloody, shit smeared dildo down their throats. I think they are fully stretched at the present time. Let us finish up in the play room so we can go work on the grapes.

The whips table was approached. I think we should start out with more mild ones and work up. The purpose is to make them very tender on the back, butt and behind the legs. As we get going, the purpose is to bring deep black and blue welts to the butt and back of the legs.

For Carla, her breasts are open turf and can be inflected with the whipping pain. Two took crops and two took leather slappers. Taking turns each made sure that every inch of the areas were beaten. Now that the skin of these areas was red and stinging to the touch, it was time to move up to a more brutal device.

Gertrude and Roseland took up the leather slappers and Elsa and Helma selected the braided quirts. These would ensure a deeper pain until the final weapons were brought into play. Elsa and Gertrude went to work on Daniels butt and the back of his legs. Roseland took hers and started on the butt and legs.

Helma was getting into the fun with zeal and said she would inflect the pain to her breasts hanging down beside the butcher block table. This went on for another ten minutes. Elsa now picked up the wide, three tail leather paddle with the rows of metals studs. Gertrude selected the many leather tail floggers. She felt the need to swing something hard and this would do, Helma took the nylon paddle with the ten metal points on it. This would do a job on the breasts.

Roseland had a different idea to Carla. She selected the hog slapper, two of the mending plates and some duct tape. Roseland thought of the fun it would be to tape the two plates to Carla's ass with tape and than with a full swing, imbed them into the ass. The other three continued to enjoy the flogging and beating of the body parts with their paddles.

It didn't take long to exhaust their fun when Elsa said it was time to use the canes on their butts and legs. They took turns with the canes. Selecting a new spot each time and bring dark blue and black deep welts to the surface. Each took ten swings. Helma couldn't wait to pinch up some of the swollen welts and squeeze them. By this time, Daniel and Carla were almost out of reality, but the fun would be continuing after a move of "TOYS" and Women to the pressing/grinding room.

As both Ilsa and Frieda walked to the tables to release the "TOYS", Ilsa looked at us and asked if we had forgotten something prior to movement. We looked at each other and she handed us two packages of fishing hooks with leaders attached. Each package contained six number 1/0 hooks. I said that we were so excited to get started down stairs that we forget. Frieda handed us two snap hooks and we went back to the bottom of the butcher blocks. Each of you will insert three fishing hooks to each side.

Each team retrieved rolling stools and started. Daniel went first. His ball sack was pulled down and the skin on one side pinched. Starting at the top, Elsa pushed the point of the barbed hook thru the sack. This instantly brought Daniel to life again. I felt the pop as the second and third hooks went thru. Gertrude took the stool and started her insertions. Pop by pop the barbed hooks went in place. The six leaders were gathered up and the snap opened. The six loops from the leaders were secured.

Carla was next as Roseland grabbed the left labia. She worked the first hook into the thin, tender flesh. Number two and three followed. My turn was called out by Helma. She took up her perch on the stool and took up the lip in her hand. Now I will work at this as hard as I can. She placed the point on the flesh and started it into the lip.

Part way in, she stopped and backed it out causing much pain. Next she wiggled the tip into the partly started hole and again stabbed slowly causing much pain. Let's see, I have two more to go. Where to go next? Maybe I should find the clit and try there. She spread the lips and brought the tip next to the clit and stabbed the point just into the flesh. Oh, I was just playing and took it out and poked the second and third ones into the lip. What a fine job if I say so myself. She placed the six leads into the clip and they were finished.

Frieda complimented the job of placing the hooks and turned to Helma and said that I see you are getting into this so very well. I was afraid in the beginning that you would not be to able and cruel as you have been today. Helma lowered her head and thanked Frieda for the kind words. Ilsa stepped over to the four women and told them to go to the whip table and select either the bull whip or a carriage whip for the trip down stairs.

Ilsa and Frieda removed Carla from her block and placed a leash to her iron collar. The chains were placed on the wrist and ankle cuffs so they would have only small steps. The leash was handed to Helma for the trip. Daniel came next, chains installed and a leash placed on his collar. This leash was handed to Gertrude. Ilsa turned and said they needed to start down to the pressing room.

They proceeded to the heavy wooden door at the back of the play room. The door led to a long sloped incline taking them to the pressing room. The lights were dim and the going slow. They got to another heaven door which opened into the century old wine pressing room.

It was a large room maybe thirty feet across. In the center was the pressing area. It was made of two stone rings. The outer ring was fifteen in diameter with a one foot thick stone ring about two foot high. A one foot space was left between the outer ring and the inner ring. The inner ring was also one foot thick and two foot high. There were two round pressing stones, almost five foot in diameter and one foot thick. In the center of each were a hole and a large pole going between the two wheels. The pole extended four foot on each side of the outside of the outer ring of stone. Two iron rings were placed at the ends of the pole with two feet between.

To start with, Daniel was led to the one side and had his wrists attached to the rings. Carla was hooked to the other side facing in the opposite direction. Ilsa came over to the women and said that you have two hours to crush all the grapes within the rings to prepare them for wine making. Elsa and Gertrude stood behind Daniel and Roseland and Helma were behind Carla. Ilsa said that it was time to start.

First a five pound weight was attached between the legs to the snap hook. Crying was heard as the fish hooks sunk deep into the flesh. There was room for the weight to swing as they pushed. The women were stationed at the three, six, nine and twelve o'clock positions around the press area. With that, Ilsa gave the word to start turning the press.

Elsa took her six foot bull whip and snapped it across the welts on Daniels butt. Roseland responded with her carriage whip to Carla's lower legs. The wheels started to turn slowly as the pair pushed for all they had. Next came time for Daniel to pass Gertrude with her carriage whip. The snap of the whip landed on his lower legs. Helma was next to bringing her five foot bull whip on the butt of Carla. Turn after turn kept the wheels turning, crushing the grapes for the winery.

Every now and than one of the two would stumble or slow, instantly bringing he sting of the whip. After a half hour, both Daniel and Carla's butts and lower legs had their welts rising and some seepage to come from them. As they passed the Women, one by one, they would give the weight a kick, sending it swinging to and fro. Daniel and Carla were just to out of it by now and little noise was heard. The time passed and the grapes were crushed and the liquid from them dripped into a barrel in the lower basement to be colleted at a later time.

The assignment finished, Daniel and Carla were released from the wooden arm of the press and their chains put back on. This time Gertrude and Helma were given the leashes and the eight of them started the long walk back up to incline to the play room. Ladies, tonight it is your turn to put your toys away. You may leave the weights on or not, it is up to you, but the hooks stay in for the night. They were led into their cell and each attached to the rings in the wall and floor. Frieda handed Helma and Gertrude the water and food bowels to place next to their "TOY". Daniel and Carla made fast work of the food and water and their bowels removed.

The light was turned out and everyone departed the room and it was locked. Ladies, you are done for the night as Ilsa and I will need to clean up the play room and set up the tools for tomorrow. The night is yours but be back in the dressing room by ten in the morning. The four went back to the dressing room, changed into their house clothes and departed for their room.

Elsa turned to the others and said that maybe they should get the supper to go and return to the room for an evenings rest. They agreed and went to the dining area, took a plate and each helped them selves to a slice of the most tender prim rib, potatoes and a wonderful mix of country vegetables. A freshly baked roll and a slice of pie completed the feast. They secured a beverage for the night and returned to the room. Each sat quietly and ate the meal. Some small talk took up the remaining time till they would turn in.

Each had so much on their mind from the day's play and sort of talked about it. Helma was the tightest wound that evening. She could not even believe the things she had done to Carla that day. She was even thinking; was she an animal or what. How could she do such things to a human being as a doctor meant to save lives, not destroy them. Roseland took her head and placed it on her shoulder to comfort her.

Don't think too much about it. Tomorrow will be even more sever to them than these first two days. I am sure that you will come thru and do what is required. Remember, you can trade places with them if you screw up. You will do fine.

It took all of us several trips here to get the full extent of the relaxations from the play. Don't even think of the "TOYS" as they are not human and will never be seen again after we finish day four. Now go to sleep and dream on. They all retired to their bedrooms and were asleep within minutes.

Day Three

Ilsa and Frieda were finishing their breakfast in the private dining room. Frieda suggested they go down to the cell and start to get the "TOYS" ready and moving. I think they will be very slow to move after yesterdays play. They got up from their table and started to the elevator. Ilsa inserted her key card and they were on the way to the lower level. The floor was reached and they went to cell door.

The door was opened and the light turned on. Neither of the two stirred with any movement so Frieda grabbed the hose and let loose with cold water. Daniel moved first and than Carla slowly lifted her head. Let's go you two; your time is passing you by. Daniel's chains were unhooked from the rings holding him. Get up and start walking.

He made it to his knees, but his legs were like rubber. You have five seconds to move or I will get the prod and stick it up your ass. Daniel asked in a low voice if he could crawl to the play room. Frieda attached a leash to the collar and pulled him to the room.

It took five minutes to get the twenty feet to the wooden bench. You are to be placed as yesterday. Daniel pulled himself up and laid his broken body on the bench. The two large belts were placed and tightened. The arms and legs were than secured.

Today, they were even tighter than the day prior. Ilsa turned and gave him a pat on the welts on his ass, causing him to scream. Good, they did a good job preparing him for today's fun. They returned to fetch Carla for her trip to the play room. She was unhooked from the rings and she was told to move. She looked up and pleaded for mercy and not be made to go to the play room today.

You are going to go and it is up to you as to how you make it. Maybe you need some encouragement, so I will give you one. Ilsa stepped behind her and firmly planned the toe of her foot into her pussy. She jumped and slowly started to crawl to her spot on the block. Now get up and place yourself on the block as yesterday. It was slow, but she made it up and was secured to the block.

Frieda made a quick inspection of the tools on the tables and brought in a mobile table with extra items for the day. The extra items included several bottles of liquids, including lemon juice and pickling solution. Dry items included salt and different types of peppers. A bowl of cut up Habanero peppers rounded out the selection.

A tray of scalpels with a variety of blades was placed in the middle of the table. Finishing off the new items were two items from the medieval period. Two reproductions of the Pear of Anguish sat there. They differed from those of the 17th century that they were made of brass to conduct electrical shocks and also transfer heat along its length.

They each had four peddles that could be opened to a diameter of four inches. There were normally sharp points at the end of each peddle, but were left off as to not injury the internal lining of the rectum. The closed pear was an inch and a half in diameter and eight inches in length.

The four Doctors arrived at the wardrobe room to make their choice of costume for the session. Because of the work to be done today, we might be better off wearing OR scrubs and shoe covers. Each one of the four selected a different color top and pants. The scrubs were downed and they proceeded to the play room.

Standing at the door of the play room, the doctor's waited the acknowledgement of Ilsa to enter. A nod of her head indicated that they could enter. Ladies, you know the day's duties which need to be done. Frieda and I will be in the corner if you need anything to perform your tasks. Now dig in and get started.

The doctor's took up their positions at the bottom of the blocks holding Daniel and Carla. Each took their hands and ran them over the deep blue to black welts on the asses and legs from the whipping and canning the day before. Even the lightest touch brought about crying and screaming from the "TOYS". Carla started begging for them to stop and it brought Helma hand to grab a handful of pussy lips. She pinched them tightly and pulled them.

Both of them still had their fish hooks still in place. I think we need to add the five pound weights to hang from them again. Frieda handed each group a weight and they were hung from the leaders of the hooks. Screams came hot and heavy as the weights were dropped to induce as much pain as possible.

Each doctor brought a wheeled chair over so they could move around easily. Let's go and choose our scalpels so we can get started. They looked at each other and decided who would make the first cut, Gertrude won with Daniel and Roseland won for Carla. Gertrude started with a large, fluid filled welt on Daniels left leg.

She inserted the tip of the blade into the edge of the welt, splashing fluid over the leg. Taking a set of tissue tweezers, she opened the skin flap. Elsa handed her the bowel of salt, which she rubbed into the open welt. Daniel bucked and tried to kick off the block. The burning had him crying and begging for them to stop. Gertrude yelled at him to shut up as he had more than two dozen more welts to deal with. Gertrude finished the other seven on his legs, pouring pickling juice into the open welts.

Carla's legs were next. Roseland took her scalpel and cut open the first of her leg welts. Lemmon juice was Roseland's choice for Carla. The acid in the juice made her jump and cry. In a shrill voice, Carla said she wanted to know why she was being done this way.

Helma walked to her head, grabbed the hair of her head and jerked her face upward. As Carla looked Helma in the face, she received a swift backhand to the jaw. Speak again and I will personally take a pair of pliers and yank out several of your teeth, do you understand me? Carla closed her mouth and the opening of her welts continued.

One by one, her leg welts were drained and filled with salt. The both of them were slowly on the way to insanity. The welts on the ass were now finished being opened and impregnated with many of the different items. Each took a hand and rubbed them over the opened welts to bring them to full attention.

Alright girls, it's time to do some stretching. Each team picked up one of the pear of anguishes for insertion. The teams decided to insert and open twice so each of the team could enjoy the feeling of inflecting the stretch. The team leaders went first. Gertrude and Helma stood next to the "TOYS" and spread the ass cheeks for a wide open shot. Elsa and Roseland each took the pear and spun it open and closed. The tip of each was placed again the rosebud opening. As with the requirements, no lube was allowed and the pear peddles were inserted dry.

The pear was inserted very slowly, rocking it side by side and corkscrewing it in. Nether of them could resist the placement, even if it was possible. Inch by inch it increased it's depth in the cannel. When they hit bottom, both Daniel and Carla exhaled in relief, little did they understand the pain to come. Now came the spreading of the peddles of the terror item within them.

We should do the opening very slowly and allow them to take in the extreme pain. A quarter of a twist of the handle at a time made the agony continue for half an hour each. The lining of the cannel was now stretched to its limits, the screaming had slowed and each of them was horse and only babbling. Let us stimulate them a little before we remove them.

The telephones were brought over to the work area and the alligator clamps were attached, one to the brass handle and the other to the bare, scared flesh, Daniel's to his foreskin of his cock and Carla to her Labia. The crank of the telephone was turned at varying rates to provide many different torments. Slow for a jerking effect and quick for a steady bite.

At this point, there was no limit to the cruelty they could inflect. Ten minutes of the telephone signaled the change of persons controlling the pain. The handles were turned the opposite direct, closing them. They were both with drawn, revealing pieces of tissue coated with droplets of blood. The pears were handed to the other set of doctors and the procedures proceeded as before. This time there was a slight difference as the bleeding made the cannel a little more slippery. Down they went into the depths of the anal cavity.

Over a period of fifteen minutes, the devices opened doing their damage. We must give them the shocking to stimulate their inners. Neither Daniel nor Carla did much complaining anymore as they were starting into a period of incoherence. At this point, Helma spoke up saying she has some of her patients that could use a good session with one of these. All four of them agreed that they had someone they wish they could use one.

Finishing the pear torture next came the finishing touch. The two fucking machines sitting in the corner were brought to the foot of the blocks. On each cart were several choices of dildos to attach. Daniel is to get a ten inch long one with a two inch diameter. One of the same dimensions was chosen for Carla with the exception of a covering of pointed spikes.

The dildos were attached and the machines wheeled up behind the two victims. The tips were inserted into the rectum about two to three inches. Each stroke of the machine would insert the entire ten inches into the already inflamed cannel.

The machines were started and the dildos slowly went in and out. The speed control was set at the lowest setting. After five minute of this speed, the controls were turned to speed up the insertion. Helma turned to the others and said we need to spice up the pressure they are having.

I think we should apply a generous coating of Habanero peppers. Pieces were taken from the bowl containing them and each one applied a liberal coating to the dildo. This brought Daniel and Carla back to reality and each begged for relief as the heat from the peppers took hold. Elsa turned to the others and said, relief is what we need.

They each removed their scrub pants and stepped to the head of the table. Grabbing Daniels head, she jerked it back and told him that he had better lick her out and drink her golden nectar. Not wanting any additional pain, Daniel proceeded to insert his tongue and lick and suck on Elsa's pussy. Carla was next. Roseland grabbed her hair and placed her super sensitive pussy in her mouth.

At first, Carla didn't do a great job, so the speed intensity was increased and salt was sprinkled on the dildo. The women changed positions and the enjoyment feast went on for over an hour. The licks were getting better with time as was the intake of the golden nectar. Not a drop of cum was missed not wanting to bring any further pain.

Total exhaustion was approaching for both the Doctors as with the two "TOYS". Ilsa and Frieda approached the tables and told them they would clean up and put the "TOYS" away for the night. The women returned to the dressing room and changed to go back to their rooms. On the way back to the room, they agreed to go get some pool time prior to supper.

Ilsa and Frieda began the messy job of cleaning up the play room and putting the two back in their cell. The arms and legs were released first from the blocks. The two straps came next allowing them to come off the block. Each tried to get off only to slip and fall to the floor. Ilsa and Frieda didn't even bother to place a leash on them for the trip back to the cell. They just each took their cattle prod and encouraged them to crawl on their bellies.

An occasional stab with the tip of the prod and the two made their way back. The limp, battered bodies were again chained to the rings and the collars attached to the wall. Food and water were served and each made an attempt to eat. Ilsa turned to them and said that they better rest as tomorrow would be far worse than the first three. You had better make peace with your maker tonight as you will not be coming back here at the close of tomorrow. As Frieda was turning out the lights, Carla began to cry uncontrollably.

The four returned to their rooms and changed into their swim suits. Each was a knock out and when they entered the pool area, compliments and even the occasional cat call came their way. Each was proud of their bodies and accepted what came. They swam and laid out in the sun till they needed to go to supper. The meal was superb as normal and they ate well. A little dancing and they returned to the room. A nice long, hot bubble bath finished the day off right.

Day Four

As the morning of the last day of play with the "TOYS" began, the four woke early and were sitting around the living room. All in different stages of dress and sipping on some very strong German coffee as some small talk helped in the process of getting hold of what was going to happen today.

Elsa and Gertrude didn't have any trouble with the final end. Roseland being very sadistic took Helma by the hand and said that all will go well today. Helma had never been in a session before where the outcome was final. Up to now, she was showing a sadistic streak during the play.

Just follow my lead and you will do just fine. Don't worry, the female "TOY" will most likely be very weak and not fight anything we do. Just to make it better, we will start out by bringing her to the best orgasm she has ever done.

I know that being an OBGYN, you have either taught others to do it or have done it yourself to patients. Let us all go and get a fabulous breakfast. They have such great food here for us and the rest of the guests. They finished dressing and proceeded to the dinning hall.

Ilsa and Frieda had already finished their meal and were heading to the cell. They walked in to find Daniel and Carla still laying half out of it. The discomfort from the opening of the welts and the Pear of Anguish had exhausted them.

The bright overhead light woke them and brought them to a state of fear. They were thinking of just what they could be in for today. Ilsa spoke to them, telling them today would be the last day of pain and torture. You will be sleeping in total comfort tonight.

We have brought you a bowl of scrambled eggs for your meal. Frieda placed the food dishes next to them and than provided a bowl of water. You will have fifteen minutes to eat and we will be back. Ilsa and Frieda went to the play room to make sure the tools were in good working condition.

Frieda rolled the large tool cart to a position just between the head of the wooden blocks. She opened it to expose some of the tool of the trade from both their pasts with the information gathering section of their past employment.

Knifes, ice picks, cheese graters, shrink wrap heat guns, wood burning sets with different size tips and a plumbers' torch just to name a few. She picked up the torch, shook the tank and applied a match to ensure it lit. A verity of common hand tools ranging from hammers with an assortment of nails, channel locks and electrician lineman pliers and even a set of tree limb cutting tools.

A battery operated drill with many different bits wound out the new tools in the cabinet. I think that all are in working condition. She asked Ilsa how often they used many of these tools to pry information from traders, spies, and political prisoner's. Ilsa replied that it was many more than she could remember.

I do miss doing the deed, but watching the work the people that pay for the privilege do is satisfying to me. I think that one of the best times was when we played dentist and used a large drill bit to drill into that prisoner's teeth. It only took maybe three teeth for him to give us all the information we needed for the General.

I think we may have company this morning. I got called into Carl's office yesterday after the session. He had been watching the session and admired the work of the four. He was most excited with Helma's excitement and work as this was her first time. He said that he will be dropping in today.

I sometimes think that he misses the old days, either the KGB or from the war. He also said that he wishes times were different, as he would hire these four to do work for him. Frieda said she understood his needs for the old trade. I think we have a 24 hours dinner/torture party coming for two dozen couples. It is always nice to have the party tables with complete feast of wonderful foods as we work on a prisoner. Also to have two or three slaves of ours that pay big money for the privilege to be here to serve them.

It is about time to get Daniel and Carla from the cell area and affix them to the wooden blocks. They returned to the cell and took Daniel first. He could hardly walk or for that fact, crawl. Ilsa and Frieda grabbed him under the arms and started dragging him to the play room. The body was lifted up on the block with his shredded back lying upon the block. He cried out in pain, but there was not much he could do.

The leather belts were applied. His arms were secured to the block and ropes were attached to the ankle shackles from above and the pair of ropes was drawn up and outward, spreading his legs very wide apart. This action fully exposed both his cock and balls, his rosebud ass hole and inner thighs. He could not have been much more wide open. His head was left to swing so the women could use his mouth.

They returned for Carla. She was trying to make herself into a ball, kind of a fetal position as much as the chains would let her. Frieda told her in a loud voice to get ready to move. Carla, you have nothing to say in this mater. It will all be over in several hours and no more pain.

The chains were undone and they pulled her from her position on the floor. She begged and stated she didn't want to go to her death.

A swift kick to her pussy and she was doubled over and she was also grabbed under her shoulders, and dragged down the hall.

She spotted Daniel in his belly up position and knew that she had to assume it or be given more pain at that time. The straps went over her belly button and just under her breasts, leaving what was left of them open and ready to use. Her arms went down to her side and her legs were fitted into the ropes from the ceiling and spread very wide. Frieda took a little more slack from her legs than they had Daniel's legs.

Being the last day, Ilsa and Frieda decided to get a little oral pleasure from them prior to the arrival of the four. You know the drill and you better not say anything about this to anyone else. We may have time with you after they are done and I can tell you that we give much more extreme torture than they do.

All Ilsa and Frieda had to do was step up and over the waiting mouths of the two. Mouths and tongues began to lick and suck very hard. When both had been brought to orgasm, they switched and received another wonderful round. Satisfied, Ilsa and Frieda took their places by the new tool cart and awaited the entrance of the four.

Back in the dressing room, Elsa and Gertrude had finished dressing. Roseland was still deciding what color to ware and Helma was kind of slower than normal. Once all were ready, they departed the dressing room for the play room. As they entered, Ilsa turned to them and welcomed them. This is your final day with the "TOYS" and there are no limits as in the past three days. I encourage you to check out the cart for the items we have brought into the room. As in the past, we are here to lend any advice to you as to what is here and how to use the items.

I have been told that Mr. Schmidt may be a visitor to the play room today. If he comes in, just go on with what you are doing. He may come over to your team and inquire as to your plan of action. On rare occurrences, he has asked if you mind if he joins in with you. It is up to you, but it would be an experience you may never get again. He is an expert in information gathering and the giving of pain.

Without any more delays, you should get going. Daniel was the first to receive attention. Gertrude started to milk his cock just as she lifted it; Elsa took the point of the heel and dug it into his balls. A silent scream came from his throat and this time, she took the toe of her boot and kicked him squarely in the balls. He tried to double up but the belts prevented it from happening.

Needing more action from him, Elsa grabbed both his nipples, squeezed, dug her fingernails into them and twisted them. Gertrude did the same thing but with his balls. He was fully awake and aware of what was gong on them.

Roseland said, I kind of like that and dug her nails into Carla's nipples, pulling them to the ceiling. With the skin already in a weakened state, small drops of blood came from them. Helma was getting so excited and grabbed her labia and almost ripped them off. Carla began to thrash and twist her legs. Helma said I like this and grabbed the bear claw.

The six sharp fingers were places at the crouch and drawn up toward the knee. Deep red lines showed immediately. I need to do this more and she switched sides. This time she drew it much more slowly up, increasing the pain level. I wonder what would happen if I placed it in her pussy and drew it outward, grabbing the labia. The screams brought such happiness; she did it several more time, switching sided as she went.

The tender lips shown in so many shades of red, and black and blue they knew they had to be in intense pain. Roseland asked Helma to share the claw so she could work on her breasts. The claw was passed and the six teeth dug into the under side of her breasts. Small rivulets of blood appeared and had alcohol poured on them and patted in.

Gertrude turned to Elsa and said we can't let them have all the fun. They took the claw from their table and started to work on Daniel's chest. Pass after pass brought bright red welts up. This is fun and I think I will keep on doing it.

Elsa went to the new table and picked up a pair of lineman's pliers. She brought them to his left nipple, placed them over them to the base and squeezed as hard as she could. The nipple being crushed was than twisted till almost being torn off. The other nipple looks left out, I will do the same to it. His nipples had been destroyed by this time, but both were still attached for now. At this point, it was a toss up as to which "TOY" was in more pain.

Helma went for her new fun toy, the crank phone. She took the alligator clip and attached them to Carla's nipples. The crank handle was now turned at many different speeds, little bites to cause jerking to fast to bring prolonged pain.

The mussels of the breasts were twitching and sweating profusely. I see you are enjoying this so much; I am going to change their location. The clips were now moved to the labia. Helma squeezed the clips digging their teeth deep into the tender flesh. This pain alone was extreme until the cranking started. Her whole body jumped and she begged for mercy. Roseland said, you can beg all day, but none will come.

Girls, let's take a brief break and look over the new tools again. Gertrude stated she was so excited and need her pussy cleaned of all the white, streaming cum dripping out of it. All agreed that they also needed relief so they took turns, moving from Daniel to Carla and back again. Roseland said a clean pussy is a good working pussy.

Now for the now tools on the table, which to use. They picked up one after another tool, looking at it thinking of how to apply it to the "TOYS". Being a plastic surgeon, I think I needed to do some art work on her breasts. She chose the wood burning tool with thin tip, a scalpel and a set of tissue forceps.

Frieda provided a cord to plug the wood burning tool into and started it to turn cheery red. Smoke began to appear at the tip. Good, I think it is ready now and I will burn little designs into her breasts. She went to the left breast and seated herself on the chair so she could draw pretty little pictures on the flesh. I will go slowly so I can get a clean picture of a tree with birds. I love to do this when I was young. Black smoke rose as the skin started to sizzle. Maybe I should add a cloud or two in the sky.

Having finished the burning of the picture, she took the scalpel and started to trace the burn lines. Next she set a stainless steel bowl next to her on Carla's stomach to hold the tissue scraps. Using the tissue forceps, she lifted the corner and ripped the skin from the shape burned into the breast. The raw area was now filled in with Habanero peppers juice. She finished with the left breast and moved to the right one.

What to draw this time, I think I will do some blocks, squares, circles, triangles. The tip of the burner flowed like it was being used by a fine artist. The edge of the knife was tracing out each shape, followed by the ripping of the skin off. This time pickling solution and a crusty layer of salt, which she ground in with the heal of her hand. I think we need to give her some time to recover prior to starting another procedure.

Elsa and Gertrude talked about what Daniel's next stimulating experience would be. I am gong to select a mixture of sizes and lengths of syringe needles. I want to decorate the area above his cock and balls. We can also use them on his cock and balls. A hammer and two inch long nails were also brought to the table. Let us first secure his balls to the wooden block. Sounds like a great idea.

Gertrude took hold of the ball skin and pulled it down and held it to the block. Elsa took a nail and placed it on the outer edge of his left ball skin. Three strikes with the hammer and that side was secured. Next the nail met the right ball skin and three taps seated the nail down. I think we are ready to start. Elsa pinched up skin just above the cock and shoved the tip of a long needle just under the skin, thru the meat under the skin and out the other side an inch later. Perfect, let's just keep going and place another dozen or two in the skin here. I like it and let's try another target. This time they started with the skin of the ball sack. Four more were shoved into the base of the sack.

Gertrude turned to Elsa and asked, how many do you think we can get into the balls themselves? Elsa said that he had large ball's, let's just start. The first one entered the sack and came to rest on he left ball. A steady push and the pop of the ball could be heard. That was so neat, my turn on the right. The right ball popped as easy as the left. By this time, Daniel was hysterical with pain and cried and screamed in total agony. The women were able to get over a dozen more on each one.

There was now a steady flow of blood. I want to see him jump from the balls; Gertrude took the crank telephone from the table. She connected the leads to the exposed tip of one of the needles in each ball. As the handle was turned, Daniel almost ripped his balls from the wooden black where his ball sack was nailed. Not sure why his cock came to attention, why not decorate it with needles also. Another two dozen needles covered his cock, some thru it and some down thru the tip. At this point, he was on the verge of being totally insane. I think he needs a break.

Helma was looking at the ceiling at this point. There were two pulleys with rope and hooks hanging there. I have an idea. She went to the table and found two long knitting needles. These will do, and she picked them up. She went to the left side, grabbed the nipple, and raised it up placing tension on the breast. The tip of the needle was now resting against the outside of the base of the breast. A steady push started the needle thru the breast.

Roseland wanted in on this fun and took the other knitting needle and slowly, but steadily pushed hers thru the base of the other breast. That is fine work, but needs to be decorated with the rope from above. The ropes were lowered and wound around both ends of the knitting needles. Helma gave them a firm tugs assuring that they would hold. With little talk, the ropes were pulled till the breasts were pulling Carla's body off the block a little. The pressure was almost unbearable. Blood was now flowing from the holes.

All stood back to admire their work when Gertrude looked toward the very corner of the play room. There was a café table with a checkered table cloth and chair. An older man sat, drinking a glass of wine and observing the proceedings. He stood and came over to introduce himself. Ladies, I am Carl Schmidt, the owner of this place of fun and pleasure.

I have been checking in on you over the last three day from my office camera. I was so impressed with your play with your "TOYS" that I had to personally watch your final day of play. In the olden days, I would have recruited you to work for me in the information gathering business. You are all very inventive and remind me of two others that I trained so many yeas ago, Ilsa and Frieda.

I am not here to tell you what to do, but I want to suggest that you need to get the big bang started as both the "TOYS" are just about done being much fun anymore. I am going to guess that you may have around half an hour left of useful reactions from them. You should make it go out with a big bang.

At that point, Carl stepped up front of each and shook each of their hands and kissed the back of each hand. He quietly returned to his table and picked up his glass and toasted them. The women returned to the table and made their selections for the final act.

Elsa and Gertrude picked up two glass bottles, leather gloves and returned to Daniel. Roseland and Helma also picked up the same two bottles, gloves, but Helma also grabbed a suture set and a pair of scissors. They than returned to Carla and began work.

Both Gertrude and Roseland downed the leather gloves and opened the jars labeled river leaches. I think we should decorate the breasts with these blood sucking leaches. Leach by leach, were placed them on the breasts of the victims. At first they didn't do much, but they would attach themselves to the flesh. Little by little they started digging into the skin to extract the blood from under the skin.

Daniel and Carla start to squirm, wiggling and screaming as the little leaches did their job. Now it was time for Elsa and Helma to begin their devious play. They downed the leather gloves and took a quarter cup scoop, opened the lid and got a scoop of red fire ants. Elsa stepped over Daniel's cock and balls and scattered them over the area. It didn't take long for the little animals to start the chewing action on what left of his package.

Helma returned to the first table and picked up a spectrum, opened the vaginal cannel and dumped her scoop deep inside of Carla. The spectrum was quickly removed, closing the exit path. Helma reached for the suture materials and said that I have always wanted to do this to the dumb drug sluts that keep getting pregnant and dropping children that the state has to take care or die in my hands at delivery.

She grabbed the labia, pulled them together and started the needle in one side and out the other. Tying each one very tightly and starting the next one down. We don't want them to escape before doing their jobs. It required a dozen well placed sutures to complete. By this time, the fire ants were well involved in biting the inside of her love cannel. All four ladies stood back to admire their work. Slowly at first, than faster the little animals did their intended job.

All at once, Daniel gave out a load scream and was quiet. He was finished and within minutes, Carla also expired. Ilsa came over to the blocks and told the women that unless they just wanted to continue on corpses, they were finished. Elsa agreed and told the other three it was time to go and change.

The four left for the changing room. A quick change to their resort clothes and they were on their way to enjoy the remainder of their two week vacations. The elevator ride to the first floor seemed to take forever. They exited and went straight to the room. Once inside, they found an envelope from Wolfgang. Elsa read out aloud to the other three. Wolfgang wrote that we at the Chalet hope that you enjoyed the experience and please feel free to use the many fun parts in our area. As normal, you will need to come and see me at eleven in the morning to be debriefed.

The women collapsed on the living room furniture and took a deep breath. Gertrude turned to Helma and asked her how she felt now that it was all over. She responded that it hadn't settled in on her totally yet. I will be digesting the events this evening. All went to their bedrooms for a well deserved hot bath and even a sauna. Roseland was the first to return to the living room wearing her tennis outfit. Elsa took one look and returned to her room and changed into the tennis outfit. They left the room for the tennis courts for several sets.

Gertrude emerged wearing her skinny two piece swim suit and asked if Helma wanted to join her. Helma said she was going to put on a sun dress and go to the top floor and just sit and look at the surroundings.

They boarded the elevator together, Gertrude stepped off at the swimming pool level and Helma rode it to the top floor. She found a lounge chair in the corner overlooking the vast country side. Just prior to lowering her wide brim sun hat to cover her eyes, a waitress startled her and asked if she would like a drink and or a snack to get her to the supper meal. She responded that a nice tall, chilled glass of house wine and maybe several finger sandwiches. The waitress departed and returned several minutes later and placed them on a small table next to the lounge chair.

I hope that you enjoy these and if you need anything else, please give me a little wave. Helma thanked her, ate one of the sandwiches and sipped the wine. She just wanted to take in the vast expanse of the mountains and think back over the last four days. She was a little bit confused as to how she felt about what she had done. Was it right of her to help dispatch the woman or not? She lay there, half awake and half drifting into bliss.

Meanwhile back at the play room, Ilsa and Frieda were cleaning the chamber. First and foremost was the removal of the bodies and their disposal. They placed them in a laundry cart and wheeled them down to the chalets crematorium. House rule number one; no bodies were to left for any amount of time. This ensured that NO evidence could ever be found of what had gone on.

They wheeled the covered cart down to the waiting truck and they drove it to a distant part of the grounds out of site of the guests. They wheeled the cart into a non-descript building. The bodies were loaded into the furnace and the controls set. The flames came on and within minutes consumed the two beyond recognition.

Satisfied that there was no identifiable trace left, they reloaded the cart and went back to the cell area. Cleanup would take hours, but it was their job and it was spotless when they finished. Tools replaced in their assigned cabinets and the tables put away. The play room would be empty for at least a week until the next event.

The Exit Conference

It was approaching the hour when Wolfgang requested them to come to his office. The women entered the outer office and the secretary told them to be seated. At the exact hour, a bell rang and the secretary told them to enter his office and be seated. Elsa went in first followed by the remaining three. Wolfgang told them to be seated and the secretary brought in refreshments. When she left, she closed the door, making the office soundproof. We can talk openly and I will start by making a statement.

I have been with Carl Schmidt, Ilsa and Frieda. They were very impressed by your skills, inventiveness, and handling of yourselves. I like to hear this as it makes my job so much more pleasant.

First, I hope that you enjoyed the rules list we put together for you this trip. I know this is only your first time Helma, but we find it is more fun to change it up from time to time. For two of you, Elsa and Roseland, you have worked together prior and I was glad you were able to give them some guidance to the others.

Helma, you stepped right up and took the bull by the horns. It is sometimes hard for a first timer to get into what was going on. For three of you, this is the second half of you four week stay. When you leave, please let the secretary know if you wish to schedule for another stay here, she can give you the necessary registration forms to fill out prior to leaving. As in the past, you have two weeks to transfer the $250,000 fee. You three may leave as this is the first time Helma; I wish to have a one on one.

The door shut and Wolfgang began to talk to her. How are you doing today? It was reported to me that you just sat and sipped wine most of the afternoon and evening on the top deck. She responded by answering she was fine. I guess that I am torn a little. He asked what she meant. I had so much fun the four days, I can hardly wait to return for more fun with another "TOY".

I did have some different thoughts the first day, but got into it the rest of the time. I guess that I just got conflicted by my life roll the day before with Frieda. Yes, she did come to me and told of the fun you two had. You are just not sure if you're are a Dominate or a submissive.

Yes that is it. I think the quiet time last evening was more of these thoughts. Yes I did very much playing with the "TOY" the last four day, but it intrigued me to be dominated by Frieda. She said that I should ask you about these feelings.

Many people have them, wanting to experience both of them. This is called being a switch, wanting to do both the deed as well as wanting to serve as a slave. We have a slave service package that may interest you. First of all, there are none of the niceties you have had over your stay. You will be kept naked for the week here in shackles and chains in the same cell block your "TOYS" were kept and treated the same.

The only difference is that you will not be harmed as you did your "TOYS" were. Ilsa and Frieda will be in charge of you for the full week. You will perform any duties they have for you without mercy. Everything they wish, being fed and watered by bowl, gagged and blindfolded when they want, and taken to the playroom for light torture and pain.

I believe you experienced a tasted of this from Friend and she said you wanted more. At the end of your week, there will a large party in the play room. You will be a slave and serve and service all, men and women. There will also be a twenty four session being done on someone else that you will be required to watch. If you are interested, the cost of this package is only $35,000.

Think about it and you can do the paperwork with my secretary prior to you departing. It is hard and draining, but all that have done it raved about the experience. As with any of the packages you participate in, you can not tell anyone else about. You are sworn to security. And you know what the penalty for talking, you become the "TOY" and you know what happens than. Wolfgang thanked her and said he hoped to see her back at the Chalet soon.

Helma left the office and said she just needed time to think over what she had just heard. She went back to the room to change. The others were just changing into their swim suits. Roseland asked her if she was going to join the pool side and she answered she would enjoy it. Helma changed and joined them in their cabana. A waitress stopped by and took her order for a prime rib sandwich and a tall ice tea.

The rest of the day, she just couldn't keep her mind on the pool and she just kept going over what Wolfgang had talked with her about. By the end of the day, she knew that she would fill out the paperwork tomorrow. By that evening, she just went back to the room and used her vibrator to pleasure herself as she thought about her next trip to the Chalet.

The rest of week passed so quickly. Swimming, tennis and tanning on the top deck. It came to Saturday evening and tomorrow they were leaving. They packed in the afternoon to be ready for the trip home in the morning. A night in the dining room and than an evening of dancing followed by a good nights sleep just made things right with the world.

Morning came all too soon and they arrived in the lobby, turned in their key cards and went to the tramway. The tram car was waiting for them. They entered the car and went down to the ground entrance. Peter was waiting by the entrance to escort them to the waiting Limo for the ride back to Dresden air port.

The return trip was as quiet as the trip to the Chalet was two weeks earlier. They arrived at the private air terminal and the same jet was standing by for them. They were helped to the plane by Peter and he wished them a pleasant trip home. He knew they would return as most always did for recreation of one type or another. Peter then went to the Limo and cleaned it up as another set of vacationers was to arrive in an hour. There was a never ending list of guests.

HELMA'S RESORT

The over head paging system was screaming. Dr. Helma Jones, Dr. Helma Jones report to the delivery room STAT. I can't believe this, I just got here and it's an emergency. I hate the fact that my group requires me to spend Tuesdays in the free clinic. Why can't I just be at the office working with rich families or women. I can hardly wait to see what the emergency is this early morning. Helma was met by her nurse at the door to the delivery room. I think you will like this.

The female's grandmother brought her in a little while ago. Ok, where is the girl's mother? The answer was the same, either drunk, pulling tricks or stoned on crack. OK, what is the girl's history? We don't have any history; she just fell in the front doors. So, how far along is she and who is her normal doctor? Again the nurse answered, we don't know as she doesn't speak any English. Than let's start with what we do know? The best we figure is that she is nine months pregnant and maybe eleven years old. I wish I had called off this morning. We need to get scrubbed up and give it our best.

Doctor Jones, there is another problem or two. First she has been beaten within the last day or two and number two is the fact, she will not give up her teddy bear. For now, get her knocked out and gets that dam bear away. Make sure you watch out, the bear may have drugs and needles in it. I don't want another team member stuck this week. It may not be her stash, but mom may have used it to get by the police. Have I said more than once this morning that I hate this place? Yes Doctor Jones, at least four so far, than make it five. I hate this place!!!!!

Nurse, help me gown up and lets get started. They got the bear away and found a kilo of crack and a dozen needles inside. Give it to security and make sure an armed guard is outside the delivery room door just in case. I have had their dealer's crash the party before and almost got several of us shot. OK, let us get started.

I need her feet in the stirrups and tied down. I will start by inspecting the area as best as I can. Helma took one look between the eleven year olds legs and turned to the nurse and said that she was bleeding very badly. I need lots of sponges and a crash cart just incase. I don't think we are going to be able to get to deliver the baby normally; we will need to do a c-section. Helma grabbed a scalpel and started to cut the young girl's belly open. The whole area burst open and blood just blew every where. The girl instantly went to shock.

We have a code blue in progress. One of you start compressions, next get some blood started flowing into her IV. Start a round of cardiac drugs and get a toxic screen drawn. I am going to grab the baby and get her sewed up. OH god, the baby is badly deformed and is still born. This girl must be a heavy drug user. Who ever worked her over did a lot of damage.

Get the ER Surgeon in here right now. I need help if we can even save her. The over head page was blearing the code blue to Labor and Delivery for two minutes. The OR crew arrive and asked Dr Jones how they could help. Don't worry about it now; she died as you walked in the door. Just lost too much blood loose and I bet you will find she is loaded with drugs and is toxic with infection. I want to see the police now and put the grandmother in a holding room.

The police arrived and she explained that the girl had in fact slowly been murdered by someone. I have the grandmother in a holding room for you to talk to. They went and found that the grandmother had fled the Clinic. She must have been in on it all along.

Helma went to the large stainless steel sink and puked her guts out and turned to the nurse. Here is number six, I hate this place! I will be back in my office and if I am lucky, the bottle of whiskey is still in the drawer. She turned to the nurse and asked if she would like to join her. She accepted and they downed the entire bottle. The day went on, maybe not as bad, but bad enough.

Six o'clock came none too soon and the clinic closed it doors for the day. I need to get home and get into a hot tub of soapy water to wash this place off for another week. Tomorrow will be every bit as much a challenge for me, but there I am in my beautiful office with wealthy patients.

The problems will be the same, but at least they speak English and pay well. You know that I am one of the best OBGYN Doctors and surgeons in the area. A taxi was called and she made it into her top floor flat near the winding river. The night was full of stars, a good meal and a stiff drink would make the day go away.

She took her bath and by the time she was done, the grill was ready and she selected an inch and a half thick steak. She placed the steak on the grill, flipped it once and sat down on the terrace dining table with a chilled bottle of wine. She cut into it and found it with just the right amount of pink in the center of the steak. A crusty role was split and creamy butter spread. Over a matter of a half hour, she finished the meal and took the remainder of the wine over to the lounge chair and laid there to watch the stars come out for the evening. Now this is a peaceful way to rid my mind of the day's events.

She lay in the chair thinking of the days of relief she had gotten at the Chalet. Was it the food, mountains, people, friends or just playing with the TOYS? Yes, I have another session with a TOY left on my reservations. She took to some daydreaming of the trip she had made last early fall. I think it is time to make another, but maybe as a slave, but she just could not be sure that she could handle it.

Maybe it was time to be with Ilsa and Frieda again. A different kind of fun, but I know it will relax me one way or another. I think they called it my relaxation project. I don't know if it scares me or interreges me as being a "slave" for a week. I need to make sure before calling Wolfgang's secretary to schedule a week. I did register and pay for the week and the $35,000 was a small price to get some sanity back.

Morning came; Helma got dressed in her expensive clinical office clothes. She went down to the garage under the complex. Where did I part my car this time, I am always loosing it? There it is, over in the corner. She used the remote on her key ring, the horn beeped and she made her way to the door. Once inside she started the tiny little red sports car, lowered the top and began her journey to the upscale area where her practice was. The peaceful trip took maybe a half hour; she entered the Doctor's parking area and put the top up. A short walk brought her to the private elevator. She placed her key card in the slot and brought the car to the parking area. Entering the elevator car, she pressed the button for the fifth floor.

The trip was short, as she exited to the hall taking her to the bank of offices. Helma entered and greeted the receptionist. She asked what her scheduled looked like today. There are three before noon and three this afternoon. Helma turned and asked, are they at least over eighteen? The receptionist checked the listings and said, yes. The youngest is nineteen. Great, after yesterday, I couldn't take it today.

Helma entered her spacious office, walked to her oaken desk, sat in her oh so soft chair and kicked off her spiked heel so she could feel the soft carpet. Her nurse entered and said her first patient was waiting in the outer office. Is she pregnant? Is she a drug addict or alcoholic? The nurse answered no, no, and no. She is even married and comes from a good home. What is her problem than? Just needs a yearly checkup and wants an IUD inserted so she can finish college without the possible of having a baby. Bring her in and I will interview her while you set up the OBGYN table for an inspection and IUD insertion. Also get all the reading material for her on the care of her IUD. The nurse answered check, check, and check. She is on the way and her name is Ruby.

Helma met Ruby at the door and ushered her in and had her sit. Ruby, I applauded you wanting to finish college and putting off a family till than. What are you studying at school? Ruby answered that she wanted to be an administrator at a school. Helma answered this was a great profession and she should study hard. Now let the nurse take you into the exam room and get you ready for the IUD insertion. The nurse had her strip down and place on a paper gown.

I entered the exam room and told Ruby to get comfortable on the table and place her legs in the stirrups. Ruby, have you ever had this type of exam before? No and I am kind of scared a little. Don't be as this will be the first of many for you. Helma first inspected Ruby's vaginal lips. No problems here, so now I need to look inside you. I turned to the nurse and said to give her a medium speculum. Helma very slowly placed it at the opening, placed lots of lube on the blades and slid it in. The screw was very slowly turned. Opening the cannel for inspection, Helma turned on the flash light on her head piece and took a good look inside.

Very nice, all the pieces and parts seem to be in the right places. Ruby smiled and relaxed some. I see you have been with a man before, did you use protection. Ruby answered yes. Nurse, kindly hand me he IUD for insertion. Helma took it in her gloved hands and placed it in its place. Ruby, how does it feel? She answered it felt fine. You can go with the nurse and she will give you all the information on the protective device I just placed in you. You will also need to return in two months so I can look at it and make sure it is right for you. Helma left the room and returned to her office.

Helma returned to her office, turned on some quiet background music and kicked back in her chair. Boy that was close. I kind of jumped back in time and remembered shoving the spectrum into Carla, without lube and opening it roughly. I have to be so careful these days. What fun it was to try to expand the two leaves and spread it very wide open, causing so much pain. I think that I am ready to return to the Chalet.

Helma took out her personnel cell phone and dialed the number to Wolfgang's secretary. The voice on the other end answered as to how she could help her. This is Helma Jones and I would like to get on the list for my personnel experience. I believe that we have an opening in two weeks and I will call you back with the exact date. Helma went back to her work, wondering when the day would be over. She went back to work and finished the other five patients for the day.

Helma returned to her flat and took up residence in her lounge chair. The hours ticked by and the wait was getting to her. Almost ready to go to bed, her cell phone rang. A recorded message came thru and said to be at the Berlin airport by eight in the morning, two Saturdays from now. The message ended and the phone went dead. Helma went right to her computer to book a flight to Berlin. The flight was due to leave for Berlin at midnight on Friday and would arrive around three am. You are to go to the private jet departure gate and wait for the flight number 603.

It was a hard night to sleep. The time till the Friday would take for ever. The days went so slow and that nasty public clinic came around again. In between patients, all Helma could do was to daydream of both her experience with the "TOY" and of what might be in store for her visit.

On Thursday, a letter came in the mail marked only with the word of Chalet on the outside. She opened it as fast as she could and read it several times. You will not need to bring anything, clothes or makeup with you. Everything else would be provided. Remember, you can not tell anyone where you are going or why. When you finish reading this letter, you need to burn it and let the ashes fly in the wind.

Helma went to the bar-b-q and lit the burners. She lit the letter and the ashes fell to the bottom. She scooped the ashes from the bottom, went to the edge of her balcony and cast them to the wind. It was happening and the long hours till tomorrow night just wouldn't tick by very fast.

The awaited hour came and she boarded the plane to Berlin. It was a quiet flight and she got into Berlin around three fifteen. She walked briskly to the private departure gate and was seated at the gate handling flight 603. With time on her hands to wait till the flight boarded, Helma took a short cat nap.

At around four thirty, she was awaken by a young lady. Is this the gate for flight 603? Helma said it was and asked what her name was? She answered her name was Judy. My name is Helma. Have you taken this flight before? No this is the first time for me, how about you. I have flown with them once before and stopped at that point. No more conversations were engaged in.

At around eight in the morning, the jet for flight 603 arrived at the gate. Helma recognized the plane. The two watched as the stairs emerged from the belly and came down. The stewardess came down the stairs with a clip board. She looked at them and asked, Judy? Judy answered and was told to go up and be seated. She turned to Helma and said welcome back to fly with us again. How long has it been? Helma answered it must have been seven months. You can also enter the plane and be seated.

The stewardess got on the plane, drew up the stairs and went over the emergency instruction for the flight. The plane taxied to the runway and was given the clearance to take off for Dresden air port. Ladies, the flight will only take less than an hour, so we will not be serving sacks. Enjoy your flight and your Limo will be waiting when we get there.

Peter arrived at the private parking area at the Dresden airport. As was his normal job of bring visitors to and from the airport to the Chalet, he made sure the snack section was ready for the trip back and waited at the deplaning ramp. Peter knew that they would not be bringing any luggage, so he left the cart at the entrance. The overhead speaker announced that flight 603 was arriving and would be at the arrival area in five minutes. Peter adjusted his uniform and hat.

The plane pulled up and the stairway unfolded to the ground. He approached the bottom and waited the women to deplane. Helma came down first. Peter recognized her and shook and kissed her hand. Nice to see you back Miss Helma. Ruby followed her down and also received the shake and kiss on the hand. Peter, welcome Miss Ruby. I know this is your first trip to the Chalet, so just step into the back and get comfortable. The two women climbed into the rear of the limo and got seated. I have provided a light snack and a bottle of house wine. Please have a quiet trip back.

The trip was in route to the Chalet when Peter got on the microphone and started to describe the country scenery. He also insisted that they try the wine as they would need to comment on its taste. Helma wasn't sure why he insisted so much, but knew that there must be a reason. She took her glass and poured both her and Ruby's glass, for the trip and both drank the wonder wine. It only took around ten minutes before the two women were uncurious.

Peter lowered the window between the driver's compartment and the women. He wanted to make sure the knockout drops had rendered both unconscious. The women had dropped their glasses and slumped onto the floor. Everything was going as prescribed. Peter got on the phone and alerted Ilsa and Frieda they should be at the rear door within an hour.

Peter brought the Limo to the main gate, inserted his key card in the slot and the gate opened. He drove the Limo around the fence to the back entrance. He parked out of site as Ilsa ad Frieda brought the laundry cart to the Limo. Peter opened the door and Ilsa and Frieda removed the two women, placing them in the cart and placing linen over them. Peter closed the door and drove away.

The cart was now pushed into the wide rear door, and secured the door. The two pushed the cart up the incline to the second level of the lower area. When they reached the second floor, Frieda used her key card and opened the play area.

The play area was empty of any items and was passed thru quickly. They rolled thru the room, down the hall to the cell area. Ilsa opened the thick oaken door and turned on the light. Several sets of iron rings were both on the floor and in the wall. The cart was dumped and both women rolled out onto the floor. Ilsa and Frieda started to prep the Woman for their play. Both women were stripped of all clothes and were completely naked. Frieda went to the cabinet and removed the cleaner shackles, collars and chains.

Each woman was fitted with a collar and chained to the wall. Next came the wrist and ankle shackles. They were fitted and a short chain went between them. Next they were chained to the floor by their shackles; all stretched out so little to no movement was possible. Frieda took two syringes from the cabinet and drew two blood samples. We will have the sample run for AIDS as all are that come here.

Comfortable that the new slaves for the week were ready. Ilsa and Frieda left the cell and shut out the light and closed and locked the door. Frieda went to check the schedule details and Ilsa went to Wolfgang's office. The Secretary announced her and she was buzzed in. Ilsa entered, closed the door and was told to be seated.

Wolfgang inquired as to the status of the women. Ilsa stated that they were sleeping on the floor. We will be waking them in several hours and explain the package they are here for. Wolfgang was pleased and told her that she would be going to the political prison in two days for the Item for the weekend party. Carl has pulled some strings and has gotten us a young hunk from prison to be used at the party on Saturday. I have been assured that he will be handcuffed and the knock out drug administered. He should be no problem on the way back. Just remember to take the envelope with the payment with you. I will pick it up just prior to leaving.

Being almost noon, Frieda and I will be going to lunch. We have a lot of scheduling to do for our two slaves. This is a good week as it brings in $70,000 for those to experience being slaves. A good week indeed, go and have a good lunch as the dozen couples will begin arriving this afternoon for the party. Ilsa left Wolfgang's office and joined Frieda in the side dining room.

The Guests Arrive

Peter changed from the Rolls Royce Limo to the tour bus. He would first drop off several visitors that were here to holiday so the private jet could take them back to Berlin Airport to get to their departures for home. They were finishing their visits/vacations. None of them knew of what the entertainment was taking place. This was also the fun place for those to relax and partake in the many fun things and good food. Each of them had paid a small fee of $80,000 per week per couple for the resort.

He took the bus to the rear and loaded the luggage onto the rear compartment. He now drove the bus to the main entrance to wait for the visitors to come down the tram. He waited at the door of the bus and helped them into the rear compartment. The door closed, he drove the road to Dresden airport's private loading area. Once they arrived, they were loaded into the return trip of flight 603. The stairs were withdrawn and they taxied for take off. Peter than reset the tour buses compartment with snacks and several bottles of house wine. He didn't have long to wait as the next plane was on final approach as 606 arrived.

The plane was much larger than 603 was, and drew its way to the gate. This time a set of portable stairs was wheeled to the plane door. The ground crew began the job of unloading the many pieces of luggage to be taken to the Chalet. The stewardess opened the door and instructed the passengers to deplane. Peter gathered the dozen couples around and welcomed them to the Chalet for their fun. He guided them to the bus and they stepped inside and took their seats. Over the microphone, Peter again welcomed them and suggested they try the many snack items and some house wine. One last thing before we start: Please turn off your cell phones.

The passengers were having a great time snacking and enjoying the scenery on the way to the Chalet. As normal, Peter pointed out the many farms and fields that dotted the country side. The trip passed fast and they arrived at the main entrance to the Chalet. Peter inserted his key card into the gate lock and it opened. This also triggered the tram operator to bring the tram to ground level. As there were two dozen people in need to be taken up, only twelve could be taken up at a time. The remaining would say on the buss.

Wolfgang as was custom, met the tram car and welcomed the people. As the last person departed the tram car, it shut its door and went back down to the ground level for the rest of the visitors. The car returned to the top quickly and the other twelve exited and joined the group. Wolfgang introduced several of the hotel staff and they would take the twelve coupled to their rooms. You luggage will be delivered as soon as possible. You will need to get checked in and ready for the tour of the grounds.

The Guide said I will collect and guide you thru the Chalet and its many activities. Even if you have been here prior, we have made many changes. Ladies and Gentlemen, you will be staying on the third floor. It is set aside for you only, so you won't be disturbed by other guests. You will be in blocks of four couples to a room. If you have friends you wish to have in your room, please let us know. You will be taken up the elevators in groups of four couples, so gather into your couples. One group at a time was taken to the third floor. Each group was shown to their rooms.

The couples from prior knew the drill, but the new groups were over come with the look and spaciousness of the suit. The guide instructed the new ones that inside their bedrooms off the living room, you will find a key that both open the main door and their individual bedroom. It is also the key to the elevator. You will need to take it to the front desk and let them know your name for the sign in.

Your guide will be back up at the elevator in an hour for the grand tour. There is also a set of rules for each couple which you will need to be read and signed by the time we get back. Your guide will collect them from you when they get back.

Please feel free to explore your rooms and once we know where everyone is, we will get you your luggage. As with the entire four guest rooms in the Chalet, there was a main living/lounge area and the four bedrooms surrounding it. Against the far wall was the refrigerator with snacks and soft drinks. A wine cooler was next to the refrigerator and an entertainment center finished off the wall. Many small and large over stuffed chairs and couches filled the space. In the corner was a stack of a dozen thick, large pillows.

Each couple selected their bedroom. Inside each was a California King Size bed with silken sheets and many pillows. On one wall were a dresser and a tall cabinet for hanging clothes. The other wall contained the bathroom. A ten foot vanity with a six foot tall mirror hung over the double wash area. A toilet with gold plated hardware and oaken seat came next. A tall cabinet was next to the vanity with six sets of towels for each person per day. A five foot wide bubble tub and a five foot wide shower were on the other wall. Finally there was a two person steam cabinet to sweat out the days play. There was not much a person could want for.

The appointed time arrived and all the couples were waiting at the elevator. The guides that had brought them up were waiting to take them first to registration to complete the forms and than to be taken to the fifth floor. As is policy, you will need to turn in your cell phones to assure you are on vacation.

The guide had them approach the front desk and present their key to the front desk clerk and sign in. Once all three groups of couples were done with registration, the guides took them to the fifth floor for the beginning of the tour of the building and recreation areas. Wolfgang was waiting at the entrance to the fifth floor. Again, welcome to the Chalet. On behalf of myself and my staff, we wish to make your visit the best you have had. You have selected the PARTY package which includes all food, drinks and recreation areas.

To the left is the dining area. There are table settings for two, four or eight persons. Breakfast is a buffet and is from 7 am. until 10 am. Dinner is also a buffet and is served at noon. Supper is our sit down meal. It is served from 6 pm. till 9 pm. I believe that you will find a vast selection of some of the best items in this area of Germany.

To your right is the lounge area with many chairs and couches to relax and have conversations in. Past that is our dance floor with a nightly band till midnight. On Wednesday evening we have a dance contest for you to try. An open bar is at the near end between the lounge and dance areas, where snacks are always available.

At this time, there are many other guests here for recreation only and not with the "PARTY" package. There may be times that you may be asked for you key card so they know which things are available. Rule number one is that you do not talk about your package with anyone other than your group. Some of the guests do not know of your PARTY Saturday.

We need to proceed up to the sixth floor so I can point out the many things available to you. They went up to the sixth floor where those that had not been there before were amazed with what they saw. The sixth floor was a partially covered area with a bar with snacks. The remaining area was open for events. We have shuffle board courts, a sandy area if you wish to sun in the sand and an area with one and two person adjustable and fixed lounge chairs. Umbrellas are available upon request.

We have several waitresses which will come and take your order; all you have to do is gently wave your hand. Let's move over to the rear parapet. As you can see the view of the many acres of the grounds are filled with many things to do. In the winter, we have full service sky slops with all equipment provided, so you don't have to bring any of your own if you want. We also have instructors if you need.

Moving to your left is our Olympic size pool. It is divided into two pools; a family type pool with a depth of only three to five feet and the other is a diving and speed swimming area of twelve feet deep. As this is an adult only chalet, you may sit around naked at the lounge area up here and the pool area. We do not permit any adult actives, please use your room and do have at least a robe on to move from your room to the recreation areas. Next to the pool area is the set of four tennis courts. They are clay bottoms and fast to play in.

New this year are several areas your might enjoy. There are seven different putting greens designed by some of the best golfers in Germany. An archery range is next. We have bow and arrows for you're to use. The last item is a riding area. We have eight excellent saddle horses. They are both for Western and English saddles. There are instructors and grooms to assist any level of riders. I do recommend that you schedule as the horses have become one of our most used attractions.

If you look in the distance, you can see our vast grape growing fields. We press our own wine and champagne right in this building. They are served at the bars and in your rooms. As for the other items, we buy only locally grown beef, chicken and pork. The vegetables are all locally grown and the cheeses are from the milk of local cows and goats. Just ask and we will do out best to get you what you wish.

You will be released to do as you wish until the Party on Saturday. You will please follow the guides for the last in briefing items left. As with your group, all those that visit, you will need to take an HIV test today. Just something we require as you may wonder between rooms and we want everyone to feel free to enjoy each others company. That completes the tour and if you need anything, just ask, now go and have a great time till the party.

Ilsa and Frieda were busy getting ready for Helma and Judy to awaken. We had better go down and get them ready before they wake up. They arrived at the cell, turned the lights on and checked the status of the two. This is great, they have not awakened yet. Frieda went to the cabinet and returned with several items. Let us first encapsulate their heads in the full leather hoods.

They slid the hoods over each woman's head and laced them up on the back. Next to come were the removal blindfolds and finally the two

79

inch diameter by two inch long dildo gag. It sat down in their throats and prevented them from talking. They opened the mouth and slid it in and buckled it so it could not be pushed out.

I have also brought two medium sized anal plugs. A little more discomfort was always a good thing. Ilsa separated the ass cheeks while Frieda wiggled and twisted them in. I guess it would have been easier if I had a little lube on them first. My bad, but they are slaves anyway and get what we want. Let us also bind their legs together so they can't wiggle the plugs out.

Ilsa told Frieda, good job. Let's leave them till later this afternoon when they are fully awake. They should be very uncomfortable by than and at least for Judy, very scared. I think Helma may be a hard nut to crack, but just give them a few days. Let's go and get some lunch. I hear they are having some great chili today. Ilsa and Frieda turned out the lights and closed the cell door and locked it.

Day two

After doing a mountain of paper work the evening before, Ilsa and Frieda went to their room to relax. Having a room to themselves, they could do as the wished. That evening, they got naked on some of ten large pillows and put in a DVD; from time to time they would kiss, hug and let their hands roam over each others large curves.

We need to shower and dress for breakfast. They each had generous servings of eggs, pancakes and bacon with several cups of coffee. Some light conversation about the new clothes in town as well as about several of the guests filled in the time while they finished. Being that they were high up in the chain and just under Wolfgang gave them special privileges. They did not have to clean up dishes or do the house keeping of their rooms. There room was on the first floor so they could be close to the play room.

I think the time has come to welcome our two slaves in the cell block. They boarded the elevator and went down one floor. Ilsa went first; she opened the cell door and flipped on the light. Both of the women were moving slightly, wiggling a little. Frieda walked over between them and gave each of them a swift kick to the ass. This brought moans and muffled talk. Frieda removed the blindfolds and gags from the hoods.

Ilsa started by welcoming the slaves to their home for the week. Helma, you know us and Judy you soon will know us. From this point, you will call us Mistress and will obey our commands. We will be guiding you to the world of slavery over the next week. You signed up for the extreme slavery package and will be treated as one. I guaranty that you will be getting your $35,000 worth of humiliation, servitude, pain and light torture training which you wanted.

I can guarantee that by the end of the week, you will be exhausted as well as very soar. This is the remains of a medieval castle and many of the dungeon items remain in working order. You will experience the stocks, rack and even a spiked chair. I believe that it is time to eat. We will deliver food in bowls twice a day along with a water bowl.

You will be allowed fifteen minutes to eat and drink, at the end of this time, we will remove them and your will not get another one till the next feeding time. If you understand, just shake your head yes. Both shook their heads and Frieda placed the water first and than bowls of dog food. Helma, you may remember feeding this to your TOY from the last time you were here. Enjoy as we will be starting soon. Helma and Judy dug into the dog food and chocked it down. Helma even thought to herself, this is what we gave to Carla and Daniel last time. No wonder they had so much trouble getting it down.

Frieda removed the empty bowls and stood back. Ilsa took the hose and started to wash the two down with ice cold water. The stimulation shocked each woman and they tried to roll around to protect their naked bodies and girly features. Ilsa turned up the pressure and pointed it between their legs and under their breasts. The ten minute pressure washing with ice cold water stimulated the slaves. They awaited their first commands with apprehension and some being scared of the up coming times.

We are about to release you from the floor and walls. Don't move until you are told to do so. They stayed as still as they could. Helma, you get up first. She did and stood at attention. Judy you are next, stand and get in behind Helma. She did and a three foot chain was placed between their collars. An iron ball was attached to the chains in between their legs. Helma, you know the way to the play room, get walking. The iron balls made it hard to walk and progress was slow. Frieda said that you both better walk faster than that. She placed the cattle prod on the butt of Helma and squeezed the trigger. She jumped causing Judy to jerk and move faster. Keep up Judy or next it will be your turn unless you wish me to change to a carriage whip and apply it to you bottom and legs.

The twenty feet to the play room was made in good time. I want you two to stand in the middle and face us. They made it to the center of the room and turned to face Ilsa and Frieda. I am going to start your slave lessons. You never look at either of us directly in the eyes unless we tell you to. Even in chains, you will stand at attention, face down and await further commands.

Frieda took the chain that joined the two of them off and they were commanded to walk to the "X" marks on the floor against the far wall. When you get there, you will stand with your face to the wall. Both women walked as fast as possible, stood on top of the "X" mark, lowered their heads and waited in total silence. Good, you are getting the knack of following orders. You are to stand perfectly still when I release the chains connecting yours wrists and ankles. With the chains gone, they could move, but dared not to. Helma, do you see the rings in the wall? She nodded yes and waited. Ilsa grabbed her left arm and drew it to the upper left ring. She tied it off to the shackle and then the right hand was now tied off to the right ring.

Very good, now spread your legs so I can tie them to the lower rings. She felt so open with her legs spread so wide. By this time, Judy was starting to think, what did I get myself into. Within five minutes, the both of them were standing, face toward the wall, spread eagle. Helma, you know of our past, but Judy may not. Judy, we are former KGB interrogation specialists. We used to gain information by any means needed, wither from general prisoners, soldiers or political prisoners.

We are experts in our means to pry it from either men or women. The tools of our trade range from whips and floggers, common tools like pliers and ice picks, a plumbers torch and even a vast assortment of medical instruments. We can carve a turkey with ease and also skin a human without causing them too much blood lose or death.

Your tortures will not get to that point, but you will at times scream and beg for us to stop. Do you both understand? Both woman shook their heads yes. According to the contract you signed, you agree to do as we say without question. Do you understand? Again, both women shook their heads yes. Very well, let us start play with you.

Ilsa and Frieda went to the table and each chose whips. Ilsa choose a six foot bull whip and Frieda chose a five foot long carriage/buggy whip. You will get your first feel of the whip. We both can pick a fly from the nose of a dog. You will feel the sting, but not suffer any damage, at least for now.

Ilsa uncoiled the whip, let it laid on the ground and than flicked it onto Helma's ass. The sting echoed thru the play room and brought a loud response from her. A deep red mark appeared and stung a lot. Ilsa coiled the whip and moved over to Helma and rubbed the thin red line. Helma just stood there without any response. Very good Helma, I am proud of you, but I will get a response from you at one time.

She stood back and let the tip of the whip fly, catching the back of both her legs, just under her butt. This time a loud thud was heard as it made contact and a kind of purring came from Helma. It seems that you like this play.

It Was Frieda's turn. She took the handle of the carriage whip and let it fly. The strike came between Judy's legs and wound up the crack of her ass. Judy tried not to make a sound, but the sudden impact was a little more than she could stand. She let out a small scream and a silent cry. She had never been abused before and it would take some time before she could handle it better. The second strike hit the back of her legs and she bent at the knees as best she could. This time she bit her lip and did not make a sound.

Ilsa and Frieda changed positions and let several blows strike the slaves. Within a half hour, both slaves received as many as two dozen strikes from each whip. They were now hanging down, their wrists taking the weight of their bodies. Ilsa and Frieda approached them and inspected their handiwork.

The Toymaker

There was a nice warm feeling and a rosy red look, but no damage was done. Remember this slave as this is only the first time to be whipped, and will not be the last. The two were allowed to hang from the wall as the two wooden butcher block tables were wheeled into the room. The slaves twisted their heads to get glimpse of what was going on. They saw the tables in the center of the room.

Helma was bought back to their use as they had been used to secure the TOYS she and the others played with. It is time to do some up close fun with you. We are going to release you from the wall. You are to walk or crawl, your choice, to the blocks and lay on them facing the ceiling. Make sure that you pussies are just hanging off the ends. Judy didn't quite understand how she was going to fit on the one foot wide by three foot log table, but followed the orders.

They both laid back and let their arms and legs droop to the side of the tables. Ilsa now applied the two inch wide belts across Helma's chest just below her breasts and above her belly button. Frieda did the same to Judy. Both of the slave's arms were forced down the sides of the table to the rings at floor level. The wrist shackles were tied to the front rings under their heads and than the legs and ankles were drawn back toward the head, bringing the vaginal area up and wide open.

At this point, the small shelves were drawn out under their head and they were secured with two straps, one around the neck and the other across the forehead. Helma and Judy were now totally secured without any wiggle room. Ilsa and Frieda stepped to the head of their table and each withdrew a five inch long folding knife from their pocket. Slaves, this is when you don't want to even move a fraction of an inch or even quiver. These knives have been used to do anything from flay the skin off a breast to cut off a nose. They are extremely sharp.

Ilsa and Frieda both went to the corner and brought a rolling stainless steel exam chair over to the base of the table. Now slaves, without using any shave cream, we are going to remove any fur you may have in your lower areas. As I said, don't you dare move, even shake in the least if you want to leave with all your parts. This will be very important when we are working on you labia, inner lips and the rosebud anal hole. As the two drew the sharp edge of their knives over

84

the very sanative areas, both slave froze and hardly even breathed. Sweat was rolling off the both of them, but they managed to stay still for the entire process.

That does it for you; they are as smooth as a baby's bottom. You can now breathe in again. Both slaves shivered a little and sighed. They both wiped the edges of their knife and returned them to the carriers in their pocket. Frieda turned to Ilsa and said; that was hot. I need some relief; I think we should show the slaves what their mouths are for.

They went to the top of the tables, released the heads and pushed the shelf holding the heads back into the table. Each of the slave's heads dropped down. Helma knew in an instant what was coming. Slaves, this will not be the last time you will pleasure us or any others we tell you to do. We will both take turns standing over you mouths and you will do the rest. You had better dig in deep with your tongues and lick our clits and boxes clean. In addition, you will drink any of our golden nectar and I suggest you don't miss a drop. As we will control you heads by pulling on your hair, we will also control your breathing. If you understand, shake you heads. Both slaves shock yes and the pleasuring of the Mistresses began.

Each slave dug deep into her vaginal opening and licked, sucked and swallowed every trace of white cream and pee that came into their mouths. Ilsa and Frieda changed slaves back and forth several times and after an hour were finished. All four Women were completely spent, but their fun was not over yet. Ilsa said that they were to have a little more pain and they both took riding crops from the table. Blow after blow fell, the tip connecting on the breasts, nipples, labia and inner thighs. Small screams came from both slaves. Frieda turned and said that this should be enough for this session. The slaves were released from the table. Judy just fell to the floor exhausted as Helma slowly slid off.

Each slave had a leash place on their collar and told to crawl back to the cell area. Each did their best to return the thirty feet to their positions. Judy did have to have the cattle proud applied between her legs for encouragement. They arrived at the cell area and took up their place at the floor and wall rings. Ilsa and Frieda attached the short chains back between the ankle and wrist shackles and secured them to the floor rings. The chain from the wall was reattached to the collar.

Slaves, you will have a treat in the morning. We have to retrieve the party favor for Saturday night's party. We will be feeding and giving you water now. You can take your time as we are not coming back till the morning. Frieda set the water bowls down and went to the cabinet for the cans of dog food for their dinner. Slaves, we will allow you to have the privilege of being able to talk tonight, this will not happen too often, so take advantage of it. When you are at work detail or in restraints, you are not allowed to talk. Ilsa turned the lights out and locked the door after they departed. Ilsa and Frieda went to their rooms, showered and than to supper.

Helma waited for several minutes after they left the area to turn and in a soft voice, ask Judy how she was. Judy answered that she was a whole lot of scared and in a little pain, but it was great. I never knew that being a slave would be as hard on the body, both physically as well as mentally exhausting. I have dreamed about this for so many years. I didn't just want to go out with someone and get beat. I was afraid of getting hurt without the suspense of performing as a real slave.

Helma spoke up and answered she had the same thoughts and when she was here before, Frieda had done some things to her to make her want to come back in this capacity. Every day at my job and some nights at home, I would daydream of this as a release from my job. I had the same idea. Helma, what kind of work do you do? I am an OBGYN Doctor and a Surgeon. Judy, what kind of high stress job do you have?

She answered that she was a bond trader. I see we both have very high stress jobs. Judy asked Helma what type of roll she had the last trip here? Helma responded that it was forbidden to even talk about it, but if I get the jest of the PARTY idea right, you might find out Saturday. What do you mean Helma? I better not tell you what I am thinking as I don't want to be a TOY here and both went to sleep. Little did they know they were being recorded to see if Helma would talk? Judy, get as much sleep as possible as you will most likely need it tomorrow. Good Night.

Day Three

Ilsa and Frieda rose in their bedroom and showered, dressed and went for breakfast. When finished, Ilsa told Frieda to go and feed the slaves as she was going to Wolfgang to get the envelope of money for the trip. Frieda went to the play room floor and entered the cell area. She opened the door and turned on the light. Helma and Judy were still asleep on the floor. Frieda quietly went to the corner and took the hose. She turned on the tap and the ice water splashed upon the two. Judy screamed in shock as Helma just took it. Good morning slaves. I hope you slept well and are ready for a partial day of slave work. Ilsa and I have to go get the Party Favor for Saturday night. You two will remain chained here until we return.

She placed the dog food into the bowls and gave it too them. I am going to give you two bowls of water for the good job you did yesterday. Frieda than knelt next to Helma's head and whispered to her that they heard everything last evening and she was proud that she did not talk of her prior visit. You passed the test and gave a flick on her nipples.

Don't tell her of anything that we do here. I do like the idea that you are trying to get her thru this experience. I will give you some extra attention this evening which I think you will enjoy. I will also let the lights to stay on while we are gone. Rest, as you will need it tonight. Frieda closed and locked the cell door, and went to the loading area to get the truck for the trip. She placed the laundry cart with sheets and blankets on the back of the truck.

She drove the truck around the fence area and arrived at the front gate. Ilsa was waiting with the instructions and envelope. She got into the passengers seat, buckled in and turned on the radio for the trip. It was around a two hour ride each way to the political prison. They were off and would enjoy the ride as it was a beautiful day.

The many Party guests were enjoying their third day. They all went to the dining room for some breakfast. Most had a full meal as some only had a bagel and coffee. As phones and computers were not allowed, they had to relax from reality. The group of twenty four broke into several different groups. Several of the men went to practice their putting skills while others went horse back riding. The women broke into groups of nude sunbathing on the sixth floor sandy beach area. Others went to the pool. A small group went back to their room and stripped naked. They planned to spend the day with each others naked bodies. Most of the members of the PARTY were gay or lesbian. Some, even thought a small part were only straight. Many sex parties were taking place over the last two days.

Frieda rolled the truck up to the non-descript building fenced in area. She gave her name to the guard on duty and asked for Sal. The guard checked their papers and made a call for Sal. Sal came to the gate, checked the paper work and told them to drive to door number three, and back in. Door three was located around the back of the building.

She backed the truck into the dock and stopped the truck. They waited for Sal to open the door from the inside. Ilsa heard the slide bolt open and the door open. Along with Sal were two heavily armed guards. Sal first held out his hand and waited for the envelope to be passed. He opened it and counted the money. With a nod of his head, the guards raised their machine guns and allowed Ilsa and Frieda to enter with the laundry cart.

With the guards in the lead, they proceeded past many cells until they came to one with a soldier standing guard and the prisoner lay unconscious on the floor. As per the pre arranged instructions, the man was naked and hand cuffed behind his back.

Ilsa went over to the man and began to inspect him. She pried his mouth open to check to see if all his teeth were there. She let her hands follow his arms down to his crotch. She grabbed his large cock and milked it some to get a reaction. It started to swell to around two inches in diameter to over twelve inches long. This will do fine as the Party Favor. Frieda also agreed, removed the sheets and blankets from the cart and readied it for the man.

Ilsa said that they would place a full leather hood over his head and place a blindfold and dildo gag in place prior to movement. Having done this, Sal indicated to the guards that the man was to be placed in the cart for the transfer. They picked him up and tossed him in. Frieda replaced the sheets and blanket over the body.

Sal indicated that he had been given a heavy dose of knock out drug an hour ago. He has no idea of what is in store for him and I don't want to know. We just don't want him to escape or ever come back. As you drive out the gate, all records of him will be shredded and he will never have exhausted. Ilsa turned to Sal and assured him that no trace of him will be around after Sunday night.

The cart was pushed out to the dock, loaded into the truck and the door closed and locked. Ilsa turned to Frieda and told her she wanted to drive on the return trip. Ilsa turned the truck toward gate, dove it thru and they were on the way home. The trip home was uneventful and the women enjoyed their day out. As the Chalet came into sight, Frieda called Wolfgang's office to tell him they were ten minutes out. They entered the Chalet grounds and drove around to the rear entrance. Ilsa backed the truck up to the dock and they unloaded the cart. They pushed it up to the playroom floor and to the cell block. Wolfgang met them at the door to the cells and opened it for them to wheel the cart in.

Once inside, the cart was taken to the opposite end of the cell from the slaves. Lisa told the slaves, you had better not make a sound or I will whip you silly tonight. Do you understand? Both shook their heads yes. The two women rolled the cart to the holding area for Party Favors and dumped the cart. The man rolled out onto the floor. He hit with a thud. Wolfgang told Frieda to remove the hand cuffs so he could inspect the piece of meat he had just bought.

He wanted to make sure that the prisoner was not screwed up to much from questioning. Happy with what he saw, he ordered that wrist and ankle shackles be placed on him and he to be hog tied. I want him to be as uncomfortable as possible. Place a collar on him and chain it to the wall. His feet should be attached to the floor ring. He will be allowed the gag be roved ten minutes both morning and evening feeding than replaced. His blindfold is not to be removed until Saturday morning. For good measure, I want him kicked in the balls at each feeding but do not cause any damage. That is for the Party guests to do, they paid the price of admission to participate.

Pleased with the prisoner, Wolfgang departed the cells. He looked back over his shoulder and told Ilsa and Frieda that they did good. As

Ilsa checked the chains and locks, Frieda walked over to the slaves and said; he is of no concern to you and do not try to talk to him. I know he is a hunk, but not for you to play with. With that, Ilsa and Frieda departed for their room to bath and change for the supper meal. The lights were turned off and the door closed.

Several hours later, supper having been completed, Ilsa and Frieda headed back to the cells. Upon entering, they turned on the light and first went to the Party Favor and kicked him gentle in the gut. He tried to roll into a ball, but the bindings he was in prevented it. Great, he is coming out of the knock out drugs. Relax; you are going to be in this position for the next day or two. You will be fed and given water in a bowl at morning and night. Twice a day, you will be washed off by hose. If you understand, nod your head, he did and went back to his more relaxed position.

You are not in the prison any more and are most likely better off for now. With him taken care of, Ilsa and Frieda turned their attention to Helma and Judy. Alright, up and at it slaves. You are to have an interesting evening in the play room. Each was unchained from the rings and a leash attached to their collars and made to crawl into the room. Both moved as fast as their chains would allow. Slaves, I want you to sit on the "X" on the floor in the center of the room. They did as told.

First to be undone were the wrist, and they were told to lie back on the floor. With that done, Lisa and Frieda each took the left wrists and attached rope to them and stretched them to the iron rings in the floor. Next the right wrist and the woman had their arms spread as wide as possible. Next to come were the ankles. They had the rope attached to the shackles and the slaves had their legs spread extremely wide. Now that we have you in a spread eagle position, we will begin the evening's pain and torture sessions.

We will not place blindfolds and gags on you. We want to hear you beg and scream for us. You will be put thru several different types of play which will take you to extreme feelings and exhaustion. Are you ready? Helma and Judy in a subdued voice, answered yes. Than slaves, let us begin.

Ilsa said that I think stimulation is the first thing to do. Ilsa and

Frieda went to the cabinet and took out a fucking machine each with electrically conductive dildos on them. The two dildo's were around two inched in diameter by ten inches long. Theses should totally fill you up and pleasure you well. Prior to inserting them into your cannel, we have to add an anal plug with electro strips down the sides. We need to apply electrically conductive gel to the items. Drip by drip, they coated the x-large anal plugs and cork screwed them in to the hilt. Next the dildos were coated with the gel and inserted in around two inches. One last thing before we turn on the machines. Wires from the fucking machine were attached, one for the dildo and one to the plug. Slaves, the way this works is that as the dildos go in and out, the machine will select a level of shock to stimulate your insides. That will vary on each stroke.

In the beginning they will be a low level shock which you will give you some pleasure. As time goes by, the shocks will increase in both bite as well as duration. You are going to be allowed an hour to have this pleasure yourself. During this time, we will be adding other things to give you even more stimulation. Let us start.

The switches were turned on causing the dildos to go in and out. The speed will also vary as time goes on. The in and out began and the shocks also went up and down. At first the shocks brought pleasure as well as their clits to tingle. About five minutes went by and the shock bit bad at their inners. Screams and bucking of their bodies increased as the time passed. We think that enough time has passed and you need a little more to think about.

From the corner was brought a cow milking machine with four suction cups. The machines were turned on and than the suction cups were placed over the slave's nipples. You could hear both the sucking sounds as the unit went to work as well as heavier screams with an occasional moan of pleasure. Being younger, Judy was even able to bring a little milk to the tubing and collection jug. By ten minutes of being milked, both the Women could only moan, no mater how many electric shocks they were receiving.

Ilsa turned to Frieda and said we need to spice up the fun they are having. Each of them picked up a freshly cut Habanero pepper and began to rub it on the dildo just as it was about to enter the slaves. Only three thrusts of the dildo brought about the firry response in the pussy channels of the slaves. It felt like a blow torch had been stuck in them. I think we got their attention with this treat.

Both slaves bucked and squirmed to get any relief they could. Judy was in a little more pain than Helma at that point. As time passed, the effects began to wear off and each woman relaxed some. The arch in their backs flattened and even Helma was back to only moaning. As the hour ended, both women were exhausted. The machines were removed and the plugs were also pulled from them. Each of them had copious amounts of white cum flowing from their womanhoods. Sweat poured from their bodies. With a shy, both the slaves took a deep breath and relaxed waiting for the next event to happen.

Let's see, where were we? Ah, yes a one gallon enema. Ilsa produced two, 250 cc double balloon Catheters. Now for a little lube and the first balloon made its way into Helma's rosebud sphincter. She groaned in a pleasurable way. Now for the air to placed into the balloons. First came the inside balloon to lock it inside the anal cannel. The outer balloon came next. Ilsa gave a good tug on the catheter to make sure it was in place.

It was Judy's turn to have the catheter inserted. She looked at Helma with concerns and wasn't sure what it was going to feel like. Ilsa said, Helma you have permission to speak to her. Helma turned to Judy and told her that it was great, just don't resist and you will love it. With the reassurance, Judy said she was ready for it and relaxed. As the first balloon took its place deep inside her, she let out the breath she was holding. Judy thought to herself this isn't too bad and wanted to feel the inflation of the balloons. The air was placed and Ilsa tugged on her catheter and found it placed well.

Judy that was the easy part, a one gallon bags with tubing were hung from an IV pole. The tubing was connected to the catheter and a valve was opened just a very little. Drip after drip entered the tubing and was now collecting inside of her. Judy, it will take several minutes for the effect to take place. Ilsa turned to Helma and hooked up her tubing. The flow of water started and she felt the warm water enter her inner tubing.

Ilsa turned to Helma and said, I bet you do this often and love it, don't you slave? Helm could only smile and asked if the flow of water could be turned up a little. I would Helma, but the entire idea of this punishment is to do it so very slowly. It should take around an hour to get as much water into you two as you will be able to hold.

As the water entered into their bodies, their stomachs, began to look like they were nine months pregnant. Frieda had returned and went to Judy and messaged her stomach causing as much discomfort as possible. Helma was next. I bet you are enjoying this very much aren't you? Helma just shook her head and continued to absorb the fluid. Ilsa looked at the clock on the wall and said that it was time to turn off the entrance of the fluid. Clamps were placed above the outside balloon to grantee no leakage would take place. The tubing was disconnected and the IV pole removed.

Frieda decided a little more punishment was due them with the water inside of them. She brought over a cordless Magic Wand and brought it to the clit of Judy. Ilsa also brought one over and applied it to Helma's clit. This was the last straw and the slaves went into orgasm after orgasm. Their vaginal areas were now covered in white cum and they moaned and screamed in joy.

Ilsa turned to Frieda and said that it was getting late and she was getting tired. We all have a big day tomorrow. Both slaves were released and told to get on their hands and knees to crawl back to the cell area. With all that water in them and being totally exhausted, the trip was slow back to cell. Now get into the position and we will chain you in. Looking like a sad puppy dog, Judy looked up and asked if they were going to leave the water in all night. The answer came quickly. I am going to release the air from the balloons and remove the catheter, but you must hold it in until I tell you to release it. Both the slaves shook their heads and the catheters were removed.

Frieda counted to ten and said, you can release it now. Large showers of water erupted from their bottoms. What felt like hours, happened in a mater of two minutes? Both women sunk into a very relaxed position on the floor. You are both so very dirty and I will have to give you a shower.

The hose opened, letting the cold water wash away the ruminants of the enema from their bodies.

They sank to the floor as best they could and waited to hear from the Mistresses. You two did very well with this set of events. I am very sure that you will be very sour in the morning. You will receive your food and two bowls of water tonight. The Party Favor had his gag removed and told that his food and water were in front of him. Eat and than get a lot of sleep as your work detail will be very demanding tomorrow. Remember you can talk to each other, but not to the Party Favor.

We will be listening and I can assure you that the whipping will be extreme if we hear you talking to him. The warning wasn't even necessary as both the slaves were out of it and asleep as they finished the last few bites of their dog food. Too bad they are sleeping, I was going to tell them that if they had wanted bad enough, I would have had Fritz screw them. He was as eager as I have seen him. The light was turned out and the door closed.

Day Four

As Ilsa and Frieda entered the cell area they found the Party Favor trying to get comfortable. He had been hog tied for over a day and a half by this time. Sorry, but you will not be released in any way till late tomorrow night. With that, Frieda kicked him in the ass to stimulate him. Little did the slaves know, but this treatment was far better than where they had picked him up from.

Good morning slaves, wake as today will be busy. They had their food and water set in front of them. Each went to it immediately. The Party Favor received his and didn't want to get into it. He sniffed it and kind of stuck his nose up at it. Out came the cattle prod and it was stuck behind his balls. Several sets of shocks had him in the mood for breakfast.

After all had finished feeding, the hose and cold water came out to give them a cleaning. The water seems colder than normal this morning.

The Party Favor tried to struggle against his bonds to get some relief, but without any success. Helma and Judy, being a slave is not only being tied or in your case chained, but also the pain, torture and humiliation of yesterday. Today is you first of two days of service and fun. The chains were released and they were told to get on all fours to crawl to their assignment.

Helma was slow, but Judy was in some pain after last evening. What is the mater Judy? She looked up and said she was just a little sore from the enema. Don't worry; some heavy labor will fix it. Ilsa looked at Helma and told her to remember what was about to happen was still a secret and not to tell Judy. She needs to find out how it is. Just remember, you already know how it works. Hope you enjoy yourself for the remainder of the morning.

They were lead thru the play room and out the heavy wooden door to the rear. Down the long hall and down the incline to the lower level they went. Ladies, this is the wine pressing room. The room had an old press in the middle. The outer ring of the stone press was fifteen feet in diameter and one foot thick. It sat almost three feet off the ground. An inner ring of eleven feet in diameter and one foot thick set inside of the outer. It was also one foot thick. Two large stone wheels at almost six feet in diameter sat, one on each side in the space between the rings. A large wooden shaft stuck thru the two wheels and protruded four feet beyond the wheels on each side. Large iron rings were at the outer ends of the shaft. Helma was now told to stand at one end and Judy to the other end of the shaft. Their wrist chains were disconnected from each other and attaches to the shaft.

This is the wine press which was installed in the early 1800s in the converted castle. They needed a place to press the vast amount of grapes. They first brought in burros to turn the shaft and later had horses. We now use slave labor to make the press stones turn. You will have till noon to press the hundred baskets of grapes. You will need to put your backs into it as we keep the grapes full in the channels. Now get moving.

One or both of us will be here to give you some encouragement to move. Ilsa picked up the six foot bull whip and gave Helma a sting on her left hip. She started to push, while remembering what she did to the

TOYS months ago. It was sinking in how much pain she had put the TOYS in when they played. She hopped that what followed after the wine press wasn't going to be as bad as they did to the TOYS. It was Judy's turn to get her first touch of the end of the whip. It was what she needed to start pushing on the shaft and turning the crushing stones.

Turn after turn crushed another basket of grapes. The fresh juice was sent down to another level and collected to be made into house wine. Both of the slaves were putting their backs into the task. Judy was laboring with the task as Helma was just daydreaming of the prior trip to this room. The dreams of her being the one with the whip, turning the flesh of each slave into red and black welts made her start to shiver and drip some white cum to the ground. Both Judy and Helma watched as the number of baskets filled with grapes slowly emptied. Helma was still a little high with joy as Judy was quickly tiring.

Finally the last basket was emptied into the ring. The sloshing of the grapes as it ran down to the filtering room and than processed into wine to age in the oaken barrels was music to the ears of Lisa and Frieda. Almost exhausted from the task, the slaves were released from the shaft and re-chained at the wrists. Down on your knees so we can go back up to the play room: they exited the wine pressing room for the trip up the incline ramp. They entered the play room and were directed to the far wall and chained to a ring in the wall. As a treat while we set up for more fun, you can get close to each other and hug, kiss and cuddle each other. Helma and Judy immediately cuddled and hugged. Even a sloppy kiss was seen.

The two were exhausted from the work detail. In the meantime, Ilsa and Frieda were emerging from one of the side rooms. They had two items of play. Both item were from the medieval times of the castle in the sixteen hundreds. First item to emerge was a spiked chair. The second was a full rack with a retching winding wheel. The rack was placed in the center of the room while the chair was set against the wall.

Frieda stood back and asked the slaves which wanted to be the first to try the rack. Judy kind of was scared of either item, but Helma spoke right up to be stretched on the rack. In a low voice, she told Frieda that she was excited to get on it. Excellent, Helma come over here and stand next to it.

Judy you will be seated and watch Helma go thru it. Just remember, we will be switching positions later. Judy was un-hooked of her chains and told to take a seat on the nails. Judy looked at the tips of the nails and was wishing she had taken the rack first. She moved back slowly and first noticed the reddish brown stains on the chair. Don't worry Judy; it is only traces of blood from the past subject to be placed here. When you sit down, make sure you are all the way back against the spikes at the back.

Judy slowly lowered herself on the tips. She just closed her eyes and sat down. Now lean back against the back spikes and get comfortable. Your arms go on the spiked arms of the chair. Again, she slowly lowered her arms onto the spikes. Now completely seated, Frieda began the process of securing her in. A two inch wide leather belt went around her waist, drawing her back in the chair. Judy screamed a little. Two belts went around her lower arms so her arms were now in contact with the nails. Let me see, what are we missing? We need to draw your legs back onto the nails which stuck out of the legs of the chair. Two more belts will finish the process. Judy felt the next around her throat and one across her forehead.

Judy, in olden times, the prisoner would be forced down by placing heavy weights on the lap. I guess that since we don't have any weights, I will have to sit on you lap from time to time. If you looked at the bottom prior to sitting, you would have noticed the seat with the nails was made of iron. To make the victim uncomfortable, a small fire was placed under it, thus burning the crouch area.

Just think of how the smell of burning hair and flesh would feel and smell? Judy was starting to turn little green at this time. Don't worry; I am all out of matches today. Judy let out a shy of relief. Judy, you will now watch your fellow slave be stretched and tortured on the rack. Just remember, you two will be trading places later.

With Judy secured and in some pain, Ilsa turned to Helma and undid her chains. Hop up on the rack and prepare to be attached. Helma eagerly jumped up and centered herself end from end. Don't worry, once I start to turn the retching wheel and take the slack out, you will be centered well. Helma was almost going into a kind of sexual trance. Ilsa went to her ear and whispered in to her ear. Helma, you are very excited being tortured, aren't you? If so, just nod your head so as not to alert Judy. Do you want me to go easy on you or do you want it rough?

Helma whispered back that pull out all the stops and make it hurt badly. Helma whispered can I please have a gag? You may, but I still want to hear the terror in you screams. Helma nodded her head yes and the hooking up went on. He legs were spread slightly and the ankle shackles were attached to chains at her feet. Now lay back so we can attach the wrist chains. A penis gage was placed in her mouth and the thick leather straps were drawn around the back of her head. Now, let me take some of the slack out of the chains.

With each click, an inch of slack was removed from the body of Helma. By click four, her body was now tight and she was in some pain. Helma, I want you to know that in the past, not only were persons both stretched to death, but other unspeakable tortures done to them. I will be applying many painful tortures to your fair skin.

I want you to imagine what they went thru. I also want you to understand that the Party Favor may be used on this rack on Saturday. You may even want to use this on you next TOY visit. As normal, you can not tell Judy of what we talked about. Helma had several more clicks of the winding wheel done and she now threshed her head slightly. I think we will let you just get use to the tightness your body is in.

Back at Judy, Frieda was just about to lightly sit in her lap. Judies eyes grew as big as silver dollars. The dull tips of the nails were just starting to dig in and cause her pain. Judy, I bet that you would do anything to get out of having the nails dig any deeper into your flesh? Judy answered that she would rather take anything else instead of the spikes. Good, let me go to the cart and find some toys for use on you. Frieda went to the cart and took out a pair of Japanese clover clips with a foot of chain between them. Now, let's see if I can get you nipples to stand up at attention for me.

Taking one at a time in her fingers, she rubbed the rosy tip between her fingers and even let her nails pinch at the base of the nipple. Nice, you are getting them at attention for me. Frieda picked up the clamp, opened it and brought it over the nipple. When it reached the base, the clamp was let close. The other nipple found itself with the clamp on it. That is a fine sight Judy; now let's place the clip of the leash on the chain.

Standing back, Frieda began to tug on the leash. As the clover clamps closed tighter with each pull, Judy let out a scream. Judy, the tone of your scream is music to my ears. Lets try it harder and see if your can go louder this time. What came from Judy's mouth echoed throughout the play room. At this point, Ilsa whispered to Helma, does it bring back memories? Helma shook her head yes and she thought to herself that she hopped that she could experience that pain. Don't worry, you chance is coming.

Ilsa went to the wheel and released the tension on the chains. Without any warning, the slack was taken out again and even maybe two more clicks brought her to attention again. Let me see, you wanted it to be heavy, right? Again, Helma shook her head yes. Ilsa went to the cabinet and took out several different medical forceps.

Helma, you know what they are and that they can cause extreme pain. Where do you want me to start? From behind her gag, she mumbled she wanted her nipples done. It was a great idea, so Ilsa took a pair and place them on her nipples. Helma winched as the clamp was tightly closed. Ilsa grabbed the handles and started to twist and pull on them.

She said, I think you used this technique on your toy. I think, that you want to know how much pain you gave her, don't you. Helm again shook her head yes between screams. Ilsa said to Frieda that she was having so much fun with Helma. Frieda turned to Ilsa and said: I knew she would. I am ready to bring more pleasure to your experience. Ilsa retrieved several pair of forceps from the cart. As you see Helma, I have chosen ones with very sharp points at the ends. Now where to place them? The area between your legs is in need of attention.

Opening the pair, she went to a point just above the "V" of her pussy mound. I will gather up some skin and close the tips. The points dug into her tender flesh and were closed till one click was heard. Helma tried to wiggle some, but the tension on her body prevented it. Just the reaction I wanted. I think I will place the next pair on you clit. Do you think it will be as much fun as you did before? I think I will make it hurt much worse. Ilsa stuck her fingers in between the labia and spread them wide. Now don't worry, after I place this set of clamps on you clit, I will return with two more and do your labia.

As the sharp points of the forceps closed on her clit, some fear started to appear on Helma's face. A shy came from her lips. One pair was applied to the labia on each side. As the tips came into contact, Helma had an orgasm. The clamps were closed tightly, imbedding them into the flesh. A popping sound was heard as they penetrated the skin. A rope from a pulley was let down and the three clamps were gathered up. Ilsa held the three clamps together and took the slack out. I think we need some weight to attach to them. A three pound weight was attached to the running end of the rope. She allowed the weight to slowly take up the slack and than dropped the last inch of slack to just drop. This brought the loudest scream so far. Small droplets of blood now ran down inside of Helma. Ilsa gave the weight a good push causing it to swing to and fro.

OK Ilsa, you have had enough fun now, it's my turn again. Frieda went to the cabinet and selected two sets of medieval finger presses. I will start at the left hand. The press was worked over Judy's four fingers till it made its way to the first finger joint. Very slowly, the screw handle was turned until the press halves came together. Enough pressure was forced onto the joint to cause extreme pain without breaking the joint. The right hand came next. Slowly the press was closed and both hands were in extreme pain.

Now for the breasts as the clover clamps are dong their job, but the ample breast meat still needs some work. A quick trip to the cabinet produced a box of one hundred syringe needles. They were only three eights inch long by twenty two gage. They were just long enough to cause pain and panic without doing damage. One by one, Frieda popped the needle from its package and removed the plastic safety cover. She brought the tip to the soft meat of the breast and pushed it into the hub of the needle.

Screaming wildly and trusting her head, Frieda decided to attach it to the back of the chair to prevent damage to Judy's head and neck. One by one, fifty needles made their way into each breast. Soon, little drops of blood made their way to tip of the hub. I like this Judy, and so saying this, she took the heal of her hand and patted the ends of the needles. She also applied a rubbing motion to cause even more pain.

Tuning to Ilsa, I don't think I should go further. Ilsa agreed and went to Helma's head and asked if she was finished for now. Please, just a little more please. Ok, but you have to leave time for the chair. With that, Ilsa took a pair of pliers from the cabinet and applied them to the big toe. This brought instant panic as the pliers were squeezed tighter together.

She continued to do this to all of her toes. Sweat was now pouring from Helma's forehead. A final tug on he rope to her labia clamps and she was done. All her clamps were removed and the tension on the chains stretching her was released. Helma's body dropped back on the rack as total exhaustion set in. Frieda and Ilsa moved to the wall and talked about where to go from there. Frieda said that Judy was so exhausted and Ilsa said that Helma was spent and had orgasms more time than she could count. Time is getting late and they have a lot of cleaning to do prior to the party on Saturday.

The slaves were both released from their piece of equipment and gotten on their knees. You two slaves don't need to be told where to go now. Helma led the way with Judy bring up the rear. They entered their cells and went to their assigned spots. Ilsa spoke first. The two of you did better than we thought you would. As a reward to you being such good slaves you will be chained together and allowed to fondle each other.

What ever else you want to do is your thing. Frieda turned to the Party Favor and gave him a kick to his balls. He stirred and was released to stretch some. Don't get use to it as you are going back to your hog tie shortly. Don't even try to touch yourself or you will think twice next time.

He twisted and turned to relieve some of the stiffness in his back and legs. Don't worry as you will be the center of attraction on Saturday. Each received their dog food and water. You will have ten minutes to finish as we have a full schedule to prepare for tomorrow. The bowls were collected in the ten minute period and the Party Favor was again hogtied. Lights out all and have a good night. Ilsa and Frieda left.

As soon as the door shut and they heard the sounds of the steps of he two go down the hall, Helma and Judy held each other closely and tried to relieve each others aches and pains form the day. Helma was still flying high with all that happened today. She never fully understood what the pain she did to the TOY was like. She thought to herself that she would make better use of the instruments and tools on the next TOY she came to work on. Both drifted into bliss and Helma had such sweet dreams of prior events she had done on her last visit. She wished that she could tell Judy of them, but knew better.

Day Five

Ilsa and Frieda woke around seven and went to the breakfast buffet. Small talk of a sale of clothes in town dominated the meal. We need to visit Wolfgang to check out changes if any. At eight thirty they both arrived at Wolfgang's office and were buzzed in. Wolfgang started the conversation. First, I want a report on the two slaves. Ilsa stated that they were great and Helma was the best switch slave they had ever had. She is also a pain slut and a half. Wolfgang turned and said he was able to watch her on the rack and knew in a minute that she was.

We don't often get one that can torture a TOY and take it so well. Frieda, as for the Party Favor; I think we will need to take him out of hogtie and let him stretch his body some. I suggest that he be put in slave chains and connected to the rings in the floor and wall. What do you think of taking the hood off and letting him see today? We will still keep the lights off when not in there for the slaves.

Wolfgang shook his head yes and said that we might as well give him some relief as this is his last painless day. Just make sure he gets fed and watered several times today. We want his strength up for the Party. You will also need to prep the slaves as to their roll in the party tomorrow. I think that since they have been so good, they and the Party Favor can have real food for breakfast tomorrow. Kind of like the last meal for him.

After two this afternoon, I will have the two men from the most trusted house staff and one from the kitchen come down and set up the tables for the party. I want them to use the two person café tables and nice café chairs. They will also need to set up the separate play room with mattresses and large pillows so the guests can have a soft place to make whoopee as the Favor is worked on. Have the slaves scrub the showers and hot tub out. It has been several weeks since we had a party there. I have noticed that this group likes their wine a lot. I will have ten bottles of the different flavors and two cases of champagne put in the wine cooler. Anything else we need to think of.

Ilsa spoke up and asked are we going to setup a special table for Carl? I forgot about that he wants to attend this one. He has some sort of interest in the Favor. He has also requested his own gown to wear, you know, the bright blue one. Those were his colors when he was an interrogator at the prison. Make sure he has access to the tool cart. He wants to perform several of his most liked procedures on the Favor. As for the group, as normal, they will always be given the chance to touch, grab and turn the crank on the phone when they want.

They paid the price to get into the action. You will be doing the pre work on the Favor and have the say, except for Carl, as to when they can request things to be done to the Favor. Make sure he lasts at least the first twelve hours alive if possible. After that, he can expire anytime. I know that you will dispose of the body in the morning, will do sir. What are you planning for the slaves this time? I know that we have used them for waitresses; but I want to put them up spread eagle against the wall. We are going to add additional straps to prevent any movement and secure the head so they have to watch the work on the Favor. This will be a good ending for Helma and have her to take another contract when she is finished with this one.

As for Judy, I am not sure exactly how she will act. I think she will enjoy watching it. Anyway, both will be open for touching and grabbing by the guests. I am glad you told me and I will arrange several waitresses to be on hand. I will have the food and drink, other than the wine, delivered by eleven in the morning. The party starts at noon and I am sure they will be ready.

I want the slaves and the Favor in place by eleven. I do want him gagged so he can't insult the guests. You can remove it when you start as the group will enjoy his begging and screaming. Again, that is what they paid for. After the party, you should get them to sign up for another Party or even be part, either as slave or torturer. I know you always enjoy the $500 bonus for each one your recruit. Wolfgang told them that this completes the prep for tomorrow and it's time to get the slaves to work. Ilsa and Frieda rose and departed for the cell block.

The women entered the elevator and wet down to the second level. All the time, they talked of what they would do with the bonus money. It was never very hard to get these rich people to come back. Frieda said that she had a new ski suit ready at the clothing shop. I want to be in style for ski season this year. As for Ilsa, she had some diamond jewelry she had tried on to be hers to place on her fingers. If we sell enough, we can upgrade a lot.

As they opened the cell door and turned on the lights, both slaves were already steering. Time to get up and work today, play was yesterday and now back to slave work. Both Helma and Judy were still hurting from there time in the play room, but it was a good hurt. The chains to the rings were released and the food and water bowls given to them. Eat up as it is to be a long day of work.

Attention was shifted to the Party Favor. Alright, you are to be taken out of hogtie and have your hood removed. You will be receiving slave chains today. This will give you a chance to stretch and get your aches and pains in order. You will not be leaving the cell block.

The rope which held him was removed, but before he had a chance to move, he had the dirty shackles placed on his wrists and ankles. The shackles were than locked together without the connecting chain. A three foot chain as attached to his collar so he could get comfortable. Enjoy the release for today as tomorrow will be different.

The hood was removed and this was the first time he had been able to see where he was. It took several minutes, but his eyes adjusted to the light. He was surprised to see two naked women across the room. As we told the slaves, they are of no concern of yours and you will not be getting to know them. If you try to talk, the hood, blindfold, and gag will go back on. Do you understand?

He didn't answer fast enough and received several kicks in the ass and stomach with one in the balls. He answered very quickly that he understood. He was now fed and given water. You have ten minutes to eat and we will be back. As they ate, Ilsa and Frieda went to the cleaning cabinet. Plenty of scrub brushes and mops to do the job. The play room needs to be done by noon as the setup crew will be here by two.

Let's go slaves. Both Helma and Judy rose to a standing position. Frieda led them to the cleaning supply closet and obtained the supplies to scrub the floors. Each took a bucket, scrub brush and a towel to the play room. Ilsa directed them to the one corner of the room. Down on your knees slaves and start scrubbing. When you are done, I don't want to see a speck on the floor. Each slave took their twelve inch long brush and dipped it in the solution. I want to see a back and forth and side to side action now. Put your backs into it now.

They put their backs into the scrubbing action; bringing the ground in dirt rising up. Now take your towel and wipe it clean. Frieda rolled a bucket with clean water up to wring out the towels in. Ilsa looked at Frieda and said, they need some insensitive to scrub harder. Frieda went to the cabinet and retrieved two six foot bull whips. The distinctive sound of the tip of the whip went thru the air and landed on each of their asses. Not expecting it, they both jumped, but went right back to scrubbing. They both knew that stopping would only bring another.

It took the two hours to scrub the room from end to end. The bucket of water had to be changed several times, but the floor shined brightly. That is it for today slaves. Each slave grabbed their bucket and took it back to the closet. The water was dumped, the towels put in the laundry hamper and the brushes put up to dry.

The slaves were walked back to the cell for the remainder of the day. Since this was the day prior to the Party, you will be allowed to have longer chains to your collars and not be locked to the rings in the floor. You may caress and cuddle each other if you wish. I suggest that you get a good, long night sleep as tomorrow will be as long as 26 hours. Do you understand me? Both Helma and Judy answered in low voices that they understood. You will also receive and extra meal and water now.

Frieda presented the bowls to the slaves and Ilsa and they departed to ready the several tool carts for tomorrow. They left and for a change, left the light on. It didn't take long for Judy to comfort herself with her head on Helma's breasts. Helma put her arm around her shoulder and cradled her head softly. They quickly fell into a deep sleep, even thought it was only early afternoon.

By this time, they knew that if they were told to get sleep, they had better. Before drifting off, Helma looked over to the man chained to the floor and set her mind into action. Not sure if she was plotting of what was to happen to him, or was she feeling sorry or did she wish she was the one inflecting the pain. Her thoughts also drifted to Judy, was she ready for what she was about to see and experience, or would she fall apart, only time would tell.

Ilsa and Frieda went to the storage room containing the tool carts. They went over the list of tools; they inspected the common hand tools, medical instruments or specialty toys. Scissors, scalpels, and even pliers were tested and readied for action. Frieda took the plumbers torch and lit it to make sure the tank was ready. Ilsa loved the battery drill with the many sizes of drill bits.

She had used it to drill teeth as well as into bones and knee joist while doing interrogations. Ilsa said that this takes her back to the times in the prison when it was their duty to obtain information or punish prisoners. Frieda agreed and said she wanted to return to the old days, but the pay sucked and all the great food and relaxation in the pool, would be sourly missed.

Next they came to Carl's cabinet. He had many of the same tools, but several special one as well. We can go thru the checklist and be done in ten minutes. Satisfied with the results, they rolled the three cabinets into the play room. It was just getting to the two o'clock hour and the two trusted workmen and the Chief Catering Supervisor were just coming. Ilsa confirmed that they were on the same page for the setup. Just make sure that you leave the wall with the rings open for the slaves. Also the wine should be the better stock. By the wall where the guest would be coming in, they set up the serving tables, portable bar, fully stocked and the wine cooler. Red and green linen table clothes were placed on the serving tables.

Next to come were the twelve café tables and chairs, comfortably spread around the room. A single table was setup for Carl. His received a golden table cloth. A bdsm center place setting consisting of cuffs, blindfold and gag went around a large candle. One never knew if the guests would want to play with each other in the sleeping room. Frieda turned and said, looking great. We can check on the total setup after when we feed the slaves.

The pair departed, leaving the remainder of the setup in the hands of the crew. I want to go up to the room and relax before supper. Ilsa and Frieda went to their room and stripped naked. Remember when we did this before work on a prisoner? They agreed that a little relaxation was needed and they went to playing with each other. Hands roamed and before it was over, a little oral was the deal for the day. Play went on until it was time for hot bath and dinner.

They went up to the fifth floor and both ordered a full surf and turf dinner. The lobster was great and the steaks were medium rare, the way they both liked them. As we need to have clear heads tomorrow, I think we should have coffee with dinner. A full serving cravat of deep dark roast coffee was placed on the table. They finished their meal and got some of the best apple pie in the area served to them. A scoop of vanilla ice cream adorned the top with several strawberries. Wow I am stuffed and ready for tomorrow.

It was too bad that the Party Favor won't get his last meal of this excellent food, only his normal dog food and water. Let's go back to the cell and wash and feed the three. It seems that the interrogation squad's job is never finished. They entered the cell and told them to get washed off. The cold water actually felt good and next came supper. Good night all and get a lot of sleep, you will need it. Ilsa took one last look at the party setup and than retired to their rooms.

Party Day

Morning came early for all. Ilsa and Frieda went to the dining room and got their plates full of egg and sausage, with some potatoes on the side. Ilsa looked at the Catering Supervisor and told her that she would need three plates like this to go in a half hour. She shook her head as she knew why. Will do, would you like a pot of coffee to go for yourselves? That sounds outstanding and maybe a few Danish's? Great, it will be a while till we are able to eat later this afternoon.

The guests were just arriving for breakfast when Ilsa and Frieda departed. The group knew they had an hour to eat and than go get ready for the Party. According to the instruction sheet delivered that morning, they should be in casual clothes and easy shoes. The group was to be at the registration desk by eleven thirty.

As they are, those that had been here to the Party before were relaxed, those that were new sat in different forms of wonder and anticipation of the upcoming events. All were at least sorry that their week of fun and excitement was to be over in a little over twenty four hours, and than back to their daily grind. It seemed that a week of relaxation was never enough. Each couple finished breakfast and returned to their room to prepare for the event.

Ilsa and Frieda went to the kitchen and took the serving cart with the three meals, coffee and pastry. They went down the elevator to the floor of the cell area where they presented each slave and the Party Favor with his or her meal. Each wondered why the real meal, but did not complain.

We are on a tight schedule this morning, so you will have ten minutes to finish. They dug into the meal as Frieda took the cart with their snacks to the dressing room/office. Ilsa turned, poured her coffee and chose a cherry Danish and said, I think that Helma knows what is going to happen today. I would also put money that Helma wishes that she could jump right in. I think we should give her a chance to tell Judy what is about to happen and get her ready. Frieda said it was a good idea and also to have a puke bucket near her as she might not understand.

Your ten minutes are over slaves. The slave's collars were undone and they were told to stand and get ready for a good shower. This time, Frieda added a little warm water to the mix. A bar of soap was handed to each and they were wet down. Now lather up, scrub down, especially the pussy and ass hole areas. We don't want the Guest to get dirty from touching you.

Each slave did as she was told and then they were rinsed down. Here are towels to dry. Helma, I want to see you over here, now. She walked over to Ilsa and she was taken aside. I am pretty sure you know what is going to happen in a little while. She nodded yes. I want to know if you think that Judy is going to be ok or not. I am not sure, but we have talked and she should be OK. That is good, but when we take you to the play room, I want you to talk to her. Tell her if she feels like getting sick, she should say something and not puke on a guest. I will give you some extra special treatment later if you do that. Is that understood? Helma nodded her head yes and returned to Judy. Let us go now you two.

They entered the play room and were told to go to the rings on the wall. Stand with your backs to the wall like you did the other day. For up to the next twenty four hours, you will be standing spread eagle, widely spread. Both were secured to the rings and looked ahead to the center of the room. There was a butcher block table, one foot wide and three foot long. From time to time tonight, either Frieda or I will come over to you and give you some food and water. You are not to beg for anything from the guests, is that understood? Both slaves said they understood.

This is how it is to work tonight; you will be witness to the torture of the male you have had in your cell block. He was a condemned prisoner and even if you don't think so, it will be much better for him than if he had been in the prison for sentence. I want the both of you to just except what is going on and keep quiet. Just remember, you can trade places with him. Judy, I have given permission to Helma to talk to you about what is going to happen. She has done the same things to another TOY in the past. As in the past, you are not to talk to anyone about what goes on here to anyone. Are we all clear about this? Yes came from both of them.

As for the guests, I will be telling them about the rules for the Party when they come down. All during the Party, they have the right to come over to you, touch and fondle you in any place or opening they want. You will NOT resist or say anything. This is a slave's duties and came from as far back as Ancient Rome.

You wanted to do extreme slavery and you are getting it now. Don't disappoint me or hell will be paid by both of you. If I have to punish you here, I will stick the cattle prod right up you pussy and burn it good. Helma, you will have five minutes to talk to Judy. Last thing, Carl, the owner will be taking part in the Party. He taught us, so you can imagine what he can do.

Helma turned to Judy and started to talk to her. You are about to see and hear things that may sicken or horrify you. This is part of the training and should be taken in. I am a doctor and I was part of four doctors that tortured two people to death a little over seven months ago. You might not think much of it or me now, but it can be exciting and was very relaxing from the life or death way we spend our lives.

If you can't bear to watch, just close your eyes and for Gods sake, don't say anything or puke. You might even find that you like it. I know by now that you enjoy the slave's way of life. I know that I will be returning for both ways in the future. I never thought that I would like the pain end, but I crave it more each day, and I think you do also. Even if you don't want to do the other side, go into it with an open mind. I know that the Party Favor will be in intense pain and will beg and scream loudly.

The group will most likely be cheering on Ilsa and Frieda while they give the pain. I don't know of anything else that will be going on in here today. Are you OK and understand what I have told you? Judy turned and said she would try her best and try to understand later. Judy now asked Helma if she would hold and cuddle her when this was over. You know I will Judy.

The last piece of the party was now to come. Ilsa and Frieda went to the cell and gave the prisoner a shot of a short acting sedative. He stopped thrashing and lay limp. Let's hurry as the shot will only knock him out for ten to fifteen minutes. They loaded him on the cart and wheeled him into the play room. He was placed on the butcher block table, with his cock and balls hanging off the table. First came the two, two inch wide leather belts one over his belly button and the other just below his nipple line.

His wrists came next and were pulled straight down the side of the table. They took his ankles and drew them back to where his hands were secured them so his legs were wide open with good access to his cock and balls. His head came next; the shelf was pulled out from inside the table end. A strap went around his neck and one around his forehead. There was no wiggle room in his bonds. He was just getting his wits back so Frieda grabbed his ball and gave them a hard squeeze. He yelled and it shook the table decorations. Good, he is with us again. I will put the gag in and make it tight. Wonderful, we are set for the Party to begin.

The Party is Beginning

The Party Guests were now assembling in the lobby. All the party goers were ready for the party to commence. Wolfgang was in the lobby and started the first twelve down the elevator. The door opened on the second floor. Ilsa was there waiting and greeted the first group. She took them on a tour and first showed them the "SEX" room.

From there, she took them to the play room. I want you to please have a seat at one of the café tables. When the second half of the group comes down, you will get a full explanation of how the evening will work. The elevator door opened and Wolfgang led the second set of party goers got off. Ilsa also took this group to the "SEX" room and than had them seated in the play room.

Wolfgang moved to the center of the room and started. You have finally gotten to the reason you picked the Party Package. What you are about to see is a modern day presentation of what was done in the Coliseum of Rome. Prisoners would be placed in front of the ruling class and slowly put to death. I will now put you in the hands of our Lead Interrogators. This is Ilsa and Frieda. Over the next twenty four hours, they have total and complete control of the scene. They will explain the rules for the Party. Please have a great time, eat, drink and enjoy the show.

Wolfgang said goodbye for the time being and departed the play room.

Ilsa stepped up to the front of the crowd. Good evening and welcome to the play room. Frieda and I will be both your guides into the experience as well as doing most of the work on the prisoner. What you are about to see is all real and the screams of the prisoner will prove it. First of all, there is no way to tell you exactly of how long he will last or if he will scream or beg.

Every prisoner is different. Frieda and I have been in the interrogation business for over twenty five years combined. We are experts in giving pain for a prolonged period of time. It will seem that there is a slow pace in the beginning, but just bear with us. We will bring him up to a very tender point and than add to his problems.

This process takes as long as three hours. We will also have rest points every hour for us. During this time, you can come up to him and look over his different areas and touch him. You can not do anything to him until after the sixth hour. At that point, if you want to try your hand at interrogation, we will be happy to assist you. All we ask is that you do not cause his death so others can play with him. If you have questions, please ask either of us.

We will also be joined by the owner of the Chalet, Carl Schmidt. He is one of the best interrogation people in the world. He will also be inflecting pain and damage to him. If you at any point feel that it is too gory, we have placed buckets around the room to puke in, or you can disappear to the "SEX" room. This process is a great sexual turn for many. You can also go and play at anytime. You can also take the table decorations and play bdsm games.

As with in the times of the Roman period, we have two slaves tied to the walls to both watch the proceedings and also for you to indulge in. At anytime you feel you wish to go over to them, please feel free. You can touch, feel, and from time to time, we will provide items you can use to inflect pain with. Exception to this is that you can not do anything to inflect permanent pain or damage. We will explain the items as we go on. I am sure that they will enjoy all the attention you give them.

To the other side of the play room is the snack area and bar. We have two people by the tables to make up the best snacks and drinks you have ever had. Please partake in the snacks which will make you happy. Get yourself settled or even come up and touch and see the prisoner or the slaves. Frieda and I will start the process on him in fifteen minutes.

Frieda moved to the place between the slaves and Ilsa stayed with the Party Favor. The group moved around the play room, some went to the slaves and caressed their breasts and vaginal areas. Others came over to the prisoner; some looked into his eyes while one of two of the women caressed his cock and balls. All proceeded to the snack table and got their snacks and a glass of wine or other drinks.

As the people began to be seated, Ilsa announced that it was time to be seated. Both she and Frieda walked over to the center of the room and opened the tools cabinet. Frieda selected several stiff scrub brushes while I picked up three stainless steel wire brushes. We will start by tenderizing his cock and balls. Frieda grabbed the ball sack and pulled it back over his cock. The skin was stretched tight and she dug her fingernails into the skin. She ran one of the stiff scrub brushes very slowly from the base of his ball sack up to her hand.

He stiffened on the block and tried to scream from around the gag. That was fun, so well let us do it over and over again. Two than three dozen times in both directions and he was even crying some. The sack was slowly turning red and warm to the touch. Ilsa changed places with Frieda and took a small wire brush and traced the same area. She stopped and milked his cock to full erection and used the brush over the opening at the end causing his struggles to increases.

Grabbing the tip of his cock, the brush was now run over the length, going around the he entire length. The abuse of his cock continued as Frieda took a nasty metal bristle parts cleaning brush and began to work on his nipples. At this point, several women placed a hand over their own nipples to either protect or message them.

The attack with many different brushes continued. Even the rosebud ass hole was not ignored. Each of his areas received a relentless attack. All the areas were turning beet red. Frieda glance at the clock and it had been an hour. Well ladies and gentleman, we have reached the first break. It is time to refill your glasses and pick up some snacks before we start hour two. For those that don't believe that the Favor is in agony, you are invited to look and touch any of the areas we have been working on. There are surgical gloves for you if you wish. I will be over at the two slaves if you wish to discuss their situation. Frieda will stay with the Favor.

Several couples approached the slaves tied to the rings in the wall. Two women started to caress their bodies and let their hands roam up into the pussy area. They are truly soft and they seem aroused. How long have they been hanging her? I answered that they were placed on the wall almost two hours ago. How long will they be here? They will be here till the end of the party, unless, they are requested to join a member later for some fun in the SEX room.

I need to add some decorations to them. I pulled out a pair of clover clamps with bright brass sleigh bells attached. Now where to attach them, any ideas? One of the women spoke up and suggested that they be placed on the nipples, so that every time the moved, it would set the bells off.

I handed each woman a pair of the bells and told them to be my guest. Judy was first to receive the bells. The woman approached her and lightly twirled the nipples in her fingers, bring them to an erect position. She squeezed the clamp open and placed it over the nipple. She released it so slow and gently. She repeated the process on the other nipple.

At that point, she reached down with her hand and ran it across the pubic mound. Judy started to moan and a finger started to work on Judy's clit. Judy put her hips into a slow rotation and a low moan came from her mouth. The woman said that she liked the reaction from Judy. On the other side, the other woman went to work on Helma. She grabbed the nipples getting them stiff. The clamp was opened and placed over the stiff nipple and let loose. A more in depth moan came from Helma and than the other clamp was placed. The woman said that she enjoyed the emotion from the placing of the clamps. She asked if she could tug on them, and I said she would enjoy the pain. The woman grabbed the one bell and pulled while grabbing a handful of Helma's labia. This added to the moans coming and she now grabbed both bells and pulled very hard.

I see you are enjoying yourself, maybe a little sadist streak in you? Yes, I have fun doing this with one of the girls at home. I have always wanted to do this to a slave. These slaves are completing a week program. They wanted to try out the service, humiliation, and pain aspects of slavery. I bet you would enjoy our program of training to be a Mistress and work with slaves, or would you rather inflect true pain?

We have a wonderful program for this. If you see me after the party ends, I can give you more information. Toward the end of the party, you can inflect real pain on the Favor to see how far you want to go. We will be introducing different items to the slaves before the evenings end.

Frieda had several couples over to the Favor. One woman was grabbing his sore balls and twisting them. He was screaming, but the gag kept it more silent. The man grabbed the nipples and pulled them away from his chest and also twisted them very roughly. I see you enjoy inflecting pain at this point. When we get a little further down the road, you may want to do some torture items of your own.

Our main point so far is to get him where the littlest touch sends him into fear and pain. The man answered that it was a great show so far and this was different from my normal work. What do you do? I am a doctor and see so much scum of the earth all the time. You may enjoy one of our toy packages. You would do the same things as we are going to do this evening.

Another woman just wanted to play with his cock and balls. She gently milked him to as much erection as she could. Very nice Favor, and with that she hulled back and backhanded his balls. He screamed again. She asked if she could dig her fingernails into the ball sack. Sure you can as long as you don't tear them off. She lifted the sack with one hand and planted her four long nails at the base of the sack, dug in and slowly dragged them up. Wow, this is fun.

The break was now over and most of the group returned to their seats. Two couples had gone to the SEX room and would return later.

This hour we are still going to roughen him up more. We will bring a different assortment of toys over to use on his parts. I am first going to use what is called the BEAR claw. It is a plastic handle with six claw like fingers. It brings a great sensation of being mulled by a wild animal without slicing them open. Frieda picked up his ball and placed the fingers against the sack. A moderate amount of pressure was placed against the skin and was drawn upwards.

The screams were the most intense so far. I think it is time to remove his gag. Lisa went to the head and unbuckled it and pulled it away. The second pass dug in deeper this time and the screams were a true indicator. Most of the audience looked intensely at him and one woman even covered her ears. I kind of thought that you would get a thrill from that, as you will be able to be heard for the rest of the night.

Frieda took several strokes down his chest, making sure to get the nipples. One man stood up and asked if he could try the claw. You sure can and he came up to the bench. He took it and drew it along the side of the cock. I like this toy; do you have one I can use with my slave during the break? I think we can spare one for use. In fact, you can use the one I have. Ilsa handed it to him and he called his male partner and they went to the SEX room. Within minutes, a soft scream came from the back room.

Frieda said I think that someone else is having fun tonight. Ilsa turned to the audience and asked if there were any other Master/ Mistress/slave couples here. Several hands went up. I did forget to tell you that if you want to have your slave naked or have then sit on the floor, it is OK. Several couples exited the room for the SEX room. Within minutes they emerged, some with collars and leashes. Ilsa spoke and said she liked the audience getting involved in the play. Now back to the Party Favor. I will use this cheese grater on his nipples and the tip of his cock. The Favor began to beg not be hurt anymore. This brought an instant back hand to the face from Lisa.

I will tell you in advance that begging only makes me want to hurt you more. Several passes over his nipples brought small droplets of blood. I need to cover the blood for now and reached for the container of salt. I sprinkled it thickly over the nipples and than rubbed it in with the heal of my hand. He now thrashed on the block.

He was a mix of anger and pain combined. Frieda got a set of pliers and took hold of his cock. The man turned into an animal and tried to get himself off the block. Nice try, these belts are strong enough to hold a raging bull. With that, she grabbed it again, this time twisting as much as crushing it. He was almost to the point of passing out. I think he needs a break so we can work on him harder next hour.

Several different persons from the group came over and inspected the work. They were impressed and from each side, they grabbed his nipples and tugged on them. Others would caress him while one grabbed his balls and punched them. This time Frieda went over to the slaves on the wall.

She brought with her a pair of crank telephones with wires and alligator clips attached. The same two women came over with a look of excitement. You two love to work on the slaves. I love how you treat them. Frieda turned to them and replied; remember they came to us wanting to experience the aspects of being a slave.

Would you like to hook them up? Sure, where do we place the clips? Place one on each of her labia. Each woman did this, now what? Take the crank handle in your hand and just turn. A slow turn bites and a quick go round will produce a large, steady shock. Judy received the first bite. The handle was cranked a quarter of a turn at a time. She shook and moaned. I like this, being the one that wanted to try being a slave, can I try it. Sure you can, are you going to do it to yourself or is your friend going to do it to you? She is going to do it.

The partner held the crank for Helma. I will tell you in advance, she loves the feel of the electric shock. The woman took the handle and just started cranking. Helma stiffened up and shook. Long moans came from her mouth, see, it is very enjoyable for her. With each jolt of the electric, the bells that were still attached to their nipples rang loudly. This is fun and I want to try it right now.

The woman dropped her panties and the partner clipped the clip to the little lips. Please make it bite at first. Several twists and she was in all her glory. The only words coming from her mouth were, more,

more, more. The woman doing the twisting stopped and ran her hand between the legs of the other woman. Wow, you are very wet, wait, let me check and she ran her hands over her lips. Hon, you made me so wet and I want to go get naked and have some fun.

They retired to the SEX room. Ilsa came over to Frieda, I think we have them sold, I can see the bonus money now. The one will make a great slave as the other will make a great Mistress. I think they need to sign up for the Mistress and slave training package. Frieda undid the clips from Judy and put the phone away for now. I think it is time for the slaves to get some water and food.

Ilsa brought over a bottle of water and gave both several sips. Frieda brought over some small finger sandwiches. Both slaves were thankful. Ilsa told the slaves how proud they were of them and that they would be rewarded tomorrow. She asked Judy how she was holding up. She answered that it was not affecting her and let's keep going. Ilsa and Frieda each took some food and a soft drink. I think it is time to pick it up a notch with him.

Just as the third session was about to begin, Carl came in and had a seat at his table. One of the waitresses came over to his table with a bottle of champagne and a glass. Good evening sir, would you enjoy a sampling of the foods we have for the guests. Yes I would, I haven't eaten all day.

She made her way back to the serving table and chose many items he enjoyed. Thank you for your outstanding service, I haven't had a chance to eat since breakfast. He munched on the finger sandwiches and drank from the champagne made at the chalet. Ilsa made her way over to Carl's table to brief him on how the Party was going. Sir, we are doing well recruiting and the guests are having fun. Would you like to join in the play? No, not at this minute, I want to get the feel of the group before I get involved.

Ilsa returned to the Party Favor and turned to the crowd. She pointed toward Carl and introduced him. This is Carl Schmidt, the owner of the Chalet. He has a vast back ground in the interrogation game with over thirty plus years doing his trade.

Carl stood up and said welcome to the group and how glad he was they came. He sat down and Ilsa continued talking to the group. This is the start of the third session with the Favor. For those of you that are a little squeamish, we will be intensifying the amount of pain and blood. If you think you will have a problem, please feel free to leave for the SEX room. No one got up and left.

We are going to start by caneing his outer thighs. Frieda brought two bamboo canes over to the table. She gave one to Ilsa and kept one for herself. They stood one on each side of the block, flexing their canes. All at once, both of them raised their weapons and brought them down on the outer side of the thighs. He immediately went into a screaming session, bucking and twisting his legs. Over and over again the canes dropped on the area. Within several strokes, black and blue welts began rising from the leg. They went on and gave him more than a dozen strokes. I think that this is a good start, would any of you like to trace the welts with your fingers.

Several came up and ran their fingers along the now raising welts. Wow, they are warm and raising quickly. They will become a very large problem for him in time. Is this the only place you will apply the cane? For now, we need to work on other parts of his skin. Frieda went to the cabinet and took out the plumber's torch, several nails and a set of pliers. She lit the torch and placed the nail in the jaws of the pliers. The flat head of the nail was placed over the flame to heat.

She watched as the head of the nail started to turn cherry red. I think it is ready, so she took it to the ring of the corona surrounding his nipple. I will start at the top of the area. She brought it neat to the skin, just as the heat was making it presents known. He started to beg for her not to touch him with the item. Frieda laughed and sunk it into the skin. Smoke rose from the spot and sizzling was heard.

His screams could be heard all the way into the SEX room, bring several peaking around the corner of the hall to see what had happened. Ilsa looked into the group and saw chills on some of the faces of group. I will let you know that this was the beginning of his suffering. The nail was reheated at the tip, over and over again. She went around in a clock pattern applying the head of the nail. Three o'clock, six o'clock, nine o'clock positions were now done. She turned to the other nipple and repeated the progress.

He was now in so much pain, his tolerance had been reached. We need to let him recover for a few minutes. Would anyone like to come up and see the burn marks? A dozen hands went up and approached him. Wow, they are deep burns. Go ahead and give them a feel. As the skin was touched, he cried and begged for them not to touch. None listened to him and continued to touch and pinch up the burnt skin. After playing with the area for several minutes they returned to their seats.

Ilsa looked at the group and asked if there were three women who would like to apply the next punishment. All kinds of hands went up. Ilsa choose three that hadn't been up before. Frieda went to the cabinet and chose four items. Ilsa had one asked who was the most sadistic and a tall blond spoke up, I have been a Pro Domme for many years and love to give pain to men. Great, please stand between his legs. The other two were told to get one on each side of him. Frieda handed the two on the side a pair of mini vice grips. The woman between his legs was handed a pair of wood connecting plates. The plates were two by four inch plates, each with thirty pair of quarter inch long spikes on them.

First came the vice grips. I want you two to close the teeth to around a sixteenth of an inch opening. Now, you need to place them on his nipples and close them. First was the left than the right nipple. He started to beg for them to come off, but this brought twisting and pulling on the priers. Please don't pull them off was heard from him. This brought a new round of twisting and pulling. His voice went silent. Wonderful job, I am proud of your work.

Let's move to his cock and balls. Frieda turned to the blond and asked if she liked to torture her slave's balls? Oh yes, that is my specialty. Have you ever used a pair of these? No, but they look interesting. This is what you do, pick up his balls and place the spiked side against the back of his balls. She did it, so now place the other one on top and make it a ball sandwich.

Wow, this is so simple; I can't believe I didn't think of it before. Before you do anything, let's let every one approach and watch you in action. The Favor was surrounded by the group and Ilsa told her to slowly close the space between the plates. She did the action and what is next? Rub the plates back and forth or make little circles. This will grind the spikes into his tender skin.

He started to try to kick and squeezed his hands. His voice was not as loud anymore as he was getting horse. Frieda looked at the group and stated the plates could also be placed with labia in between. Frieda took several pair of plates from her pocket and gave them to several of the people. Please try them on the slaves, but don't damage them. They moved over to the slaves and place the plates on them. With just a light squeeze, they did their jobs. Helma and Judy let people know of the intense pain they were in.

Several couples took the plates and withdrew to the SEX room to try them out on each other. These are such great fun and only around a dollar a piece. Frieda said we need to let him rest for a few minutes, but let's leave him with a reminder of his predicament. She picked up several Habanero peppers and shoved them up his rectum. The effect was instant and would last during the break. His rectum was on fire inside, all the way up several inches. Applause was heard from the group as the break started.

Members of the party wondered around the play room. Some were checking out the Favor's condition as others went to the slaves. Frieda was with the slaves. Three women approached and asked if they could ask both of them some questions. Frieda told them it was OK. Is the package what you thought it would be? Helma started by saying it was so much more than she expected. I want to be sure what it truly meant to submit to the different parts of being a slave. Judy jumped in by saying several parts of the training was a surprise and she was glad for the many different aspects.

Other than the bondage and pain, what were you put thru? I think that the humiliation was hard at first and the work was hard. Maybe it was the food we were given during the last week. What do you mean about the food? Helma answered this one. We were given a can of dog food, twice a day. It was not tasty, but did get us thru the day. I am sure that by the time I get home, I will have lost several pounds. That is a welcomed side effect of the training.

I understand that there are several different packages for the slavery journey? Judy answered; we both selected the extreme package. Helma stated that it was the most challenging package and may be a little harsh for the beginner. I had never thought of myself as a slave before, but it brought me to places I would never have experienced otherwise. I am sure that I will go home very satisfied and relaxed. I have a very stressful job and it is hard to just shake it off. I know that I will be back many times to come, and I found that I like the pain aspect of the training.

Judy added that her work was also stressful and with no outlet for the need to not be in charge. Is their a competition between slaves? Helma said, I don't think so as it hard enough to just keep up. We did find that we depended on each other for comfort by the end of a training day. Will you try to find someone and be a slave when you get home? Both answered at the same time, NO. After doing it with these two training Mistresses, there is no substitute for their excellence.

Ilsa spoke up and said it was time to start the forth period on the Party Favor. Frieda walked back over to Ilsa and waited for the party goers to get their refreshments and be seated. Ilsa spoke up and introduced Carl again. He will join us with this session. Carl spoke up and told the group they might want to bring their chairs up and circle around to get a better view of what was to happen. They moved their chairs around the block, unless they were the submissive of a Master or Mistress which meant they would be sitting on the floor. Several of the submissive were either holding onto the leg of their owner or were stroking and petting them. By this point, all were ready for the true pain session to come. Carl spoke up and said this was a great way to show the slaves affection for their owner.

Carl went to the outer legs and ran his hand over the red, black and blue welts made by the cane beatings. They had swelled up and were fluid filled. We need to make him much more comfortable and reduce the swelling. Several in the group laughed under their breath. Ilsa, go and get me my favorite toys to reduce the swelling. Don't forget the juice and salt. Ilsa retrieved a scalpel, several surgical spreaders, and tissue tweeters. What we are about to do is first lance the welt and than "treat" it. Frieda, I will also need several thick towels. She placed them on the floor on either side of the Favor. She gave the last one to Carl.

Carl took the scalpel and lightly traced the raised portion of the welt. A red tinged looking fluid ran from the cutting. This is the simple part. Now we place a surgical spreader between the flaps of skin and slowly spread the skin apart. Moans and than screams came from him as the skin was spread wider. That opens the middle so we can access the inner section of the welt. I will use tissue tweeters to gain more access, and will allow us to pour some of the pickling solution in the wound. Animal like screams were now coming from him. Ilsa, tell him that he has almost two dozen to go, so be less noisy.

Now that the solution has had it effect, we must pack he wound. Frieda handed Carl a container of salt. He poured it into the wound. This time Ilsa covered his mouth to cut off the sounds. Carl turned to the group and asked if anyone would like to try this procedure? Four or five hands went up. Carl told Ilsa to oversee the finishing of the draining. It was maybe twenty minutes to the completion of the draining. That was fun, kind of takes me back to my old life. Frieda, go and get my fishing gear.

Frieda stepped to the cabinet and took out a dozen large fishing hooks with leaders attached. A package of fishing twine was with the hooks. Now that he has settled down some, let's have some other fun. Carl moved down to between his legs. I want to go fishing and you all can help me. Carl picked up the ball sack and flattened it on one side. I will start at the top edge of the sack and now watch as I insert the first hook thru it. A loud popping sound was heard as the tip of the hook entered and exited the sack. Everyone see how easy this was.

There are eleven more hooks in the package and it would be a waste not to use them. Frieda, I want you to distribute them to those that want to go fishing. One by one, the hooks found their target and were popped thru. Now I will attach the twelve lines to the leaders, he handed the ends of the line to twelve different people. Please return to your seats and draw the line tight. Here is where the fun starts; I am going to have Ilsa point at a different person at a time. When she points at you, give the line a tight yank. He will give you the best play you can have.

Ilsa started to point and he had his ball skin pulled or yanked. For over an hour they played the yank the balls game. Ilsa collected the lines and took them back to the table. I think it is time for a break. The group was having so much fun, they came over during the break and felt and grabbed the open welts and looked at the damage to his ball sack. He was at the point of total exhaustion and almost passed out. Most of the others refilled their glasses, some retired to the SEX room. It was approaching midnight and there was still some fun to have.

Many questions were being asked of Frieda and Ilsa. Is there a private package to interrogate a person? Can I bring my slave and use the equipment? What other type of equipment do you have here? We will try to answer them, one at a time. We have many different packages from slave and Master/Mistress training to slave training. You can have either private or group sessions with your slave, or like the two we have today, several slaves being trained at a time.

As for equipment, well, this was a medieval castle at one time and we have many of the pieces used to interrogate prisoner ranging from a rack, stocks, the Spanish horse and also a spiked chair, our two slaves have experienced two of them. You can ask them how they felt during their torture training. We can sit down with you and help you plan another vacation of play and training. I will tell you that if you are in slave training or bring a slave, we keep them in the cell area next to the SEX room. We will always be here to explain the use of the equipment or areas to your needs.

Carl called all to their tables and thanked them for their visit and hopped they would return. I will again let Ilsa and Frieda complete the event. I am not sure how much he has left to endure what is coming, so I suggest we work to his conclusion. Ilsa spoke up and asked if there were any suggestions of what they wanted to see.

The tall blond Mistress rose and went to the cabinet. She selected the pair of horse shoe nippers. She examined them to see how sharp they were. Great, they are what I was hopping for, and proceeded to nip away at his toes. Just a nibble at first on the toes, than down to the first joint; I think this is great. Anyone want to try this? Several more guests came over and took their turns. Within ten minutes, the first section of his toes was gone.

Another one went to the cabinet and selected a pair of channel lock pliers. He approached and placed them over one of his balls. Oh so slowly, he closed them, crushing the ball in its sack. That looks like fun said another woman. He turned the pliers over to her and she made short work of his other ball.

Several others picked up scalpels from the cabinet and selected different parts of the body. I have always wanted to skin a person. Little bits of skin were now being removed. Small amounts of blood were now beginning to flow down his sides. Two women talked and decided that they wanted revenge on their x-boy friends and went about skinning the skin from his cock.

Let's also cut his balls from the sack. All the intense play brought about a slow death. Ilsa checked him and said, I am sorry, but the Party Favor has left us. This will conclude this portion of the play, but you can still play nicely with the slaves if you desire. Frieda and Ilsa wheeled the Party Favor from the room to a holding room to wait to go the crematorium in the morning.

People continued to party, the wine and Champaign flowed as well as did the food and other drinks. Some just got naked in the play room while others went to the SEX room. The hours ticked by till it was noon again. This concludes the party package. If you get dressed, we will escort you back to your rooms. By one in the afternoon, the last of the group had been escorted to their rooms.

Returning to the play room, it was time to take Helma and Judy down from their places on the wall. Both Women dropped to the floor as they were released. Ilsa and Frieda both took them under the arms and carried them back to the cell. We will let you rest for an hour or two and return. At that time, you can request your final ordeal. You will be on your way home by three tomorrow afternoon. We will get you some good food to eat and a glass of wine to drink, enjoy. Ilsa and Frieda took the body to the ramp down and placed the body in the laundry cart. We can get him to the chamber and dispose of the body in time to get back to our outstanding slaves.

They both returned and went to the cell area. The slaves were finished eating and were resting. Ilsa told them that they did a great job today and will get their wish. Judy, you can go first. I want to finish off my time strapped to the block facedown. I want the fucking machine with the electric shocks. This time, I want the moving part to go in my ass and the other electrode in my pussy. I want to go real slow and enjoy each stroke. I would also like the milking machine attached to my nipples that are hanging down the side of the block.

They strapped her down to the block, hands and legs tied to the side of the block. The ten inch dildo with knobs on it was inserted just inside the cannel. The other electrode sat neatly up inside her pussy. The motor was dialed to its slowest speed and the shocks were a low mixture as the dildo went in and out.

Judy, do you want a gag or blindfold? I don't think so; I just want to enjoy it. The machine ground in and out. The suction cups of the milking machine were slipped over her nipples and started. Judy moaned and let out so many happy noises. Frieda, moved to the dildo going in and out and gave her a surprise, she coated it with Habanero pepper coating. This brought a great big smile on her face. We will return in several hours, now just say put.

Helma, have your thought about your wish. Yes, I have been thinking of he man we spent several nights with. I want to be tightly hog tied with no movement. I want a full leather hood with blindfold and large gag. Helma, I think this is a good end to your adventure. Frieda and Ilsa began to tie her into a pretzel. Hands and arm tightly tied behind her and her legs into a ball and attached to the neck. I don't think you will be able to move now.

Before I place the hood on, is there anything else? Yes, I want to be kicked like he was and the cattle prod would be nice. Sure and what else. I want an extra large anal plug inserted. We can fulfill that request. The hood was laced tightly on her head and the blindfold and gag place on. Now for the plug Helma, I will let you have some lube unlike him. Just as she was to have the plug inserted, Habanero peppers were rubbed over the plug. This brought a smile to her face, even though she knew about it. Two kicks, one to the ass and one to the stomach finished the wish. We will be back in an hour or so to check on you and add to your torment. A quick trip to check on Judy, and turn the shocks up a little and they went to the dressing room.

Six hours had passed and it was time for the two of them to be released. Judy came first, the fucking machine was backed away, the plug in her pussy removed and the milking machine turned off. Well, we got a little milk for you to try. Her arms and legs were untied and the belts undone from her body. She was spent and had to be helped to a sitting position on the floor. Bet that hurts on you rear hole from being done for six hours. Judy only smiled with happiness.

Now it is time for your sister slave. Helma, are you ready. She shook her head yes. First off were the blindfold, gag and hood. Frieda pried the plug from her ass and they started to untie the ropes. As the last one came loose, she crumbled into a ball on the floor. Helma, can you crawl or do we have to carry you? I will try, where are we going? The two of you have earned a night I the SEX room. The settings are much softer than the stone floor you have been on for the last week.

Judy greeted Helma as she entered the room. Can we just crawl into each other's arms for the night? Helma answered that it would be nice. Ilsa chimed in and said that you have six hours to sleep and we will be back to get you ready for your return trip to civilization. Helma and Judy, should we turn the light out or not as we leave for now? Both wanted to be able to see each other, so the answer was no.

The night was filled with much touching and cuddling. Many kisses and several session of oral sex completed the night. At eight that morning, Ilsa and Frieda returned and started the process of getting them ready for travel. If you both will follow us to the dressing room, you will shower with lots of hot water, fine soap and shampoo. The clothes you came in are waiting, washed and ready for the flight home. Judy and Helma decided to shower together as they had formed a close sisterhood during the week. They dried off and dressed. We have brought you a fine sampling of food for your last meal here this time. Having watched you over the last week, I know you will both be back.

They finished their breakfast and coffee. Ilsa came in and said it was time to leave. They all walked thru the play room, down the ramp and out the service door. Peter was waiting with their Limo. All four of the women hugged and kissed. Helma and Judy entered the Limo and the trip to the airport began. Even thought it took an hour and an half, the trip just went too fast. Peter drove up to the private entrance and flight 603 was waiting for them. Peter helped them out and reminded them that they couldn't talk about their experience any more. They understood and boarded the flight. The trip to Berlin took an hour and they held hands all the way. As they departed on their separate flights home, Helma hugged Judy and said she hoped that they would meet back here again someday.

Home again

It was the first Tuesday back since her trip to the Chalet. She dressed and called a cab for the trip to the free clinic. Helma tripped into the front door and proceeded to her office. Her nurse approached her and asked how her vacation. Great, but a little short and I am moving a little slow today, too many fun things to do. They were just relaxing over coffee when the overhead page came on. Doctor Helma Jones to the delivery room stat. Helma turned and said, I hate this place.

DOCTOR JONES, CALLING DOCTOR JONES

The secretary for Wolfgang answered the intercom and it was Carl Schmidt, owner of the Chalet. I want to have a meeting with Wolfgang in my suite in one hour. I will give him your message sir. She rose from her chair and walked to the door to Wolfgang's office. She knocked and a voice from within said please enter. Sir, Carl wishes you to join him in his suite in one hour. Did he give you any indication of what he wanted? No, he sounded pleasant and happy. Wolfgang thought for a minute and told her to clear the rest of his day and get his note pad and two pens ready. He must be going to talk about changes for a new season at the Chalet in the up coming year.

As the time approached, Wolfgang went to the bathroom in his office, checked his hair and his tie. He put on his suit coat and stepped into his otter office. He turned to his secretary and asked if he looked straight for the meeting. She said he was ready and here is you're your note pad and pens.

Wolfgang exited the office and walked to the end of the hall to the elevator. Upon entering the elevator, he inserted his key card into the rear slot and pushed button marked "S". The car sped to the fifth floor and opened the rear door upon to a vast open area filled with plush chairs and couches. A massive oaken desk sat against the wall with a view to kill for of the area surrounding the Chalet. Wolfgang stood at attention and awaited Carl's entrance.

At the appointed time, Carl opened the door from his private living space and entered. Carl started the conversation by saying good morning and welcome. Please take off your coat and tie, get comfortable. Wolfgang did as he told him to and laid his coat and tie on the end of the closest chair. Wolfgang, please join me at the bar and pour yourself a glass of my private stock of brandy. Wolfgang did as he was told and asked Carl if he wanted one also. Carl answered that he still had his glass he had been sipping on. I want to go to the chairs by the window and talk about the up coming year.

Wolfgang, first I want to say that you have done a great job of promoting and running the many services of the Chalet. You have earned a 10% raise this next year. Thank you sir, it has been a great year, both on the resort side as well as the lifestyle side. We have almost a complete booking for the rest of the year. I have been working to fill the few open sections.

We are predicted to have a snowy winter and the ski lift is ready. I have added a carriage, hay wagon and sleigh rides in the country. Carl added that both Ilsa and Frieda were to get 5% raises. They have run the lifestyle section with great zeal and professionalism. Sir, I am sure that they will appreciate the raise. They apply themselves as much as twelve to fifteen hours a day when we have the packages in house.

Wolfgang, I want to bounce an idea off of you. I think we need both a Medical Doctor in house as well as assistance for Ilsa and Frieda. I was thinking about bring aboard Doctor Helma Jones. After watching her in both the Dominate role in the "TOY" package and her in the slave training role, I feel she would be a wonderful addition to the staff. What do you think about her? Sir, I watched her as she did both and had full reports from Ilsa and Frieda. Both were pleased the way she acted in play, both ways.

Wolfgang, I want you to make the necessary inquiries on her; work, play and housing. I will send our investigator in her area and start what is required. I will also run this by Ilsa and Frieda for their input. Very good Wolfgang, now let us take a tour of the area to kick some ideas around for the next year.

We should start at the dining room and have lunch. They left the office and exited thru the back door and into the private dining room. They entered Carl's private dinging area and sat at the table for two. Carl pushed a call button and his private waitress entered. Cindy provided both with a menu to select from his special selection.

Wolfgang turned to Carl and said he would be honored to have him select the meal. Carl turned to the waitress and ordered a two inch thick stake with sautéed onions and mushrooms. A fresh mix of tendered, buttered vegetables with a slice of the strawberry topped cake for dessert. A bottle of the private stock of the Chalet's wine to complete the dinner will be a great touch. Cindy, I also want you to be in your topless outfit when you serve. Cindy answered of coarse sir and I will be back with your steak as fast as I can.

Cindy went to the head chief and he dropped what he was doing and started on the order. He knew that Carl liked his steak medium and his onions and mushrooms well done with lots of creamery butter. He turned to Cindy and said I see he wants you in your best outfit to serve him.

Cindy was a female of her late thirties and very well built with her thirty eight DDD breasts. Cindy took a serving cart and collected the best linen napkins, polished silver wear, and crystal stem wear and took it to the Carl's dining area.

She entered and stared setting up the table. Sir, the Chief said your steak will be ready in about five minutes. She twirled the wine in the ice bucket and asked if she should pour wine for them. Carl answered yes and the two glasses were presented. Cindy, please come over to us and present yourself to us.

She walked over in front of the both of them and wiggled her ample breast for them. Carl took one of her nipples in his hand and softly caressed them till they were hard and stiff. He than invited Wolfgang to join him and he gently twisted the other nipple. You see Wolfgang; I told you that this "slave" would be a great addition to our programs. Wolfgang agreed and continued until Cindy reminded them that their meal would be ready by now and she slipped away from their hands and went back to the kitchen.

She received the two plates with the steaks and vegetables from the chief and placed them and the strawberry covered cake on the serving cart. The trip back to the dining area took only a minute or two. She placed the dinners on the table and stood next to Carl.

He snapped his fingers and she knew what was required. She stepped to the rear of the area and stripped naked. With a click of his fingers, Carl indicated that she should assume a position next to him, on her knees. She assumed the position and made sure her head was lowered and her hands were on her knees. She didn't raise her head or say a word during the meal, even when Carl petted her on the head and ran his fingers through her long brunet hair. I see that you are keeping yourself as we discussed when I hired you. Without raising her head, she said yes in a very low voice.

Carl and Wolfgang eat their meals and started on the cake. Wolfgang spoke and indicated what a wonderful meal Carl had ordered for them. There was much small talk during the meal, both about the Chalet actives as well as how their lives were. Carl indicated that they should retire to the couch and sip their wine. They both walked to the couch; with a snap of his fingers, Cindy crawled over between them and sat awaiting the next order.

Carl just looked at her and she instantly knew what was required. She took her hands and began to cuddle his cock and balls, bring them to an erect position. The next click brought her to unzip his trousers and place her hands on his cock. She rubbed it till it was erected, than placed her lips on the tip. Within minutes of licking, she swallowed the full length down her throat.

Very slowly she brought him to conclusion, took a linen napkin and wiped it off, gently replaced the cock and balls in his pants and zipped them up. She turned to Wolfgang and asked if she could please him. He replied that it would be a pleasure, but he had a very busy afternoon. Wolfgang stood and thanked Carl for a wonderful meal and entertainment. He left the dining area and proceeded back to his office.

As Wolfgang entered his office, he told the secretary that he needed to talk to Ilsa and Frieda ASAP. Send them in as soon as they arrive and he retired to his office. It only took ten minutes for the two women to arrive. Ilsa looked at the secretary and asked what was up? She said that she didn't know, but he was in a very good mood. She went to the office door and knocked. Wolfgang spoke to have them enter and bring in some soft drinks for the three of them. Ilsa and Frieda entered and were told to have a seat and get comfortable.

Ladies, I have just finished a meeting with Carl. He is both impressed with the work you have been doing and told me that we are having a good year thanks to you and your recruiting. He authorized a 5 % raise for the two of you for your performance this year. The women turned to each other and a smile came to their faces.

Next on the agenda is the matted of acquiring an additional person to our staff. He wants to have both a full time Doctor on site as well as an assistant for you. The two smiled again and asked if he had Doctor Helma Jones in mind. Wolfgang turned and said, you read my mind. Do you think the she would work well with you as both an assistant and also as a slave when necessary?

It only took less than a minute to answer. Yes, we enjoyed working with her both times, working on the "TOYS", as well as in slave training. Wolfgang did remind them that they would have to share her with the Medical duties around the Chalet.

Ilsa spoke and said that they could work with this. Frieda than asked if she would be sharing the four bedroom suite with them? As of right now, that is the plan. I could see from the last time she was here that the three of you got along well.

Now that this topic is finished, we need to talk over the upcoming events. Ilsa answered that there was nothing on their radar until the beginning of next month. We have a group of four coming in for Master/Mistress and slave training. Great, that will bring in $200,000 for a weeks work. This will also give me three weeks to see if we can get Helma on board. I will start the process of getting her here and the two of you can have a week's vacation.

The two departed the office and Wolfgang asked the secretary to enter. She came in and was seated in front of Wolfgang's desk. I want you to get our man started to get an investigation started on Doctor Helma Jones for a possible hire. She asked how deep he was to investigate and how fast? I need a full and deep job investigation done. I need it by the end of the week so have him start now. The secretary left the office and pulled Helma's card. A quick phone call started the investigator on his task.

A week later

Monday morning arrived and a thick package was waiting on Wolfgang's desk. He opened it and was satisfied with the results. He told his secretary to have the investigator go to Helma and present an invitation to visit for a week, all expensives paid. She has to be on a plane to Berlin and hop on Flight 603 by Wednesday. The secretary made the call and set everything in motion.

Tuesday morning brought Helma to the free clinic where she had to work. As normal, Helma was about to utter her fifth statement of "I hate this place" to her nurse, when a call over head requesting her to return to the office. Helma just shrugged her head and said, what dip shit wants me know? She entered her office and saw a well dressed man in his late fifties. The first words out of her mouth were what agency are you with and what did I do wrong this time? It has been a very bad day for us.

The man introduced himself and said he was not from any agency. I am here with an invitation from Wolfgang at the Chalet. Helma's eyes instantly perked up and asked why? You are invited to enjoy a full week on the Chalet. These are your tickets to Berlin and than Flight 603. May I tell him that you will be on your way? Helma thought a minute and told him she would be glad to come. The man left and went to inform Wolfgang that she was on her way.

Helma made several calls to clear her schedule and told her nurse that she was leaving early today. The nurse asked if she was sick, and got a response of just from this place. She finished the few patients in the waiting room and called for her cab home.

Arriving home, she went to her flat on the top floor and found an envelope which had been slid under her door. She opened it and found the instructions for her visit to the Chalet. She only had three hours to get packed and be at her airport. She read the letter further and it said: Thank you for accepting our offer. Please bring an assortment of clothing ranging from your bathing suit to dinner wear and a formal dress.

After reading the letter, she brought out her large traveling suit case and began to pack. What to wear, what to bring and what was this all about? The questions flew through her mind as she finished packing. A quick shower and a beautiful light blue traveling dress were slipped on. She called for a cab to take her to the airport.

The cab arrived within twenty minutes and she was now on her way downtown to the airport departure gate. She grabbed her suit case and went to the ticket gate. The agent checked her in and took her case to be placed into the belly of the plane. You plane will be departing in around in twenty minutes. Please go to the gate and check in with the agent.

She made her way to the check in desk and presented the ticket to the person sitting there. The agent took her ticket and told Helma that she should go to the head of the line. Helma wondered why, but did as she was told. The time for boarding came and she was told to go on the plane with the first six persons in line.

At the door to the plane she was met by a stewardess and told she was in 2A. Helma looked at her and asked if she was sure? Yes, you have a first class ticket and are to be in our best section. Helma thought to herself, WOW I have never sat in first class before. She took her seat, buckled in and waited for take off.

The plane rolled down the run way and became airborne in seconds. Once they leveled, the stewardess came over and placed a glass of champagne on her tray table. Helma just looked at her and thanked her. She was told that her meal would be here shortly. Helma had never flown in first class before and was a little over whelmed.

The flight was short and the meal was exquisite. She started to daydream as the flight continued to Berlin. The Person sitting in 2B turned to her and asked if she was going on business or holiday? Helma turned to the passenger in 2A and answered that she wasn't quite sure.

For the rest of the flight, Helma went over so many questions in her mind as to why the trip and visit. Had she said something to someone about what went on at the Chalet? Was this a trip to become a "TOY" or a "Party Favor"? So many thoughts passed through her mind that she missed the fasten seat belt announcement and was told by the stewardess to get ready for landing. She snagged her belt and the plane was on the ground and they pulled up to the gate.

Helma made her way to the departure gate for flight 603. Having done it two times prior, she knew the way well. The attendant at the gate said that the plane would be there in an hour and that she should please have a seat. Helma turned to the man and asked if there were to be many others on the flight? He turned and said that she was the only one scheduled to depart to Dresden. This made her more uncomfortable and so many questions ran thru her mind.

The plane taxied to the gate and the stairs came down from under the plane. Helma saw her suit case loaded into the belly of the plane and she was welcomed up the stairs and into a seat up front. Please buckle up so we can get on the way. We have several passengers to pick up and return to Berlin.

The plane departed and picked up altitude quickly. She just looked out the window wondering why she was being requested to come to the Chalet. If it was a last trip, than why did the note want her to bring so many different changes of clothes. The short flight began its descent into Dresden and taxied to the private gate. As the stairs descended to the ground, Helma prepared to meet what ever was to come.

Helma walked down the stair to the pavement and saw the Chalet Limo at the gate. Peter was escorting the four people from the rear and to the stairs of the plane. He made sure that the guest's luggage made it to the ground crew. Now that the departing guests were on board, Peter took Helma's bag and placed it in the trunk.

Peter escorted her to the rear of the limo and got her seated for the trip. Peter greeted her and asked if she was thirsty? Thanks Peter, but I am still confused. Do you know what is going on and am I in trouble? Peter just looked at her and said one word, NO. Please make yourself comfortable and enjoy the ride. Peter placed the window between the front and rear compartment up and drove to the Chalet.

The trip took its normal of just over an hour. The countryside was beautiful this time of the year and Helma took it all in. They arrived at the front gate and Peter placed his key card into the slot of the gate.

It opened and they proceeded to the tram area. Peter opened the door and escorted her to the tram doors. He turned to her and said, welcome and enjoy yourself.

The doors opened and Helma stepped inside. The tram operator closed the door and they started the trip to the main entrance. The trip was short, maybe 500 feet and up 50 feet. It traversed up and over the old mote of the hundreds of years old castle. The trip was as breath taking as the first time she came to the Chalet.

The tram arrived at the main entrance and as the doors opened, Wolfgang met her. He greeted her and asked her to follow him to his office. She had done her out briefing there after her first trip to the Chalet. They entered and went past the secretary and entered his office. He told her to be seated in the chair across from his desk. She slowly made her way in and sat down.

Wolfgang started the conversation by asking how her trip was and if she would enjoy some soft drinks. Helma, still not sure why she was there, but said yes and the secretary brought two cold glasses of drink in for them to enjoy. Helma, first I want you to relax, you are not in trouble, on the other hand, I am about to ask if you want to join the staff of the Chalet.

The dumb founded look on her face was priceless. She spoke up and said that she was so scared that she had screwed up and was going to be a "TOY" or "Party Favor". No Helma, you are OK and as a mater of fact, Carl was the one that suggested we ask you to sign on board with us.

Now that you know of our plans, let me do the talking for a few minutes. I will answer all you questions in a few minutes. Your employment is a two part job requirement. First, we have been expanding a little more quickly than even we thought that we would. We have a need for a Doctor of your expertise on the premises full time.

The Skiing time is coming and you know how many injuries can occur, as well as just nicks and pains that occur for both guests and staff. The second part of your job would be to work with Ilsa and Frieda. You would be both an assistant to the play and could also be used in the way you enjoy as a slave in certain packages.

I can see by the look on your face that you have at least one if not a million questions. Helma swallowed and took a deep breath; can I ask some questions now? You may, but I think I can answer most of them before you ask. We have done a complete investigation of your life over the last week. In fact, the man that came to the clinic and gave you the information was the investigator.

I know for a fact that you are at the point that you were not sure if you wanted to sign another contract with the Doctor Group you were working for. Second, your lease on you flat was coming up for renewal. Helma shock her head yes to both.

The offer is for a one year contract at first with a salary of $250,000 to start. I know that this is a little less than you made, but you will have full room and board here. We know that you are paying over $125,000 a year for your flat and much more on the meals you go to.

You will also have full access to the recreations on the Chalet grounds when not on duty. The big perk is that you will no longer have to go and do gratis work at the clinic, and we know how much you hate that. I do not need an answer this minute, but by the end of the week, you can stay or go. Let us go to the dining area and have lunch. I can give you a few more details there.

Wolfgang led the way and they were seated in the private dining area for upper level employees. Let us go to the buffet and chose a sampling of today's menu. They each sampled a little of so many items from the long serving table. They returned to the table and sat and ate.

Helma, I will talk to you about the Doctor half of the employment. I will give you a large office and examining area. You can have a large budget to order the tools and supplies to outfit it. You may also want to include a portable X-ray machine for the sprains and breaks from the actives. We will get an assistant with the necessary skills to assist you. Anything too deep for you to treat here will be flown to Dresden.

I just don't know want to say Wolfgang. Again, you have till the end of the week to make up your mind. If you do accept, we will close out your lease on your flat, pack and move your furnishing to our storage area. We will also have your shiny red sports car shipped down for your use. As for the other side of your employment, I will let Ilsa and Frieda talks it over with you.

At that point, the women walked in with their trays and sat down at the table. Ilsa spoke and said that she could see that Helma was a little over whelmed with what had taken place over the last hour. Relax, it is a great deal and there will be no pressure on you. During your stay with us for the week, you will stay with us in our suite. Helma just couldn't get any words out at that time. Let us all finish our meal and we can go back to our or your new room.

They all finished their meals and Wolfgang excused himself to return to his work. The three women departed the dining room and went to the elevator. Ilsa led the way and inserted her key card and pressed the first floor button.

Helma, you will receive a staff card like ours which will allow you access to almost all areas. They exited the elevator and went to the first room on the left. Frieda using her card to open the door and they entered. As you can see, this is the same setup as the other floors in the Chalet. You will be staying in bedroom number three. You will find you key card inside.

We may not have all the same goodies as the guests, but I think you will enjoy them. I believe that Peter has already placed your suitcase in the room and you can unpack and put you clothes away the way you wish. As the plans for your hire here aren't fully put together yet, we don't know if you would stay with us or have your sleeping quarters in the Doctor's suite.

If you wish to stay with us, we can put in a good word with Wolfgang. Both Frieda and I tend to enjoy ourselves in our off time and you can join in if you wish. As you know, we are both bi and do enjoy lying around naked with each other. We are pretty sure that you are also, but you would be welcome to bring males to your bedroom.

As with Wolfgang, we feel that you have many questions for us, both as your schedule and the perks due to senior staff. To start, you are on the same level as we are and are required to work some long days and nights. I am sure from your pervious visits that you know how we had to not only do the setups but take care of slaves.

We do a lot of training of those that come here. In fact, in two weeks, we have four couples here to do basic to some advanced Master/

Mistress and slave training. This is the most basic package we offer and does not include any serious inflection of pain or death. We do not work 24/7 and do get many hours off to enjoy the Chalet. As for your other job, the hours and emergencies are unknown and will be a little like being a Cruse Ship Doctor.

I understand that they will be interviewing a Paramedic to be your assistant. He or she will have a bedroom in the medical suite and be the front line person to treat those in need. They are not senior staff and will not have access to the other areas you will. One last thing for now and than you can ask away. After your Advanced Slave Package, did you make up your mind as to if you are a Mistress, Switch, or slave?

Helma sat on the couch and began to compose her answers as well as questions. To your questions of my status, I for the most part am a pain slut slave. I do like the other side also, so I guess I am a Switch. Is this going to be a problem? Ilsa answered that it was not and that was a good answer. Just what is my job to be when I am working with you?

Frieda answered and started by saying, you are going to be a guide to those in the many packages. You will assist in the training or working with the Masters/Mistresses as well as the slaves. We are still working on the details for now as we only knew a week ago that we would have an assistant.

If I were to say right now, I think you will be our training aid, at least at the beginning. This means that you will be used as a slave for some and a person to teach them how to use equipment as well as to be with the slaves in the cell to get them thru. I think this will be kind of a perk in itself.

We know how you enjoy being used in the cell as well as the play room, are we right? Helma just shook her head and said that she at times wanted it so badly; she almost went to a Pro Dom in the Town where I live. I knew that it would in no way come up to the standards or level of pain as the two of you provide.

Ilsa turned to Helma and told her that the training for the position would start in the morning. She also asked what she might want to do for the rest of the day. To say that I am still overwhelmed would be an understatement. Could I just hop into the tub for a bubble bath and give it some further thought. Ilsa and Frieda said it would be a good idea and they retired to their own rooms. We will be back here at 5 this afternoon for supper. Please join us and dress in formal attire as we are taking you out dancing and partying this evening.

Helma shook her head yes and they all retired to their rooms. Once inside, she put her things in the wardrobe cabinet and dresser. For a brief instant, she just stripped naked and lay on the bed with her eyes closed. Am I dreaming or is this the best thing that has ever happened to me.

Other than maybe the nurse in the town that worked with her, she did not have much of a life. Now for the opportunity to not only have her own private practice, "NO" free clinic time and the chance to be in the cell area and play room, what else could be this good. Time passed and she went into the bathroom, drew a steaming hot bath, added some scented bubble bath and slowly slipped in.

She rubbed her hands over her body, allowing the water to slowly sprinkle over her body. I want to run down to Wolfgang in the morning and ask where do I sign up or do I make sure that is what I want. If I stay, will I never want to return to a normal life? Decisions to make and time was getting short. The water was getting cooler and she knew that it was time to rinse and dress. She selected a light blue pair of crouch less panties and a pair so shear nylons.

The big decision came next, do I or don't I put on a bra? I will skip it so my ample breasts and nipples will be on full display. The Dark blue evening dress slid over her shoulder and a set of four inch heals finished the outfit. Several quick strokes with a brush to her long hair and she entered the central living area.

Ilsa and Frieda emerged at about the same time. Both the women were astonished at the beauty Helma displayed. They approached her and commented how she wore the dress and how beautiful she looked. Helma swirled around and thanked them for their comments. Frieda approached Helma and cupped the ample woman flesh held within the dress.

I almost have forgotten how wonderful you breasts are. Helma blushed a little and both women embraced in a long kiss. Ilsa turned and asked where my hug and kiss are? Helma immediately responded by placing her arms around the waist of Ilsa and she also kissed her. If this was going to be the way the evening was going to be, WOW.

We need to be on the way to the dining room now. All went to the elevator and pressed the fifth floor button. On the way up, Ilsa reminded Helma that all the visitors in the Chalet were very Vanilla and did not know of the packages in the play room. Helma nodded she understood and they exited to the staff dining area. They picked a table in the corner and prepared to order. As part of the senior staff, you have access to the great menu items as the Visitors. By this time, Helma was starving and ready for dinner.

They picked up their menus and began the selection process. Ilsa and Frieda chose a thick steak, potatoes and butter spring vegetables. Helma decided to try the prime rib with potato and salad. They each decided to have ice tea for their drink as they would be in the lounge later.

The order went back to the cooking area and it was only a mater of ten or fifteen minutes till their orders arrived. Frieda asked if she could get this back where she was from and Helma said never. A basket of fresh baked bread was placed in the center of the table and all began to eat.

The dinner proceeded along with some small talk. When they finished, Frieda turned and ordered some cheese cake with strawberries for all three. It arrived and Helma could not believe the size of it. It was least three inches in height and a generous topping of the red berries.

The cake was so thick and creamy and was enjoyed by all.

Having finished, they departed the dining side for the dance and lounge area. Frieda and Ilsa each took one of Helma's hands and escorted her to the lounge. A waiter approached and asked what would the three women like to drink? Ilsa answered for the three and ordered champagne. This is to celebrate your first evening with us. Helma sipped the tall glass and laughed as the bubbles tickled her nose. Frieda asked Helma if she liked to dance. I do, but I am just so excited this evening, I want to go to the window and sit looking out at the country side. The view was breathtaking and she just inhaled it for a half hour.

The orchestra was beginning to play and several couples walked to the dance floor. Frieda asked Helma if she would like to dance with her, and the two entered the floor. It was a slow dance to start and they just held each other so very close. Ilsa broke in and she took over as Helma's partner. They also were very close.

The evening continued with both slow as well as fast dances. Helma did not recognize that they were the center attraction on the floor. A blush came to her face, but the girls just danced on. Helma wished the evening could go on for ever, but she know that there was training to do in the morning. The three returned to their rooms.

As they entered, Ilsa suggested they go to their bedrooms, undress and return to the living area for some quiet fun. Helma was so high on emotion by now; she could not get to her room fast enough. The three settled into a large stack of over stuffed pillows in the middle of the area.

All three of the women were very beautiful. Long, lean bodies, all well shaven. Ample breasts were now flopping and each women let their hands roam over each other's bodies. Frieda now dropped down between Helma's legs as Ilsa took on the nipples. Loud sucking and licking sound were now heard.

The Roman orgy play continued till Helma was totally exhausted, but it was not over now. Ilsa now said, slave Helma, get down and service us both till we say it is time to go to bed. Helma was a little surprised, but jumped into the task ordered by the two. The three were totally spent by midnight and just dropped off to sleep in each other's arms. Helma was lightly purring as she slept.

Day Two

A light touch on Helma's shoulder brought her to a semi awake. She rolled over and sat up on the side of the pillows. Frieda said its time to get up sleepy head. We are going up to breakfast in an hour, so you need to get a shower and get put on light work clothes. Helma stumbled to her shower, got in a hot water shower and than toweled off. She brushed her teeth and brushed her hair.

A nice light print top and pants finished her morning tasks. She emerged to find the others ready to go up to breakfast. They went to the buffet and sampled the fair. Several cups of coffee got the conversation rolling. Today, we are going to go down to the cell area and play room. We need to go over all the play toys.

Ilsa said it was time to go down to the play room level. Helma asked if she could try her card and was told to go ahead. They entered the elevator; she slipped her card into the slot and pushed Level L2. The car went down and opened onto the play room level. Ilsa turned to Helma and told her that they would be going over the many rooms and all the items within them.

They started in the play room. We know that you have been in this room twice before. Do you still remember the rings in the wall? Helma shook her head and said she had day dreamed of the times being hung there. Can I go over and stand there for a minute? Sure, we want you to be happy and enjoy yourself.

She walked over and placed herself, back against the wall. Next, she spread her arms and legs wide and closed her eyes. For the next several minutes, she became so at ease. Enough fun for now, we need to show you the other rooms off the play room.

This is the storage area, tables and chairs for parties. The second room contained the portable bar, lunch tables and the wine cooler. The door to the rear is where you went down to the first level where the wine press is located. We will go down later to show you where we bring the slaves in and bodies out.

Back to the cell area down the hall. The first door is where we have the clothing and costumes, where you and the other three picked out your clothes. On the other wall are racks of different articles of costumes such as pony or cat and dog. You will see how this enters into play when we discuses the basic Master/Mistress, slave package coming up in two weeks.

Off to the right is our office down here in the cell area. There are two desks, our personnel costumes for play and also a shower to finish off the days play. We also have several lockers for our own clothes; one will have your name on it. There are also an assortment of paddles, crops and whips on the board over here. We are completely stocked, even with a refrigerator to have a supply of treats and drinks.

Last on this level is the cell area. You know it from both sides. Once when you came to get your "TOY" for play and also as your dungeon cell for the Extreme slave training package you went thru. Again, Helma dropped into sub space, remembering how she felt being chained in this room. There are enough rings in the floor and wall to handle six slaves or prisoners.

The storage cabinets on the far wall contain the items we use or need to keep the prisoners and slaves in place. There are two different types of gear in them and are separated into two separate cabinets, first, a slave, either like you were or first time for training, or prisoners. Because the packages for slaves are expensive, we tend to use the clean, stainless chain and shackles where prisoners are made to use the rusted ones.

A separate cabinet contains the assorted hoods, gags, and blindfolds. As with the chain and shackles, the nice ones are for slaves and the older ones are used ones for the prisoners. There are also items to persuade them to get both slaves and prisoners to do as you want. These can include anything from a whip to the cattle prods. We also have the food pantry. I am sure that you remember your dish of food.

We have several different types with the different "guests". Prisoners get the low grade dog food. Slaves get either a spam type can or one with better cuts of meat in gravy. You as an extreme slave package received the lower dog food. As you remember, it did not do you any harm, even if it wasn't very tasty. Helma turned to them and said I remember the horrid taste.

Helma, we will start your training for hooking up a slave. We want you to ask any questions you wish. First, we will use you as a demo model. You need to go to the office and strip naked, use your locker to hang up your clothes. Helma eagerly went to the office and removed her clothes. She quickly returned and said I am ready to learn. We will use you so you can experience as we talk.

They walked over to the cabinet containing the shackles and chains. Frieda selected several sizes of wrist and ankle shackles. The first set they put around her wrist were way too loose. When closed, you can see how much they twist around could cut into the skin. That would be OK for a prisoner, but not a paying slave. On the other hand, a prisoner would get a set that was as tight as possible to cut and chafe.

The correct set was placed on Helma's wrists and ankles and closed. Next we need to chain you up. For new slave training, we normally place the wrists in front of the body. As with you for the extreme slave package, we went to the rear. The chain comes in short and longer lengths. The longer ones let the slave move and relive the cramps from lying, as the short ones begin to place stress on the joints. They can be hooked or locked to the shackles.

Now lay down on the stone floor, between the rings on the floor and the one in the wall. The hooking up of the persons in place is also dependant on if they are slaves or prisoners. Prisoners have no wiggle room to get relief from the stress. New slave trainees will be allowed to have room to stretch and move, unlike the extreme slave program as you were in, and only had a little room to move.

The Ankles always go to the furthest ring from the wall. The wrists go to the center ring on the floor. Your neck collar is to be attached to the ring in the wall. The length of the chain will depend on if you want them to be able to sit only or lay dawn. With certain persons, we can also use leather straps to bind their elbows behind them and also hold their legs together. Do you understand the way we do things Helma? She answered she did and understood why thing were done the way they were when she went thru the extreme training.

We can also add several different types of discomfort to the mix. I am sure that you remember the assorted sizes of dildos and anal plugs we used on you. For the training session today, we are going to attach you in a prisoner position. Helma's eyes perked open wide and she could hardly wait. First spread your legs wide so we can insert a plug up your ass and dildo up you womanhood.

She willingly spread her legs and accepted the plug and dildo. They were both large in size, filling her fully. Her legs were quickly strapped tightly together. The ankles came first being locked together without any chain and than to the ring in the floor.

Frieda asked her if she was doing OK, and she shook her head yes.

Your wrists will be next. Frieda placed them behind her, inserted the lock to the shackles and than to the ring.

A leather strap was placed between her elbows and pulled tight. To complete the attachment of her to the cell, a short chain was locked to the collar and than to the wall. This chain will only let you have some room to relieve stress and eat, not enough to sit and or to lie down.

Helma, I told you that there would be plenty of perks to this job. Helma shook her head and said she remembered being told this. I will be placing this full leather hood over your head and working the lacing up the back.

The hood was form fitting and was very tight. I think you need a leather blindfold, and one was fitted in place. You see Helma; you are going to spend the night down here to experience how a prisoner is to suffer while waiting for his or her sentence.

At this point, Helma was so far gone into sub space; she would or could not beg for release, in fact, she was glad for the chance. Before we go up to supper, we are going to give you yours. Frieda went to the cabinet and opened a can of the dog food, placed it into a bowl and placed it in front of her. A bowl of water finished the feeding. The lights were turned out and Ilsa and Frieda went to dinner.

Ilsa and Frieda partook in a wonderful dinner meal. A bottle of wine and some small talk helped finish off a large slice of chocolate cake. They decided to go down to see how Helma was doing. They turned on the light as they entered the cell; Helma was in a semi trance and made a small cooing noise. Frieda was removing the two bowls when Ilsa stepped up behind Helma and placed the two points of a cattle prod to her pussy lips. Ilsa pushed the button on the prod giving her a hefty shock.

Helma jumped as far as her bonds would allow. She almost said something when she remembered the punishment for talking. That was a good girl and I will give you a treat. Frieda came over to her and said open wide. I am going to stuff an over sized gag into you mouth, but first I need to coat it with a little of both of our white cream from the orgasms we just had.

They each plunged the dildo gag into their pussies, coating it with the thick white cream. Wonderfully done and now it is time to insert it. I think she will need a little bit or incentive, so I will stick the prod up her ass.

With the pushing of the button, Helma almost screamed, but it was cut short by the gag being shoved up into her mouth. The gag was pulled tight and the buckle in the back cinched up tight. Night, night Helma, we will return in the morning before breakfast.

Day Three

Several times through out the night, Helma knew she heard someone in the cell arca, but no one came over to her. My head was still swimming and both my shoulders and legs were in pain from being bound so tight. I am getting so hungry and cold from the stone floor.

I am beginning to think my mind is playing tricks on me. The thought that this is how the prisoners are kept made me wonder how they didn't go crazy. Again I think I hear foot steps coming toward me, when a hard spray of cold water overtakes my body. It must be Frieda as I still remember how she would wash use off in the mornings.

Ilsa spoke and asked if I enjoyed my night. Still being gagged, it was hard to answer. So you don't want to talk, than let me give you some encouragement. She took the cattle prod and placed it between my legs. She turned it loose and I jumped the best I could. Well Helma, you can hear me and I see you are enjoying the perks I told you about. I settled back down and relaxed some. I think it is time to get you out of the bindings you are in.

She started by undoing the strap around my legs. As the blood rushed back down to my lower legs and feet, I felt so much relief. Helma, I can see that you needed that. Next to come was the strap around my elbows. Again, my arms came alive and my hands tingle, and than burned as the nerves came alive.

Now Helma you can see the effects of being a prisoner in this configuration for days. The locks were taken off, releasing my ankles, wrists and finally my neck from the rings holding me. I fell on my side and curled up into a fetal position. I just lay there until the feeling started coming back into my body.

Helma, I just want you to lie still for a while. Frieda came to my head and removed the gag. Now close you eyes and hold them closed till I tell you to open them. She removed my blindfold and told me to very slowly open my eyes. The laces on the hood came next and I was now released from my predicament.

Helma, when you are ready, sit up against the wall for a few minutes while I remove your collar and shackles. I did as I was told and think that I was never as exhausted as I was now. Ilsa said that I was down in this position for over twelve hours and have experienced what few had. This punishment is normally reserved for those here as prisoners waiting the final punishment.

Frieda looked over at me and asked how I was feeling. I replied that other than being a little sore and tired, I felt great. It was the best experience I could have asked for from the both of you. I think the best part was licking the cream off the gag all night. It tasted so good and lasted well into the night. It also brought back the memories from the Extreme Slave Program I went through.

Before you get a shower and get dressed, you will need to learn to clean and disinfect the bondage gear. First you will need to place the locks, shackles and collar in the pail in the office. There you will find a bottle labeled medical grade disinfectant. A little bit in the pail, fill about two thirds of war water and let it set for ten minutes. While they soak, take the gag, blindfold, and hood to the table.

There is a bottle of spray cleaner/disinfect there. Spray the items and use the towel to rub it in and than dry them and place the gag and blindfold over the line. Now turn the hood inside out and place it on the hook to dry. Going back to the pail, you will need the stiff scrub brush to work on the shackles and collar. Now rinse and dry them off prior to placing them back in the cabinet.

Having completed my assignment, they told me to go into the shower and wash and rinse off and get dressed. Once I finished this, I got dressed and we all headed to the dining room for breakfast. I was famished from the small meal late yesterday afternoon when I was bound.

I ate enough food for two people. We finished eating and Ilsa told me to get a carafe of coffee so we could go to the room and talk about the night. I went to the counter and filled the container with coffee; plated a half dozen of the morning pastries and we went down to our room.

Upon entering the room, we got comfortable on the couch and started to debrief the events from the past day. Ilsa started by asking if I had a good time. I answered, a good time, no, an outstanding time, yes. I asked if this would be available to me if I took the job. Ilsa replied that it would be available as long as time permitted. This is one of the perks that you will be allowed along with many others.

Frieda turned and said that this made it for sure that I was a slave for sure. Tell us how it felt being bound so tightly. At first it scared me a little and than my feelings of joy set in. I won't say it didn't hurt some or a lot, but I just dropped into sub space so deep I just cursed through the night.

I did think I hear someone in the cell area several time last night. Yes you did, I know for a fact that both Carl and Wolfgang visited to see how you were doing. They were pleased at how well you withstood the extreme bondage they had requested us to put you through. Other than that, Fritz, our dog may have come thru on his nightly patrols. I thought I felt something wet sniffing me, but wrote it off as a good dream.

We have a little more training this morning for you. Helma, are you rested enough to go back down? I answered yes and we went back down to the play room level. Ilsa started the tour by opening a room we left closed the day before.

Helma, this is the large equipment room. It contains both the block tables you were attached to as well as the OBGYN table you used. Against the other wall were the instruments of medieval torment and torture we use for a Medieval Package. Along the far wall were racks, spike chair, hand and foot stocks, adjustable height head and hand stocks and pillories. A full steel iron cage in the form of a human body was hanging from the ceiling.

Smaller items sat on a table against the far wall. Two different head cages or branks, one a half head and one a full head cage, both with iron mouth pieces to keep the wearer quiet. This is a scavenger's daughter. It has a place for the head, wrists and ankles to be secured. When properly place into the unit, the wearer had their legs spread wide and the hands secured just below the neck. It puts lots of tension on the mussels, leaving no relief, only to be rolled onto the wearers back or side.

These are finger, hand and foot presses. They arc spiked presses to place the item into and slowly close until the spikes inside close. It is extremely painful. For the breasts, we have several breast presses. We have two basic kinds in steel and wood. The steel ones we can either place in warm/hot water or an ice bath. The effects are awesome. In addition, we have plain and spiked wooden ones. All are slowly tightened, flattening the breast.

For a more realistic experience, we have an Iron Maiden. We first show it to them with real metal spikes inside, blindfold them and than replace them with rubber ones. Last, but not last, we have an eight foot round wheel of wood. It is on a stand that allows us to attach the victim on and than spin.

By now Helma, I bet you want to jump up on any and all the items. She could only stare with very wide eyes and shake her head yes. Don't worry, we will be placing you on all the items so you have a feeling of how they work and feel, but now we must finish the tour.

We all went out the rear door to the play room and down the incline to the wine room. I know you have been here, both as a slave crushing grapes and as a Mistress with your "TOY". If we go the other way down the hall, we will come to the unloading area. The famous rolling laundry basket with sheets and blankets was waiting for its next delivery of human slaves. Frieda opened the door reveling the dock area and truck. This is where we bring in the unconscious slaves for transport to the cell area.

The tour being completed for now, they went back to the elevator on the play room level and up to the dining room. It is lunch time Helma and the end of work today. You are to have the rest of today off as well as tomorrow are yours to do with as you please.

Wolfgang suggested that you use the time to both enjoy yourself and to make your decision as if you will take the job or not. We will be available to talk with both days. Please ask any questions you have as we want you to make the best decision you can. They ate and went their separate ways. Ilsa and Frieda returned to the room.

Helma decided to go to the sixth floor and sit under a beach umbrella and sip on an ice tea to go over all the options. Thinking to herself, there was so much going for her if she stayed. The only question is if she would miss the outside world. I don't have real friends back at town and as for the clinics, they were just a job. Here she could still do her skill as a doctor and also work with the slaves. A great side effect was that she could live the life as a slave a good deal of time. What a wonderful thought as it relaxed her so much.

Dinner time came and she joined the other two in the Dinning room. So Helma, have you reached a decision to stay or go. Helma responded that she had, but wanted to tell Wolfgang first. She asked if Ilsa could make an appointment for her to meet with him tomorrow afternoon. I just want a little more time to enjoy the resort and enjoy myself, but I am sure that you will be very happy with my choice.

They finished their meal, Ilsa and Frieda stayed to dance and Helma went up to the sixth floor to watch the night's skyline. The stars were so bright and there were so many. She never saw so many in the town she was from that it astonished her. Around midnight, she returned to the room and crawled into bed for a nights sleep. It may be more comfortable in the soft bed, but not as much fun as the night prior.

Day Four

Frieda knocked on Helma's door and said it was time to go to breakfast if she was going. Helma answered that she would be coming up later. Ok, you do as you wish, but we made a three o'clock appointment with Wolfgang for you. Be prompt as he is a busy man. I will, but now I want to spend some time in the bath. She drew a hot bath, added bubble bath and slowly lowered herself in. I felt so good to just relax and think if she had made the right decision the night before.

Minutes passed into an hour and she drained the tub, rinsed and toweled off. Not sure of what she wanted to do, she put on a light shirt and pants to go have breakfast. She wasn't very hungry, but managed some Belgian waffles, fruit and hot tea.

Finishing her meal, she went to the sixth floor to hang over the railing and take in the morning sun. Do I want to do some swimming or should I try horse back riding. Swimming won and she went to the room for her suit and down to the pool. Helma was a good swimmer and did almost twenty laps. She found herself a lounge chair and did some sunning.

The afternoon was coming and she went up to get into more formal attire. She got herself ready with a nice dress, stockings, high heals shoes, brushed her hair and made here way to Wolfgang's office. She entered at about ten till three, told the secretary she had an appointment and was told to have a seat.

Three o'clock came and the secretary received a call. Miss Jones, Wolfgang will see you now. Helma rose, knocked and was told to enter. Upon entering, she was told to be seated in the chair across from the desk. Wolfgang greeted her and offered her some refreshments.

Wolfgang started the conversation. I understand you have made up your mind on the offer. I will say that both Carl and I were very impressed the other night when we looked in on you. Helma thanked him and said it was both exciting as well as relaxing.

Miss Jones, I know that this is a big decision for you and I know that you have been thinking deeply about it. Yes sir, I have and have decided that I would like to accept the officer. I believe the Doctor part will be much like what I do now, but the other half of the job will be so exciting. I will be very happy rooming with Ilsa and Frieda as we get along so well. Helma, will you need time to return home to pack or will you let me arrange for you items to be shipped? Truthfully, I don't think I ever want to return there again. That is great.

The secretary will draw up letters for you to sign, both canceling you lease and quieting your partnership in the doctor practice. She will also have you sign a contract for a year at first to work here. That will be fine sir. You will be sharing time both with setting up your new office and ordering equipment and supplies and well as being with Ilsa and Frieda for additional training.

You have the rest of the day off and start in the morning. Report to your new office on the first floor at nine in the morning and we will get you started. It is located at the other end of the hall from where you are staying now. Good bye Miss Jones and welcome aboard.

Helma returned to her room and was greeted by Ilsa and Frieda. So Helma, what did you decide? I told Wolfgang that I would be staying on and was very glad for the offer. We are so glad for you. We were hopping that you would stay and we hope that you will stay in our room. I wouldn't have it any other way. There are so many things I want to talk about with you. First, is it correct to call you by Ilsa and Frieda or do I have to call your both Mistress?

Helma, we are very laid back and unless we are in scene mode, we are equal, just as we would call you Doctor in the office or when you are on call. Sounds great, can we celebrate this evening. I am so giddy and just want to burst with my new life. Sure, we need to go to dinner and we can just go from there. You do understand that we need to go over so much more in the next two weeks.

They all bathed and dressed for dinner. It was just so heavenly and I could not even get into dinner. They ate and went back to the room with a bottle of champagne. Ilsa and Frieda both congratulated her again and they toasted with several glasses.

Helma, is there something special you wish to do this evening? Helma answered and said she knew it was late, but could they go to the play room for an hour or two. Sure, did you have something special in mind? Yes I did, I would like to be place up against the wall, facing it and spread eagle. A good whipping and flogging followed by some forced oral on you. I am sure that I will need one of you to use the prod on me to encourage me to suck deep. Frieda answered that Helma, you are a true slave and pain slut.

They headed down to the play room. Once inside, Helma went to the office, stripped and went to the shackle cabinet. She selected sets of shackles for her wrists and ankles along with the connecting chains. She walked to the play room and stood, face to the wall in between rings in the wall. Ilsa proceeded to hook her up as tightly as she could. She than asked if she would require a hood or gag? No, I want to hear myself scream as you strike me.

Frieda appeared with Lisa's bull whip and she carried a carriage whip. Helma braced herself as the first swing of the bull whip as it made contact on her ass. The tip of the whip bit into her flesh, but she didn't make a sound. Next to come was the carriage whip. It made contact with the legs, just below the ass. This did bring a muffled scream as the two switched between the bull whip and carriage whip. As the beating continued, Helma was between screaming in pain and begging for more and heaver hits.

After a half hour of beating, Helma was in sub space and had a glassy look to her. Ilsa decided that it was time to get some well deserved relief from Helma. They released her and she fell to the floor. Crawl over here slave, you have work to do for us. Ilsa said that she would go first and Frieda would provide the stimulation to get her moving.

Helma placed her lips to Ilsa's womanhood and began. Each lick went deeper and caressed the swollen clit and the white cream began to flow. Frieda, she is not going deep enough for me, warm up her ass hole.

Frieda placed the two points of the cattle prod to her rosebud and let loose. Helma just rocked back and forth and licked and sucked slowly. Ilsa was becoming so exhausted by now so they changed places. It made no difference whose womanhood Helma was working on, the effort never slowed. Both woman were completely satisfied and knew it was time to return to the room.

Helma, we are going back to the room. You need to clean the shackles, chain and floor we kind of got all wet before coming up. Ilsa and Frieda departed the play room for the living area. Helma was in no hurry to complete the task and just sat on the floor, relieving the event. She eventually came around to her scenes and washed the shackles and mopped the floor. Getting dressed again was a different story. She just didn't want to put that dress back on. Over coming her dreams, she dressed, turned the lights off and returned to the room.

When she returned to the room, both Ilsa and Frieda had bathed and put on some night wear. Helma, we are going to bed now and will see you in the morning. Helma went over to the women and gave each a hug and big kiss. She went to her bedroom, showered and crawled into her bed. She didn't even seem to know that she was naked. Night to me and lights out and I hope that I have wonderful dreams.

Day Five

Morning came all too soon for the three. They dressed in casual clothing and went to breakfast. Small talk filled the meal of their day's work. Ilsa and Frieda would be doing the preparations for the training program. Helma, on the other hand would be planning for new office. In her mind, she was going over what type of equipment, tools and supplies she would need to set up her new Medical practice.

Helma went down to the first floor and down the hall to the new office. She was surprised that her name was already on the door. Doctor Jones was in two inch high letters. She stood back to take in the sign. She had been a Doctor for almost 20 year and never had her very own practice. She said "I love it" and entered the space.

A man with a clip board was sitting on a chair in the middle of the large room. My name is John and I do the ordering for the Chalet. I am Helma, the new doctor, but I bet you already guessed that. Helma, I just wanted you to get a sense of the space you will have to work with. It is basically the same as your living quarters. The lounge I guess will be the waiting room and where your Paramedic will sit. John went to the one bedroom and pulled out a portable table and another chair for her. We need to get started with a layout for you office.

John, I have never had so much space to work with or even had a say in it setup. Doctor, just relax and we can get thru it. First, do you want to have your desk in this area or in one of the rooms? I think centered against the back wall will be good. Let us start with an assortment of soft chairs and couches on the side walls with a few coffee tables for reading materials for patients. Several two drawer filing cabinets should be placed by each desk. The Paramedic's desk should be near the front door so they can check them in.

One room should be my exam room. I will need an examination table with a set of retractable stirrups for the women. Several large glass front medicine cabinets and a large wardrobe cabinet for their clothes should go on the far wall to be used for supplies. The second room will be a treatment room.

There should be another examination table, rolling exam chair, and storage cabinet for supplies. We will have to do something with the carpet on the floor as it will become messy with blood or plaster casting material. I can just see suturing up cut fingers or casting sprains from the slopes.

The third room will contain the portable x-ray unit. A nice soft padded table to lie on in the center of the room and a desk for the computer for the unit to sit on. I know that we will need to fill in pieces and parts as we start to get the office going. I will need a catalog of instruments and a portable autoclave unit. I will work on the list over the next day or two. Thank you John for putting up with me, but I never had a choice before. They spent the rest of the morning deciding on colors and placement of the equipment.

Helma shook hands with John and went to her room. She found Ilsa and Frieda sitting in the lounge area, folders and note books lying all over. I think I am exhausted from just picking out furniture and placing it. Wow, you two have so much that has to be done, I would never have guessed.

Ilsa said that it takes a lot of planning for each program they worked on. We did almost three days just on your slaving training. Helma, this will be your first program that you will be working in. After lunch, we will show you what goes into a good experience for the parties.

Lunch came and went for the three. We will be spending the rest of the day in the office next to the cell area. They arrived and each took up a seat around the desk. Helma, this is the folder for the next training program. Enclosed are questioners that the Master and Mistresses filled out and submitted.

You should remember when you first came here; you were required to fill out a different one for the "TOY" Package. Yes, I remember now, I never thought the questions would end. We take the questions and answers to get a better feel as to you needs, wants and skills.

This package will bring us 2 Masters, 2 Mistresses and 4 slave trainees. It consists of 3 female slaves and 1 male slave. All the slaves are very new and need lots of training. The Masters and Mistresses are in varied skill levels, but only a slim amount. This means that we will have to bring them along slowly in the week they will be there.

Helma, what part do you see yourself playing in the training program? I think I could be on either sides or at least a training aid for you. Great, this is how we talked about it. Your main function will be to be with the slaves and talk over what makes a great slave. Am I going to be in shackles and chains during the training? In the beginning, you will be down here in full gear.

We will have you as a demo model during the first day when the Master/Mistress starts out. For say, you could be placed on a piece of furniture or how the shackles are placed on. Starting the second day, they will be responsible for the up keep of their slaves, feeding and watering much less the hosing down, to clean them up.

The first day for the slaves, they will be shackled, chained with short chains to allow some movement and a fully laced hood with blindfold and gag. This will start some loneliness as well as some hopelessness. It breaks down their will and inner soul. The purpose of this is to bring the Owners into the scene and make them the person that will take care of them. Your first thing is to make sure that they don't go too far to the down side.

Your roll will change from day to day. For instance, you will be showing the Master/Mistresses the proper care of the toys used as well as the feeding. You will be down here for much of the time because we will be wining and dining the other side. Unless you wish not to, we can send down a normal great meal from the main dining room, or you can eat the slave menu.

As these slaves are I training, they will get pampered with chopped up spam, not dog food, although we will tell them it is dog food. Also as a perk, you can be chained up as they will be or even like the other day. Something we can talk about the day before they arrive.

The day passed faster than Helma dreamed they had. Her normal duties mainly consisted of getting her Doctor's office setup. The equipment was arriving daily and John, with the help of two other maintenance men, set up the desks and cabinets. Helma was thrilled with the two oaken desks and the shiny stainless cabinets and tables.

Both Wolfgang and she interview several Paramedic candidates for her assistant. They decided on a younger, maybe 24 year old male named Dave. He was out of school for three years and was a member of the ski rescue team in the village. It didn't hurt that he was a hunk and very good looking. They sat down several days in a row so they could talk over how Helma operated. They were a good match for each other.

When not working with Dave, she was down in the play area. She wanted to understand as much of the equipment as possible. The rolling toy cabinets with the many hand and medical tools were picked up and even played with them. Many times, she would place clamps or the electrical leads on her self and played with them. Once she even got excited by the crank generator and brought herself to orgasm. There was always a good deal of clean up following her playing. She once almost got herself caught in the head and arm stocks.

Day before the Arrival

Helma, Ilsa and Frieda were sitting around the lounge area in their room. Helma, this is the day before your first program that you will be on duty. The member's of the program will be here by around noon tomorrow. Wolfgang will handle the Masters and Mistresses, giving them the grand tour of the grounds and taking them to their room.

We will be meeting Peter at the back door with the four slaves. They will be uncurious from the spiked bottle of wine as you were. We will have to bring them up from the first floor to the cell area and get them comfortable. You will first draw the blood vials and we will get it tested for Aids. Your Paramedic assistant will draw the others. Are there any questions so far on what you will be doing? Helma said that she was fine and would pick up things as they occur.

The three women went to the room, bathed, dressed and went to dinner. They arrive on the fifth floor and went to the dining area for the employees. Each selected a wonderful selection and began to eat. Along came Wolfgang and sat down at the table.

Are you ready for tomorrow and each said they were. He also asked Helma how she liked the office which she set up. Sir, it is the best array of instruments and furniture I have ever had, great. I will work hard to make you and Carl proud of me as your selection for the house doctor.

On the other hand, I hope the biggest thing I have to take care of is tennis elbow. Helma that is what I want to hear. I will let you three finish your meals and do as you want but remember, it will get busy in the morning. They finished and went back to the room. Each undressed and poured a glass of wine, picked out a large pillow and laid on the floor next to each other. By midnight, they each retired to their own room.

Day of Arrival

As he had done hundreds of times in the past, Peter arrived at the Dresden airport private loading area. For this trip, he brought the special limo. This one contained two sections to it. Flight 603 was on its final approach for landing. He wheeled the luggage cart to the entrance and stood by. The small jet landed and taxied to the gate. The stairs came down from the belly of the plane and the stewardess began the deplaning of the passengers.

As was protocol, the Masters and Mistresses came off first. They were dressed in fine tailored clothes. Peter welcomed them and both shook hands and he kissed the hands of the females. He escorted them to the front half of the limo and got them seated. Top of the line snacks and wine were waiting for them to partake on the trip to the Chalet.

When he was sure they were enjoying themselves, he returned to the ramp area for the slaves. They, unlike the first set of visitors, were dressed in casual clothes. They were escorted to the rear compartment and shown the snacks and wine that was waiting for them. Peter told them they were to try each as it was part of the training.

As he closed the door, they were already into the wine and snacks. Peter knew that it would only be maybe ten minutes before they would be passed out and ready for the arrival. Peter started the drive back to the Chalet. He closed up the windows between the passengers and himself. The ones to the rear were completely cut off from those in the front half of the limo.

Peter took glances at the slaves and saw that they were all passed out at that point. He used the intercom to inform the passengers in the front half that there slaves were now completely out and they were in good shape. They will be out for around nearly twelve hours and that the trainers were going to take good care of them. As normal, Peter pointed out the highlights of the country side on the drive. At around fifteen minutes out, Peter called Wolfgang of their arrival at the Chalet.

Ilsa received a call and turned to Frieda and Helma that they had around fifteen minutes to be at the loading dock. They headed down, retrieved the laundry cart and went down to the door for the arrivals. Helma was so excited, being her first time at being on this side of the training. They would wait for Peter to call them and inform them they should be outside waiting.

Peter arrived at the front gate, inserted his access card for the gate to open. This function also informed the Tram operator to bring the car to the lower level room. Peter opened the door to the limo and helped the guest out. The tram door opened and the guests were about to enter when Peter stated that their luggage would be taken to their rooms and the others would be bedded down for the night.

The tram door closed and started its ride over the old castle mote to the main entrance level. Wolfgang met the group as they departed the tram. He also shock hands and kissed the hands of the females.

Peter now drove around to the back and service entrance to the chalet. First he stopped at the door where he unloaded the luggage where a bell hop was waiting to take it to the room. Peter than drove around a distance and came to the loading dock where Frieda pushed the laundry cart next to the rear doors of the limo. Between the three of them, they loaded the four unconscious slaves into the basket. Once loaded, Helma spread blankets over the four and than they pushed them into the dock doors. Up they went to the play room and on to the cell area.

As they arrived at the cell area Ilsa told Helma, we are going to show you the ropes in getting the slaves put up for the night. First of all, they are not going to be placed like you were. They are to be babied some and will be treated better. We need to undress them all and place their clothes in the storage area. I want you to pick out the correct shackles for each of them.

Helma went to the shackle cabinet and selected one of each size. First, next to the wall is Roxie. Helma selected a medium set of cuffs and placed it on her. Very good, now complete the set and place short lengths of chain to them. Now lock them to the two rings in the floor and a chain long enough to let her lay down comfortable. Helma finished her task on Roxie and stood back. That is correct, now we will place Wilma, than Lynn. Helma completed the shackles and chains for these two. Michael is the last. His owner has requested that we keep him separate and add additional security to his cock and balls.

He will be placed two sets of rings away from Lynn. Before he is chained up, we will install a locking cock and ball cage and chain it to the foot ring. Frieda handed Helma the device and they separated his legs, slipped on the cage and locked it in place. A two foot chain was attached and ran down to the foot ring.

Helma was thrilled that she had let her place the cage. He is so large; I would enjoy playing with him. As long as they are uncurious and their owners are not here, you can run your hands over them. This is a side benefit. Ilsa turned and asked Helma if she could finish securing the slaves with lacing on the full head hood, blindfold and two inch diameter by two inch long penis gag. Make sure they are buckled tight. We have to go up to greet the other four of this group. Be ready to meet the group down here after the lunch hour.

Ilsa and Frieda went up to their room to change into a more formal set of clothes. Having changed they found the group being given the full chalet tour by Wolfgang. He turned and introduced Ilsa and Frieda to the group. These two women will be both your go betweens and also teachers. They will be joining us in your room after lunch.

Let us go to the fifth floor and try the buffet. Ilsa and Frieda led the group to the fifth floor and selected a table against the far wall. The group followed Ilsa and Frieda and selected from the buffet and returned to the table. Ilsa started the small talk by reminding them not to talk about what they were there for.

They finished their meal and all returned to the room on the second floor. Ilsa used her key card to bring them in. Each of the four was impressed with the way it was laid out.

Each of you will find your bedroom which we marked for you. Inside, you will find you own key card for the week. It will get you into the front door of the living room and the individual bedroom. It will also be necessary to operate the elevator.

At this time, please take a seat and we can get started. While you are here for the training program, both Frieda and I will be your instructors. We understand that you may have already done some work with your slaves. We ask that you forget this for the week and let us guide you to better understand your slave. We will take you through the many facets of the Master/Mistress, slave world.

We have over twenty years between us in the many aspects of what makes a great slave. You will be given several ways to approach ways to work with them. In the five days we have to work with you, we will give many different samplings of play, up keep and discipline.

During your time here, your slave will be kept in the cell area of the play room floor. You will need to have one of us with you when you visit them. At first, you may not agree with our method, but it is meant to break them down so we can build them up in the best way.

We have placed a copy of both the in house rules and also the training schedule in you room. We will take you to the cell area so you can see your slave. At this time, they had been given a knock out drug in their wine on the way from the airport. It will be wearing off by around eight this evening. If you wish to go down and cuddle them and let them know you are here, we can do this. Let us go down so you can see them and meet the third member of our training team.

They loaded onto the elevator and Frieda inserted her key card in the special slot and placed the down button. They stepped out and were greeted by Helma. This is Helma and she has a double roll here. Besides being an assistant to the training, she is the Chalet Doctor. Helma will be in both rolls as a slave and a training aid. She has done both and is a Dominate.

They entered the cells area and were somewhat shocked to see the slaves chained to the floor, hooded, gagged and blindfolded. They are being kept this way to start the breakdown process. They have ample room in the chains to move around and stretch. For today and tomorrow, we will take the responsibility for feeding and giving them water.

Since they are beginning slave trainees, they will be fed a diet of chopped up spam, twice a day. If they were here on the more in depth training or an extreme slave program, they would be fed real dog food. It will not harm them, just ask Helma as she went through the extreme slave program. Helma responded by saying, it was not very tasty, but it reminded me why I came here.

Starting tomorrow evening you will be required to provide full care for your slave. We will show you how we feed, water and bath them as a Master/Mistress should do. This is very important as it build trust between both of you.

At this time, I want you to go and stand at the foot of your slave. It was easy for Michael as Anna went right to his feet. The other three slowly went to their slave. Not as easy with the hoods on is it? You should be able to know your slave without any hesitation. Belinda said I know Wilma by her labia. They are large and stick out well, so she took up her lace at her feet.

Christen and Hans took better looks and they finally knew which was which. I know the mole on Roxie's breast anywhere. This left Lynn. Hans stood back and picked out the size of her nipples as her trade mark. All now stood in front of their slave. Ilsa said very well. After tomorrow they will not have a hood, blindfold or gag unless you wish.

It can be used as a punishment or even a perk if they like them. It is time to leave now.

The group was confident that there slaves were in good hands. For now, it is time for you to go up and prepare for dinner. Helma will be here taking care of the slaves. After dinner, we will meet in your room and will bring you back down for the first feeding in the cells. After this, you will be able to enjoy the nightly fun in the lounge and dance area.

Frieda led the group to the elevator and took them up to their rooms. Ilsa stayed behind to talk to Helma. I want you to stay with them as they will be waking up shortly and will be both some scared as well as disorientated.

You can handle them in what ever way you wish to, but do not remove the hoods or gags and blindfolds. You can talk and reassure them, even stroke them. We will return around 7:30 this evening. With that, Ilsa started to depart but turned and told Helma that she would bring her a meal from the dinner menu.

Ilsa and Frieda went to the dining hall and ordered their meal. Frieda, I want to keep an eye on the new group. I am not sure how they will adjust to what they saw in the cells. It can be stunning to see someone you care for or love in the restrained position.

The group of four slowly walked into the dining room and chose a table near the far end of the hall. Anna was the one that spoke first. She began the ordering process choosing the prim rib. Belinda and Christian chose the steak dinner and Hans ordered the turkey.

They were soon served their meals and began there dining. Anna was doing most of the small talk as the four dug into their meals. Ilsa had Frieda order a fine meal for Helma to deliver it to her. The meal was delivered and Frieda took it down to Helma. Ilsa stayed behind to keep an eye on them as they finished their dessert.

Frieda arrived in the cell area and gave Helma the dinner she had ordered. She found her down on the floor between the slaves, talking and reassuring them that they were OK. Helma told them that their feeding was only an hour off and they should just lie back till than. From under the gags could be heard little bits of questions and even Lynn was softly crying. Frieda placed the tray of food on a tray table and Helma ate her two inch steak and potatoes. You could see the slight movement among the slaves as the smell of the food drift down to the floor.

At the appointed hour, the four Masters/Mistresses, escorted by Ilsa arrived to witness the slaves first feeding. Ilsa told the group not to talk and distract the slaves. They entered the cell area and stood to the side. Ilsa signaled to Helma to start. She first selected four bowls of water and placed them next to the heads of the slaves. She first told the slaves to stay still as she removed their gags. Each slave was relieved to have the gag out.

They started to ask questions and plead to be let out of their chains. Helma stood back and in a booing voice told them to be still or they would be punished. Wilma began to rant and she instantly received the tip of the cattle prod against her ass cheek. The switch was pushed and she jumped as far as her chains would allow. Now, is there anyone else that wants to push it now? The other three sunk back onto the floor and were quiet.

I have placed your water in a bowl next to your head. I am going to get your meal for the evening. She went to the four cans of spam, opened them and smashed them into the bowls. The basic meal was shown to the Masters/Mistresses to assure them it was real food.

She placed the bowls next to the water bowls and told them to dig in. You will have ten minutes to eat and drink and than I will remove the bowls till morning. Being blindfolded, the slaves could not see what they had been served. Helma looked at them and said enjoy the food, the guard dogs do. One or two of the slaves kind of coughed, but with the promise of the cattle prod, chocked down the feast till their bowls were empty.

Anna and Belinda were very much impressed with the meal. Christen and Hans kind of stood to the side and wondered why the slaves ate their meal. Ilsa took them into the play room and started to explain the breaking down process.

We use the short watering and feeding periods along with the hoods and total withdraw from reality as a way to get their attention. They will be this way till you serve them tomorrow evening. At that time, you will remove their gags, blindfolds and hoods. This will bring you and them closer together. If you feel that they need it longer, you can replace these items.

It is time for you to go up and enjoy yourselves. Helma and Frieda will remain to pick up the empty bowls and replace the gags. Don't worry the four will be watched and taken care of. While Frieda picked up the bowls, Helma proceeded to replace the gags. Two of the slaves begged not to have the gags replaced, but were instead given a taste of the cattle prod.

Slaves, in time you will understand that what ever treatment you are required to take, it is from your loving Owners. Helma gave each of them a tender stroke of her hand on their nipples. Even Michael purred and relaxed as she brought the human touch to them. Frieda departed the area, slammed the door and went up to their room for the night.

Day One of Training

Most around the Chalet were stirring from a night's enjoyment. Ilsa and Frieda were up early to go to breakfast and than to training. They ate their breakfast and Frieda proceeded to the cell area. Ilsa stayed behind to catch up with the four Dominates. Good morning and I hope that you slept well.

Today is the first day of training for both you as well as you slave. We understand that you may have had some work in this before, but we ask that you work along with us. We have been doing this for many years and we want you to learn as many things as you can. When you finish your coffee, we will proceed down.

As they arrived, Frieda was about to hose off the slaves for the first time. Ilsa escorted the four down to a point where they cold see what was about to happen. A good slave is a clean one. We wash them off with a hose, but you may just want them to bath or shower. Even having them get into the shower or just wash you in the tub are up to you when you get home.

We hose them off after each meal so they will be clean for you to work with. Please step this way and watch as Helma preps the meal for them. She selected four cans of spam from the cabinet, opened them and placed the contents into the feeding bowls. She used a fork to break up the block of canned meat. We tell them it is dog food to humiliate them. This is another part of the breaking process. Again, you can feed anything you wish when you leave although some continue to feed this at home.

Helma placed the bowls in front of them and than returned for the water bowls. Meal time for you slaves. She started to remove the gags and the four began to maul the mashed down the meat. Good isn't it slaves, like I said last night, the guard dogs enjoy it well.

I want you to remember that Mistress Frieda is standing ready with the cattle prod if you have a problem with the top of the line slave food. They finished their meals and water within the ten minute period and the bowls were removed. I know that you all were thrilled and now it is time to replace the gags.

Slaves, your first treat is coming. You will be cleaned off. At this point, Frieda picked up the hose and started at one end of the line and directed the cold water into all the crevices of each slave. Starting at the feet and working up to between the legs and than to the neck line. The icy water got them moving and there were almost some complaints, but they remembered the prod and stayed quiet. She finished the last one and than sprayed off the floor. Several of the slaves had peeped overnight. As you can see, we will be controlling every part of your stay.

With the first lesson completed, Ilsa had the four steps into the costume and dressing room. As your slaves go back to resting, we will go over dominating attire. There are so many different ways to dress to play or show. It depends on what type of event or play you are going to. A formal event may require full formal attire or even a tux. Women's formals should be slightly tight fitting, but allowing for unrestricted movement. If you wear flowing dresses, you may get tangled up in them as you lead your slave down the isle or into a dungeon.

Most trips to dungeons may require an outfit which is your hall mark. For instance, Men will wear pants with a ruffled shirt and women may wear the customary leather corset with a low cut bra. Most of those new will either add or subtract from this. For instance, a man may want to go in shirtless and show off their chests. Women often will wear only a corset with their breasts open and swinging. Either of these will get everyone's attention. You want to make it your own look.

Another widely used outfit is the use of riding apparel. A nice set of riding britches with a fancy shirt or blouse, high top black leather boots, maybe laced or not. It is always a trip to demand your slave to lace them up. Differences can be obtained by mixing or matching the colors of the outfits. Some like the stand brown or tan. You can get custom colors or having lace sewn on. The ways to vary your style is endless.

We do have Dominates that prefer to go naked or just with boots. I guess what I am trying to say, there is no patent way to be dressed. It is what ever makes you feel the best or most dominate. As for us, I like the full leather corset with boots and, Helma enjoys wearing scrubs with a set of walking shoe.

The way your slave is dressed is just as important as your outfit. Even though it is the basic idea to drag them into an event naked, there are drawbacks. The biggest one is the weather. If it is winter, you don't want a blue skin slave or one dripping wet from a rain storm. Myself, I like to put mine in a leotard with tights or fishnets. Even a unitard is sharp. You can color coordinate with your outfit.

Your choice is sometime determined by the invitation from your host. Do they want breasts swinging or fully covered? Also, the place you are going will give you an indication. If the party is on the 70th floor pent house, you would be required to cover them up, maybe with a flowing robe or maybe even a fur coat. Most dungeons will most likely be in a part of town surrounded by apartments or homes where those living might call the authorities about nudity.

I think that you get the picture of where we are going. What we want you to do over the next few days are to try on what you might like. We have over three hundred different basic costumes for both you and your slave. If you like something, we can give you the maker and address where to order.

They made their way thru the many racks, trying on what made them feel good. None had even thought about how to dress for play. I want you to set out your clothing for tomorrow. I will tell you that it might get a little messy in the morning, so a set of casual clothes would be the best.

As for tonight, you will remember how much fun the cleaning of the slaves is, dress accordingly. You will be responsible for the feeding and cleaning of your slaves for the next several days. We like to get them fed by either 6 in the morning and 5 in the afternoon. This allows you to do the maintenance on them and get cleaned up and go to meals yourselves.

Before we let you go till the 5 o'clock feeding today, I along with Mistress Frieda will show you around the playroom as well as the storage areas and toys you will be using. They departed the cells area for the play room. You will be doing most of your training in this room, with one day of hard labor on the next floor down. We will explain each steep as we go. Please don't be afraid to ask questions of any of the three of us.

We want to show you some of the many toys and tables we have here. You may not get to use all of them now, but we think it is always fun to look and touch. Frieda opened the storage room door to expose the vast array. Some were a little shocked, some were excited, but all had many questions. Please let yourselves explore the many items and the tool carts. Do watch out when you get into the carts as they have many items in them, both pointy as well as sharp.

They went from one piece of furniture to another. If you feel the urge, go ahead and sit or lay on them. You will be using the items in the front half of the room. The rear contains our selection of medieval toys or in some cases, torture items.

The group was like a bunch of kids in a candy shop. What are these clamps for or what is the OBGYN table used for? Why do you have straight razors on the table? All are very good questions. The first thing in the morning, you will be placing your slave in the OBGYN chair and use the straight razor to clean up hair off from between their legs. This is a confidence building skill. We feel they will respect you more if you do it rather than us and we like a clean slave.

One or two of them turned green and asked if it was necessary. You have to build trust between you and your slave if you want them to perform for you. Yes, you may never have used a straight razor before, but we will show you how and we have a good supply of band aids as will as a surgeon on hand. We will even give you a zip lock bag for any pieces and parts you may come up with, I'm only kidding.

It is getting almost time for lunch, so you are dismissed. Frieda will take you up to your room so you can get ready. I suggest that you spend the afternoon talking over the day so far and to go over both the rules and the training schedules. Remember, you need to be at your room by 4.45 so we can bring you back down. One last thing, remember there are many guests at the Chalet that do not know of this training or area, so don't talk about this with anyone else. If asked, just say you are here to relax, which is not entirely wrong.

The four Dominates finished their lunch and returned to their room. Talk about the morning began to flow. Some were not exactly sure of what they had gotten themselves into. Hans said that he had never seen Lynn in such a sexy position, totally helpless and gagged. Anna chimed in that the cock and ball cage on Michael was great. First time he wasn't able to move from me. Christian and Belinda agreed that seeing their own slaves chained did bring them to almost orgasm, but were worried about their safety. Anna took charge and pulled out the rules and training manual and started going over the contents.

In the training book, it explained what they had just seen. We at the Chalet believe the best way to build trust and respect in your slave is to bring them down and let you regain all in you. Tonight at feeding, you will prepare their meals and water bowls for them. It will be time to remove the gags, blindfolds and hood just prior to serving. We suggest that you remove them slowly as this will be the first time in almost 24 hours they will have their freedom of them.

At this point, a gentle petting or even a kiss will go far. Do NOT let this become a begging session for their release from the chains. They will be required to be secure all of the time, except when we move to training. Also remind them that there is to be no loud talking when they are alone.

The appointed hour arrived and the Dominates moved to the elevator waiting area. Ilsa met them and they started the ride down.

Are there any questions for us at this time? Each turn and said no. You will be allowed to stay with them for a one hour period and than you must go back up to dinner.

After feeding and cleaning, you may want to cuddle them. They are yours and you can do as you wish. Anna, you will need to decide if you want the cock and ball cage left on or taken off. Also, do not tell them they are eating spam, only dog food. It shows more need for them to obey you and your use. Last, but not least, always ask questions as they come up for you, but never in front of the slaves.

The group departed the elevator and walked over to the slaves lying on the ground. One by one the masters and Mistresses approached their slave. Hans went first, removing the gag from Lynn's mouth. He than went for the blindfold, shielding her eyes from the overhead light. Lynn saw who was working on her and thanked him. Slowly unlacing the hood, her full head came into view.

She both sobbed as well as thanked him. He cuddled her head in his hands and kissed her. He took his hands and ran them down the breasts and stopped at her nipples slowly placing her nipples between his fingers on them and rubbed them. His hands now crept slowly to a point between her legs at the labia. Again, he slowly felt and played with them till she gave out a loud shy of pleasure. Lynn finished with many thanks to her master.

Roxie went about same with Christian. She showed her gratitude with many kisses and thanks. Belinda walked over to Wilma. The gleam in her eyes told the story. She and Belinda were deep, passionate lovers. The kisses were deeper and the hand action in her crouch area brought her to orgasm. Belinda knelt down beside her and whispered to her. Belinda placed her self over Wilma's face and snapped her fingers. Wilma instantly and without hesitation, began to lick at the Mistresses pussy lips.

Michael was last. Anna turned to Frieda and asked for the key to the cock and ball cage lock. Frieda handed it to her and she unlocked the caged package. A giant shy of relief came from his gagged mouth. She fondled his cock and than grabbed his balls, squeezing and twisting them roughly. Anna turned to Frieda and told her that he was very use to this treatment and loved it.

A small amount of pre cum came from the tip of his cock. Anna now removed the gag and ordered him to kiss her. He did as required and it lasted over five minutes. Anna now removed the blindfold and hood. Michael gently shook his head and in a low, soft voice, thanked his Mistresses.

The group now went about opening the cans of food and placing it into the bowls. The foods along with the bowls of water were placed next to their slaves. Each owner gave their commands to eat and all the slaves did as instructed to.

It may have been the fact that the slaves were getting used to the taste of the food or the fact their owners gave it to them. The bowls emptied quickly and the water licked from the bowl within the ten minutes. All bowls were removed and set on the counter.

Next came the cleaning. Each Master/Mistress took their turn with the hose and directed the cold water over the bodies of their slave. It was aimed at the bodies coming from the feet and up the legs. Each slave was than commanded to spread their legs as far as the chains would let them.

The ice cold spray made it way up the front and moved to the rear of the space between their legs. All the slaves gave a cold burr and shiver, but accepted the cleaning. The spay of water continued up to the breasts and around the heads, washing the hair that had been trapped within the hoods. At this point, Helma handed each Dominate a towel to dry off their own slave.

With the drying complete, the Dominates proceeded to touch, kiss and cuddle their property. From the looks on both the Masters and Mistresses faces and the more relaxed bodies of the slaves, you could tell all was well. This went on until Ilsa gently tapped the Dominates on the shoulder and reminded them it was time to go up. She said that Helma and Frieda would tend to their needs. All went to the elevator and went back up to the dining room.

With the hoods, blindfolds and gags removed and the fact that they had been reunited with their owners, the slaves were much more relaxed. Frieda spoke and started by telling them that they had been good up to this point.

She said that they were very privileged to have such good owners. You have been brought here to become the best slaves you can for your owners. Tomorrow we will start the training process for the both of you. You should try the hardest to do as your owners tell you.

They will also be in training to learning the fine points of play. Now go to sleep as tomorrow will be long, trying and even painful training. You can talk softly between yourselves, but be aware that both your owners as well as we will be able to hear. The four slaves shifted to get better looks at who was next to them. Frieda and Helma turned the lights off and closed the door.

Frieda and Helma joined Ilsa and the four at a table in the dinning room. They ordered from the menu and were all waiting for their food to arrive. Ilsa turned to the four and congratulated them on the way they handled themselves today.

I am sure that it was hard to see them in the condition they were in. They will become better to take the training and discipline they will receive. The food arrived and all ate slowly and enjoyed. They finished and the four went to the lounge area and got a drink and did some dancing.

As they were about to go back to their room, Ilsa went to the group and again reminded not to say anything in the public area and reminded them to be ready to go down to feed and clean the property in the morning. Get as much sleep as you can and don't drink too much as you will need a steady hand. Good night all and enjoy.

Day Two of Training

The group was waiting at the elevator at the appointed time. All entered the elevator, except for Helma who had gone down earlier to turn on the lights. Ilsa took the group to their slaves and told them that they were now on their own to feed and water. I will be here if you have questions. Frieda and Helma went to the equipment room and moved the OBGYN table to the center of the room.

Each of the four dominants went to the cabinet, removed a can of spam and emptied it into the bowls and drew water. One by one, they knelt next to their slave, gently caressed their faces and placed the bowls so they could eat and drink. Each slave ate and drank their meals.

After ten minutes had passed, the bowls were removed and the hosing off of the slaves began. They were so ready for their cleaning; each slave eagerly spread their legs for the washing. A quick toweling off and they were ready for the days work out.

It is time for each of you to go to the costume room and get dressed for the day. As they proceeded to the room, Ilsa told them to bring a leash with them as they emerged for training. You will be having your slave crawl on all fours to the play room. Each of the four took the outfit they had picked out the day before, dressed and emerged ready and willing to start.

As you release your slaves from their chains, start with their legs. Have them extend and move them slowly to regain full feeling in them. Next to come were the hands. They released them and rubbed them to get feeling back into them. You should now cuddle them and get a big hug from each.

The collar was next to be released. Once the collar is released, place the leash on the ring and have your slave get up on their hands and knees, remember that they have been chained to the floor for almost two days and will be a little shaky. Once all were up, they were lead one by one to the play room.

Once in the play room, Ilsa told them to take up a place next to the OBGYN table with the slaves in a sitting position next to their owners. Each did as told and all were very attentive and listening for their next order. From now till the finish of training, this is where you will be within one hour after we bring you down for morning feeding.

Today's lesion is one of both trust and obeisance. Controlling your slave is most important. It will make you look important as well as a well trained team. It will be up to you if you have them crawl or simply walk behind you.

How they wait is another position you will need to decide. Some want them to simply stand next to them, or they can lay on the floor or even sit like a dog next to you. Either way, they should always be to your rear and to your right rear. This is the traditional way from history, just like with an expensive dog at a show.

Little things are your decision as do they keep their eyes down or are they looking at you. Myself, I like to have a slave trained to except hand signals to move or sit. Verbal commands can be lost in a crowd and they may not do as you want. You can customize this as we go. Never should you let your slave accept orders from another Dominate unless it is prearrange. Just these little things will make you the couple to stand out.

Let us practice commands. I will demonstrate with Helma. Helma walked over to Frieda, handed her the leash and took up her a kneeling position. Helma held her head down and waited for Frieda to start. Frieda started by placing her hand under Helma's chin and had her rise her head. Next, Frieda snapped her fingers and Helma rose to a ready to move position. Frieda took the slack out of the leash and they began to move around the room. As you can see, the slave is looking straight ahead and carefully watching for instructions.

She will only move with her Mistress as long as the Mistress is moving. Once she stops, the slave should freeze in place waiting for the next command. Frieda turned to Helma, snapped her finger and Helma came to a sitting position and lowered her head. This all looks so easy, but it takes training and much practice to accomplish the precision of what you have just seen. Frieda had Helma stand and removed the leash.

I want you each to do as we showed you. Don't worry if you get it wrong the first time. To tell you the truth, most wind up either pulling the leash or tripping over each other. I will walk you through it several times. The Dominates stood with the leash in their hands. Each slave got to their hands and knees and stayed very still. The slave's heads should be facing down at this time.

Owner's now place your hand under their chin and raise their heads to look at you. Now take up the slack on the leash, snap your fingers and start walking in a circle around the chair. This should look like you are at the grand dog show, guiding your dog around the Judges.

The group started out well until one pair slowed up some and the couple behind them stumbled over the set in front of them. Frieda commanded them to stop and start over again. Let us try this again. Set your slave and start. This time the walking went much better. Now have your slave stop and get them into a sitting position. This went better than Ilsa had expected and all were at attention. Very well, you have completed your first lesion.

I want you to practice this for the remaining portion of the morning. Over the next hour or so, the group practiced the lesson of the morning. It is approaching the dinner hour. You need to walk your slaves back to the cells area and chain them up as you found them.

The slaves set themselves up to accept commands, head down in the sitting position. Each had their head raised and than walked back to their position. The chains were replaced and the slaves lay down. Now go and change to you dinner clothes and we will go up to lunch. You will have two hours to dine and be ready for this afternoon's work. All went up to the dining room, selected their meal and sat at one table.

The group finished their meals and proceeded to the play room. As the elevator opened Ilsa emerged first. She turned to the group and told them to go and change into their costumes for the afternoon. When you have changed, proceed to your slave, unchain them and report to the main play room. Take up positions as this morning around the OBGYN chair. The Dominates changed clothes, readied their slaves and walked them into the play room. They stood with their slave next to them, the head facing down.

This afternoon we will be doing four different things at the same time. To determine the order you will perform the task, I want you to draw numbers. Frieda produced a small pail with four poker chips with a number on them. I want you to draw a chip and step back.

Each Dominate stuck their hand in the pail and picked out one of the chips. Ilsa asked who had number one and Hans answered he did. Good, you take Lynn and stand at the foot of the OBGYN table. He prompted his slave and they walked over to the table and he had her sit. Number two was drawn by Belinda. You will be against the wall next to Mistress Frieda. Christian was the third to answer. Take a place next to Mistress Helma against the wall. I guess that leaves you Anna. You stay right here.

This is how we are going to do your training today. Number One will be the first to shave your slave. Number two and three will get training in both hooking your slave to the wall as well as experience with the crop, paddle, flogger and last the bull whip. Number four will have the time to practice walking your slave.

With the slaves at the stations, Mistress Ilsa told everyone that they would have forty five minutes at each station. Ilsa started by having Hans get Lynn into the OBGYN chair and her legs into the stirrups. Once Lynn was situated in the chair, Ilsa took the straps from the drawer and handed them to Hans. I will show you how to secure her to the chair.

First came one above and below the knee. A strap was fitted around each wrist and one around the neck. Now they took the two large two inch wide straps and placed one just below her breast and the other above the belly button. As you can see, she is fully attached and has little movement.

Frieda and Helma came next. They had one of the slaves stand with her face against the wall and the other with their face outward. We will now attach them spread eagle against the wall. The rings in the wall will provide attachment places for the chains to the shackles. Start by spreading the legs apart as far as they can go, and secure them to the rings near the floor.

Each did as they were told. Now we will go to the wrists and attach them to the upper rings. Both Frieda and Helma inspected and told them to take a little more of the slack out of the ankle chains. This left both slaves taunt without movement. Great, this will become apparent why we spread them soon. Now take a blindfold and a gag and place them on the slave. We don't want to accidentally loose an eye or snap off an ear. We don't want them screaming or begging for now.

Ilsa turned to Anna. You are to practice your commands and lead your slave between here and the cells. I want to see improvement when you are finished. You may also want to give your slave some encouragement as you work him out. Anna turned to Michael and raised his head and snapped her fingers. They began to walk back and forth between the play room and the cells. I will be watching you, so don't cheat.

Ilsa returned to Hans and told him that it is important to have a cleanly shaved slave. Hair is unsightly and can get in the way of play. She asked Hans if he had ever held a straight razor or shaved anyone before. No I haven't, but can hardly wait. Good, I will show you by doing the first several strokes. First is to clean the total area between her legs with an alcohol soaked rag. Hans did this and was now told to take a wet rag and clean her off with water.

Next to come was a shaving mug with shaving brush. You are to work the brush around in the cup and work up lather from the cake of soap in the cup. Hans did this and than applied a light covering to the pubic mound and down to below her anal opening. Make sure you get both the inside and outside of the labia. Hans worked the brush around and covered all the indicated areas and handed the cup and brush back to Ilsa. I want you to go to your slave and whisper to her that you are not going to cut her and she should not speak out. He did this and gave Lynn a kiss. This calmed her down.

Hans, we will start at the top of the pubic mound, just under the belly button. You pull the skin tight and bring the razor blade to this point. She slowly brought the blade down against the skin and slid it against the furry mound.

It is easy, but you need to go "SLOW". Don't worry, you can do this Hans. Hans was handed the razor and repeated the shaving of the mound as Ilsa had done. That is it, you did a great job. Your slave is doing a great job also, but you might want to quickly reassure her again. He did as requested. Now finish the pubic mound and we will go further.

You now will remove the hair around the anal area. He lowered the blade and scraper the fur from this area. Great, now finish that area and we will move to the labia. They are more tender and thinner. Start by pulling them outward and take the fur off the inner side and than the outer side. Hans did the task in time and was relieved when he had finished.

You did well and did not even draw any blood. I want you to take the wet towel and clean the area off. He slowly toweled off the area several times and her face showed relief when he was sure no blood exhausted. For the remaining time, you may cuddle and stroke your slave, but leave her restrained. The two cuddled and kissed as Lynn softly thanked him for the job and not cutting anything off. Ilsa stood back and smiled.

Frieda was working with Wilma and Helma had Roxie. At some time during a play session, you will find it time to whip, flog, crop or paddle your slave. These are normal parts of play and can be both memorable as well as sexy.

Christian was handed a multi tailed leather flogger. I am going to start you with one made of dear skin. We will work up from here. You will be working on her shoulders, rump and the back of her legs. You want to stand back to almost and arms length, bring the flogger up to almost over head and bring it down in a steady move. Let it fall on the skin and follow thru till it leaves the skin.

She showed Christian several times and handed the flogger to him. I will make it easier for you. She took a water based marker and placed XXXX on her shoulders, upper back, rump and upper legs. These are the areas that are safer to strike. Stay away from the spine and soft organ area in the lower back area. It spoils an evening if you have to take her to the hospital for damage to these areas.

It was his turn to flog Roxie. He raised his arm and let the flogger fly. He struck the left shoulder. He turned to Frieda and said this was great. This is good as most that have never struck anyone before are scared. I want you to continue to flog her on the different areas. He continued till he could get the tails to fall in the same place more than twice. After gaining confidence, Frieda replaced the flogger with one made with heavy leather, two foot long tails. Now practice, lightly at first. He did and brought shies of joy from Roxie.

Helma began outlining the safe spots to strike on Wilma. These consisted of her breasts and nipples, hips, the area between her legs and the thighs. We have two different types of crops to work with. The main different types are the one with the narrow tip. This one will cause more pain than the one with the wide tip.

Helma took the wide tipped one and placed several strikes on her breasts. Wilma gave out a low scream and kind of bit her lip. These will hurt and are great as a punishment item, also to guide a slave along. She handed her the wide tipped crop and he gave it several tries. Very good, now let it fall over her hips and tights. She did as shown and was handed the small tipped crop. She repeated the steps and stood back.

Frieda stepped up and said to take a slow rest prior to changing to the paddle and whip. I want you to go to your slave, cuddle them and give them a kiss. Also reassure them that they did well and you are proud of them. They did as requested and ran their hands down the front and backs of he slaves. The process gave both the owner and the slave more confidence to continue. They stood back and repeated the training by changing tools to the whip and paddle. This went well for both owners and slaves.

A timer rang on the wall indicating that the forty five minutes had expired. Ilsa told each to undo their slave and move to the next station. Each of the lesions was repeated and than they moved on. By the time that they finished, all four couples were exhausted. Time has come to put your slaves away for the evening. As it is almost five in the afternoon, go ahead and feed and water them. You will also need to wash them off as they are all sweaty. When you finish, change back to your regular clothes and you are done for the night.

The Dominates worked hard at placing the chains back on, feeding and washing off the slaves. They ended the session with many good hugs and kisses. They changed and prepared to go up for dinner. Ilsa reminded them that they were on their own in the morning to perform the necessities for their slave.

After this, they were to select their outfits and bring their slaves out for training by nine. Ilsa took the group up to ready for dinner. Frieda and Helma finished up small chores and joined Ilsa for supper. Helma turned to the other two and said she never know how much went into the different programs they worked on. Frieda turned to her and said it will come easier as time go on. Ilsa told her that she did very well today. Tomorrow, you will be in charge of the wine pressing session by her self.

Day Three of Training

The slaves lay chained in their cell, waiting for their Owners to arrive for breakfast feeding. The elevator door opened and they entered, lead by Helma. Ladies and Gentleman, you are on your own this morning. When you finish feeding and cleaning, I will take you back up for breakfast. Each of them went about securing a can of spam from the cabinet, placing it in the bowl, smashing it up and placing it next to their slaves.

The ten minutes for feeding went by and the bowls were removed. The hose came out and each slave was washed down. A quick toweling down, some cuddling and a kiss and they returned to the elevator for Helma to take them back to their rooms.

Just before eight o'clock, Helma met them at the elevator and returned them to the cells. Again, you are on your own. You have till nine to select your outfits for the day and have your slave in the play room all lined up. Each tried on different costumes and took a leash from the shelf. They attached the leash and with the appropriate instruction to their slave, proceeded to the center of the play room.

Helma was giving instructions for the day. Today is both hard labor day as well as how to use punishment toys on your slaves. You will spend half a day at each, go to lunch and return to do the other half. I am going to be in charge of the slave labor half on the next level down. I want to tell both you and the slaves that between teaching sessions, do not tell the other half of your training.

Mistress Anna and Master Hans will be with me on the lower floor. Mistress Belinda and Master Christian will wait here for Mistress Frieda and Ilsa. While you are waiting, you should practice your handling skill as you will be tested on them.

If the two in my group will follow me, we will go to the rear door and down the ramp. With Helma in the lead, the two sets snapped to and began the walk/crawl down the ramp. They reached the large wooden door and Helma inserted her key card to open it. As she opened it and turned on the light, the group saw the large outer and inner stone rings with two stone wheels and a wooden shaft through the middle. This is our grape pressing room. We squeeze the grapes to be turned into the Chalet's world renowned wine and champagne. This is the slave labor training area.

I want you each to take your salve to one side of the wooden shaft. By this point, you will be able to do the hook ups with my instruction. Have your slave place their hands on the shaft and use the hooks in the rings on the shaft to hook up their wrist shackles. Anna and Hans both did as they were told. Now I want you to place the one foot piece of chain between their ankle shackles and hook it in place. With both slaves in place, Helma took Anna and Hans aside and instructed them to select either a flogger or whip from the shelf. We will now practice the skills you learned yesterday.

You and your slave will be learning that being a Dominate and slave is not only parties and showing them off. A slave must also be able to do manual labor when required. The labor they perform maybe as simple as house work and in this case, heavy work, all benefiting you or your group.

I will start by placing grapes between the inner and outer rings. When I give the order, you will walk behind your slave and get them to move. You are to use your striking tool to encourage them to move. We have a total of one hundred baskets of grapes to crush before they are finished and can go back to the cells during your lunch. I will tell you in advance that you must keep them moving to get it finished.

Helma said to start them moving and stood back. It was hard to start both for the slaves to push and for the Owners to use their whips and floggers to strike the slaves. Progress was slow at first as the two wheels crushed the grapes. Basket by basket of grapes was dumped into the pressing area and the wheels ground it into juice and pulp. The crushed mixture emptied into a holding tank in a different room.

At first Michael and Lynn were slow at moving the crushing stone wheels. The application of the sting of the whip on their rumps got their attention and the pace was speed up. At first Lynn was taking a step and a half for every step Michael took as he was almost six inches taller. After several complete turns of the wheels, they began to get into sink and they were together.

Back on the upper floor, Ilsa and Frieda arrived to find Christian and Belinda putting their slaves through their paces. Ilsa turned to Frieda and said that they were improving nicely. Ilsa told them to have their slave sit and rest by the wall under the rings. She walked over to them and talked about their upcoming training for the morning.

Today's topic is the use of the many toys used in the discipline and punishment of a slave. A slave may need to be punished for any infraction of your rules or just plain screwing up. The use of pain is always the best way to get their attention.

You went through the use of striking tools yesterday and today will be the use of smaller toys. This is not only a bad thing as you will find that many slaves very much enjoy the use of pain as a reward. Now wait here until Frieda and I set up the stations.

Frieda had already opened the door to the toy storage and brought the two toy cars out. Next to come were the wooden tables, each were only one foot wide by three feet long and three feet tall. They were placed one on each side of the room. Rolling stools were placed by each block table. We will be taking you through how and what to do; one on one training. I will take Mistress Belinda and Frieda will take Master Christian.

Now I want you to bring your slave over, and have them stand with their rumps against the bottom end of the tables. Belinda brought Wilma over to my table and Christian took Roxie to the table with Frieda. The top drawers of the cabinets were opened reveling straps for tying the slave to the table plus gags and blindfolds.

The slave is to lay on the table with their rears just sticking off the table. Now go to the other end and pull the small shelf out from the head of the table. This will be a head rest for your slave. We will first start by placing a two inch wide strap around them at the belly button and than one just below the breasts. Next is to secure the ankle and wrist shackles to the bottom of the block.

This should ensure that they will not thrush on the table during play. To finish off the securing, first place a gag and blindfold on them. With that done, use two one inch strap to secure their heads to the shelf. One strap is to be loosely secured around the neck and the other tightly over the forehead.

I want you to now slowly stroke your slave, making sure to touch every part from the neck to the knees. On the way down, cup the breasts and twist and pull the nipples. Lightly at first and than apply pressure and bring the slave to attention. You should either get an indication of pain or pleasure levels.

Moving further down, pinch the labia, pulling and twisting. Be prepared as you may start them to orgasm, but don't give in at this time. This is something that they must earn from you. The rubbing and petting of them will get them sensitized to receiving what is next.

This is not a torture session, only punishment session. Over time when you know wither they are pain sluts and do in fact want it hard or extremely hard. You are going to get the basics and can either add or subtract in time. Let us start with the breast area.

Look in the second drawer and pull out ten clothes pins. Start by pinching up some skin at the base of the breast. Take a cloths pin and place it on the pinched up skin. Now go around the breast at quarter intervals and place another pin. To finish off this breast, place one at the base of the nipple. Now doesn't that look pretty?

At first till you get used to your slave, only leave them on for ten minutes or till they start to turn blue. You can make interesting patterns or flower designs placing more pins on. I have seen a slave with as many as fifty clothes pins on each breast. You can have a little fun by waving your hand across the tops of the pin or even giving them a little pull upward.

You do not need to waste any more clothes pins on their breast, move down and pinch up a section of their labia. I normally start at the top of the labia and work down. Place the pin down as close to the bottom of the folds. You can flick these also and bring pleasure to them, or did I mean pain, it depends on the slave.

Ten minutes had elapsed since the first cloths pins were placed on.

As you can see, the skin around the tip of the pins should be turning many different shades of blue. This is a sign that it is time to remove them. Slowly start at the base of the breasts. Give each one a little tug and maybe twist it.

As each one was removed, the slaves wiggled, trashed and tried to scream. Christian said that he was very much enjoying the removal process. Belinda was a little more aggressive in the removal. She also pulled hard as she released the pins from their tender skin. Unlike Roxie, Wilma was enjoying the discomfort and even giggled.

Now that the pins were removed, Ilsa told the two dominates to message the reddened area. This will both assist in the return of the blood in these areas as well as bring pain. It is time for more fun for you and maybe even the slave. I want you to go to the cabinet in the third drawer and find several different scrub brushes. Let us start at the tips of the nipples.

Using you hand, cup up the breast so the nipple is sticking straight up. Start by running the softest of you brushes over the tip of the nipple. At first the reaction will be of pain and will go to pleasure. Back and forth the different types of bushes were run over the nipples. The nipples became more sensitive with each stroke. You can bring all kinds of fun to the nipple by squeezing and twisting it now.

If you think this is fun, move down to the labia. Draw the brush from deep between the legs and up toward the pubic mound. After several of these motions, use a return brush movement to excite the labia from the other direction.

Every so often, stop and run your finger over her clit. She should shudder and moan. You may even get her to come to orgasm, but don't let her cum too much as we want it to last for a while. Christian and Belinda got into it so much that Ilsa and Frieda had to stop them.

We want to keep the punishment and fun up for a little while longer. Another popular toy that is a favorite of the Dominate is the anal plug. In the forth drawer are many different types of and design. Question, have either of you ever used one on your slave before? Christian said no, but Belinda said she loved to insert one in Wilma. Christian, I want you to choose the small one, one inch in diameter to start with. Belinda, you can choose one that suit's your fancy.

She chose a larger one, over two inches in diameter and shaped like a pigs tail. That is a great selection. Before you start the insertion, make sure you place plenty of water based lubricant on it. Us the basic rule of "P" for plenty.

Now place the tip at the little rose bud opening and gently start it in. You can have much more fun by cork screwing it in, a little at a time. Wow, this is fun and the slaves seem to be enjoying it very much. For more fun, remove it maybe half way and than back in. Belinda said she loved the slurping sound as it entered, was withdrawn and reentered. Enough fun with the plugs now, now removes them and cleans up the runny lube.

Belinda turned to Frieda and asked if she could do something a little more painful to her slave. Frieda asked what she had in mind, and Belinda said she saw a pair of pliers in the cart. No problem, I want both of you to get a set that are comfortable to you and we will start at the nipples.

This can be very painful as well as destructive to the skin so we will take it slow. Place the tips of the pliers over the nipple and slowly close the handles till just before they completely close. Each slave came to life and trashed widely on the table. Rock the pliers back and forth as well as lift them up. At this point, the slaves were trying to rip themselves from the table. You must be careful as you could rip the nipple right off.

Take the pliers and go down to the labia. Remember, these little flaps of skin are much tenderer and will damage much faster. Just the sure touch on the lips will send shivers down the spines of the slaves. Now apply some pressure and pull outward. Roxie could be heard begging for mercy but Wilma was begging for more intense pain. The pliers were switched back and forth on each lip.

We are now running short of time and there is one more play item we want to introduce you to. Frieda and Ilsa went to the storage closet and each brought out the fucking mach on its base and plugged it in. The two slaves have done well and deserve an electrifying relief. We have installed a bi-polar dildo on the end of the fucking machine.

Below on the stand you will find a set of controls. The dildo is an electric probe. It does two things at a time. First, it acts as normal dildo going in and out. The secondary effect is that you can give them an electric stimulus on each stroke. You will find out if and how much your slave enjoys the sting of the stroke.

Bring the tip of the dildo up to and insert it about two inches into the vaginal opening. First, go to the knob labeled stroke and turn it to the number one position. The dildo started it's plunging in and out. Each slave started to enjoy the movement and you could tell how much they were ready for an orgasm.

Now choose the one labeled with an "E" and turn it to setting number one. With each stroke, one on the inward and one on the outward stroke the slave felt a light shock. About every five strokes, turn each knob up one place.

Both the strokes and shocks increased bringing uncontrolled need to an explosive orgasm. After maybe twenty minutes, both slaves were spent and needed released. The machines were turned off and removed. Large quantities of white fluid came oozing from the opening. Each slave was fully exhausted. I want you to slowly release your slave and do a lot of cuddling and kissing. You must reassure them that you love them.

Time was approaching the eleven thirty hour and it was time to put the slaves away and go up for lunch. Helma was just bringing the group up from the grape pressing room. The slaves were returned to their cell positions and the group entered the elevator to go up for lunch.

When we return from lunch, each team will switch places and do the others training. You all did well and hope that you learned many ways to have fun with your slave. Just as the group was about to step out of the elevator, Belinda whispered in Lisa's ear; do you think that I could do a turn on the fucking machine? Lisa replied, I think we can handle that later on this evening after the sessions.

The group enjoyed their meal and went back to the play room and did the others training. All were both surprised at what had happened as well as how much fun it had been. They took their slaves back and chained, fed, cleaned them and did lots of cuddling. As the group exited the elevator to return to their room to rest before dinner, Frieda turned to Belinda and whispered that she wanted to show her some of the recreation items. The other three Dominates departed as the elevator door closed.

The elevator returned to the play room floor. Both Frieda and Helma lead the way with Belinda following. Ilsa told me of your wish and we are here to grant it. First, you will need to answer several questions. First, you do understand that to experience the fucking machine; you have to play the slave side? She turned and said yes. Next, you are not to tell anyone of the events to come in the next two hours or so, again, she answered yes. Last, you will be our slave and do as we tell you. Belinda thought for a second, first of all what had she gotten herself into and than said YES I will.

Belinda, you have exactly two minutes to go to the chair against the far wall, strip naked and neatly fold your clothes, place them on the chair and return in a slave position. Belinda sped to the chair and stripped and folded her clothes. She had returned within the allotted time and was on her knees, head down and her hands on her knees. Frieda turned to her and said what a good slave she was.

Slave, stand and present yourself for inspection. Belinda looked at her not knowing what to do. That is right, you never got taught this in the shortened coarse your are in. The present position is standing with your feet apart about two feet, hand locked together behind your head and face down. This is what we have slaves do to be ready for inspection.

Helma steeped behind Belinda and placed her hands up under her breasts. Slave, I saw a little flinch in your body. A slave does not move or object to any touching done to her body. Helma began to squeeze the breast very roughly. She than reached a little further around and grabbed the large nipples. She closed her fingers and squeezed the nipples very hard.

The nipples became very hard and stuck out to rosy red points. Very good slave, you are learning. Frieda lowered her hands and began to explore between the legs. Each hand grabbed a pussy lip and pulled and twisted them. The slave stood as still as she could and bit her lip in pain. Slave, you see how it is to be on the other side of the event.

Both Frieda and Helma stepped back and waited. Slave, you are to thank your Mistresses for the wonderful pain they have given you. Slave, now get down on you knees, thank us and than lick our boots. Belinda instantly dropped to her knees and licked the boots, starting at the toes and working up to the tops. Very good, you might make a goods slave in time.

Now go and position yourself at the base of the block table. You remember, just as you had your slave do earlier. Belinda quickly moved to the end of the table and stood with her head lowered. Very good, now assume the same position on the table. Now you will understand the feelings your slave did when you ordered her to do this. Lay back on the tables and let your arms and legs hang down the sides of the table.

Helma handed Frieda half a set of wrist and ankle shackles. They each knelt by the side of the table and placed them on Belinda. First to come was the wide belt to go just below the breasts. Next was the belt just above the belly button. They went to the bottom of the table and attached the ankle shackles to the rings and than to the top and repeated the process to the wrist shackles.

Slave, are you now understanding how your slave felt? She answered yes. Last, but not least came the head. Frieda started with the penis gag. She prepped it by rubbing on and in her pussy to get the womanhood taste on it. She pushed into her mouth and tightly buckled it in place. Next to come was the leather blindfold to be buckled in place. Are you getting the picture of how helpless a slave feels?

She shook her head, than the two straps were placed around her head. The first strap was placed around her neck and than the one across the forehead. Knowing that Belinda had not expected all this, Helma cuddled her and than placed a kiss on Belinda forehead. We will be doing the same things you did, except that we are going to put a twist on them.

Helma produced a bucket of clothes pins and a ball of string. Let's see, you placed five pins on each breast and nipple. We will be placaing a dozen around the base of the breast and four around your nipple. There will be a difference as we will be placing a string under each one. This is called a zipper and you will better understand its operation later.

They than went down to the labia and place six pins on each with the string running under each side. While we wait for the numbing effect to take effect, I think you will receive an anal plug. Let me see, you used the pigtail plug. I will allow you plenty of lube before I insert it.

Helma went to her ass checks and spread them wide, exposing the red rosebud hole. Frieda placed the tip against the hole and began twisting the plug into the hole, a little at a time, some in and than some out. This went on for over five minutes until the base of the plug made contact with the fleshy bottom. Are you comfortable yet?

Belinda didn't have time to answer before she felt the smack of the wide tip crop make contact with her pubic mound, smack after smack brought her to tears, but she refused to beg for mercy. Wonderful, she is learning well. She is ready for her next lesson. Frieda went to her breast and began to wiggle and pull at the clothes pins. This began to bring life and thrashing from the slave. Helma did the same with the pins on her labia.

Both areas had started to go numb and they knew it was time for the big step. Slave; ready yourself for what is coming. Helma started first and slowly pulled the string, ripping the pins from the lips. The scream from under her gag could be heard all around the play room. Did you like this added touch slave, now for the breast area? Do you want me to go slowly or all at once? She didn't answer fast enough, Frieda let them rip. The pins flew all over the room. Again, screams and crying were heard.

Both areas were still on fire as Helma brought the many tips of the heavy leather flogger down on her breast and pussy area. The crying and screaming were uncontrollable now. At least ten hits each to the breasts and pussy and they let her settle down. You see, being a slave is not as easy as you may have thought. Oh, the plug is still in and Frieda began to wiggle it in and out and all around within her tender ass. When Frieda was sure that the effect had been well felt, the plug was slowly removed and the tip of the crop was brought down onto the rosebud hole.

One last thing before you gets the fucking machine. If I remember, you wanted to use something a little harsher on your slave. Both Frieda and Helma each picked up a pair of pliers and began to pinch up the skin of the nipples and pussy.

The calm of Belinda was short lived as the teeth of the tips of the pliers dug into to her tender flesh. Wiggling and pulling the flesh made her trash even more than before. She was getting very sore. I think she is ready for some fun now. Both Helma and Frieda stopped the work on her tender parts and did some cuddling of her.

Well Belinda, it is time for you to receive the fucking machine. Helma rolled the platform with the machine resting on it to a point at the bottom of Belinda's ass. This morning, we used a smooth bi polar dildo for the job. For you, I have decided to use one with rubber spikes on it. This will bring you around with such excitement as it goes in and out.

The tip was place around two inches inside of her. Are you ready slave? With what ever energy she had left, Belinda mumbled yes from her gag. Frieda turned the switch to the number one position causing the dildo to enter and withdrew. A small smile could be seen on Belinda's face.

Are you enjoying this slave? Great, now let me increase the in and out and add a little electric charge. This got the attention of Belinda. A kind of smile appeared on her face. Let's try an increase of two on each switch.

It was now a toss up of if she was happy or going out of her mind. Frieda turned to Helma and said it was time to get some pleasure from her ourselves. They went to her head and took the straps off. Do we want to remove only the gag or the blindfold also? I think she should get to see what she will be giving pleasure to.

Belinda, we know that you are bi, so we will give you something to lick and suck. Frieda stepped over her face and grabbed the hair. I am going to draw your face up to my womanhood and you will service me. You are to lick and suck my clit and pussy very tender and you will not loose any of the wonderful white fluid of my orgasm, do you understand? Without waiting for an answer, her face was securely pulled between Frieda's legs and the pleasuring began.

It took Frieda over ten minutes to achieve full orgasm. Helma said it is my turn now. She traded placed with Frieda and secured Belinda's head in place. Frieda went down to the controls and increased both the in and out and also the shocks. It was now coming to the twenty minute mark when Helma exploded into her mouth. She stepped back and the controls were slowly taken down to the off position.

The dildo was removed with a big shy of relief from Belinda. You have been a great slave to us and it is time to go up. First came release of the wrists and than the ankles were released, than the two belts around the main body came next. Don't try to get up, let us help. With one under each arm, they lifted her to a sitting position. Helma stroked her sweat drenched hair as Frieda covered her body with a blanket.

Fifteen minutes had gone by until Belinda regained her composure and started to cry with happiness. Frieda now asked her if she both enjoyed herself as well as better understanding what a slave goes through. She came to grips with what was being asked and answered that she had more questions than she knew where to begin.

Helma spoke first, are you confused as to what you are, a pain giver or receiver? For me, I thought I could only give the pain, but than I took the extreme slave package and found I could enjoy both. Belinda answered that she would have to take some time to think it over, but I did like both. I will say that was the best orgasm I have ever had.

The two helped her to get dressed and walk to the elevator. Frieda told her to take her time to go over her thoughts and take a hot bubble bath. We can meet on the sixth floor deck tonight and talk over the events of the afternoon. You are in overload right now.

I am sure that your friends are getting ready for dinner now. Don't worry; we will take care of your slave this evening. If you want to further explore your slave side, I suggest you think about taking the extreme slave coarse, Helma did and she is a better person for it. It is time for you to go to your room and get your head cleared up and relax. We will check in on you later and talk.

Day Four of Training

Day four start as the ones prior. The slaves were fed, watered and cleaned. The Dominates met with Ilsa, Frieda and Helma in the dining room for breakfast. Ilsa started the conversation by saying that they were to gather back in their living room. The group finished and returned to the group's room. Ilsa began by telling them that today was the last day of training. We will split it into two different directions. It is common to participate in horse and pony play. It is every bit as popular as regular horse and pony work and can be as expensive. We are going to expose you to the basic concepts of it.

The completion of the day will be used to what you wish to do or try. When we are finished today, you will have your last full day tomorrow. During this time, we suggest that you spend the day being close to your slaves. Go swimming, play tennis or just lay in the sun getting tanned. Show them that you both love as well as respect them.

Pony play can and does have many different directions to go. You first have to question what path you wish to go with it. The biggest thing you have to remember is that they are no longer human, they are animals. They have no cares or worries. They don't talk, just whinny, bathroom habits, and can and do wonder off from you. You can not punishment them for what they do. You have to teach them how to act and use reinforcement to get them to do what you want them to do.

What are you going to do with them? Are they going to be "My Little Pony", show ponies, cart or sleigh ponies, or possibly in Michael's status as a work horse for pulling a field plow? What I am saying is that there are many ways to use them. Depending on if you stay close or join other human pony clubs, you may even be part of teams.

Costumes come next. For yours, you can go Country or English. The main difference is the Country can be as easy as blue jeans and a shirt with cowboy boots and English are breeches, either a tight fitting shirt or formal one. As for your pony, it depends on your taste as well as the rules set by your club.

Many want their ponies to have pretty costumes with no nudity and some want partial or full nudity. For females, a lacy corset with bouncing breasts is a common look. As for my pony, I like them in a leotard or unitard. At the least, your pony should have a high top lace type boot for good ankle support. These can be regular or custom made with hoofs and a tail. The looks are endless.

Housing of them; I have seen them go from a custom made stall in a sixty six floor pent house to one in an old barn. Most consist of wood railings with a gate and many rings to tie off the harness. The flooring can be rubber matting to straw and or saw dust and even just a dirt patch.

There are normally buckets for feed and water. They are required go to bathroom on the material you pick. Even wash down areas can be as simple as a concrete pad with a cold water hose; similar as your do now to a private stall with hot and cold water.

The feeding of ponies can vary in different ways. Feed can range from a bucket of oats, carrots, apples or other vegetables. I have heard of those that receive fully cooked meals, but the common factor is that they eat out of a pail.

You should always have a treat in your pocket. Some use a cube of sugar or candy piece to a carrot or apple slice. Remember, they don't have hands so you will have to hold it or toss it in the stall.

Now for the expensive pieces and parts which make up a horses wear, we come to tact. Western tack is plain in nature but can be laced with silver conches and barding. Halters and bits, halters, saddle and even a regular or turnout blanket.

The accessories are endless. Many, if not all will have to tailored to your pony and custom made. We can supply you with makers of this gear. Don't forget the use of hobbles to keep the feet together.

I know that I have brought up so many questions. We will try to get you started with many items in the play room. If you do want to get into this way of enjoying your slave, I suggest that you attend one of several human pony schools that exist for schooling. They normally are part of very expensive horse or racing farms. Now if you go with Frieda and Helma, they will take you to the costume dressing room to choose your outfit for today. Belinda, if you will stay behind, I have the answer you asked of Helma yesterday.

Belinda, now that I have you alone, I want to know how you feel after your play with Frieda and Helma last evening. I never know how the other side felt and see her in a different light. There was nothing wrong with how you were doing; they just thought you wanted to see the rougher side of play. I know you were a little scared to start, but were acting as if you wanted more of it.

We watched as you worked on Wilma and found she enjoyed the pain side of play. You know what she liked and maybe you might want to take a step deeper than you are with her. If you wish and I suggest you do in the free play section today. Place her back on the block table and we can show you how to play harder than you were.

Don't let the fact that you enjoyed the play on yourself effect you playing. Helma was the same as you until she went to the extreme slave program herself. You can be a secret person we refer to as a Switch. Just think about it and we are always here to help you.

Ilsa took Belinda down and she chose a western outfit to wear for play. Now that you all have selected outfits, bring your slaves out and have them sit in front of your table. We will go over how to chose tact and place it on your pony.

The gear on the tables is all custom made and much small than what you get for real horses. For today's training, your horse will be in a leotard, except for Michael, he gets a set of tight spandex briefs. Even your trainers enjoy a tightly displayed package.

First thing to place on is your head harness package. It consists of a rubber coated bit and the straps to attach it. Next pick up a pair of ears. Some are tall, some short and even look like a mule's. They will either stand up or flop over. For now pick out what you want to try. To complete the harness, you will need to place a set of blinders on the sides. These keep your pony from being distracted by your neighbor. A set of reins will complete what you will need today.

Step to the center of the room and have your pony on your right side. We will be going in a clock wise patter to start. I will tell you in advance, Mistress Helma came down and briefed your ponies on what a pony was and how to act. They are not to talk, just whinny. They may and do wonder off and have short attention spans. I guess what I am trying to say is that they will be a handful. On the other hand, you can use the leather reins to pop them across the ass.

We will start with a simple move of going around in a circle. Let your horse get to the limit of their reins and start walking. Simple short steps are best to start with. Just like humans, ponies need training on how to put one foot in front of the other. The step should be done with the bending of the knee and bringing it up with each step. Great, remember all that we do today takes endless practice to get it down right.

Good, now let us improve the costume of theirs. We need to add a tail for them to swish back and forth. Go to your table and select a plug tail. This plug sets up inside of them a little different than the one you used yesterday. It is designed to stay in until you pull it out. It may be uncomfortable at first, but they will get used to it. Later on, you may decide to use one that attaches to their costume. Now back to walking.

I want you to stop and remove the reins and attach a five foot lunging line to the right side of the bit. Instead of being next to them, you will be to their side when they move. Start by walking. This is the same as before. This action is always slow. We will change to a canter. This is kind of like skipping. Fine, they are doing fine. Step up the canter to a trot. This is a run and we don't want it too fast for now. If the ponies are enjoying it, I want to hear a whinny from you. All came back with a loud whinny and continued.

Have your pony walk back to the table for an additional piece of gear. Many owners like to have their ponies with their hands and arms behind them. We will use an arm binder to encase the arms and hands. They come in both buckle types and full lace ups. The lace ups can be pulled tighter and will cause some pain for prolong periods of time.

Since our time is limited, we will use buckle up ones. Have your pony place their arms behind them and hold hands. Run the sleeve up their arms until the top touches just below the neck. Place the straps around the shoulders and chinch them tight. Now, start at the hands and buckle each set up to the shoulders. Fine, you now have more control of them. Back to the ring and have them go through walking, cantering and trotting again. This will be much more difficult than without the arm binder.

Are you having fun yet? A series of whiney was heard as well as Oh yes from the owners. You can continue for a few more minutes and than it will be time to put them up for lunch. Prior to taking them back to their cells, a good owner has to rub them down and wipe them down. It may also be a great time to thank them for their ride and performance.

A cuddle and maybe a small piece of candy go far also. This done and the slaves back in chains, the group went up to lunch. We need to be back by one to get a full four hours of play in. While at lunch, you need to think of some idea of what your want to put your slave through. The only thing that is out is more grape crushing. We did not get any more in this morning.

The group returned from lunch. They were met by Frieda and told to get their clothes changed and have their slave sitting against the rear wall in the play room. They quickly changed and retrieved their slave and walked them to the play room. Ilsa walked to the group and spoke to them.

This afternoon is the final part of this training program. I asked the Dominates to consider what they wanted to do the last several hours today. I would suggest that you also take input from your slave so the both of you can do exciting things.

Anna spoke up first. Michael and I want to continue to do pony play. Christian came next. Roxie and I want to spend the afternoon going through costume room and try on the many outfits. Hans was next and said he wanted to put Wilma in the OBGYN chair and work on her. Well, that leaves you Belinda, what do you and Wilma wish to try. I took you suggestion and want the block table and the cart of heavy duty tools. These are all very good choices. Except for Christian and Roxie, each of the pairs of you will have one of us to help you along in your play.

These will be the team assignments. Helma, you are to work with Mistress Anna on pony play. Frieda, you will go with Master Hans and the OBGYN chair. I will work with Mistress Belinda and the block table. As for you Master Christian and Roxie, I will come in and get you started and than return to the block table. Let us start and get the most out of the afternoon.

Mistress Anna took Michael to the table and selected different pieces of tack. Helma made suggestions as to how to change up the pieces and looks. Anna selected a studded pony head gear. The bit gag was placed in the mouth and buckled in the rear. Blinders were set in place for the games. She told Michael to place his hands together and prepare to receive the arm binder. This time a lace up binder was slipped on and attached around his shoulders. The laces were beginning to be pulled up slowly, taking out the slack and causing him some discomfort. Helma than told Michael at accept it and enjoy the pressure on his arms and shoulders.

Let me show you a more fun way to place the tail in place. Helma led Michael over to a waiting rope and hook which hung down from the ceiling. She attached the hook to the "D" ring at his hands and pulled his arms up tightly and bending him over. Now spread your legs pony. Christian did as he was ordered. Anna went to the table selected the plug tail for this play. She placed a little water based jell and than pushed it in. He whinnied and stomped his feet as the tail hit bottom in his ass. Anna, I want you to chose a six foot lunge lead and attach it to the left side of his bit.

Helma went to the storage closet selected jumping rails in several heights. I am going to set them up in a line against the far wall. I want you to bring your pony to the far end and get ready. Anna walked her pony down and waited for further instructions.

Helma stood next to Anna and told her this is how it works. I want you to slowly walk up to the first rails, have him jump over and than approach the second and than the third. The first rail is six inches above the floor. The second is twelve and the third is eighteen inch. I want you to go slow and build confidence until you can do it at a slow run. This will build a large trust factor between the two of you.

Anna brought Michael to the first rail and he jumped it with ease. They walked to the second one and he stepped/jumped over the second one. The third one took a little more thought and drew a little more caution, but he did jump over it. Helma told Anna to continue this until she had it down.

Ilsa turned to Belinda and told her to get Wilma secured to the block while she went to the costume room. Christian and Roxie were already trying on the many items. What a wonderful selection your have already made. As you can see, there are so many types of clothing you can wear in a scene or to go to a party.

If you find items you like and wish to have sets of them, place the number, size and colors on this order form. We will forward it to the venders we use and they will contact you with costs and options. From there, you can purchase what you want or they can send you catalogs to use. These venders are top of the line quality suppliers and can be trusted.

Frieda was with Hans as he had Wilma get into the OBGYN chair. I want you to get her secured in as you did the first day. He assisted her in getting her feet and legs into the stirrups and strapped into place. I want to place a full hood on her. Frieda went to the storage room and selected one. Hans slowly pulled it over her head and laced it tightly to her head. I choose not to use a blindfold and gag so I can see her eyes and hear her. Question, what if she screams loudly?

There is no problem as this is the upper level of an old castle and no one has ever been heard before. Hans helped her lay back in the chair and placed the two leather belts around her. You see slave, you are now tightly bond in place. With her head in the head rest, he strapped her tightly in place. This is how I want to play with you in the future slave. Do you enjoy the no wiggle feeling of this scene so far? In a soft voice, she said it was a great feeling and to please use her in any way he wanted.

Ilsa returned from the costume room and checked in on Belinda's progress. I can see you paid attention yesterday. Before we go any further, check that you slave can breath smoothly. She did and went to her head. I want to blindfold her and place a large penis gag in her mouth. I don't want to hear any screams or begging. As yesterday, Belinda took the gag, worked it up inside of herself and than placed it in the mouth of her slave. The slave made the sound of approval and sucked hard.

The shelf was pulled out and her head was tightly bond. Belinda stood back and said I want to check to see how well she is secured to the table. Lisa suggested that a good test was to take her nipples in her fingers, squeeze them tight and twist hard. Wilma squirmed on the block as best she could, but no movement was detected. Belinda, you did a great job.

Ilsa took Belinda aside and asked if she remembered what was done to her? She shook her head yes and Ilsa said, go ahead and get the clothes pins and string. Go ahead and place as many pins as you can around the base of her breasts. You tie the string to the first one and than just make sure the string goes through each of the rest. With the size of her nipples, I would use at least five or more to circle them. Go ahead and finish both breasts and than do the same to her labia. I am going to stand back and watch as you are doing a good job. Belinda went about her job with zeal.

Hans turned to Frieda and asked for suggestion as to where to start. Well, since this is an OBGYN chair, I think that you should do an internal inspection on her. They both went to the rolling cabinet and selected a medium size Collins speculum. There are several makers, but I like this one best as you can get into the area and explore better. I will show you how to insert it and you can do the work. As long as you take it slow at first, you won't do much of any damage. Unless you want to shock her, I suggest that you rub it between your hands and warm it up.

He did this and approached Lynn. Now slide it in between her puss lips and down to the base of the instrument. I think the most fun is to open it very slowly. For a woman, this procedure is normally very humiliating. Also, if you know medieval history, they used an instrument like this. It was called the Pear of Anguish. Once inserted, it was opened, causing the tender skin inside the person to expand and rip and tear. You can tell that she is being interrogated as a witch and you are using one.

Anna had Michael kind of skipping and running over the rails. Helma asked her if she was having fun yet and she said yes. Now we ask the pony. Michael turned his head, shook it yes and whinnied. See, he likes the challenge of being a pony. I think you found a fun way to play.

Let me take the rails down and I will come back with some traffic cones. Helma set the cone up in a zigzag pattern. I want you to run him through it and increase speed as you go through each time. She did and both Owner and pony looked very professional. With each complete trip, a loud whinny was heard from Michael.

Hans turned to Frieda and said this is fun and enjoy it very much. Remember, until she knows your skills better, you need to check in with her. He went to her head and asked her if she was ok. She answered that it was a great feeling and to proceed.

Frieda and Hans went to the cabinet and opened a drawer of medical instruments. Frieda pointed to several items and they returned to the speculum opened area. I want you to take the pointed probe and just lightly press the point around inside of her. With each touch, she both made a small twitch of her bottom and also a shy of joy.

Now try the tissue forceps. He picked them up and she told him to start to pinch little parts of the internal skin. The points on the ends of the forceps took hold of skin flaps and as he closed them, he lightly pulled them outward.

The sounds of joy came with each pull and a little bit of cum started. Unless you want a full blown orgasm, move the pinches around. He did and drove her mad wanting to have the big one. Last, before we give her a rest is the Warrensburg wheel.

Take the small wheel with the many teeth on it and roll it around her insides. Lynn was going wild by now. I suggest that you go up and cuddle her some; he did and she loved him so much.

Belinda was brushing the clothes pins back and forth on the zipper line. She looked at Ilsa and said it was time to pull them off. Ilsa asked her if she was going to pull slow or fast. I am going to go very slow, one by one on her pussy lips and than rip fast on her breasts. Ilsa motioned to wait for one minute while she called for total silence in the play room. The room went totally dead and Ilsa gave the go ahead. Belinda went slowly on her pussy lips bringing a low moan and than the big rip on her breasts.

Clothes pins went flying and a scream that woke the dead came from the gagged mouth of Wilma. Applause came from the other

Dominates. To bring things to a head, Belinda began to pinch up the skin that only a minute before held the pins. The skin was red and extremely painful. She climbed on top of the blond body and rubbed her body on top of the slave.

Hans picked up a wide tip crop and was beginning a pattern of strikes on Lynn's breasts and nipples. She squirmed and moaned out load. The strikes continued going between her breast meat and the nipples. The speculum she still had in place was working its way in and out with each swat. Frieda turned and told him to start to tap around the opening and even tap the tool itself. She was being driven wild with desire to cum.

Hans took the tip of his finger and started to message the swollen clit. The results were instant. She shot her orgasm almost eighteen inches from her body, again and again. After maybe five large loads, Lynn dropped off into a trance type sleep. I think she is spent for now and needs some rest and a kiss, which Hans was already doing.

Ilsa asked Belinda if Wilma was slow at orgasms or not? Belinda answered that it sometime took a lot of play to bring her to one. Do you want to give her a great big stimulation? Yes, what do you suggest? Go to the bottom drawer and let's get some electric play items. The bottom drawer contained several conductive dildos and anal plugs.

Select the ones you think she can be fitted with and bring the E-stimulation box and wires. Place the connectors from the wire attached to the E-stimulation box to the ones on the plug and dildo. The dildo is an inflatable item and should be placed in first. Belinda pushed the rubber balloon item into her vaginal cannel till it seated itself deep inside. Now pump it up till it is tight. With each pump of the inflator, both pleasure as well as discomfort was felt by Wilma. You can either place the plug in place with just lubricate jell or we can add a little more sting to it.

Ilsa handed her several crushed Habanero peppers in a bowl. Just coat the tip of the plug with jell and than roll it around in the peppers. Do I want to put it in fast or work it around slowly? Ilsa looked toward her and said your choice. Belinda thought for a minute and worked the plug in and out, twisting it as she went. Wilma's anal shaft began to burn from the chemical action of the peppers. She tried to bring her rump straight off the bench.

I like the effect it is causing her. Now taking the box and reading the instructions, a medium intensity setting was chosen. The setting knob set the duration and how often it would spark. She set it to be an ever changing mixture. That should set her in motion I think. With that, Belinda flipped the switch on the box to set the fun in motion. A little shock followed by a large one, short relaxations periods and than several shocks, one after another.

This was all too much for both Belinda as well as Wilma. Belinda took the straps from her head, removed the blindfold and the gag and slid the shelf from under her head back into the table. Wilma's head was now moving up and down and all around. Belinda dropped her head next to Wilma's ear and whispered that she needed to be serviced. Between the pulses of electric shock and the burning, Wilma shook her head and Belinda mounted her mouth.

Both of her hands grabbed the long flowing hair of Wilma and gave her much encouragement to lick and suck hard. The oral went on for maybe ten minutes when both the women exploded into intense orgasm. White cum dripped down the sides of Wilma's face as Belinda moved to place her lips on the hard, red tips of Wilma's nipples.

The action of Wilma's body continued until she was becoming numb to the shocks. Ilsa suggested that she was shot and done for the day. Belinda agreed and turned the E-box off, released the air in the dildo and removed it and the anal plug. Wilma was covered in sweat and was purring like a cat in heat.

Both Belinda and Hans decided it was time to release their slaves from their position. Ilsa said it was time to get ready to go up anyway. Very slowly the arms and legs of Wilma and Lynn were released. They went limp and remained at their sides. The large belts came next. Ilsa told both not to let them move for a few minutes, just cuddle them and provide a blanket for warmth. She also had the table pulled back out to support the head of Wilma.

Helma was helping to remove the tack from Michael and place his horse blanket on. She handed Anna a brush and told her to rub down her pony. She did and many whinnies were heard. Helma said a girl and her pony, a great sight to behold by all. By this time, even Christian and Roxie had gone through every one of the many costumes and accessories in the dressing room.

With Frieda and Helma watching the slaves as they recover, she called all the Dominates to the center of the play room. Over the next hour, I want each of you to escort your slave into our office and let them have a hot shower and put on the clothes they came in. It took almost an hour to get all moving and showered, but the slaves looked refreshed and a little bewildered. They wondered if they had done something wrong.

With the showers done and getting dressed completed, Ilsa had the group reassemble in the play room. Today is the last day of your formal training. For tonight and tomorrow, you are on your own. I expect the Dominated to take your slaves back to your room and help them with a hot bath and lots of cuddling. You all have been a good group and now better understand the Master/Mistress and slave rolls. I hope that you better understand the service, pain and loving sides of the lifestyle relationship.

Tomorrow, I think you should reflect on what we introduced you to and how to build on it. Sometime tomorrow, Wolfgang will gather you together and give you an out briefing. Remember and make sure your slaves understand that they are not to talk about this other than in your rooms. I will take you to your room and we will all meet you in the dining room for supper. For you slaves, I am sorry, but dog food is not on the menu. All four slaves laughed.

All went to their room, bathed and preceded to the Dining room. A large table for twelve was ready for them in the rear corner of the dining room. Ilsa, Frieda and Helma were seated at the head of the table. For all of you that have been on a limited diet for the last several days, I think you will find some great dining tonight.

I checked up on the deck on the sixth floor and the evening is cool and the sky is cloudless. I suggest that you all go up and just enjoy each other's company and reflect. You can stay up there as long as you wish and both the snack bar as well as the regular bar will be open till midnight. Tomorrow, you can do as you wish and enjoy the recreation areas. All ate well and the three trainers retired to their rooms.

Their last day went fast for some as well as very slowly for others. Swimming, tanning, horse back riding filled the day. A little after the lunch hour was finished, Wolfgang gathered them in their room. I hope that your experience here in the introduction training went well and all had fun. I know it was hard for all, but also refreshing.

You were shown a good beginning to this life style and remember we are here to help you expand the experience at a later date. We office many different programs to delve into, including a great Medieval tour or even an extreme slave training program to try. All you have to do is call and we will send you details. Enjoy the rest of the day and be ready as Peter will be taking you to the Airport in the morning.

The day turned to evening and than the last night came. All slept good and at six, a wakeup call woke them. They had their last breakfast and than packed. Wolfgang met them in their room and took them to the lobby. Ilsa, Frieda and Helma were on hand to wish them good bye and they loaded on the tram for the trip to the ground. Peter was waiting with the Limo and got them seated.

The trip back to the Dresden airport was a cheerful and somewhat sad moment. They arrived at the private gate as flight 603 was arriving. Peter shook hands and wished them well and thank you for visiting. They boarded the plane and it took off shortly afterward. Peter returned to the Chalet and got ready for the next group of visitors.

Wolfgang invited the three into his office. A bottle of wine was opened and all raised a glass. He asked the women how the week went. Ilsa answered that all had a good time and she thought that most if not all would be returning soon. I even think that Mistress Belinda will be coming back to experience the extreme slave package for herself. She is a natural Switch and pain slut if I have ever seen one, except for maybe Helma. They all laughed and Wolfgang dismissed them to go ready the play room as another group would be arriving in three day. Wolfgang said a job well done by all.

CHALET MEDIEVAL

I lsa and Frieda sat in their living area discussing what to do with the beautiful day at the Chalet. I think we should spend the morning at the pool and the afternoon on the sixth floor sunning in the sandy area. It has been a long month with the several different play scenes we had to put together. What do you think Helma? You need to get out of the living area and away from the computer.

I have a little more research to do on a personnel project. Frieda asked what are you researching. I have been working on a special project for myself at this time. It must be special as you won't even let us see. Are you going on vacation or a trip? No, but I will let you know, maybe by the end of the day. Go and enjoy yourselves and I will join you later.

At that moment, Helma's phone rang. Doctor Jones, can I help you? Doctor Jones this is your Paramedic Dave. What can I do for you Dave? I need you down at your office. What kind of problem do I have waiting? Two are simple ones and one that need stitches. OK, make everyone comfortable and stop the bleeding. They are and I have placed a pressure dressing on it. Great, I will be there in ten minutes.

Helma walked into her office, looked between the three people and made her way to Dave. OK Dave, where do you suggest that I start. One has tennis elbow, the second fell of a horse and has a sore rump and third is a cook's helper with a cut leg. Take the one with the tennis elbow and get her into x-ray and shoot a set for me to look at. Do you think the one that fell off the horse is bad? No he hurt his feelings, not his rump, but the stable was just worried. As for the cook's helper, you need to see her wound. Where is she waiting? I had her go to the casting room and had her take off her pants and placed a dressing on it for her to hold. Great work, I will go to the casting room.

Good morning, I am Doctor Jones. The woman on the casting table was looking sad and in some pain, pointed to the bandage on her lower leg. She took her hand off the bandage and some blood trickled down her leg. Wow, that is a nasty looking cut, how did it happen? I was slicing some vegetables for the dinner meal and the knife slipped out of my hand. I tried to get out of the way, but didn't make it. The worst thing is that I almost broke the tip off my new knife.

Let me take a look and we can see how bad it is. I got on my rolling stool and put her foot on my knee. I see you did a good job of cutting it up, I hope the vegetables faired better. They both laughed. Is it serious? No, but I well need to place several sutures in it. Is it going to hurt, Doctor Jones responded only if you want it too? I am going to have Dave scrub it up and prep it for sewing. I will have him give you a shot to help deaden it up. I will be back in fifteen minutes when the shot takes effect. Thank you Doctor.

I went to Dave and told him what I wanted him to do. He told me that the x-rays were clear, but she was in a little pain. I walked into the exam room and greeted her. The woman said she was in some pain and asked if she was in bad trouble. I told her no and took a look at the x-rays myself. I walked her over to the light box which held them and showed her that nothing was broken.

I believe that you went after a ball the wrong way. You have a light sprain or tennis elbow. I am going to have Dave put your arm in a sling and I will order you some pain medication. You need to stay away from the tennis court for two days and come back on Thursday morning so we can look at it again. If it swells or turns blue, have the front desk call me and I will look at it right away. Thank you Doctor.

Dave, I need a sling for the tennis elbow and some low strength pain meds, you know the ones I mean. I will check on the man with the horse problem and than go and stitch up our cook. When you finish the tennis elbow, have him go to the exam room, strip and lay down on the exam table. Will do Doc.

The cut isn't as bad as it looked before. I went to the casting room and spread the wound open a little to check its depth. How are you feeling now that Dave gave you a shot? It is still a little sore, but I feel much better. We can't have that, so I will just have to cut it off. The cook looked at me and I said that I just wanted to make her a little more relaxed. She understood and joined in laughing.

Just lay back and I will have to put maybe six stitches in it. I took out a set of surgical gloves and called Dave in to assist. I will need some silk sutures from the cabinet and a suture set. I went to work and make six of the prettiest little loops and knots I have in a while. Sorry, but I will need to pull the last one a little tighter, hold on. She did and I closed it all nice. Dave will finish by bandaging it up and give you another shot for tetanus.

You are to stay off of it for two days and keep your leg dry and elevated. I want you to come back Friday before your shift and I will check it out and remove the stitches. Dave, have someone from the kitchen bring her personnel items down and get her home. I will let the chief know you are OK.

Now, I am on my way to John Wayne. Well sir, did the Indians win or did you get away. I am sorry Doctor, but the rules said I had to come see you. I know I wrote the rules and am glad to see you here. Not often do I get to see such a handsome man on my exam table.

Just tell me how it happened and where the pain is. I guess I missed the saddle when I through my leg up and spooked the horse. I don't think I was more than two or three feet off the ground when I missed and fell on my butt.

I see and what a beautiful butt it is. I ran my hand over the affected area. I see that you winched a little. Was it a sharp pain or just my cold hand? Doctor, you are wonderful, you made the pain go away. Thank you but I need to do some pinching and feel around for any indication of broken bones.

I don't feel anything and it is only a little black and blue. How do you feel now? I'm not sure, I think you need to run your hands over it again, and maybe a little bit further up. Sure will and run my hand up and this time bumped into his cock and balls.

Must have been the cure he was looking for as he sat straight up and kissed me. I think you are going to be OK. I will give you a day's supply of muscle relaxers, a days pain killers and see you in two days. If the pain continuers, have the desk call me and I will pat it again and make it better. I do think you should stay off the horse for a day. Thanks Doc, you are great and thanks for the understanding. I have watched you in the pool for a day or two and wanted to meet you. Great, now get out of here.

Once all the patients left, Dave cleaned up the casting room and the examination room. Dave said it looks like we made it through another set of dire emergencies today. You are correct and that is more than enough for today as I have some more research to do.

Helma walked down the hall to her room. I think I will change into my bathing suit, do some swimming and maybe get a little tanned up on six. She changed and made her way to the Chalet pool. I feel like doing maybe ten laps in the computation pool. She found a free lane and dove in. She swam back and forth till the last lap was finished. Placing a towel around herself, she made her way to the sixth floor, placed the towel on the sandy beach area, place a wide brim hat on her head to cover her eyes and drifted off.

Helma did a lot of day dreaming for the next hour. It has been so busy the last several weeks and more packages to come. I need to relax and also more research on my personnel project. I will go down to the play room after dinner to relax and think.

Helma joined Ilsa and Frieda in the dining room. They already were seated at their normal table in the staff dining area. Ilsa asked Helma what happened to her during the day. I answered the phone right after you left, the Titanic came in and the emergencies just floated into my office. Wow, anything very bad? No, but I hope we don't get any of the poor vegetables we get tonight aren't from the cook's helper I had to sew up after she cut her leg, don't ask.

They enjoyed the meal and went back to the room. So Helma, what are you going to do tonight? I am going to work on some more research and do a little relaxing in the play room. Do you want any company or is this personnel research? No, I just want to think and do some day dreaming. OK Helma, just don't get too tied up, HA, HA.

Helma didn't even change, just got on the elevator and went down to the play room level. I think I need to check out the medieval toys in the storage room. She opened the door and turned on the low lights and stripped naked. Scanning the room, she went from one torturous item to the left. What am I looking for? She started by jumping up on the rack. She slipped the ropes around her ankles and lay back.

Shutting her eyes, she imagined herself being stretched limb from limb. This is great but I need something a little more challenging. Releasing myself, I moved to the spiked chair. She thought back to the day she was placed on the stiff rubber spikes and was tied in. Both Ilsa and Frieda made it seem so real during the Extreme Slave Package, I felt like I was being interrogated for being a witch.

To complete her fun for the evening, she went to the toy cabinet, took out a spiked dildo, mounted it to the top rail of the Spanish horse, picked up a hand held veterinary cattle prod and mounted the dildo. She let the dildo slid up into her so slowly.

Once it was all the way up, almost eight inches inside her, she closed her eves and placed the cattle prod to her pussy lips. She squeezed the trigger time after time till she was having orgasms as often as she could recoup. After maybe ten orgasms, she stopped, got off and than cleaned and returned the items to their storage areas. I think I have enough information to go to Wolfgang, but better pass it by the Ilsa and Frieda first.

I returned back at the room about the same time that they did. Ilsa, Frieda, I want to talk with you. OK, but let us go to our rooms, get naked and return to the living area. They each ducked into their bedrooms and reappeared bear and looking great. Well Helma, what do you want to talk about? As you know, I have been doing a lot of research over the last week or so.

What I was doing was to get information on the medieval days. Frieda asked, are you that old or just like the period? I just got to thinking about the vast store of medieval toys in the play room. I want to propose to Wolfgang that we do a Chalet wide medieval week long fest.

What do you think of the idea? Ilsa answered it sounds different and interesting. Great, I think I will go and ask for time to talk to Wolfgang tomorrow. Hope he at least listens to me. He will if you can show him he can make lots of money. Now let's cuddle up and enjoy.

The three cuddled and kissed for a good part of the evening. Hands roamed and so did the mouths of each other. All did oral on each other and by the end of the evening, all were worn out. They just dropped off to sleep where they were.

Morning came and the three went to breakfast. On the way back to their living area, Helma broke away and stepped into Wolfgang's office. The secretary greeted her and asked, Doctor Jones, what can I do for you? I answered by asking if I could get to see Wolfgang for a few minutes today. She answered, let me see. She walked to the door, knocked and entered. Wolfgang, Doctor Jones would like a few minutes if you have the time. Sure, show her in. I entered his office and she left. Doctor Jones, please have a seat. I did and he asked if there was a problem.

No Sir, things are going great. I just wanted to shot an idea past you. OK, I am all ears for you. Over the last week, I have been doing some research on a theme for an event for the Chalet. First, we have all that medieval equipment in the play room which almost never gets the light of day.

What I propose is that we put together a medieval week in the whole Chalet. What I mean is it would be a mix between an October fest and Halloween party. We could have both Vanilla events in the upper area as well as a torture style event for four to six slaves/prisoners in the lower area.

I like the idea, but how much will it cost us? I don't know if it would be cheaper to have someone come in and cater the entire event or secure the items and have them for recurring events. Helma, I can see you have done a good deal of research on the subject.

Give me some of the ideas you came up with. I think it would start with a carriage footman at the drop off point, make the tram operator a draw bridge operator, the front desk man as an innkeeper. You would not have to change the dining schedule till the Dinner meal. We would have to get other entertainers which we could get locally from the guilds.

I need some idea of the cost before I go to Carl with the package. What can I do for you to get you started? If you could call the dining manager and get me some time with him, it will help. I will call him and you should be able to get with him this morning. Helma, you know that I am not going to pay you extra as a party planner. I have my own ideas which I will enjoy during this event. I bet you do and I can hardly wait to hear them. I will be on my way and thank you My Lord. That will be enough for now Helma.

I made my way up to the Dining room Manager's office. I knocked and he told me to come in. So Doctor Jones, what can I do for you? I was pitching an idea to Wolfgang for a week long medieval event. Sounds good, but what do you need from me. I need to know what the difference in cost for the meal.

We could use the same menu for breakfast and lunch, but it would be a full banquet setting for dinner. I have a sample menu for the evening feast. You know the event favorites like turkey legs, sides of ham and beef as well as a roast pig on Saturday night. Are you talking to bring it out here and cut it in front of the people? Yes and have your serving wenches take it to the people. I think that we could have the tables in a "U" setup.

Just off hand, I don't see more than maybe a thousand dollars more a day. What about table clothes and eating wear? I am working on that, except that we would have to get tankards to serve drinks. Boy, you are getting into this aren't you? I have been researching it for a few weeks. I have heard that you have been talking about new tables and chairs for the dining room. I want to buy heavy wooden tables to use everyday.

You know Doctor Jones, I have done several of these before, not here, but you have thought of the many things involved. I will get a list of most items we need and have it to you in several days. By the way, thanks for fixing up my cooks helper. My pleasure and thanks for the help.

Helma now went to the maintenance director. I knocked on the door and from inside, was told to enter. Good morning, I need your help. Doctor Jones is there something wrong with your office. I said no, but I need some information for a project I am working on. Sure, what do you need?

I am doing some research for an upcoming event. It will be a medieval style event and will be mostly on the fifth floor. Could your people easily change the wall light fixtures to medieval styles and than back and how much time would you need? Is the fifth floor the only area? No, the other areas would be the main entrance, the front desk and maybe the connecting halls and even the chandelier in the dining room.

No problem, maybe two days at the most. We would also need an area for a bond fire near the pool area and an area for standing pillory stocks and a prisoner holding area. I don't think maybe a few days extra if we can work around the normal crowd. Wonderful, I will put it in writing and get it to you in a day or so.

I was beside myself with the progress I had made today. Everyone was so cooperative with me. I need to go back to my computer, search for many of the items and print out the information on them. So much work to do and no time left.

As I entered the room, Frieda was sitting on the couch watching a movie. She said you have been a busy little beaver today. Yes I have and the day is still early. If you don't mind, I am gong to get into something comfortable and continue to work. I selected a light green, short sleeve spandex leotard. I know it will make me feel great and I know you enjoy watching me in it. Frieda nodded yes and went back to her movie.

Day led to evening and than into the night. I must have gone through two reams of paper and lots of toner. I spread the different categories of items around the living room. Slowly, I assembled them into packages and placed them into folders. I wasn't going to give Wolfgang any excuse not to take it to Carl. Ilsa returned to the room and commented on my outfit as well as the mess in the room. I think you have created a monster of this event.

Information Is In

Helma was just finishing her breakfast when the Dining Room Manager came over to her table. Doctor Jones, do you have a minute to talk. I said yes and we each got an additional cup of coffee. Sorry it has taken several days to get the information together you requested. No problem, are we on tract with the event. Yes, the numbers I have provided you will show several things.

First, only changing the Dinner meal will cost maybe two thousand dollars a day for the meals. We would have to put on several more cook helpers and servers for the week. We already have outfits for the servers and bartenders so a change is no problem, except for the cost of them.

As for the dining room furniture, you were right. I was going to ask Carl for funds to replace the tables, chairs and linen, and some of the plates and order tankards. Your idea for a heavy duty wooden table with chairs will add atmosphere to the normal dining. I love the pictures of the type of tables, but would ask you do not get chairs with cloth coverings. Spills would make a mess of them.

I also did some research on the fabric drapes and bunting to adorn the walls. I heard from the Maintenance supervisor that you want to change the lights. Yes, I found many different types which fit the medieval design. The change would only be for the dining area and not the lounge and dancing areas. I think these areas can stay with the common theme we now have. Doctor, what about a castle crest? I have to check with Wolfgang to see if we already have one or else.

Do you have any objections on the entertainment I listed? The jester, pickpocket, jugglers, and even a taro card reader will add to the medieval atmosphere. I know we can get most of these people from the surrounding area theater guilds.

As for the harpsichord and player, that might be a little harder to get. I will work on these people along with the jousting events. Don't worry, that will be in the back yard, not in the dining room. Will we or you have a problem if I place a chained villager up here? She would be a villager that tried to over throw the king. I don't think it will be as long as Carl doesn't think it will.

When do you think you will present the package to Carl? I am planning on it by Friday. I need to practice my pitch for the event. I can show him we will make money and keep them coming back. Good luck and let me know as soon as you can. I will get back either way and let you know.

I left the dining room and went to find the maintenance manager. He was roaming the halls checking on the carpets. Good morning sir. What have you done with the information I supplied to you? I looked it over and talked to my maintenance people. They all said it would be fun and it could be done in a mater of maybe three days. As for the manufacture of the village square and hand and foot stocks, just give us drawings and I can start the work on it.

I decided to go back to the room and finalize the information I had received from the Chalet Managers. Ilsa and Frieda walked into the room and asked if I was getting it ready. I said I was putting the finishing touches on it and was glad. I can't even begin to estimate how many trees I had to cut down to do all the copying.

I have put three binders together, one for Carl, one for Wolfgang and one for the two of you. I hope that you take the time to review it. They each agreed and made their way to their bedrooms. I worked through the afternoon assembling the binders. They sure looked good.

First thing in the morning, I went to Wolfgang's office. His secretary asked if she could help me. I said that I had these binders for him. She took them and I was told he would call me if he had questions. I decided to go to my Doctor's office to check on the supplies.

Dave was inside reading a medical journal or was it a girly magazine on anatomy? How are things going in the office today? Dave answered he had cleared the cook's leg and removed the stitches and re bandaged her leg. She healed nicely and I cleared her for work in the morning. The only other thing was the man that fell off the horse. He wanted to know if you might want to feel his sore ass again. I think he has a crush on you Doc.

Dave, I have a question for you. OK Doc., shoot. Do you think you can run the office by yourself? Sure, but are you telling me you are leaving? No, we might have an event in the Chalet that will take all my time for a week. I will be available if we have a dire emergency. I have been watching your work and am very excited about your progress. I don't think I ever had a nurse as good as you and the work you do. I am going to my room and relax before lunch. Have a great day Doc.

I was just finishing my lunch when Wolfgang caught up with me. He leaned over my shoulder and told me to be in his office by two and be in nice business attire. I said I would be there and asked if I was in trouble? No, just be there.

I arrived at fifteen minutes till two. The secretary said to knock and go in to his office. Sir, how can I help you? You started this package and you are going with me to see Carl in a half hour. Are you ready to answer question? Sir, I have been going over the material and proposal for maybe a month. They left the office and went to the elevator to go to the fifth floor office/suite of Carl Schmidt.

Wolfgang walked to the door and knocked. Carl said to enter and we did. He was standing by the window and welcomed us in. Come over to my desk and have a seat. The copy of the proposal was lying open on his desk where he had been reading it. So Doctor Jones, I can see you have spent a considerable amount of time in this. Yes sir I did. I hope it didn't cut into any of your other duties. No Sir, it was all on my down time.

First, I have some questions for you to answer. What brought the idea of a medieval event at the Chalet about? Sir, I kept looking at the many pieces of equipment in the play room storage room. I asked and was told that it hadn't been used for a package in years and I felt it needed to be incorporated into an event. Doctor, I see you have done a considerable amount of research on what will need to be done. Yes Sir, as you can see, I even priced it out wither you rent the items or buy them outright.

You came up with a number of around $300,000 for us to own it and have some outsourced items. Yes Sir, but if you see the bottom line, 64 rooms with only one person in a bedroom at $35,000 instead of the normal $30,000 for a normal week, brings in around in an additions $640,000 for the week. This doesn't even account for the four or five

Owners and prisoners in the lifestyle section. We should be able to bring in another $80.000 for four prisoners.

I see you have done your homework on this project. I believe that I have covered most if not all the bases Sir. Wolfgang, what are you likes or concerns on this program? I think it will be fun, but some work. As you can see, we will need maybe a week closure to be ready, but if done right, we could have them maybe twice or three times a year. As for the cost, most items are one time buys and than put away. Just think of the publicity we can get and bring in many new clients.

Doctor Jones, I see you have cost it out and the profits will pay for it self. What do you want to get out of it? Sir, what I want to receive is the fact I would be the woman from the village being accused of trying to kill the King. This is why I wanted a Hollywood makeup artist. I would be in costume, a slightly torn peasant outfit, with welts, black and blue marks all over my body.

I could be led around the Chalet in chains and an iron ball and staked out in the town square. Either Ilsa or Frieda could flog or whip me every so often, and when not there, I would be in the cell area with the other prisoners.

I even thought that the prisoners could be placed in the stocks in the square. I would insist that they be somewhat experienced slaves and their owners agree. With the theme week, it would fit in and they would enjoy the experience.

Wolfgang, I am going to release the three hundred thousand dollars to get started. I want both you and Doctor Jones to give me weekly updates and I want a date for the event by the end of the month. I will give orders for the Department Managers to cooperate to the fullest.

Before you leave, I want to know one thing. Just who do you have in mind to be the King for the final night's event? I answered that would be you Sir. King Carl the lionhearted. You will need to have a Queen. If you don't have a person in mind, you could have your waitress dress for the part. Doctor, I think you read my mind. What about Wolfgang? I have already called him "My Lord" and it struck a nerve. If I will be a King, than you can be a Lord. Now go out and get started.

Wolfgang and I went back to his office. As he walked in passed his secretary, he said to bring something hard to drink. She went to the cabinet and drew out a bottle of ten year old brandy and two glasses. Helma, have a seat in the comfortable chair and we need to celebrate. Helma, I have never seen Carl get so excited about a new program, much less turn loose that much cash at one time.

Wolfgang called his secretary and asked her to have John the purchasing manager come up immediately. It took ten minutes for John to knock on the door and be welcomed in. John, I am sure that you know Doctor Jones. Yes Sir, is there a problem? Yes and no. Have a seat and have a drink. He poured himself a brandy and had a seat. John, first of all, Carl has released $300,000 for a new program at the Chalet. Second, you and Helma are going too joined at the hip.

I don't understand Sir. Helma has made a proposal for a medieval fest at the Chalet. She will be giving you lists of pieces/parts to order, everything from light fixtures to dining tables. You will need to go to the Department Heads to finalize what items are needed. I believe the Dining area will get the largest share of the new items.

There are also items which will need to be made, and I think locally will be best. A small amount will be contracted out, as a jostling event. A what Sir? You know when two riders charge each other on horse back with poles. We will also be hiring many local actors and entertainers. The big thing is that Carl wants it to be an event quickly. You and Helma will sit down in the morning and get started.

Helma and John departed the office and agreed to meet in the staff dining room in the morning after breakfast. John said that he would make the calls to arrange the Dining Room and Maintenance Managers to join. Your job Helma is to have lots of coffee and Danish ready for the meeting. They both laughed and went their separate ways.

Helma returned to her room and changed into her set of leotards. She wanted to both relax as well as look sexy. She was enjoying her victory as well as prepare for the many hours of work to come. When Ilsa and Frieda returned from the days work, they saw her lounging on the couch and asked how it went.

Well, we are all going to be very busy in the future. Carl bought the entire package and released the money to start. I have appointments with the many Managers in the morning. I would like you to attend and have your input heard. I know that they only know of the Vanilla side of the event, but you will be deeply involved in it. We will also have to work out the lifestyle side.

The three put on something more formal and went to dinner. There was much small talk among them and even a quick visit with the others that had heard of the up coming event. Before they knew it, two hours had passed and dinner was over. Ilsa said we should celebrate this evening. Frieda turned to her and asked if she had anything in mind? Ilsa looked at Helma and told her to go to the play room and strip. We will join you in a few minutes.

Helma went to the room and got undressed. I wonder what they have in mind for me. As they walked in, they told Helma to go and get wrist and ankle shackles and stand facing out by the rings in the wall. She quickly did as she was told and knelt in front of the rings on the floor with her head down. Frieda placed her hand under her chin and instructed her to stand. Ilsa pushed her back to the wall and began to hook her up spread eagle. Frieda, I think we should start with a good whipping. They went to the cabinet and each selected a six foot bull whip.

They took turns letting their whip tip fall on Helma's body. The first blow was placed on her breast, one on her legs and than both on her pussy. Helma was now in seventh heaven and purring.

Ilsa asked if she was enjoying herself and the answer was a loud yes. This went on for several minutes till she was red all over. Frieda went to the cabinet and drew out two cattle prods. Ilsa said to do her in two different places at a time to confuse her. She was soon shaking as she withered under the shocks. I want to do something we haven't done to her in some time.

Ilsa took out a box of syringe needles. Where do you think we should start? I want to place some I her breasts first. Strips of ten needles were opened and each woman took a breast and stuck them in. Some were placed around the base and than some in the nipple.

By this time, Helma was enjoying herself so much. It is time to bring her to orgasm. They went to her labia and placed five in each of them. Both rubbed her clit and the white cream flowed. Helma was now crying in joy and was going limp where she hung. Frieda and Ilsa slowly removed the needles and little trickles of blood flowed down Helma's tender skin. They unhooked her from the wall, got her dressed and they all returned to the room for a hot bath and sleep.

The appointed time of the meeting of the minds arrived and each of the managers and Helma were seated in the main dining room. John started the conversation by saying: we have a bunch of work to do and no time to get it done. During the evening hours, John had made copies of Helma's proposal for each of the managers. It was time for input from each of them.

The Dinning room Manager started. I believe that I have the biggest portion of the ordering to do. The tables that Helma specified are great. Heavy wooden at eight foot long with eight chairs each. I will need sixteen to feed the one hundred twenty eight guests, plus at least four more for the head table and four extras. This is a total of twenty four.

These are catalog items and have a six week delivery time table. As for tankards, I need four hundred. Most of the rest of the items we have on hand, except for the sets of table clothes and napkins. There are also the decorations, wall hangings and several sets of crests, and costumes. I believe that the several clothing and drapery companies in the area will be able to fill them.

The maintenance manager confirmed that the lighting fixtures would be around four to six weeks to order. His men would be able to change them out in two days. John looked at Helma and told her that she needed to go into the town acting guild and discuss the entertainment needs. You may need to go to Berlin to get a quote on the jousting event. They can be housed in the stable and in town. As for the stocks and tent, we need to get bids from the local carpenter and Rental Company. These will be bought, but they can secure them for us.

John continued to get ideas and projects from each. From the looks of this, I think we can tell Wolfgang that it should be ready within ten to twelve weeks. This should bring us to around the second week in September, still warm, but with cooler evenings. I can just see sitting around the blazing fire and sipping ale and rum. Helma, you are also responsible for the lifestyle end of the week. Make sure that you have Ilsa and Frieda plan those events and decide on their costumes.

Coming Together

Days were turning into weeks. The items were slowly arriving and stored in the storages buildings. Everything was still on schedule. Helma and John were together more than they were doing their normal duties. John had invited Wolfgang and Carl to the storage building and showed many of the items such as the tables and light fixtures to them. Carl was very impressed with the progress and decided to change out the tables and light fixtures early as it was a converted medieval castle anyway.

The costume makers made several visits to get measurements from the staff for their clothes. The only one that couldn't make up his mind was Carl. He wasn't sure how long his robe should be and if his Queen should show a lot of cleavage or not.

These are the little problems and each fixed itself as they went along. Helma was working with the theater guild to recruit the need players. A Footman, a draw bridge man, guards, village peasants were just a few. They would each have to be trained as to their duties.

As for the house staff, their training went on daily. The bar and serving wenches each had three costume changes. Grounds keepers, cooks and the Chief all took turns doing their duties and learning to talk in the times of the 1400s pereiod.

It was all taking shape. Little by little the tables were in place, lighting fixture were hung as were the tapestries. Two of the coat of arms adorned each side of the lobby desk. Even a set of armor stood in the lobby. It was time to put out the word of the event.

Wolfgang brought in an advertising firm, photos were taken and brochures printed. The travel agents that handled the normal trips to the Chalet took reservations. The four weeks gave each guest time to get their costume ordered and altered. As for the lifestyle side, those reservations went as fast as they could be signed up for.

With four weeks till the event, all available space was filled. This made Carl very happy as well as Helma as she was sweating it not coming together well. Carl called a general meeting for those managers involved as well as Helma. He started out by saying how impressed he was with the way it was coming together. Having seen the final parts, I think I want to make this the every day affair.

We can take down the decorations between events, but the tables and lighting will stay. It adds so much to the atmosphere of the castle and will add to guests coming back. I was not sure that it could be done, but I want to personally thank you. I am authorizing a five thousand dollar bonus for each of you. One thing, I want a dress rehearsal the week prior to the opening event.

Helma, Ilsa and Frieda were requested at Wolfgang's office to talk over the lifestyle portion. They arrived and were seated. We are almost there and if I remember right, we do not have any programs until than. Ilsa opened her appointment/schedule book and said it was clear. Good, I want the three of you to set up the play room as a medieval dungeon. I will give you an extra ten thousand dollars to get decorations. You will have two weeks to get it together as Carl wants a tour. Ilsa assured him that it would be done.

The final inspection of the Chalet was today. The Managers, Wolfgang and the three women gathered in the dining room. Each went over their areas in detail. The dining manager started and showed how the tables were arranged in a big "U" with the head table in the center of the "U". Carl, are you going to officiate each night or just the last evening? I will do a walk through in costume daily, but I think my Lord Wolfgang will do the nightly meal. Don't worry; I got you a well built lady in waiting to be at your side.

The lighting came next. The chandeliers and the side wall lights came on. They had a look of having a flame in them and gave them a low light. This is great as you know how those Princes and ladies get frisky. They went to the main entrance and saw the decorations and crests. What a wonderful entrance you have created. There are big name hotels in Berlin that do not have such grander to them.

At this point they went to the rear of the Chalet. I see you have a quaint town square. The tent is a good addition to allow for sun or rain if it should get bad. No town square should be without its stocks and tether ring.

Helma, do we have actors for the stocks? In a way sir, I will be using the lifestyle guests to fill them during the day. They will be instructed as to what to and not to say and act. I believe that their owners can even flog them for entertainment.

We will have a soft deer skin flogger for them. As for the ring, I will be made up as village woman that had planned to overthrow you. This is where the makeup artist comes in. He will make it look like I have been to the dungeon for an interrogation. Bruises and welts will be covering me. I will be wearing a low cut peasant dress, ripped in the front with ample cleavage flowing out.

I see you have planned this out well. John, you and the two managers are finished here. The rest of us will go the play room. I want to see how you have it set up. They all boarded the elevator and went to the play room exit. As you can see Sir, we have it in subdued lights in the cell area.

As of right now, we have five prisoners to house till their turn in the dungeon. They will only be used outside during the afternoon. I will be outside on and off all day to entertain the guests. If you look over your shoulder and on the cabinets, you will find many hungry rats, all parched to attack. I had them made to look very real.

The prisoners will be held in a different way than we normally do. They will be shackled and chained in the front. Their arms and ankles are chained to each other and an iron ball attached to their ankles. We even got larger diameter chain than we normally use. A collar with a six foot section of chain will be attached to the wall.

I will be in the center space between them. I may be in chains or even the scavenger's daughter with a collar and chains; I will be working on their brains to get them into the mood. I figure that I can play a little crazy from being tortured for a long period of time. Wolfgang turned to me and said, a little crazy, when is this different than normal. All laughed.

The tour continued to the main room. Carl stated that he had forgotten how much medieval furniture we had. Yes sir. I have done a good deal of research into the medieval ways and have set it up this way. We have even added things to make it more real the last night. A fake fire pit and irons, a vat of bubbling tar which is really waxing solution at a low temperature and I even got a Pear of Anguish made. It is limited so it can't do any damage. Against the rear wall is a chair for the King, you Sir. We have made sound effects of persons screaming to play for the prisoners.

The plan is for the prisoners to be worked on each day after dinner. Their owners can come and do work on them. The largest part of the play will be during the last day they are here. We plan for it to be mild the first days with it getting more intense the last evening. As you know from the past, you know how much I enjoy being tortured. They can take turns on me and the last night you will order my demise in the iron maiden.

Well Helma, you have brought back many of my KGB memories. I may even get into the inquisition of you myself. Do you think you would enjoy that? Sir, I can hardly wait. I am sure the prisoners will be impressed. I think that you have gone all out and if it comes off as you planned, we may do this several times during the year. Thank you sir for your kind remarks and I will make the best entertainment you have seen.

The tour ended and Wolfgang and Carl departed. Ilsa turned to Helma and asked her if she know fully of Carl's past. We did much work with him and he is much worse than when you were here on the "TOY" package. You may regret wanting to be on the receiving end of his work. Helma answered, I hope so and am looking forward to it and remember, I am the Doctor and can fix myself. They closed up the play room and returned to their room to get ready for lunch.

Almost There

Carl called Wolfgang for a final report on the medieval fest. Wolfgang met him and they talked. Carl said I want to go to the sixth floor and look over the parapet at the goings on around the Chalet. As you can see, we set up a straw bail arena for the jousting events. The show will be arriving in the morning to practice. We decided to use straw bales for seating as this is the way it would have been in the olden time. It look so real I can almost see it for real myself.

The town square and tent were close to the other events. They did a great job of reproducing the head and hand stocks, pillory and the hitching post with ring. This is a great way to show the way it was back than. Next to come is the place where we will have nightly bon fires. Again, we have place straw bales for seating. There are also several areas with a place to get a tankard of ale or even brandy. Carl asked about night lighting. We have torches to light up the way and also some dark areas for those that want to make out. This is excellent.

Are we ready for a full run thru with costumes? Yes we are Carl. Tomorrow we will run thru it fully. Remember, the guests will start arriving in two days. With the sure number of them, it will take maybe six trips for Peter from the airport. What about the prisoners and their owners? They will come in later on a Sunday morning flight. I will brief them separately and they are on the first floor.

Friday morning came and the full staff along with those hired as extras and entertainers filled the dining room for inspection. Carl took charge himself. I want to welcome you to the Chalet medieval affair. Today will be a last minute inspection and to make any changes needed. He went from person to person looking at how the costumes fit. Next, he had them bow and welcome guests.

For those of you that are full time, I expect the best you have ever done and for those we brought in, remember, if it is a success, you will be back several times a year. The people you will be working for are for the most part well to do and had to shell out a lot of money for this event. They come from all over Europe and even a couple from the US. They speak many different languages and if you don't understand, excuse yourself and get one of the translators.

I want you all to take your places and get ready. Wolfgang, I am going out the back way where Peter is waiting with the Limo. Carl got himself seated in the back seat and indicated to Peter to go around. Peter drove to the main gate and stopped. The Footman opened the door and bowed and extended his hand. He led Carl to the tram car manned by the Draw bridge keeper. He escorted him into the car and took Carl up to the first floor. From there, he was escorted to the desk by a paige and the innkeeper greeted him. Lord Wolfgang greeted him and took him to his room. From there he went to the dining room and was seated. The serving wenches brought him empty plates of food and the entertainment went on.

Carl was impressed with the degree that every one worked so well together. He told Wolfgang that he was satisfied and it was a go in the morning. Wolfgang dismissed all the staff and told them to be here in costume by eight in the morning. The first guests would not arrive till around ten.

Guests Arrive

All the senior staff was up early and were finishing breakfast with Wolfgang. I want everyone at their top of their way. Everyone responsible for a section, make sure the costumes are straight and every one is ready. I am going to get my Lord outfit on and will be in the lobby. Helma, you had better get your makeup done even though the prisoners won't be here till tomorrow. Ilsa and Frieda, you get your guard/torturer outfits on. Just think you can wear your outfits on the main floor for a change.

Peter was just arriving at the Dresden private arrival and departure gate. He was driving the larger bus to be able to fit forty passengers at a time. He walked through the seating to check the snacks and wine they could snack on during the trip. He heard the announcement of the arrival and had the luggage rack at the entrance. The door to the plane opened and a set of stairs rolled up to it.

The stewardess began to motion the passengers down to the tarmac. Peter ushered them to the bus and got them comfortable on board. Using the intercom in the buss, he told them to enjoy the ride and that he would point out the surroundings.

He made good time and arrived a few minutes early. He made

a final announcement that their luggage would be brought to their rooms for them. He opened the door and the Footman greeted them and showed them to the tram car. In groups of twelve, they boarded the tram for the trip up to the main entrance.

Wolfgang was there to welcome them and showed them to the in keepers desk to sign in. From there several Paige's escorted them to their rooms and explained the key card system and that Lord Wolfgang would be having them in groups to be shown around the Chalet and when meals would be served.

Carl was watching on the closed circuit system of the goings on. He was pleased and called Wolfgang and let him know. By eleven o'clock the last of the first group were processed in and taken to their rooms. Peter was on his way back to the airport for the group arriving at two. Wolfgang went around the Chalet and checked in with the group leaders. It seemed that all was going well and he returned to his office.

The arrivals continued all day until the one hundred twenty eight visitors were in the Chalet and in their rooms. At five thirty, Paige's went room to room and had them come to the dining room. They were seated by the serving wenches and a meal was brought to them. From the head table, Wolfgang went over the many aspects of the Chalet. As they finished their meal, they were told that the formal medieval fest would begin in the morning. He told them that there were complete instructions as to what was offered to entertain them through the day and if they had questions, just ask any of the Paige's or staff. They finished their meals and departed. Some went to the lounge while others went to the sixth floor to take in the surroundings.

At this point Wolfgang took a deep breath until he went into his office. There he found Helma in all her makeup. She looked as if she had been hit by a garbage truck and left by the curb. It is great and you will make a great prisoner. Thank you, the artist worked a good part of the day on it. She turned around and he could see the "welts and scars" from the many pretend beatings.

He said that it had been a long time, but he could not have done this to her better for real in the past. You had better go and get some sleep as tomorrow will be a long one. Remember, you will have your meals brought to the room for you. I can't afford to have your roaming the dining room looking like this, and next time, wear your iron ball, chains and collar.

It Starts

The sun was rising over the Chalet on the first full day of the medieval fest. The many guests were getting up after a glorious night in paradise. Most were taking the time to read the instruction booklet on their living room table. For the most part of the day, up till four o'clock in the afternoon, vintage clothing was optional. Breakfast was being served in the dining room by the costumed serving wenches. As the guests were seated at the new tables, they had a better view of the decorations by daylight.

Wolfgang was in his Lord outfit and was roaming between the many now going to the buffet to make their choices of food. He sat at the head table and clanked a serving cup to gain their attention. Welcome again and I hope everyone had a wonderful evening.

The day up till four is to be for your recreation. Swimming, tennis, horse back riding or the putting greens are all ready for you. For those of you that made it to the sixth floor, the lounge chairs, beach sand and towels are available. There is also an open tavern for you to secure soft drinks, ice tea, and a tankard of ale and of course, the Chalet's best wine. Many features are listed in your book of rules in your room.

Please make sure that you check out the town square. Besides a medieval tent, there is a town criers board with the many events later on today. Partake in the many forms of entertainment such as jugglers, tarot card readers, roaming mistral, and even a pick pocket. Just down from the square is the Chalet prisoner holding area. There are both a pillory, hand and foot stocks for those troubled villagers. If you have the urge, we have a guard on hand to fit you into one and offer to take a picture of you there. From time to time, some of the prisoners will be placed there. A placard with why they are being held will be posted.

The prisoners are being held on many different charges. These range from being a town drunk, shifty merchants, horse thief and even a woman who tried to over through the King. I would suggest that you don't get too close as they may be "violent". Each will try to make their case as to why they shouldn't be there. If you feel so adept, you can chose a tomato and through it at them, just be careful of the head. One of the Chalet's jailers will be on hand to show you the use of a flogger or whip. If you wish, they will let you try your hand with a soft flogger.

To finish off this morning, I will excuse myself. As the Lord of the Chalet I have many duties. Feel free to spend your day as you wish. As you go about your daily actives, you may run into the King of the Chalet, his Majesty, King Carl the Lion hearted. Fell free to talk with him as this is his Chalet. Just remember, after four this afternoon, you need to be in medieval attire.

Helma was sitting in the makeup chair getting her welts and bruises touched up. Ilsa looked at her and said it reminded her of the old days. When you are finished, we need to go to the play room for your chains. The artist worked and Helma put on her raged villagers outfit. It was a plain tan blouse, full skirt and her breasts almost fell out of it. The pre cut tears opened the rear to expose her welts. OK prisoner, it is time to go down and get the rest of your costume.

They arrived in the cells area to complete the outfit. I think we should use the old rusted shackles and collar. I agree Helma and Ilsa reached into the cabinet. She selected the rustiest set she could find. Great, now for the heavy chain and ball, which she was fitted with.

Ok prisoner Helma, pick up your ball and let us get you settled in the town square. Remember, you are here to be interrogated as to being part of the over through of the King. Don't worry, I have practiced my pleas and begging for a week.

They went to the door leading to the square. Ilsa was wearing her jailer outfit and carried a ten foot bull whip. As they entered the court yard area, Helma made slow steps, dragging her ball behind her. At one point, she even made herself trip and land face down in the dirt. Ilsa took out her whip and snapped it across her ass. She stood up again and made it to the post with the ring on top. A short section of chain was secured to the collar causing her to sit in the dirt.

The show caused several of the guests to gather around the two of them. Ilsa stood in front of Helma and announced to the guest that this village woman was part of the plot to take over the Chalet. Some of the women guests looked at her and turned and shielded their eyes from her, as the men made their wives or girl friends comfortable. This wench has been in the torture chamber for a week and still hasn't broke. Never fear, we will get a confession from her and she will be burned at the stake.

Helma started her roll and began to rant and rave. I have been accused of these crimes and am innocent. I didn't do anything to deserve this. Ilsa turned and told her to be quiet. Helma started yelling at her as Ilsa took the flogger and gave her several swings of it on her shoulders. This brought some cheers from the growing crowd. Many even got into the act and called her a lyer. Helma tried to crawl to the crowd, but the chain to her collar was way to short. Helma began to beg for help and this brought some rotten tomatoes.

The crowd was changing and new spectators were coming and going. At this point, Lord Wolfgang showed up and told the jailer it was time to place her on the rack and try for more information.

Ilsa unhooked the chain to the collar and started to drag Helma back into the castle. Just inside the door and out of sight, Wolfgang was waiting. Helma, you were great, but you need to get ready for the arrival of the other prisoners. Helma picked up the iron ball and they started to the cell area. As they were leaving, Wolfgang said, Helma you were great, but don't think you will get a raise for your acting career.

Ilsa and Helma met Frieda in the cells area. Frieda asked if she wanted to clean up some prior to the arrival of the others. She said yes and went to the office, showered and changed to a clean outfit. Ilsa suggested that they have some lunch and she and Frieda went to the Dinning room. About an hour later, they returned with a full assortment of today's fare. Helma ate as if she hadn't taken anything all day. Remember, you will be eating the same gruel as the prisoners starting this evening. Play the roll to its fullest with the prisoners. They are all experienced slaves so they kind of know the routine.

Peter was waiting for flight 603 to arrive at the airport. He had the Limo with two sections. The front was for the Masters and Mistresses.

The rear seating area was for the slaves. The plane taxied to the off loading area and the plane's stairs came down. As was the practice, the stewardess helped the Dominates off first. Peter shook hands and kissed the hands of the females. He escorted them to the front half of the Limo.

Once he was sure the passengers were comfortable and had their snacks and wine, he returned to the ramp. He motioned to the stewardess to send the others down. There were five slaves for the trip. He welcomed them and took them to the rear compartment.

Once seated, he gave them some snacks and soft drinks. The good stuff was reserved for the front compartment passengers. As arranged this time, the slaves were to be kept awake as they would carry the luggage for their owners. They departed the airport for the Chalet.

The limo arrived and was met by the footman. He escorted the group to the tram and than up to the main floor. They were met by Lord Wolfgang and they got signed in. He took them to the suite and each unpacked their owner's clothes. He instructed them to leave the prisoner in the living area for their instructions and be taken to the cells. The rest of the four were given the tour of the Chalet.

Ten minutes passed and Ilsa and Frieda showed up in their guard costumes. They both had a six foot whip on their belts. Since none of you have been here before, we will go over the rules this package. Your owners have brought you here to spend your time in our dungeon. While there, you are prisoners of the King and Lord of the Chalet.

As time goes on, you will receive punishment for your crimes of the village. We will read the charges in the morning. Your punishment and interrogation will take place in the medieval dungeon setting. In addition, you will spend time in the stocks and pillory in the town square. We will go over the details in the morning. Now go and change into your costumes.

Once they changed, Ilsa and Frieda guided them to the elevator. Until the last evening, you will not return to this area. They loaded them and went down to the cells. As they entered, Helma was in one of her acts. She crawled around the floor, ranting and raving. She turned and the scars of the "whipping and interrogation" showed.

The group slowed and was wondering if they would get the same treatment. This is prisoner Helma. She is accused of trying to kill the King. She has been under going interrogation for over a week now. We know that we will get a confession soon and than she will be burned at the stake or which ever the King wishes.

As for you, you're Masters and Mistresses have sent you to the dungeon cells for interrogation and punishment. They may elect to come and see you but you are under the control of Jailer Frieda and me, Jailer Ilsa. During the day, you will be on display in the town square in chains and stocks or the pillory. You have been accused of different crimes which I will tell you about.

During your time in captivity in the square, you are not to talk of this area. The rest of the visitors are Vanilla and know nothing of the lifestyle. Yours owners have agreed that you should make them proud by acting as the accused. You may try to make your case to the citizens in the square, pled that you were falsely accused or beg for your release. Also, either jailer or your owner may flog you.

During the evenings, you will be treated as any slave. We have a fully equipped medieval dungeon and will take you there after dinner. We have full authorization to use you as we feel. You are all experienced slaves and are expected to do as slaves. Except for the trips to the square, you will be chained in the cells area.

Twice a day you will receive food and water. It is better than we normally serve slaves. The gruel comes from the kitchen. It is left overs and scraps from the Dining hall. You unlike Helma have edible food, she gets caned dog food.

Time to get you fitted for your iron shackles and chains. One by one, step over to the cabinet and Jailer Frieda will select the proper size. Once you have them fitted, I will assign you to your spot on the floor. Unless you want to, you can stay in your clothes. I did forget one thing; you will each get a chastity device. The three men will get locking cock and ball cages and the two women will get a chastity belt. All will be locked on to keep you from getting friendly with one another. I do understand there is a married couple here, too bad; you can cuddle if you want.

First against the far wall is Donald. You have been accused of being a horse thief. Have a seat on the floor and I will lock the chain to your collar. Second is Amy. You are the town whore. Third is Justin. You are the town drunk. That leaves Craig and Windy. You operate a meat store and were short changing the Chalet cook. I suggest that you practice your lines as tomorrow in the morning; you will be taken to the square for at least three hours. By the way, it doesn't matter if it is sunny or raining, you will get to be there for the villagers. One or both of us jailers will be there to watch over you. I did forget one thing; there are baskets of rotten tomatoes for the visitors to throw at you.

I suggest you get acquainted as it will be along time till Sunday. Sunday afternoon and evening, you will have the sentence proclaimed on you. At that time, you will be put through the total expanse of the dungeon by either the jailers or your owners. We have real medieval tools and toys to be used on you. It is real and you will hurt at that time. We will be back at around five this afternoon to feed you.

Both Ilsa and Frieda left the cells, closed the door and turned the lighting down. As soon as the door closed, Helma started her acting. She looked at the other prisoner and shook her chains, and cried and begged. I didn't try to kill the king. I am innocent and should not be here. Please help me as I can't stand the pain anymore.

They take me out to the post in the square and bull whip me all day. You see my welts and the black eye they gave me. I even hear that the king is going to have me branded in the morning. This Sunday, the King is going to pronounce sentence on me. I don't want to be burned at the stake. I'm too young to die.

Helma was now trying to crawl over to Craig. As she reached the end of the chain to her collar, she reached her hand to his and cried. The entire five prisoners were very startled by her actions and were either afraid or felt sorry.

I don't even know if I will last till Sunday. The Jailers are so hard on me. Both are hardened interrogators and Jailers. You better stay in their good graces. Amy began to huddle in a fetal position and cry. Helma thought to herself that she had made a good start.

The appointed feeding hour came and Frieda entered the cell area with a cook pot and ladle. She went to the cabinet and took out five bowls. She handed each one a bowl and than ladled a scoop in each one. This is your feed for tonight, make sure you eat it all and enjoy it. Windy asked if they were to get a spoon or something to eat it with. Frieda answered all and said to use you fingers or starve.

It smelled bad, but they each tried it. Well for you prisoner Helma, let me get yours. Helma spoke up and begged for what they were having. No Helma, you get your dog food. Remember, the guard dog loves it. The can was opened and poured in a bowl. Frieda walked over to her, gave her a kick in the stomach and put her food on the floor.

I have to get the entertainment area ready for you tomorrow. I hear the people of the Chalet are ready for the show and you will be the targets. I need to go and practice my whipping and flogging tonight. Sleep tight as you will need it tomorrow.

Ilsa and Frieda went to the room of the slave's owners. They knocked and were invited in. We wanted to insure you that your slaves are in good hands. We prefer that you don't visit them until tomorrow when they are displayed in the square. You can tune the closed circuit TV in and watch them over night. They will not be hurt, at least bad until next Sunday.

Every night, they will be chained to a wall in the dungeon and flogged. You may apply the punishment if you wish, or we will do it either way. On Sunday afternoon, King Carl the Lion hearted will over see the interrogation of them. Again, you may do it if you wish or we can help. They have been fed and should be talking and go to sleep for the night. They will be awakened at five for breakfast.

Monday at the Chalet

The day started with Ilsa being called to Wolfgang's office. How are things going with the prisoner? I think they are getting something different than they are use to. Frieda is going to the kitchen to get their gruel for the morning. Not sure they will like the bland taste of sticky, dry oatmeal. As was discussed, Helma is eating her favorite dog food.

You got to hand it to her as she is playing the role to the maximum. She has several of them scared to go to the square. It should be a lot of fun today.

Wolfgang said that he had gotten many great comments from the guests after Helma's appearance yesterday. Most are convinced that she has had her back whipped to welts. I want you to have a "C" placed in a prominent place on her left breast. Make sure the makeup artist has it look like a fresh brand. Tell the crowd that she is a liar and had been punished. Will do sir. I am going to flog her today and even let the gests try their hand at it with the dear skin flogger. I know that she is enjoying this way too much.

Carl called me and said that he is considering giving the three of you a big bonus. It appears that many of the guests have made inquirers as to when the next fest is. He is even considering having one every other month to start. I want you to think over something during the week. Is it time to offer Helma a sisterhood here? I will talk it over with Frieda and get back to you. I have to go as it is time to feed the prisoners now Sir.

Frieda opened the door to the cells and brought the foal smelling pot of the morning gruel in with her. Feeding time prisoners get ready and eat fast. As she passed Helma, she sprung out at her and screamed that we are not animal. I won't eat that slop any more. Alright prisoner Helma, you will starve till dinner. The others just held out their bowls and received a dipper of the stiff oatmeal.

This is the morning you are to be put on display in the square. Guard Ilsa and I will be taking prisoner Helma out first. When I return, Justin, you are to be ready. Remember you are the village drunk and act accordingly. Ilsa showed up and took out a stick with a nose on the end of it. She looped the rope over Helma head and around her throat. I have her, place the iron ball on her leg chains and unhook her chain to the collar. Frieda did the tasks and they dragged Helma out of the cells area and to the elevator. Once inside the noose was removed and Helma stood up and picked up the ball. Wow, I thought I was going crazy playing crazy.

They exited the elevator and went to their room. The makeup

artist was waiting as was a fine selection of breakfast. Ilsa turned to the makeup artist and told her that a big "C" brand was to be placed on her left breast. Helma looked at Ilsa and asked who wanted me branded? It was Carl's idea and he wants you to show it off today. Remember, it just happened and it is tender to the touch if I pinch it. Helma asked if she was to get flogged today. Ilsa answered yes and also whipped. Don't worry, I can pick a fly off a pin tip and not draw blood. Good as it will be a long week.

The refreshment of the makeup was finished and Helma finished her meal. Time to go to the square for today. Remember that you are going mad and I have to put the rope around you neck again. With Ilsa in the lead and Frieda bring up the rear; they went out with Helma being dragged behind. Even thought it was early, the crowds were starting to form. Ilsa yelled to stay clear of the prisoner. The ball dragged behind Helma as they arrived at the hitching post. The chain was locked to her collar and the rope removed. Ilsa said that she would stay with her while Frieda went for the village drunk.

Frieda entered the cell and told Justin to stand. She locked the iron ball to the chains at his feet. Justin, I want you to remember to play it for all it is worth. I will be carrying a whip and I can open your back up just like Helma's, do you want that? No jailer Frieda, I will do as you request. They departed the cell and went to the square. Ilsa stepped to the foot stocks and opened it to accept Justin's feet. Now sit your ass on the narrow wooden bench so all can see you. He did as she said and than raised his hands to cover his face.

A group of at least twenty was gathering around the area. A sign describing his charges and punishment was in front of him. A gentleman approached Justin and said: let's see the face of the town drunk. Reluctantly he dropped his hands and all laughed at him. Can't hold your ale can you? It doesn't happen often sir. I had a fight with my wife and she pitched me out of the house. It won't happen again Sir. The sign stated that each time you are put here, you will receive a flogging.

Frieda answered that was correct and asked the Gentleman if he wanted to try it. He eagerly accepted the challenge and Frieda gave him the dear skin flogger. She showed him how to hold it and swing it to land on the back between the shoulders. He made several practice swings and than landed one on the spot. Justin made sure to thrash a little and groan. Wonderful, that wasn't too hard, was it? The Man answered no and handed the flogger back. A woman stepped forward and asked if she could try. Frieda said yes and showed her how. By the time the crowd had all tried it, Justin was sobbing.

As the crowd walked in front of Helma, Ilsa pulled back her blouse and showed the fresh branding. The King ordered it this morning. It is still very tender and Ilsa pinched it to show them. Helma let out a scream in pain. That is enough prisoner, and she stepped behind her and let the whip fly. Helma jumped as far as the chain would let her. Now stay quiet wench or I will let it fly again.

Helma started to beg for her to not do it again. Several members of the crown picked up tomatoes from the basket and let them fly. They struck Helma and splattered. Pieces of tomato went everywhere, including down her blouse. The crowd chanted that it serves you right for trying to kill the king. Helma just begged them to believe her that she was wrongly charged. All laughed again and continued to go their own way.

Dinner time came and most of the guests went to the dining room. Frieda came to Justin and gave him a dipper of water. He thanked her and said he had never had so much fun. I am glad as tonight will change that. I will be flogging you with a full heavy leather flogger. You are allowed to talk to the others and tell them of your experience. We will be going in shortly.

Ilsa took a dipper of water to Helma. She asked her how she was holding up. Helma said that it was great but could she give her a few more strokes with the whip. When everyone returns from lunch, I need you to make a disturbance and scream at me, I can do this for you.

Around two, a different group came to see the prisoners. Helma went into her ranting again and Ilsa took her whip and let it sail. I will teach you to be respectful witch. The group cheered again and got into the whipping. Justin also got a few softer flogger hits on his back.

It is time for the prisoners to go back to their cells. Frieda released Justin and walked him back to the building, the iron ball dragging with each step. You can pick up the ball for the rest of the trip. They got back to the cell and Justin was told to sit back in his spot and the collar was locked. Frieda took the ball off and placed it aside.

Frieda returned to the square to assist Ilsa bring Helma in from the post. This time, a leash was attached to her collar and she also dragged her iron ball behind her. Ilsa walked behind swinging the whip and hitting the ground next to her. Again, they went to their room and Helma cleaned up the tomatoes. Were there any problems today Helma? No, this is everything I had dreamed of when I was planning the event. Good, I have some snacks for you and than back to the cell.

Helma was now back in her spot, chained and waiting for feeding. Ilsa walked in with the night's pot of gruel. As was getting to be the normal, each prisoner held out their bowl, all except for Helma. What is the mater prisoner; you are getting a treat this evening. Helma lunged out and tried to kick at Frieda. Ilsa reached for her whip in her back and applied several strikes to her ass. Helma backed into the wall she was chained to and settled down.

Hold out your bowl slut or you will go hungry till the morning. She finally put the bowl out, but only received a half dipper of the food. Frieda turned to the others and asked if anyone wanted Helma's other half share? Three bowls came up and begging started. The remainder was split between the three.

Prisoners, this is the first day of your punishment. After dinner, we and possible your owners will be back to apply a good whipping to each of you. They looked at each other and wondered what type of whipping they would get. Would it be like in the square or the sting of the whip like Helma just got. Only time would tell, so they settled back to wait for the appointed hour.

The feast in the dining room was in full bloom. Merriments and great medieval food was being served. Ilsa and Frieda joined Wolfgang in the staff dining room. They would get their portions served to them. As the feast was finishing and the guest were heading to the lounge and dancing area. Ilsa approached the four owners of the prisoners and quietly asked if they wanted to be part of the punishment in a half hour. They all nodded their heads and followed the women to the elevator.

Once on the elevator, Ilsa told them that their slaves were doing well and not to accept the begging they might do. They exited the elevator and headed to the cell. As they approached their slaves, Amy began to beg for forgiveness of Mistress Katherine. At this point, Mistress Katherine drew her spiked heel back and kicked her in the ass. Remember prisoner, you are accused of being the town slut whore.

We want each of you to unhook your slave from the wall and place a leash on them. They than lead their slave into the medieval furnished dungeon. Several of them slowed or stopped prior to be taken to the far wall. Ilsa turned and asked, does this scare you already? Except for prisoner Helma, you will not be getting placed on any of the nasty items.

Master James and Mark, please bring your slaves to the wall where the rings are in the wall. Frieda told the owners to watch as she hooked them up. You will be responsible for hookup starting tomorrow. In turn, Frieda had the prisoner spread their legs and chained them to the rings. Next came the wrist and they were pulled as tight as she could get them. They indicated to have Amy brought over to the pillory and place her hands and head through the holes in the cross beam. The beam was closed and locked.

This left Craig and Windy. Mistress Julie was motioned to bring them over to where a hook was being lowered down from the ceiling. It came down to a point where the wrist chains were hooked. The rope with hook was now raised bring them to a point where they just were able to touch their toes on the floor. A thick strap was now placed around their waists to hold them face to face.

Ilsa brought a selection of whips, crops and flogger to the room. From the information you provided, you stated that your are experienced in the use of these items. For the first night, please feel free to punish your slaves with whatever item you wish. Frieda will be here to assist you until I return from whipping prisoner Helma. Ilsa walked around the corner and to Helma's side. You are doing great, but I will have to simulate whipping you. Helma turned and whisper: no, please whip me hard, I need it and they need to hear the sound of the whip hitting me. As you wish Helma, turn your sorry ass over and prepare to be whipped. Ilsa let the whip fall time after time and Helma screamed out in agony, or was it joy?

In the dungeon, the punishments were being given each prisoner. Some was harder than others, but all were crying and begging to stop. After a half hour, the first session was finished. Please bring your slaves back and hook them up for the evening. All did and each slave was cuddled by their owners. As these are your own property, you may do any sexual thing you wish to them.

Julie had her two masturbate each other. Mark and James each had theirs slaves do deep oral on them. Katherine had Amy first work her clit to an orgasm and than lick it clean. The owners and slaves were pleased. Poor Helma only got a kick in the ass for her relief. The group left the prisoners in the dim light and went up to party.

Helma was curled up in a ball, lowly crying. Justin asked her if she was in much pain. She said that this has been going on for over a week she thought. I can't be sure as I have lost track of time. Amy asked her if the punishment would get worse as time goes on. It did for me: do you see what the king had done to me today. She pulled her blouse aside and showed them the brand she received this morning.

I heard them tell your Masters and Mistresses that the King will personally oversee our punishment on Sunday evening. I know that he will likely order my execution. Donald said that they had better get so some sleep as tomorrow would be here sooner than they wanted.

Tuesday at the Chalet

The morning came as they had in the past two days. The breakfast slop was served and it was time for Helma to be lead to the square. Frieda looked at Helma and said: are you going willingly or do I have to beat you? Frieda slowly looked at her and nodded her head yes. Helma placed a leash to her collar and they left. Once on the elevator up to their room, Frieda asked her how she was doing. Helma answered, great and they entered the room. Her makeup artist began touching up her welts and branding. Helma was given a tray of food and she ate it eagerly. I kind of feel guilty as they only get the gruel and I get fine food. Never mind, I have a date with the adoring public. They left and entered the square where she was chained to the post.

It was Donald's time to be presented to the public. He was placed in the single pillory. His hands and head were secured and his ass was hanging out. As each new day came, the crowds grow in size. They were all getting into the sights. It was beginning to get to be the biggest attraction at the medieval fest.

Frieda stood in front of Donald and read the charges to the crowd. This man is accused of being a horse thief. He is not much better than a man that steals his neighbor's wife. He will be punished with the feel of the whip. The King has not decided how lashes he may get, but the standard is seventy five to one hundred. I can assure you that he will be a bloody mess when the whipping is finished. His wounds will be filled with salt and it will be rubbed in hard. The crowd cheered and said it would be a just punishment.

The day progressed as the day before and the prisoners were taken back to their cell. Helma was taken to the room where her makeup was touched up. As she had her supper, Ilsa told her that she would be placed in the spiked chair while the others were whipped. She asked if it was possible to have her clothes removed. And Ilsa answered, as you wish.

The prisoners were fed and watered and told to be quiet till their owners returned to punish them. It seemed like hours, but the appointed hour arrived. The prisoners were brought back into the dungeon. Tonight, I want you to have your slaves undress and place them in the corner.

The assignments will go this way. Donald and Justin will be on the wall. Windy and Amy will be strapped together and their arms drawn up in the air. Craig, you get the pillory.

This meant it was time for Helma to be brought out. Frieda and Ilsa went to get her. She was already undresses and crying for pity. They grabbed her under the shoulders and dragged her to the spiked chair. They picked her up and slammed her onto the protruding spikes. She let out screams and begging to be given mercy. Shut up prisoner, the King has spoken and you get the chair tonight. They belted her into the chair, pushing the spikes into the soft flesh. I think we need to blindfold and gag her.

The whipping and flogging started on the other prisoners. Frieda stood by Helma and invited the others to grab and pull her breasts and nipples. Each in turn took their turn doing this to her. It gave incentive for Katherine and Julie to go behind their slaves and grab and twist their slave's nipples. James and Mark got into the act by grabbing the balls of their slave and put a crushing hand on them. Craig thought he had gotten away free when Julie came up behind him and swatted his balls with the crop in her hand.

The time increased to three quarters of an hour so the slaves could be given more punishment. The Owners were so happy to get into it, they almost didn't want to quite. Time for them to get some rest for tomorrow so each were released, ordered to get dressed and returned to the cell. Frieda decided to give Helma a little extra before returning her.

She sat in Helma's lap, pushing the spikes deeper into her ass. Sorry Helma, but this will increase the red points look in your ass. This time, they had Helma crawl back to her spot in the cell. Her red ass was swaying back and forth. You will be left naked overnight to remind you of what is coming to you this Sunday.

She collapsed to the floor and cried. She lay with her ass pointed toward the group. Amy asked if she was OK. Helma gave no answer, just laid there. Windy tried to reach across and comfort her. Her hand was only inches away, but did not touch it. Donald now asked how painful it was. Helma managed to answer in between sprits of crying. I thought I was going to die in the chair. The spikes are so sharp. Just wait till Sunday when you will get put into it. All were quiet and slowly dropped off to sleep.

Wednesday at the Chalet

Wednesday came and it was Amy's turn. She was placed in the sitting foot stocks. As before, Frieda stood and read the charges. This slut is accused of being the village whore. This is an acceptable profession in the village, except that she failed to give her portion to the Sheriff. She will receive three dozen strokes of the whip and be branded with a large "H" on her left breast. Amy almost fainted with the reading of the charges and punishment, as if was for real. She almost lost her breakfast. Amy was getting into it well.

Many of the male guests came up to her and picked up her chin and looked her in the eyes. Her owner came to her, grabbed her hair and slapped her across the face. She leaned down to her ear and whispered that he was proud of her. She returned a smile before getting another slap.

Helma's part was not getting as much inter play as the other prisoners. She was glad that they were getting involved as much as they were. As the day progressed, Ilsa gave her the daily dose of flogging. Helma turned to her and spit on her boots. Ilsa grabbed her hair and pulled her head back as far as she could. Now open your mouth slut. Helma was slow and got her face slapped. She opened her mouth in pain and Ilsa stood over her and spit in her mouth. This seemed to go over well with the crowd. It seemed that they wanted her to be in pain more often.

As the afternoon came, the prisoner's were taken back to the cell. Dinner was served and the nightly actives were started. You have an hour to do as you wish. We will be in the cell with Helma. The owners did as they wanted to punish their slaves. Whipping and flogging went on for the hour. They placed their slaves back and went up to party.

Thursday at the Chalet

It was the turn for Craig ad Windy. They were taken to the square and placed in the double pillory, side by side. Frieda stood in from of them and read the charges. This husband and wife team runs the store where the Chalet Cooks get the food for the staff. Over time, it was found that they were giving him lower quality meats and the weight was short. They will each be whipped and branded with a "T" on their chests. The "T" is for thief. They will be run out of the village and never let back.

The time came for Helma to be brought out. She could hardly crawl out to her spot. Now prisoner Helma, this time you are to be placed in the single Pillory. She was placed in and locks placed. Frieda stepped behind her and ripped her blouse totally open, exposing the welts and burses.

Today, I am going to give her the prescribed whipping and flogging she deserves. Ilsa stood on one side as Frieda stood by the other. Ilsa raised her whip and let it fly. Helma screamed out in pain, this time for real. Next came Frieda with her heavy leather flogger. Her swing brought a similar response. Helma was now receiving blow after blow. The crowd cheered loudly as Helma screamed louder each time. After twenty swings of each the whip and flogger, Helma slumped down, almost passing out from the pain.

The punishments were complete for the day. The three were taken back to the cell. Helma was dragged back. She refused any food and lay quietly on the floor. Helma's back was visible to the others. This time the welts were very real. All the rest were very concerned if this was in store for them on Sunday. Time passed and the nightly punishment was completed. Comforting was done and the group went to party.

Friday at the Chalet

Ilsa and Frieda entered with the morning meal. This time, the prisoners were allowed a little honey on their oatmeal. All gladly accepted it and dug in to breakfast.

Ilsa turned to them and told them that their trips to the square were finished. There were several big events and they would be a distraction. Turning to Helma, she told her and the group that the King wanted to see her in his private quarters. She will not be back tonight as the King want to have his way with her and determine how she will die. They grabbed her under the arms and dragged her out. Once on the elevator, they made sure she was all right.

She was laid on the stack of pillows. They undressed her and placed her in a steaming hot bubble bath. The hot water brought her back to the living. Wolfgang wanted you to have a day to recover before Sunday. As I am sure you have guessed, you will be tortured for real that day. The others will also get a taste of the items. Your game book is going as planned. When you feel up to it, Wolfgang wants to come down to see you. Helma just splashed a little in the bath with her head down.

Wolfgang walked in as Helma made her way to the living area of the suite. I am here to say just how happy both Carl and I are with the medieval fest. The comments of you and the other prisoner have been pouring in and are wonderful. Carl is now thinking of having one of these fests monthly. Besides making a lot of money for the Chalet, the Guest are making inquiries as to if they could be a prisoner at one in the future. This made Carl very happy and we know that when Carl is happy, all of us will be happy.

You will be here over night. I will have a great meal served to you here later. If there is anything else you need, just ask. Helma retired to her soft bed and fell instantly to sleep.

Wolfgang stayed and talked to both of the women. Have you give any thought to the idea of making Helma a part of your sisterhood? Carl wants to know so that we can initiate her after the guests and prisoners leave the dungeon Sunday. We have and very much want her to become one of us. We know that she can function on the normal packages as well as the medieval ones. Her main ingredient was done when she was part of the "TOY" package. This is good and I will tell Carl to be ready then. He will be happy as he hasn't done any real torture in some time.

Saturday Arrives

The final day for the medieval fare guests have arrived. Instead of only being the evening affair, it was to be an all day one. All the costumes were bright and plentiful. All through the Chalet, events were going on. In the back yard, the Jousting matches were in progress. Knights were perched on the backs of their steeds with full armor and lance. As they charged each other, the crown cheered their favorite. As the lances contacted the armor of the other, they would break and splinter. The loosing Knight would fall off his horse and be carried away.

Archers were busy in the next pit. A display of their skills included hitting the bull's eye of the target to knocking an apple off the head of a scare crow.

All during the day, King Carl the Lion hearted with his Queen in hand walked around over seeing the events. He would present silver and gold coins to the winners of the events. He was enjoying all the excitement of the goings on. Lord Wolfgang was also making his way around.

Along with the other act such as the pick pocket, like the Artful Dodger, a mandolin player, jugglers, and even Gypsies doing card readings, time went so fast. As the dinner time arrived, King Carl gave the order to go to the dinning hall. The guests came in and were seated at the great wooden tables set in a "U" pattern.

There was almost twelve feet from the backs of the inner people. After all had been seated, King Carl and His Queen entered and went to the head table. The entire group rose up and waited for the King to be seated. They than took their seats. The King than lifted his tankard of ale and pronounced that the festivity was to began. Serving wenches were busy going from person to person, taking orders for drinks.

The Head Chief and his second brought in the Roast pig and placed it on a table in front of the King. Next to come out was a ten foot long by six foot wide rolling table. On it were selections of food of the highest quality. There were sides of Ham and tender beef, turkey breasts and legs and other fine foul. There were even several types of fish and seafood adorning the table.

Many types of vegetables and potatoes were on the cart. Gravy and soups, pickles and relishes over flowed the table. As the cart rolled down the isle, the wenches would take the orders, the Chiefs cut the meat and the other items were added to the plates. There was so much merriment around the tables.

The serving went on for over an hour. Seconds were served and than came the dessert cart. It was filled with pastries, pies and even a flaming rum cake. There was not an empty stomach when they finished the meal. The King raised his tankard and proclaimed the entertainment should begin.

From the rear came many dancing girls. Some in gypsy outfits and others in belly dance outfits. Cheers went up as they would stand behind a gentleman or maiden and let their scarves drop on them. Many had their cheeks rubbed and even a pinch from a gentleman was felt by the dancers. The dinner and entertainment went on past ten.

From the dance floor came the sound of the band. Its featured harpsichord made the guests start to sing. Some went to the dance floor and did what ever they felt matched the music. Others went down to the area where the bond fire was going in a full roar. Many couples sat on the bales of straw and watched as the fire crackled. Many of the couples sat arm in arm and cuddled as they hadn't in many years. Even a few disappeared into the shadows and made love. Any and all was acceptable for this night.

The merriment continued on for most of the night. Many barrels of Ale were consumed along with many bottles of wine, champagne and brandy. Happiness was felt and seen every where. It must have been at least four in the morning before most went to bed.

The opposite was true in the cells. The prisoners had been chained in their sitting position for over a day now. Helma had her makeup redone and returned to her place with them. Low conversation was herd between several of the prisoners. Windy asked Helma what had happened when she was with the King. She started her story for them. I was chained to the corner of the room. Jailer Frieda was within several feet of me with her flogger in hand.

The King walked over to me and said he wasn't sure of how I was to die. He stated that the nights events would determine what punishment and how long it was to last. I started too pled for my life, but I felt the lash of the Jailer's flogger. I quieted down and just listened. Tonight condemned prisoner Helma, you are to do anything I require without hesitation. Yes King Carl, I will do anything you wish.

I want you to start off by stripping of your clothes. I did as told and stood their waiting for instructions. Come over and stand in front of me so I can see the many marks on your body. I walked over and stood with my hands folded in front of my body. He ran his hands over each of the welts and pinched them. I see the brand I had placed on you is healing. Yes Sir it is. He than grabbed the scabs and yanked on them. The pain was terrible, but I stood there and said nothing.

His next orders set me back some. He ordered me to assist in the undressing of the Queen. She was a large breasted woman. You are to start at her neck and lick her all the way down to her toes. I did and the Queen moaned with pleasure. She grabbed my head when I got to her nipples and had me stop there and suck on them for ten minutes. I continued down and she stopped at her womanhood. With both hands she grabbed my head and stuck it between her wide spread legs. I was made to bring her to orgasm many times over. My mouth was filled with her white fluids.

When she was finished with me, the King ordered me over to him. You are to unbuckle my pants and take them down to below my knees. I knew what was coming, but did as I was told. Prisoner Helma, you know what is expected to happen.

I took his cock and placed it in my mouth. He ordered as loud as he could, suck it and you better do it good. I did it and made a good job of it, but he must not have been pleased. He took my head and slammed it over the cock until I chocked. He than motioned the Jailer to start flogging my back. The pain reminded me that I needed to do a good job. He orgasmed many times until he was empty or any more fluid. He finally let my head go and I fell back to the floor.

He looked at the Queen and said what do you think I should do to her? She answered that there were many punishments I could be disposed with. Normally, I would have you skinned alive and than tied to the pole and burned as a witch would be.

I might even have you pulled apart on the rack while the Jailer applies white hot irons to your body. Your offences are extremely bad, but you did do a great job. I will determine your sentence down in the dungeon. I will not make you suffer as much as I normally do. Now get down and service us again, and this time also do the Jailer.

After several more time that night, they took me out and whipped me at the post. (Remember, she was in her room sleeping and is a great story teller). I was just brought down here and am here till tomorrow night. Windy turned and said, I feel so sorry for you and wish I could do something for you. Never mind as I brought it on myself.

I just wonder what the king has I mind for you tomorrow. Have you seen his many pieces of torturous furniture they have in the dungeon. I understand it goes back as far as the 1400s.

Sunday Morning at the Chalet

The many guests at the Chalet were up early packing. They would first have breakfast and than Peter would take them back to Dresden airport for their flights to Berlin and on ward to home. Lord Wolfgang was by the innkeeper's desk thanking them for their visit to the Chalet and the first medieval fest. All could only say how much they enjoyed their visit and would recommend it to their friends. Please mail your comment cards back so we can improve on your visits. If you have questions, please call and I will personally answer them.

Group by group took the tram down to the waiting bus and Peter to drive them back. This went on all the day until the only guests left were the Slave owners. They spent the remainder of the day lounging, swimming, tennis and resting for the night's event.

At just before four, Wolfgang gathered the four Slave Owner's to the dining room for an early meal. As the group was about to be seated, Carl walked in and thanked them for their visit. All six were seated at a single table and were served by Carl's personnel waitress. Julie turned to the group and asked, wasn't this your Queen last evening? Yes she was and a good one at that. She took the orders of the group and went to the Chief to have them prepared.

Carl started off by thanking them for letting the Chalet use your slaves as part of the square's events. They played their parts well and in the evenings, did very well in the dungeon. You stated that each of them was an experienced group of slaves. This week was very trying for them as well as slave Helma. In case you didn't know, she is also our Chalet Doctor; in fact, she put most of the medieval event together.

I think I will need to pay her as an outstanding Actress. When you leave, ask your slaves how she acted and the stories she told them. It was designed to get them into the mood and play along. I was even told that several of them believed that she was seriously hurt by the jailers. We have an outstanding makeup artist, even though some of the latest welts are real. She is our Chalet switch, which can play both sides.

During the week, Helma set up the scene occurring in an hour or two. Please do not tell your slaves in advance of Helma's real work, as she will "die" for her attempt on the Kings life. I am not sure how deep into play you have put your slaves in prior to coming here. We want you to be able to take them back in time and experience the medieval side and punishment of being a prisoner.

We have one of the most extensive working dungeons in the area. Many pieces of the furniture are from olden dungeons in the area. Facts show that several have been used to torture some for information or even death.

I know that you may have read or seen items like the rack or spiked chair. What you most likely don't know is how far you can work with them without doing damage to your slave. Both Jailers Ilsa and Frieda will be on hand to show you the ways to use them. Do not be afraid to ask for help or have them do it for you.

You may want to place a hood, blindfold or gag on your slave, it is not needed. Our dungeon is made of the old castle base with three foot thick walls. I can assure you that they can scream as loud as they want. It will drop your slaves deeper into sub space if they witness and hear what is going on to the others. I have found that a scared, experienced slave will enjoy the experience better.

Several waitresses began to bring the dinner meal to the table. As Carl's personnel waitress bent over to serve him, he reached under her dress and took a good feel. She just giggled and went on her way. The group enjoyed the food and made small talk. As it approached five thirty, Carl said it was time to get ready for the trip to the dungeon. Wolfgang will take the group down at six. I will join you a few minutes later. You may change into your costume if you wish as I will be going down as the King. They all left and readied for play.

At six o'clock, Wolfgang gathered the four and they went down to the dungeon. I want to tell you that by now, Ilsa and Frieda will have had your slaves strip naked and be waiting for you. As they exited the elevator, the group saw five naked, shaking, scared human beings sitting on the floor. Even Craig and Windy were cuddled together to comfort each other. Ilsa and Frieda stepped over to greet the four and take them on a tour of the dungeon and its equipment. We would like to suggest that you place them in a holding pattern until we can get them onto one of the more terrorizing pieces of equipment.

As they wondered between large and small pieces, they touched and would feel them. Mark placed his hand on the spikes of the spike chair. These are sharp, but not deadly. You are correct, but the effect and after seeing Helma's back and ass from sitting in it, they will be scared.

Julie walked over to the Iron Maiden and felt the large spikes inside. They look so real, but are soft and pliable. It is to give a feeling of the effects of being impaled. Even the hot wax is at a mild temperature to simulate hot tar. Other items such as the heretic's fork and thumb screws will cause damage if wrongly used. The rack, according to the history behind it has taken many people to their deaths.

Are there any questions at this time? No one said anything.

The group returned to their slaves and placed a leash on each. Ilsa told the slaves it was tine to go to the dungeon and face their punishments for their crimes. James started the procession into the dungeon. He turned to Frieda and asked for a suggestion of how to hold him. I would place him in Gibbet cage and raise him off the ground. He will swing and be able to see the rest of the play. You can also poke him with a stick or beat on the cage.

Katherine came in next. I hear that Amy was mouthy and loud during her stay. Can we bind her to the post and place a Heretic's fork on her. Sounds great and will keep her quiet. She will learn quickly to stay quiet.

Julie was third to enter. I want the two of these prisoners place spread eagle against the wall so I can flog them. I was so happy doing it over the last few evenings. Make sure that they are spread as wide as possible. Both should be facing the wall at first and I will turn them when I am sure they are ready for the front side to be whipped.

Mark came next. I want Justin hog tied and placed in the corner, maybe with an anal plug inserted. Sounds like fun. Please go over to the tool table and pick out the sized plug you want inserted. There are also some hot peppers to apply to the plug if you wish. Mark responded, wow, what a great idea.

Last to appear was Helma being pulled and begging all the way. Ilsa led her to the wall where a Scavenger's Daughter was waiting. Her chains were removed first and the device opened. Frieda slipped it around her neck and bolted it together. The two rails ran down at a forty five degree angel. At around shoulder level, her hands were placed in iron cuffs and than her ankles were at the lower end.

The device made the victim sit, legs spread and hands at an uncomfortable height. They never could get relief no matter what way they tried to move. To keep her from talking, a Branks head piece with a spurs mouth piece inserted in her mouth. The spikes on the spur will keep her from getting mouthy.

All stood back and enjoyed the way their slaves were secured to await their punishment. Julie started off the fun by flogging her slaves. Each slave drew many strikes to their shoulders and butts. First Craig and then Windy let out screams as the leather tails found their targets. Every forth strike was targeted between the legs of the prisoner. This brought about even louder screams and even some begging for mercy.

James stood next to Donald in the Gibbet cage. He used an iron bar strike the cage and also to make it swing. A few pokes up from the bottom openings found their mark of his cock and balls. Katherine decided to make Amy try to open her mouth. She crept up from the rear and began to tickle her inner thighs. Mark went over to Justin. He was having trouble with the plug in his ass with the peppers rubbed over it. He walked up to him and rocked him back and forth to further insert the plug. All this fun was taking its toll on the slaves.

From the hall, Carl entered the dungeon and took his place on his throne. He looked over the different scenes and was pleased with the results. Has there been a decision as to where you go from here? Katherine raised her hand and said I want to place Amy in the spiked chair.

Even with Heretic's fork against her throat, begging and pleading was heard from her. Amy was released from the fork and untied from the post. Katherine dragged her by the hair to the chair. Amy took one look at the spikes and dropped to her knees and begged and cried not to place in the chair.

Katherine had nothing to do with her. She motioned for the Jailers to assist her place Amy in the chair. They grabbed her by her underarms, picked her up and placed her in the chair. The straps began to tie her in tight. The large two inch leather belt went around her waist and her breasts secured her in the chair. The points instantly started to give her discomfort as she wiggled. Her weeping and crying was heard around the dungeon.

Mark decided to place his drunken slave on the rack. The Jailers took Justin from the Gibbet cage and dragged him to the ominous looking rack. They placed him on the rack and had Mark slip the ropes over his feet. With him secured at the feet, they laid him on the rack and had Mark place the ropes around his hands.

Justin began to flail around, but only until the slack was removed. Ilsa told Mark to remove the slack very slowly. Inch by inch came out of the ropes, bringing his body to a stiffened position. Once you get him tight, add one more click and let him set for a while.

James now had an idea for his horse thief slave. I think the Spanish boot will do him well. Donald was dragged to a chair and tied into it. The boot itself was and Iron replica of a pair of boots together. It was split in half to allow the victims feet and ankles to be secured inside. The halves were placed around Donald's feet and drawn together. Iron straps were placed around the two halves to hold them together.

Now secured, Donald tried to wiggle, but his feet were tight inside. Frieda now handed several wood looking wedges made from very firm foam and a rubber mallet.

What you want to do is insert the large wedge between his legs and drive it in slowly. The other wedges are for the front and rear of the leg. Just the thought of having his leg bones shattered started Donald screaming for mercy.

Julie now though what to do to her two slaves. I want to do two different things to them. Let me take one at a time. Bring Craig over to the wheel. They released him and dragged over to the eight foot diameter wooden wheel. She told him to step up on the blocks under the wheel. Each of his feet were now spread and ties to rings on the wheel. At this point, he had his arms spread and tied to the rings at the top.

The wheel was now leaned back slightly. The wheel was on a hub which allowed it to be spun around. Frieda pulled the pin allowing it to move. Julie took the edge and started it spinning. Round and round it went. Craig was getting dizzy and almost puked. She stopped it with his head at the lowest point, had the pin replaced and grabbed and twisted his balls. Craig screamed and bit his lip.

Julie went over to the Spanish Donkey. She looked at it and asked what the hole was for in the top of the unit. Ilsa responded that it accepted any number of different dildos. Julie was intrigued and went to the table. She picked up each of the five different styles. She took the eight inch long by two inch in diameter one with little rubber points on the sides. This will do fine and she inserted it in the hole. A little lube and we are ready to go.

Windy was taken down and dragged by both Jailers over to the unit, with her hands tied behind her. Her eyes opened to the size of silver dollars and she struggled even harder. Julie grabbed her hair as Ilsa and Frieda lifted her over the top of the donkey. They each spread a leg and lowered her onto the dildo. Julie reached down between her legs and spread the labia far apart.

Windy was now lowered onto the dildo, a little at a time. She struggled all the way down, but finally hit bottom. Windy tried to flail her legs until Julie placed a five pound weight to each ankle. Ilsa suggested that they attach a rope from the ceiling to her wrists and pull the upward in a strapado position. That should keep her from struggling too much.

This left Helma to her punishment. King Carl told Ilsa and Frieda to release her from the Scavenger's Daughter rig and bring her to the

Garrote stand. Helma was placed, sitting on a narrow board seat. A thick leather belt was placed around her waist, drawing her back to the upright piece of 4 x 4 lumbers. Her feet were drawn back under the seat and secured to the rear of the post. Her arms and hands were tied behind the post. A two inch wide iron band was placed around her neck and locked in place.

From behind, a large "T" threaded handle was turned driving a block (block was made of foam) into the back of her neck. Helma began to struggle as the block cut off her movement of air in and out of her lunges. She struggled as best she could, but the turning continued. Even Helma was scared for the first time during this play. She tried to scream, but nothing came. After the third turn, Helma lost control and peed on the floor.

King Carl ordered the turning to stop so they could torture her more at her death. Carl surveyed all that was going on in the dungeon. He gave the two thumbs up and said he was pleased.

Katherine turned to Frieda and asked what more she should do to Amy. She is looking to comfortable sitting on the spikes. Have you thought of sitting on lap and wiggling on her lap? That is a great idea, but what about a little more after that. As Katherine sat in the lap of Amy, Frieda brought over a set of thumb screws.

They look very vicious, are they? Yes, go too far and they will break the joints. Show me how to put one on her left hand. You place the hand on top of the plate and the bar over the joints of her fingers. Now you very slowly twist the thumb screw down till it makes contact with the joints. Only add more twists until it gets snug and nicely tight. She will be so scared at this point she will do anything you wish. The procedure was now repeated on her other hand.

James had almost hammered the wedges fully into the Boot. Donald was feeling the pressure of the foam wedges pressing on the bones in his ankles. He had Donald's hands tied in front of him and attached to a rope coming down from the ceiling. From a crank on the wall, his hands were drawn upward toward the ceiling. He was now in a standing position, with his cock and balls standing out. James took a wide tip crop from the table and began striking his balls. Donald was crying and begging for relief, but none came. When he was finished with the balls, James started to work on his cock. Donald didn't know what hurt most at that time.

Mark, it is time to release Justin's arms a little. The rope was loosened and than the slack was taken out an inch more than before. Justin trashed his head side to side as this process was repeated several more times. Mark also went to the table and selected a heavy leather flogger. He began to work all the mussels and torso of Justin. He was good at snapping it as it landed causing extreme pain.

Craig was next to feel the sting. With the wheel in the position of his head lower than his feet, his cock and balls were hanging down. It seems that your two friends have had been cropped and flogged, so I will do something different. First she grabbed his balls, crushing and twisting them. Let me take a look around. I see a pot of boiling tar.

She went over to the pot which had the hair removing wax in it and scoped up a ladle of the substance. Craig, you should see the way the tar is boiling up. I am going to pour it over your ball very slowly. I want you to enjoy the last of them. They have been a bother to me and now I get my way. She grabbed his cock and pulled it out, expositing the balls. Very slowly, she dripped the wax (no more than 100 degrees) over his balls. Craig came very close to passing out.

Julie now moved to the Spanish Horse with her slave Windy seated on top. She reached down and began to rub her clit and to watch her rock back and forth. I see you are able to move way too much so I will add another five pounds of weight to each foot. This drew her down, increasing the pain of the dildo. Ilsa came over and suggested that she reach down and spread the labia apart further. This will make her sit on the top edge of the horse and increase the pain. She did this and went back to the messaging of the clit. Windy begged to be able to cum and was given the OK.

The time had now passed midnight. Carl suggested that it was time to release them so no permeate harm would come to them. Each in turn was released and told to stand over by the Iron Maiden. It is time for Helma to learn her fate. I have decided she will be dispatched by being impaled in the maiden. They released Helma from the Garrote. She fell to the floor, totally exhausted. Take her and secure her in the Maiden.

Ilsa and Frieda dragged her over and stood her inside, belts were placed around her waist, legs, ankles and arms. Her head was left loose to thrash around. Prisoner Helma, you are to feel the spikes of the Maiden as she is closed. Ilsa and Frieda began to close the door, bring the spikes closer to Helma's body.

Just before they closed the front, they invited all to see as the spikes came in contact with her breasts. Helma was pleading to stop, but the King just laughed. Ilsa had all step back and the front was pushed shut. Helma let out several loud screams and than it was totally quiet. At this point Helma found the packet of fake blood and smashed it. The red substance oozed from the bottom of the Maiden. Several of the slaves actually cried.

King Carl stood and declared that the medieval fest was finished for all. I would advise you to take your slaves to your room for some fun. Make sure that they each have a long and hot bath. This should be a bonding time for all. Lay with them and do a lot of cuddling. I have made sure that the Kitchen is still open and all can get a "real" hot meal for them and yourselves. Enjoy the night as you will need to pack in the morning. You will be leaving after breakfast.

They departed for their room for the evening. Ilsa and Frieda went to the Iron Maiden and opened it. They found a totally exhausted Helma standing inside. She was covered in little red marks where the foam spikes had pushed into her. Carl walked up to her and said you were wonderful during the total event. Thank you Sir. I had a great time all week.

That is great Helma, now I want you to go and get a shower in the office and report back here in ten minutes. You are to stay totally naked and come back and assume a slave position at my feet. She lowered her head and quickly was off to the shower.

During the time, Carl had Ilsa and Frieda move the furniture away to the sides and make sure the rack was the center piece. We are going to do the Sisterhood ceremony as soon as she is back. Get my private cart out as I will need my interrogation tools from it. They hurried to complete the assigned tasks.

The Sisterhood initiation

With all the excitement of a five year old, Helma dashed to the office and took a hot, five minute shower. Little did she know what she was going to be asked when she finished the shower? A few towels later and she crawled back into the room. She saw Carl sitting in his royal chair and ended her crawl in front of him. She stopped in the slave kneeling position, hands on her knees and head down. She tried to contain her fast paced breathing and be as quiet as possible. Never before had she been commanded to be in this position by him.

The two women, Ilsa on her left and Frieda on her right stood perfectly quiet. They both knew what was coming as they had both been through it before. In his most official voice, Carl told Helma to raise her head and look straight at him.

Helma, you have been with us for a half a year now and have been extremely good at what ever you were asked. I have conferred with Ilsa and Frieda and they agree that you are ready.

The proposal I am about to make has only been done to a dozen women before, Ilsa and Frieda being two of them. I am going to make you a proposal which you have to say yes or no to right now. Nothing will be said if you say no, but there are many advantages and perks to accepting. We want you to become part of the Sisterhood.

Helma, at this time you only know a small part of what goes on around here. In addition to the workings of the Chalet, we run an interrogation service. We do this work for Governments as well as private Companies and Persons. It maybe for pay, but many times it is for favors that keep us running.

I first want you to remember that you did a "TOY" package which was mild in nature. You, along with the other three Doctors destroyed two human beings over a period of four days and walked away clean. As an interrogator, your task is different. What I am asking is can you

259

put aside your oath as a doctor not to intentionally do harm to a human being? Think deeply as once you agree and start, the only way out is to the crematorium.

Frieda, please bring the small table with the contract and place it in front of her. Frieda did as requested and returned to her place. Helma, in front of you is a life contract to work here with us doing what is required to obtain information or bring a person to a very slow and painful demise. Your one year contract will no longer be valid and this one will. I will explain further so you fully understand what goes on.

From time to time, we will receive a person here to interrogate or punishment. They may be male or female, young or old, it makes no difference. With the training you will receive from Me, Wolfgang, Ilsa and Frieda, you will be able to extract what ever is requested.

As I stated it may be international secrets, industrial secrets or just plain revenge for something they did. We just supply the personnel to complete the contract. We even will take contracts outside of the Chalet. This is where the other ten of the sisterhood come in.

You will work with those from other countries. They may come here and you can assist them or you may go to where they are and assist you. It will take a long time to train in the endless ways to inflect pain to obtain the information.

Unlike what you did before, the information may be needed right now or you may be required to draw out the interrogations for days, weeks or longer. Right now, between those of the four of us in the Chalet, we have more than a hundred combined years in the field. Myself, I started over forty years age in the KGB and also cross trained secretly with German SS officers that escaped from the Nazis of World War Two.

If I haven't turned you off yet, I will continue. Both during training and after, your status will be elevated to part of the senior staff here. Only Wolfgang and I are higher in rank here at the Chalet. Helma, do you have any questions so far? You may speak now Helma. Sir, I have several questions. First, will I still be the Chalet Doctor? Yes you will and still have your helper. Second, will I still work on the packages of our guests? Yes Helma you will and I will say you do a splendid job at it. May I read the contract before signing? I insist on it and again, ask if you come up with any other questions.

Helma read and reread the five page contract. Sir, I find all in this contract fine with me. I fully understand what will be expected of me in the future and want to sign it. Carl nodded and Ilsa handed her a pen. There are a dozen placed to sign Helma. She went page to page signing on the lines marked with an "X". Both Ilsa and Frieda than signed as witnesses and the contract was handed to Carl. Welcome aboard and now it is time for you initiation into the Sisterhood.

Sir may I ask what the initiation consists of? No Helma, it is to be a surprise, but I know you will get through it. You will be placed through a mini interrogation over the next forty eight hours. The treatment and pain will be very real and intense, far worse than anything you have done in the past here. There is no way you will be able to prepare yourself, just experience it. You will be introduced to a part of Ilsa, Frieda and Me that you have never seen before.

Helma, stand and do as you are told. She did and was guided to the rack. Lay, face down and stretched out to be hooked up. She did as told and Ilsa placed the rough ropes over her hands as Frieda looped the ropes over her ankles. Helma, the rack has been in use for over a thousand years and has been found to be very effective.

Over the next six of more hours, you will be pulled to the point of feeling that you have broken. This will not be the case as they know every trick in its use. Are you ready to start? Sir, I am ready for what ever comes. Very fine, the rules are simple. You must endure what ever is done to you over the time limit. You will not be given a blindfold or gag. Just the sounds of a person's screams are music to our ears. Your entire experience will be recorded so we can re watch them and your screams will be recorded and used for those in any slave program to come. If at any time you want out, you must say my Name, Carl.

The two women each took hold of a wheel on either side of the head of the rack and began he removal of the slack. Click by click tightened the stress on her joints, and brought her to attention. Just when Helma thought there was no more to be gotten from her body, they found another inch. Frieda ran her hands down along the arms and legs to feel for the limits being met. Sweat was now running down Helma's face and shoulders. Ilsa gave her several swats of her hand across her ass. It was as if Helma didn't even feel them.

Fifteen minutes went by in this position and Carl gave the command to let out the rope. The release was only maybe two inches, but it felt like haven to Helma. No more than two minutes later, Carl ordered her to be stretched again. This time, they went an inch or more further. Again Frieda felt the tension in her joints and the process was stopped. Carl walked over to her and asked how are you doing? She shook her head in a yes fashion and the torture continued. Carl went to his cabinet and drew out his favorite twelve foot, twelve plat bull whip. You have never seen me at work before Helma.

I am going to whip you ten times over the next two hours with two minutes of rest between. Carl stepped back to the distance he wanted and let fly with his first strike. The snap was felt between her shoulders. The sting could be heard through out the dungeon. A large red stripe appeared on Helma. That is number one, you are to count each strike or I will just add another for fun. Helma understood as the next one landed on her left ass cheek. Two Sir was heard and than a loud scream. That is correct and we will proceed. As the twelfth strike fond its mark, Helma yelled twelve and her head slumped back on the rack. You are doing very good Helma; you get your two minutes rest.

Each set of twelve was followed by Ilsa and Frieda running their hands over her now swelling welts. Helma, they are so warm and red, you will be proud of yourself. The process continued until the twelve sets were complete.

You are now going to be released, but may not like the feeling. As the rope became limp on the rack, Helma felt the mussels in her arms and legs come to life. Her joints as well as her back, ass and legs were on fire.

Carl gave the order to turn her over and begin the process over again. Helma thought the first set of stretching was bad, but being on her back with the welts was worse. Ilsa joked with Frieda that Helma would wind up maybe three inches taller when they were finished.

Helma didn't laugh, only groaned in pain. Carl walked over to her and looked her in the eye.

The first part was easy compared to what is coming. He walked to the top drew of his cabinet and took our two pair of vice grip pliers. He set them so only a sheet of paper could be inserted between the tips. Helma, take a deep breath. She did and Carl clamped a pair on each of her nipples. The pain shot through her nipples, than her breasts and into the brain.

The pliers were than pulled away from her chest and twisted. Such lovely screams, don't you think Frieda? She shook her head yes and went to the cabinet to retrieve two more sets. She handed one pair to Ilsa and they adjusted them the same way. This time the target was lower. Each woman selected a spot on her labia and clamped. The screams were much more intense and Helma tried to pull herself off the rack. The ropes held her firm on the rack. They also began to pull and twist. I think she is getting the idea of how much we can do to the human body. Carl told the Women to stand back and let the prolong pain set into Helma's savaged body.

After ten minutes, all the pliers were removed. Ilsa said that we should give her some attention. Each Woman took a nipple in their mouth and clamped their teeth into it. The feeling was now back and she let out further screams. Carl stood back and told them to each get their whips and work on her from both sides at once. They did and the tips fell starting at the top of the breast and working to the tip of the toes. Carl picked up a thin bamboo cane and started striking the soles of her feet.

Helma's front now matched her back in the number of welts. The women were ever so skilled and managed to caress the tips of her nipples with several strikes. Carl said that I think she is enjoying this to much. Bring me the magneto and wires. Frieda went to a large drawer and removed a box with two brass bells on it and wires leading from it. The box had the markings of Western Electric Telephone Company.

Helma, this was part of the 1920s phone system. It has a much more intense sting than the smaller army field you have used before. Frieda and Ilsa knew what to do next. They each took the alligator clamps attached to a wire and grabbed one on each labia. They placed the teeth on the tender skin and pinched the teeth into the flesh. Wonderful, now hand me the magneto. Helma, this box has a crank handle like the phone you used. The two brass bells will ring each time I crank the handle and you receive the shock. Stand back so I can demonstrate.

Carl grabbed the handle and gave several full turns. Helma instantly arched her back and screamed very loud. All looked at each other with joy as Helma suffered deeply. I will continue to crank the handle while you go and get the next portion of the fun.

Fried and Ilsa went to the office and retrieved several buckets of leaches. Each downed a set of rubber gloves and picked up one bucket each. Helma, you remember these from the "TOY" program. These have not been fed in a week and are very hungry. Helma shook her head yes that she remembered but wasn't sure how they would feel or where they were going to be placed.

As Carl continued to inflect the electric shocks, Ilsa and Frieda started to place the leaches on Helma's breasts. I think about a dozen on each breast should do the trick. They started to place them around the base and up the sides of the breasts. Between the shocks and the leaches, Helma was jumping around the rack. Ilsa took out a wide strap and placed it around her stomach. She was now settling back down on the rack. The mouths of the leaches were now in their sucking motion and burrowing into her skin.

With her now occupied, Frieda took a three foot metal spreader bar from the closet. They let the foot rope loose from the rack and spread her legs apart and attached the feet to the ends of the bar. A chain now hooked the bar to the foot of the rack and the tension reapplied. Carl stopped giving her the charges of electric and the clips were removed. Even with the leaches digging in, Helma thanked the two for removing the clips. Don't get excited Helma, much worse is to come.

So far, all your experience has been external. We need to fix that. Ilsa took the largest Collins Speculum from the cabinet and plunged it into her. She than spread it as far as it would go, bringing the screams to a fever pitch. Frieda now took a Q-tip and rubbed it around inside a Habanero pepper. Frieda loved this part.

She peeked inside of Helma and found her pee hole. First she started rubbing it around the opening and than up inside it. She twirled it until she was sure all the surfaces were covered. The heat built fast and Helma thought a blow torch was up inside her. Nice reaction don't you think Ilsa. The area would stay inflamed for a half an hour. The speculum was removed and a little relief was felt by Helma.

Carl was very impressed with the events and said she needs to get off now. Frieda rolled the fucking machine over to the foot of the rack. While she plugged it in, Ilsa went to the drawer and selected a one foot long studded dildo and attached it to the arm of the machine. They now inserted two inches of it into her. Carl gave the word to start and the machine was turned on.

At first the strokes were slow; but than went all the way in. Ilsa set the control for automatic which varied the speed. The timer was also set for forty five minutes. She should be raw inside by the time it is done. The leaches had been feeding and were full, they started to fall off.

Carl went to Helma just as her time ran out on the machine. Ilsa removed it and copious amounts of white fluid along with specks of blood came out with the dildo. She has gone thru as much as we needed to see. Over the next thirty six hours, I want her placed in a prisoner position in the cells. There is to be no slack or wiggle room. You know what else I want.

Helma's exhausted and broken body was removed from the rack. She could not move, much less stand. Ilsa and Frieda grabbed under her arms and dragged her to her spot on the floor. Before Carl left, he ordered that she was not to be fed or watered during this time in confinement. At the end of the time, I want you to take her to the room and pamper her so much. She is to get two weeks off to recover. The two of you need to help her in and out of hot baths and bring her meals in the room. I will stop by off and on during the two weeks. I feel that we made a good decision with her.

The first shackles were placed on her wrists and ankles. A collar went on her neck next. Frieda went to the cabinet and selected a full leather hood, blindfold and x-large cock gag. These items were placed on and laced up the back. Helma's hands were placed behind her and the shackles locked together. Several wide straps pulled her elbows tight together.

Before the ankle shackles were locked, Ilsa choose an anal plug and a spiked dildo, both X-large and stuffed them in. The legs were pulled together and the shackle locked. Several large belts went around her legs to prevent her from dislodging the dildo and plug.

To get her attention, they stuck the cattle prod between her legs and let go. Helma, you are sentenced to thirty six hours like this. You are not to be fed or watered. We will check in on you every so often and use you for oral sex. If you do an outstanding job of it, we may pee in your mouth for fluid. We will leave Fritz the guard dog down here for company. Enjoy the feelings. Ilsa knelt down and whispered in her ear, you did well and are part of our Sisterhood; Ilsa got up and kicked her in the butt. Helma, you now understand the interrogation side of the Sisterhood. They exited the cell and she and Frieda went for a good meal.

HELMA AND THE SISTERHOOD

I lsa and Frieda exited the elevator on their way back to their room. Both women were exhausted and sweaty from the last 24 hours of working the medieval fare as well as the initiation of Helma into the sisterhood. They decided to soak in a hot bubble bath and than some time in the saunas in their bedrooms.

Time passed oh so slowly as they relaxed from the last days work. As they finished their sauna, they toweled off and met in the living room. A bottle of fine house wine was uncorked and glasses filled. They took their glasses to the stack of large pillows in the middle of the room, shed their towels off and lay naked next to each other.

They drank their wine and small talk started of the last week's events. They knew that they would have to put an after actions report together of the fun as well as the problems which came of the first event. The evening dinner meal was approaching and both women were hungry. They returned to their bedroom and selected simple attire to go to the dining room.

The Chalet was mostly empty by now. The many guests who had spent the week were on their way home. They entered the private dining area. Wolfgang was already seated and munching on his steak. The women sat at the table and a waitress approached to take their order. Within minutes, she returned with salads and a soft drink for them. She said that the main course would be served in around fifteen minutes.

Wolfgang started the conversation by asking how Helma was. Ilsa responded that when they left the cell, she was extremely uncomfortable and going in and out of reality. She will be having a very painful thirty six hours bound up. As prescribed by Carl, she can not move much as well had been gagged and plugged. The hood is tightly laced and she can either chock, chew or lick on the penis gage for relief. We will be checking on her every six to eight hours.

Do you think she will need any relief prior to the time of her release? Frieda looked at Wolfgang and snickered. You know how much of a pain slut she is. Ilsa chimed in saying, remember how much of a pain slut she is. She is most likely having her tenth orgasm by now. The only problem she will have is to know that her ordeal will be over. As required, she will not get anything to eat or drink till her restrictions are over.

The women's meals of prim rib with potato and vegetables and a roll arrived. They began to partake of the meal along with small talk with Wolfgang. Time passed quickly and a dessert of two inch thick cheese cake with strawberries arrived. Wolfgang ordered brandy for them and they raised their glasses to the latest member of the sisterhood. The glasses clinked and the ten year old drink was enjoyed.

Remember we have a meeting in the morning about the medieval fest and I want a report on Helma. He left as did the women. Let us go down to check on Helma and than we should go back to the room and pick up where we left off in the stack of pillows.

The Visits to the Cell

Ilsa and Frieda entered the elevator for the trip down to the cell area. The pair entered the area and turned on the lights. A low moan could heard coming from where Helma was bound. It was almost eight hours since Helma had been secured for her final part of the initiation.

As they approached Helma, Ilsa stepped behind her and planted the toe of her foot into the extremely bruised ass. Frieda headed for the cabinet and selected her favorite cattle prod and placed the tips as far between her pussy lips as possible and gave several long and intense jolts. The stimulations woke Helma to a semi conscious state.

Ilsa started by saying, glad to see you are still with us. Ilsa stepped to her head and loosened the strap on the gag in her mouth. With her mouth having been stretched wide from the gag, Helma struggled to move her jaw. Now reality began to set in. Frieda kneeled next to her and told her that she needed to come back to reality. Helma worked to regain control of her mouth and than realized how hungry and thirsty she was.

Ilsa asked her how she was doing. Helma replied that she was doing fine and very much enjoyed her stay in captivity. That is good as over a forth of it was done and that time for release was on the horizon. I am sure that you don't remember what we told you on the way out after binding you. Helma's mind still in a sort of haze shook her head no and lied it back down.

I will refresh it for you. You will be required to service us both now and when we return in the morning. Helma seemed to grasp what was going on and said yes. Both Frieda and I will sit over your face and you will service us until we are satisfied. Remember, the sooner you do a good job, the sooner you will receive our yellow fluid to somewhat quench your thirst.

To encourage your endeavor to do a good job, Frieda had brought over the telephone magneto and will hook the alligator clips on your labia. The clips were installed, one at a time to the lips. As each clip bit into the very tender skin, they were wiggled back and forth to make sure they bit deeply into the flesh.

Ilsa went first; squatting over Helma's parched lip and grabbed her head, drawing it tight to her womanhood. The word was given and Helma started to lick with everything she had. As Helma liked the taste of both Ilsa and Frieda, it would not take much encouragement. It would not matter how good Helma did, the crank handle of the magneto was turned sending biting volts of electricity racing thru Helma's lower body.

After several rounds of pleasure for Ilsa and Frieda, the clips were removed from Helma. She lay her head back down on the floor in exhaustion. Not so fast Helma, you know what is to be replaced. The penis gag was picked up, but before being replaced, each woman inserted it in and out of their vagina, coating it with the white cream from the play. Helma opened her mouth and gladly accepted the gag.

Good girl, now for a little extra fun before we leave. Frieda brought over two 18 gage by two inch long hypodermic needles and two corks. She handed one set to Ilsa. Frieda started by taking Helma's nipple between her fingers and rolling it around, turning it into a stunning tower of flesh. As she held it out, she took an alcohol pad and cleaned the area behind the rosebud nipple. Ilsa than uncapped the needle and brought the tip to just behind the nipple tip.

With a slow, twisting motion, the needle was inserted thru one side of the area and out the other side. The popping sound of the needle entering and leaving her tender skin was music to their ears. The cork capped off the tip of the needle to prevent it from working out over the next eight hours. The two reversed jobs and the other nipple received its needle. Little droplets of blood were seeping from the points of where the needle entered and left the nipple.

The two stood back to admire their work and complimented each other on their work. I think that this should just about finish the work, except for one thing. Frieda threaded two thin pieces of string and ran it thru a pulley in the ceiling over where Helma lay. The ends of the string were brought to the needle ends and tied around the ends of the needle. I think that we should add a little fun to the game. With that Ilsa brought over a two pound weight and the ends of the strings were tied to it.

The weight was dropped pulling pressure on the needles. The freshly inserted nipple in Helma nipples tugged at her skin and she let out a sound somewhere between a groan and a scream. That should help her enjoy the next eight hours. Ilsa and Frieda both kick Helma in the ass and gave the weight a good push on their way out. Good night Helma, sleep tight, we will return later.

The woman returned to their room, took off their clothes, and both entangled themselves in a ball on the pillow stack. Many deep embraces continued throughout the evening till they both drifted off to sleep.

Morning came and both took a steaming hot shower and dressed for another day's work. Their second trip to check on Helma was to be completed first. They went down to the cell area and as they entered, they saw Helma trying to wiggle around to get the weight to draw tighter on the needles. Nice try Helma, we will do the inflection of pain on you. With that the leads from the magneto were replaces and several long cranks were preformed. Helma laid there and kind of let out a purr of affection.

Frieda and Ilsa each took hold of the weight and pulled it down causing the needles to be yanked hard. The nipples came to full attention and Helma was not purring anymore. It seems that you are at full arousal and ready for the mornings fun. We will do the same as last time, except that we will add to the incentive to do a great job. As Ilsa took the gag off and began to seat herself over Helma's mouth, Frieda produced a syringe of liquid Habanero sauce. She inserted it into a hole in the end of the large spiked dildo in Helma and placed the twenty CCs of the liquid directly into her love box.

It did not take long for the effects of the extremely hot pepper juice to take hold of her. In Helma's mind, a hot blow torch had been brought to the entrance and turned up fully. She started to buck and scream lowly. The serving went on as before with the women trading places often.

When the two had finished being pleasured by Helma, they removed the alligator clips, put the magneto away, and replaced the gag. Ilsa turned to Frieda and said that she had been so much fun for the day, let us remove the needles.

It could have been a simple process, but that was not to be. The strings were untied, leaving the needles and corks in place. Each woman took one side and removed the corks.

Ilsa said that they should remove them very slowly, inflecting as much pain as possible. Ilsa started and took the hub of the need and twisted and pulled it till it exited the nipple. The same was repeated by Frieda on the other side.

Each of the nipples was swollen from the invasion of the needles to their targets. Each nipple was grabbed and violently twisted between Ilsa and Frieda's thumb and finger. The pain was intense and brought some bleeding.

271

We can't leave her bleeding over the next eight hours. A cup of salt was brought and liberal amounts were worked into the wounds. This should control the bleeding and give her enjoyment.

The Women each took their turns of kicking Helma. Blows were dispensed to both her ass as well as her breasts. We don't want her to get too comfortable in the last third of her stay. Ilsa turned to Frieda and said it was a warm day so they should get a few laps in the pool before dinner.

They left the cell and returned to their room, changed into their swim suits and went to the pool.

Initiation's Over

Ilsa and Frieda were sitting in the dining room finishing a wonderful meal of baked chicken. Wolfgang came in and sat at the table next to them. He started the conversation by asking how the meal was. Frieda answered that it was the great quality as normal. Are you both aware that Helma's time in the cell is almost over. Yes, we are going down after dinner and release her.

Ilsa commented that she was doing great and that she has earned her spot as one of the sisterhood. I know that Carl will be glad to hear this. Do you think that she will be back on her feet within the two week period? I think so, she is young and hardy. Anyhow, she loves being abused and in pain.

We will have a hot bath ready for her and the cook is getting a large helping of chocolate pudding, some lime jello and a full cheese cake with strawberries covering the entire top for her for her snack. She should be back to solid food in two days. We will baby her over this time period as well as going over the many rules that come with being one of us.

The pair of women departed the dining room for their room with the goodies. Ilsa began to full Helma's tub with super hot water. I think I will add some of her perfumed soap beads. Frieda was busy putting all the many pillows in a pile, fluffing them as she placed them in the center of the living room. I think she will be glad to just lay on them for the rest of the night. I will also place a pile of blankets for her on the table. She will be a total loose at least over night and need us to help her.

I think we are ready so let us go and retrieve her. They took the elevator down to the cell area. Frieda, get the laundry cart ready and I will start to get her awake. Frieda loaded the bottom of the cart with many pillows and covered them with a sheet. She also included three blankets to cover her for the trip back to the room.

Ilsa silently approached where Helma lay on the floor. She knelt down next to her head and whispered to her; Helma, it is time to awaken and be released. She took her hand and gently caressed the side of the hood covering Helma's head. Sweetie, it is that time, just relax and we will get you out.

Frieda went to her other side and unbuckled the gag. As she removed it from her mouth, she gave a shy of relief. Over the many hours she had been wearing it, her mouth had been kept open and her mouth was soar. Helma, in a weak voice, thanked them both.

Honey, we have to release you a little at a time. I don't want you to try to get up and move until I tell you. First we will release the straps holding your elbows together. One by one Frieda undid the straps and took them off. She began to rub her arms back to reality. Next came the straps holding the legs tight together. Again her legs were gently rubbed getting the circulation back and some blood moving. Helma, just lay there and sweetie, don't move too much.

Your hood is next. I want you to keep you eyes closed until I tell you to open them. Ilsa began to let the laces holding the hood tight loose. As slack came to the hood, it loosened from it place encasing her face and head. Slowly, the leather hood was pealed from her head, leaving the face that had turned into a prune finish.

Frieda turned the lights down to minimum in the room. Ilsa placed her hand under Helma's head and began to stroke her matted hair. You can now slowly open your eyes and join the world again. A big smile came to Helma's face and she muttered some barely recognizable words. Don't try to talk now, just relax till later.

Helma, we will release your arms and legs now. First to come were the shackles from her ankles. Both her ankles had turned a darker shade of black and blue. There was even some chafing of the skin. Frieda spread her legs and the butt plug and the spiked dildo from within their cavities were removed. There was an instant relief and slight thanks. The dildo was covered in many dried white layers of Helma's orgasms.

Ilsa turned to her and said you had fun while tied up. Helma shook her head yes and asked if they could save it for her to look at later. Yes you can have it than and even lick it if you want. He legs were allowed to sink back together again.

Last will be your arms. Frieda moved behind her and let the shackles drop from her wrists. Helma tried to move, but was unable to as she had been restrained for such a long period of time. Just lay there like a pile of wet noodles so we will do all the work for you. This was comforting as she was not able to do much more than twist her wrists some. Don't worry, the feeling will return in a short time and you may wish we had left you chained up.

A cold glass of water with a straw was brought close to her mouth. Frieda held her head up slightly and told her to go slow and just sip. The cool water felt refreshing to Helma and helped to wash away the hours of her own saliva, not to mention the many orgasms she was forced to take from Ilsa ad Frieda.

You are doing very well my sweets. I think it is time to get you sat up against the wall. As she was sat up, a blanket was place around her shoulders and they scooted her up to the wall. They sat on each side of her to help support her somewhat limp body. The two of them began to caress the tired body. Life was now beginning to return and color came out to the arms and legs.

Helma, can you talk some yet. She answered that her head was clearing and the feeling had returned to her body. The first full sentence she spoke was to thank the two of them for the experience they had imparted on her. Your welcome and now you are one of us. You passed the test and came through it well. Do you think you can stand with our help? She nodded her head yes and they each place their arm under hers.

They very slowly helped her over to the laundry cart. Helma, you are getting the top of the line ride back to the room. She was gently lifted and slid into the pillow lined cart. Several blankets were placed around her and than the one over the top. Hold on tight my darling, next stop is our room.

The two guided the cart to the elevator and placed it and themselves on board. The doors closed and the car went to the first floor where their room was. The doors opened and the cart was pushed to the door. They entered and the blankets removed. Helma was already trying to get out on her own, but was told to relax. Her eyes had a sparkle in them and she had so many questions for them. Relax, there will be plenty of time for them and for now, stay still.

Helma was helped to get out of the cart. For the next several days, we will be doing the heavy lifting for you. For now, it is time for your body to absorb the feeling of a bubble bath and some aftercare with us on the pillow pile. Helma smiled at them and let them place her in the tub. The hydro jets were turned on and the smile on her face was worth a million. We will be in the next room, so if you need anything, just let us know.

Helma sat soaking in the lightly scented bubble bath for what she thought was days. Ilsa and Frieda returned and told her that it had been over an hour and that there were some snacks waiting for her. Did you get me a steak and French fries? No Helma, being a doctor you should know better. You will start out on some lime jello and than some pudding. Helma muttered chocolate pudding? Yes as we know it is your favorite. Later this evening, we will partake in one of the chief's best cheese cakes with the x-large strawberries.

They removed her from the bath and gently patted her dry. I didn't know just how wonderful I could feel after a bath. We are glad to hear this. Now we will guide you to the awaiting pile of pillows to just lay and blow off the night. Don't worry; we will be lying with you all night. Helma's half broken body was let slip into the pillows and a light blanket was placed over her. Don't talk too much until in the morning. You will have plenty of company in the morning as both Carl and Wolfgang will be visiting to see how you are doing. The lights were turned down and a lot of caressing of Helma's body started.

Day One after Initiation

As early morning came, Ilsa and Frieda slipped away from the pile of pillows. Each returned to their bedroom and selected a sun suit and comfortable shoes for the day. Once dressed, they went to Helma's closet and selected a set of light sweat pants and a colorful print top. Returning to the living room where their new sister lay on the pile of pillows, they gently woke her and assisted her to dress.

Helma, we want you to just lay here and rest. We are going to go to breakfast and a meeting with Wolfgang. What would you like to your first soft hot meal? Maybe some oatmeal with brown sugar and boiled raisins or some scrambled eggs with a pile of crisp bacon. Helma looked up at the two of them and said that either or all would help fill her empty tummy. Also I could use a whole pot of the chief's prize winning coffee. Ilsa turned and said she would place her order and they would return with them soon.

Ilsa and Fried proceeded to the private dinning area and first presented Helma's order to the Chief and than took their plate and selected breakfast. They returned to a table with Wolfgang sitting with his meal. Greetings were exchanged and all slowly ate. Wolfgang started by asking how Helma made it through the night. She is well and looking forward to a full breakfast. She is also full of questions and wants to know more about her new roll around here. That sounds like she made it without any mental problems.

Except for a considerable amount of stiffness, she was doing well after a full night's unrestricted sleep. She has already been told that both you and Carl will be making visits today. This is tradition with new members of the sisterhood. It is around 8 now; I have a few problems to take of so I will be there around 10. I will call Carl and find out when he will come by. Make sure that you inform Helma that she is not to get up and move. She can remain in the pillow stack.

Frieda went to the Chief and picked up the order. He said that he also included several hot, freshly baked biscuits. This should make our Doctor happy this morning. The two of them exited the dining area and returned to the room. They knocked first and entered the room. Helma was sleeping lightly and she came to life with the smells of the morning's food. Just in case you forgot the rules for the next day or two, we will be doing the lifting and you are to work on getting your strength back.

You went through an ordeal that only the extreme prisoner's go through. Hon, just sit up a little in the stack of pillows and we will bring your serving tray over.

Helma's eyes started to open as wide as silver dollars with the arrival of her food. I didn't think that I could be so hungry after my little ordeal.

Helma began to take in some of the eggs with some grape jelly on her biscuits. She started to sip on the hot coffee and found it refreshing and started to remove the crusty taste and feeling in her mouth. How did you sleep last night? I must say that it was kind of mundane compared to the last 36 hours.

Yes, I was able to move, but the lack of pain and being required to service the two of you were lacking. I guess that I am a true "pain slut". I have sat thinking of the many differences in my personal idea of myself over the last several hours.

These are things that we have all gone through after the initiation process. Remember, you are only the thirteenth one to experience it and make the trip from outsider to one of us. What happened to you was meant to wash out someone that might be too weak to perform the upcoming chores. Don't think of it now as we will be going over a great deal of training in the next month or two. Finish your breakfast as Wolfgang will be her shortly.

After a short time, a knock on the door was heard. Ilsa went and escorted Wolfgang along with Carl into where Helma was sitting. They both said good morning and proceeded to sit on the sofa across from her. Carl started by asking how she was doing? Sir, I am doing well, just moving a little slow. Understandable after what you were put through. I hope that you understand that we had to make it rough on you. Yes sir, I do and as weird as it sounds, I had fun and enjoyed it very much. Wolfgang turned and said I always knew your enjoyed the submissive as well as the pain side we offer here. What you endured was only a taste of what you will be putting others through.

Starting in around two weeks, Ilsa and Frieda will start you into an intensive training program. It will include the fine art of interrogation as well as bring a slow and painful death to those assigned to you. For now, just lay back and relax. I will allow you to visit with your paramedic and make sure your office is running right. Other than that, you are to spend time in the pool, sunning and getting a great tan. I will be calling you into my office around every other day. I want you to feel free to talk over your experiences.

Training Begins

Helma's recovery was progressing quickly. The first few days were spent lying around her room. Ilsa and Frieda spent most of their days working on their daily paperwork and planning several new and up coming programs. Helma was still getting her meals brought to her and getting stronger with each meal.

By the forth day since her release, both her inner strength as well as her clearing mind got stronger. Ilsa and Frieda not only talked to her, as well as much cuddling. I want to get out of this room. I am going crazy sitting around. Helma downed her light blue sun dress and departed for the sixth floor for a day of lounging. She selected a full lounge chair and requesting one of the helpers for an umbrella and a floppy hat to shade her face.

The combination of both the week in slavery for the Medieval Fest as well as the initiation scene took a toll on her body. She was very conscious of the many burses as well as welts which were still visible on most of her body. When asked, she would replay that they got out of hand at the play scenes in the court yard.

She was enjoying laying and soaking up the warm from the sun. A soft tap on her shoulder brought her to a state of awake. Wolfgang was standing over her with a smile on his face. I am glad that you are back on you feet and away from your room. Helma replied that she just didn't like being cooped up. I just had to stretch my legs and enjoy the beautiful view. So, how are you recovering? Helma answered that she still ached in the shoulders and hips, but other wise fine.

Since we are alone up here, I need to talk to you. Sir, am I or did I do something wrong. On the contrary, Both Carl and I are so very proud of how you took the initiation ceremony. We hope that you understood why we were so nasty to you. Your understanding of the pain and discomfort that you will be imparting upon those you are brought before you is critical. Have you had any second thoughts to the fact that you will be destroying both body and souls?

I believe that my trip here to take part in the TOY package removed deep feelings of inflecting the pain and torment on a human being. There were and are many time that the conflict of being a doctor that I am still mauling over. Do you think it will get in the way of performing the job of the sisterhood? No, I can guarantee you that it is a job which I will do to the max of my ability. I know that I can separate both sides of my inner being.

I know that it will be some time before I will be as good as Ilsa or Frieda. They are so mild mannered, but with the personnel experience of their savage side, I will get the necessary training I need to do the job. I will need to separate the scenes from those I have done here with the information gathering or just revenge on the body of an unlucky person.

Helma, I am glad to know how you feel. I want you to get back into the Chalet routine this week. Visit you Doctor's office and work with your assistant. He has been doing a great job treating the general population and should be complimented. As the fact is, you may be unavailable to be with him on a daily basis. Let me know if you think he needs additional training, equipment or even a helper. I will meet with him in the morning and talk over the job in more detail.

After Wolfgang departed the lounge area, Helma decided to stay a little longer till the dinner meal. She was excided about joining Ilsa and Frieda in the staff dining room for the first time since the Medieval Fest started. The cooling breeze and the sun shine were bringing her back to her former self. As the sun was starting to slowly be swallowed up in the west, she started to make her way to the dining room.

She entered the dining area and sat at the table being occupied by her room mates. So Helma, how did you do on your first day out? It felt so human and brought myself to a wonderful state. I did many hours of digesting the two days of the initiation along with the requirements of the life contract I signed. I have no regrets by signing it and wish to do many hours of talking with the both of you.

Turning to the waitress, she took the menu and spent the next ten minutes studying the fabulous choices. She looked at Ilsa and Frieda who were patiently waiting to order. Sorry, but it had been a week and a half of eating what was placed in front of me. No complaining of your choices you made, but I feel like a totally new person. Helma looked at the waitress and started to order it.

I want to get the surf and turf meal. A two inch stake, medium rear and a large lobster, broccoli with cheddar cheese sauce, a fresh beaked hard roll, butter and a piece of apple pie. Frieda turned to her and asked what else she could add to empty the kitchen out. The three of them just laughed and ordered their own meal. The meal was served and all ate their choice.

They finished their meal and returned to their room. Small talk on the way back brought an idea all could agree to. They each went to their bathrooms and took a hot bubble bath, downed a robe and met in the living room. They entered the elevator and went to the sixth floor. The sun was almost totally gone by this point. A light cooling breeze was blowing across the sandy area.

The women went to the sandy area, disrobed from their sun dresses and lay in the sand. Helma was in the middle and was doing snow angles in the sand. Frieda and Ilsa just chuckled and joined her. Helma said, this is living and I need to do this more often. They cuddled in each others hands and watched the stars come up. Around midnight, they went back to their room and quickly showered and settled in for a good nights rest.

Helma woke early the next morning. She penciled a note for Ilsa stating that she was going to her office. She downed a more business attire and walked down the hall to the clinic. As she entered, she drew Dave's attention and even a quiet cat call. I am glad to see you back Doctor Jones. It's been over a week since you checked in. I will say that

I did watch you during the time you were chained in the courtyard. I believe that I even might have hit you with a tomato.

So that was you Dave. I think that you might want to practice your aim for the next festival. Will do Doc. What is on the agenda for the day? First, I want to let you know that I got so many great comments on your performance. Even Wolfgang told me that you worked your wonders on those that came in for treatment. I will ask you about the time the guest tripped on her long dress and came in for a look see. I find it interesting that you did such a great examination of her body. I hope that it was OK, but she was such a hot babe.

I don't care as long as you had her permission to run your hands over her tender lovely ass. My only question to you was did she enjoy it as much as you did. Doc, all I will say is that she asked if I could join her in one of the dark areas in the court yard for a cool drink and some fooling around. I explained to her that it wasn't allowed to be with a paying guest, but did invite her back to check out her hurting rump. She made three more trips back.

Alright Dave, I need to talk to you. Over the last week, I was involved in more of the events within the Chalet. After talking with Wolfgang, he has informed me that I will be spending more of my time with Chalet activities. What I am trying to tell you is that you will be in charge must of the time. Do you feel comfortable doing the bulk of time? Dave thought for a minute and answered.

If this is what is on the horizon, I would ask for some advanced training in the emergency side of my duties. I could also need an assistance, maybe an EMT to assist and do the receptions work. Dave, I think I can sell these ideas to Wolfgang. Have you done any research on training which is offender locally? I will do this afternoon as my assignment.

Do you someone in mind for the assistant? I do, she is on the ski rescue team that I use to work with. Her name is Heidi and is a very hard and knowledgeable worker. Great, I want to talk to her as soon as possible. If Wolfgang gives me the OK, I want her on board to start training. One question, are you involved with her? Dave answered with a two word answer, kind of. I don't care, just don't use the examination table to enjoy the longs hours here.

Helma wished Dave a great day and departed the office. She walked down to Wolfgang's office. The secretary greeted her and asked what she needed. I would like to talk to Wolfgang if possible. She checked his schedule and buzzed him. Sir, Doctor Jones is here and would like a few minutes with you. Very good, have her come in. Helma knocked on his door and was invited in.

Helma, how can I help you today? Sir, I did as you requested and talked with my assistant Dave. He would like some advanced training as well as an assistant. He will supply me with the different training programs he would like to take. He also has another person in mind from the ski rescue team for his assistant.

These are not absorbent requests and I will approve the requests. I think you should interview his new assistant and make sure you are feeling good about her. You understand that we can't pay her as much as Dave, but will increase hers rate as well as Dave's salary as time goes on. I have a request for a larger expense item. OK, lay it on me Helma. I would like to get a four wheel ATV equipped as an ambulance to bring those that get hurt on the grounds. Get me the specifications and I will get it ordered.

Thank you sir, as you know, I will be starting my advanced training with Frieda and Ilsa. I will carry my phone with me so I can handle emergencies if they arise. Very good except, your training comes first and let Dave handle all except dire emergencies. Helma agreed and departed the office and returned to her room.

As the week pasted by, Helma tied up the loose ends. She interviewed the EMT helper for her office and made sure that Dave was well versed as to his job and what he could do. Helma also had fully recovered from her time in the cell and the welts were almost gone. It was Friday afternoon and she along with Ilsa and Frieda decided to blow off the weekend as Helma's in depth training was to start on Monday.

The weekend was slow in the Chalet as no packages were in progress and people were coming and going for their personnel relaxation. The two days were spent between going to the pool to do laps, hitting a few balls on the tennis court and a ride up into the country side on horse back. They splurged in the dining area and finished their evenings together in the living room, naked and in each others arms. Ilsa turned to Frieda and Helma and stated that the time was just going too fast.

Helma's training starts

The three of them went to the dinning room for breakfast. All enjoyed the variety of items on the buffet. As they sat enjoying some strong German coffee, Wolfgang joined them at their table. Niceties were exchanged and he asked them to his office when they finished. They said they would follow him down to the first floor office.

Wolfgang entered the outer office and turned to the secretary. I will be having a long meeting with the three women and I do not want to be disturbed except for Carl or if the Chalet is on fire. She nodded that she understood and asked if refreshments would be required. Wolfgang responded by asking for a pot of coffee and some ice tea. These items were delivered and the door shut tight.

Wolfgang took his seat at his massive desk and indicated for them to have a seat. Helma, you will be starting your training today. The girls will be taking you into the depths of the sisterhood. Any and all training you get is top secret and can not be transferred to anyone.

Ilsa, are you going to start in your quarters or in the sub basement? I will start in our quarters and move down. Good, your training aid will be here later today and you will have to bed him in. Carl has been asked to handle the work on a political prisoner. We are not being paid for his use and there is no record of his transfer to our facility. There is a full set of notes in his envelope which will be accompanying him. Some small talk concluded the meeting and all departed.

The three women departed Wolfgang's office for their room. Frieda said that she was going to the kitchen and secures a large carafe of coffee and some snacks to get thru the day. Ilsa and Helma entered the living room. Ilsa turned to Helma and suggested that they put on comfortable clothing.

Ilsa went to her room and downed a sloppy set of jeans and a light T-shirt. Helma put on her favorite as well as the others, green, short sleeve leotards. Frieda entered and gave Helma a cat call showing how much she liked her choice in attire. Frieda asked Helma if she minded if she dressed in a unitard? No problem, I would like to see you in it.

Within minutes, Frieda returned wearing her shimmery purple unitard. She walked over to the couch and took up place next to Helma. Ilsa, bring the senior member of the sisterhood at the Chalet, handed Helma a several inches thick binder. This is our operating manual for what we do. Over the next few days, you will be required to read and memorized the contents. Helma took the book and opened it to the title page. Her name was embossed in gold on the page. I am so proud to receive it from you. You will be required to keep it in the lower dungeon safe.

Helma had a lost look on her face. Yes, we said the lower dungeon safe. We will be taking you down there at the close of the day. You will need this new key card to access the area. A totally blank key card with the number three on it was handed to her. Wolfgang and Carl have the Master cards.

Helma opened the book to section one. The label had the words on it "Person of interest". This is how we identify who we are going to work on. There will never be a name of the person as we don't have to know it. There will be a picture of the person or persons which we will be working with. There is also a description as in the height, weight and sex of this body. We will show you later this afternoon.

Section after section was gone over. The most important sheet is what they require from us. It will describe what you are to do with them. Good deals of them are to be interrogated for secrets, governmental, industrial or other. We also are entrusted to do revenge on them. Never mind the reason why they are being destroyed by us. Other details will be included such as intensity or type of pain they want them to be put through.

The biggest thing you need to understand is that they are here for only thing; go out in as much pain as possible. You must never get involved with them or feel sorry for them. They maybe younger or older than you, male or female, and very good looking or ugly in appearance. All you can see them as is the project you have been assigned. Any questions so far? No. but I will need some time to memorize the contents better. You will be given the time, but only in the lower dungeon.

Ilsa received a call stating the person they would be working on is on his way. Helma and Frieda put on a set of jeans and light shirt for the trip down stairs. They went down to the normal dungeon area. Helma looked around and said that this is where she was used to playing in. You are right; follow us down the ramp and past the wine pressing room. As they passed that door, Ilsa indicated for Helma to open the next door.

As she opened the door, a set of lights came on showing another long ramp going below the wine pressing room. The ramp led to a large room with fifteen foot high ceilings. The first thing Helma notice was the walls were covered in rings to attach people. The far corner had an oaken door which when opened shown four sets of cells. Each cell was three feet by three feet by eight long. A heavy barred door with lock on it finished the top. The other end was the stone wall of the structure. Rings for attachment were all around the inside of the cell.

A second door finished the area. Helma opened it and found a desk, several chairs and a set of lockers. A small refrigerator stood in the corner. A heavy duty safe was inset into the wall. To open it, you will need to insert the entry card and enter your sisterhood number and birthday. Helma tried it and it opened. She found both Lisa's and Frieda's instruction books stored within. This is where you will place your book in from now on. If you wish to study it, you will come down here.

Helma, there is one more item in the safe. It is a key for the toy chest in the large room. Like the safe, it takes your key card and key to open. Let's go and open it and show you the new toys you will use during you work.

Helma opened the toy chest and took a step back. WOW, these items are a lot different from the ones in the dungeon. I don't even remember anything this bad from when we did the "TOY" program. You are right Helma; these are meant to inflect more pain and torture on a victim. Remember, we are in the business of either retrieving information quickly or just the prolonged agony.

Ilsa turned to Helma and told her to pick up any item and we will explain its use. Helma selected two different floggers. The first had many thick leather tails, each with metal shot balls on it tips. This is designed after the ones used in the roman times. It is called a scourge. It was meant to not only open flesh, but could break bones. I can see how it would do this.

The second one had a wooden handle with six tales of different length of barb wire. We use this one to inflect much pain. The barbs will also open the flesh in many places. Depending how hard you swing it, you can just barely make it enter the skin or a hard swing will make deep openings. The open area can than be flooded with a pickling brine or rub salt into. The combination will normally bring screams and terror to even the hardest nuts to crack.

Helma picked up one item after the other. As you can see, many of the toys are the same as up stairs, but with some changes. She picked up the pear of anguish. Almost like the one up stairs except it is made of solid brass for great passage of electric charge through it and into the body. The second this is that the sharp points on the ends of the leaves will cut into the inner lining of which ever hole your place it. Third, try spinning it around some. The leaves spread open to almost six inches across. Just think of the damage which will occur.

By half way thru the chest Helma was in a semi dropped state. Frieda turned to Ilsa and said that I bet she wants to try the new toys. Ilsa turned to Helma and snapped her fingers in front of her face. Snap out of it Helma, you can only fondle these toys. Most of them would make you unable to work with us or even "DEAD". She snapped out of her trance and back to reality.

Don't worry Helma, when we demonstrate some of the items and procedures, you will be the torture dummy. Step over to the middle of the open area. They did and Ilsa proceeded to show Helma the many ways to stretch a person. She pointed to the ceiling first. There are five different electrically operated winches. We can lift a body in several directions at once.

Guiding her hand around the floor of the chamber, Frieda pointed six different points where winches with cables and hooks were attached at the wall. We like to refer to this as being like stretching by the four horses. We can operate each winch by it self or all at once. We have even once had an arm tore from its socket. It is a feeling to "Die" for.

Helma, this will be your first try at being a torture dump. You are to go to the office and strip of your clothes. Once you return, lie on the floor and wait. You might want to bring your gag with you as this will get very painful. She did as commended and returned within two minutes. She dropped to the floor and waited for Ilsa to start her adventure.

Now Helma, spread your arms and legs in an "X" pattern. We are asking you, but a prisoner is forcibly spread. At this point, Helma was so excited; she spread and held the position. Ilsa and Frieda brought sets of steel shackles and placed them on her wrists and legs. A steel collar was than placed around her neck. Next came the gag, her favorite, the penis shaped gag. Prior to inserting, both Ilsa and Frieda inserted it into their womanhood and coated it in their thick white cum.

The insertion into her mouth brought pleasure to Helma. She always enjoyed the taste of her two friends and sisters. The hooks and cables were brought from the four winches and attached to Helma's wrists and ankles. Ilsa now brought the remote control box and showed it to Helma as she lay on the floor. From this box, we can take out the slack and go from there. Ilsa pushed the button to control the four winces all at the same time.

The first press will just take all the slack out of the cables. The slack was slowly removed; bring Helma to a taunt status. As you can see, we are just at a tight position, maybe a little uncomfortable. Helma agreed and shook her head. Now, let us see how much you enjoy the next moves.

The next click on the button brought only a half inch of slack to be removed from each winch. This isn't bad, just only uncomfortable. Another push brought Helma to a rigid position. There was no more wiggle room in her arms and legs. Helma, can you understand the fear of the prisoner? She again shook her head yes.

Now, you will feel the tremendous pressure that can be exerted on them. Another press of the button and Helma let out her first cry of pain. You are now beginning to feel the torment of the pulling. I want you to try to remove the pain by wiggling around on the floor. As hard as she tried, no relief could be found.

Ilsa stood over her and asked if she thought she could handle another half of slack be removed. Helma shook her head yes and the button was pushed. Helma immediately let out a blood curdling scream. You can see how effect this is to get the victim set to answer questions. Again she shook her head yes.

Just to add to their agony, let us do some play on your body to show you how much fun you will have. Frieda went to wall where the bull whips were hanging. Ilsa went and got a three foot section of cheese cloth, folded into a section of about eight inches by eight inches and places it over Helma's mouth and nose.

Ilsa and Frieda glanced at each other and proceeded. Frieda with the procession that came with many years of wielding the whip let its tips fall across Helma's tender pussy lips. As Helma was absorbing the pain on this area, Ilsa squatted over her face. This is our version of water boarding. A little at a time, she let her yellow fluid soak the cheese cloth. The effect was instant. Helma was struggling to breath and for the first time actually begged for it to be over. The begging at first did no good to relieve the situation.

After several minutes, the soaking of the cloth as well as the whipping stopped. Ilsa removed the cloth and Frieda put the whip back on the wall. Ilsa again took the control box and pressed the button to let the cables reverse. This let Helma's body come back to resting position. They removed the hooks from the shackles. Helma's sweat covered body went limp and she was sobbing.

Ilsa removed the gag from her mouth. Helma lay on the floor in a sobbing, limp fetal position. The two women both got down and cuddled her. It took several minutes for Helma to regain her thoughts. Helma, are you with us? She shook her head and asked if she could have a blanket. One was brought for her and laid on her.

Helma tried to sit up, but could only make it part way up. The first words from her were that this is very painful. I was more scared and in more pain than at any time since I have been here. I thought that I could take it, but it didn't click. The stretching was bad, but the feeling of drowning and being whipped made it worse. I am beginning to understand how it works now.

As she regained the feeling in her arms and legs, she sat and than stood. They escorted her to the office so she could redress herself. Slowly, they got ready to depart the lower dungeon. All materials were returned to the toy chest and safe and it was secured. Helma said that she thought she could make it back on her own, but standby just in case I might need help. The trip was slow back up to the elevator and to their room.

Helma went right to her bedroom and drew a steaming hot bath, added some bubbles to it and sunk into it. The other women did the same. Once they felt human again, they returned to the living room. Helma started the conversation by saying that she had never felt so helpless and scared. I know that another click of the button and I would have dislocated my ankle and wrist sockets. I know I will be sore in the morning.

Frieda than turned to her and said that this is as close to being pulled apart on the rack as can be. You now have an understanding of our job. This is not like the Fifty Shades of Gray we practice in the normal dungeon with the slave packages. Your job is to inflect as much pain and suffering as possible, per the instruction sheet. We did let you off some.

We could have placed a hook on your collar, and another in your case, to inert the pear of anguish and pulled you from all angles at once. If you would have been a male, a rope would have been placed around your cock and balls. All Helma could say was Ouch. They proceeded to the evening meal and relaxed.

Over the next several days, the three women spent many hours together. They would talk over what the instructions on what was to be done to the victim. They also went to the lower dungeon to go over the storage of prisoners and the many new tools to use on them.

Helma caught on fast. She was so fascinated with the feel of the tools. She would take them out and touch and rub or place each of them on her body. At one point, she took out the pear of anguish and spun it around. She thought how it would feel. She asked Frieda if she could insert into her own vagina. Frieda told her to lie on the floor and spread her legs. Ilsa bent over her on one side and spread the tender little lips.

Frieda took the tip of the leaves and inserted up inside her. Much care was used as to not nick her insides with the sharp tips. It finally settled in to the depths of her inner area. With that, Frieda asked Helma if she was ready to be stretched.

A quarter of a turn at a time of the handle expanded the four leaves. The pressure grew and the pain came I steady waves. Helma requested another turn to feel the full extent of the process. By two more turns, she was again begging for it to be removed. Frieda turned the handle, closing the instrument and removed it.

As the torture instrument was removed, Helma let out big shy of relief. She took a look at the leaves and noted that there was a slight covering of red. Her first statement was that I hope that as an OBGYN doctor, I never put any woman into that much pain. Frieda told her that the tool would have been shoved in roughly and made sure that the points jammed into the surrounding tissue. You also only got maybe half the turns to open up the canal. Helma, just remember it can go up the rectal cannel of either a male or female.

Helma crawled/walked back to the office. I can see how this item can bring both the information from them as well as destruction of the body. Remember, the item is made of solid brass and electric shocks can be added to the pain. You can also apply tension or weights to the handle and pull it out as far as possible. The pressure on the openings is a max process.

Helma, I understand that you have only had a weeks worth of training. You should be able to assist in the interrogation of a person. You will get your chance to practice this training. Wolfgang has informed me that we will be getting in a male tomorrow. We will walk you through the entire routine starting in the morning. Now, let us go up to dinner and enjoy the rest of the evening.

Her first try at Real Pain Giving

A truck without any markings was pulling up to the main gate. A security member from the Chalet pulled up to the gate. After checking the paperwork, they told the driver to follow the security jeep to the rear entrance. The driver acknowledged the instructions and both vehicles proceeded to the loading dock.

Security alerted Wolfgang and he than alerted Ilsa of their arrival. The three sisterhood members took the elevator to the lower level and thru the play room. The laundry cart was brought to the door at the dock. Ilsa indicated to the driver and he should back to the door.

Ilsa accepted a sealed envelope and the cart was wheeled into the rear of the truck. Frieda and Helma saw a sack resembling a mail bag in the front of the truck. Frieda took her pointed toe of her foot and kicked the bag to check for movement. None was seen, so the bag with its contents was loaded into the laundry cart. A hand shake between Ilsa and the driver concluded the transaction and the truck drove out.

As Frieda and Helma began pushing the cart in the door as Ilsa opened the doors leading to the lower dungeon. Once inside the dungeon, they rolled the cart to the cell area. Its contents were dumped on the floor. The bag rolled over several times and came to a dead lump on the floor. Frieda instructed Helma to unlace the bag to expose it contents.

As the man's head was exposed and it was checked against the photo in the sealed enveloped. The remaining laces were removed and the naked body of the man was seen. He was a man of European decent. His body was around that of a five foot eight inch man of medium build. Burses were covering his body and face. He had already been worked over severely.

The first cell was opened and his unconscious body was tossed inside. Frieda selected sets of rusty hand and ankle shackles and placed them on him. Next to come was a steel collar. The wrists were first to be attached. They were secured to the top end of the cage. He was stretched taunt and they pulled his legs toward to the lower ends of the cage. A rope was run through the attachment of the collar and drawn tight to the top of the cage. Several wide belts were placed around the man securing him tight to the bottom of the cage. There was no wiggle room to move.

Helma was getting into the prisoners dilemma. She looked at Ilsa and asked if she can grab him to see is he was coming too. Ilsa said that it was OK, but don't do any permanent damage, at least not yet. Helma knelt next the cage a reached in. Taking her hand, she applied a tight clutch of his ball. With a quick snatch, she both squeezed and dug her fingernails into the sack. A low groan was heard from him.

This sounds like he is coming alive again. We had better try a better stimulus. Helma took a hand held veterinarian cattle prod and jammed it into the area between his balls and rectal opening. She squeezed the trigger sending an electric charge into the area. He instantly came to life and tried to trash around.

Welcome to our little dungeon. As you can see, you are not in charge and at our whims. Just lay back, as if you have a choice and enjoy your holding area. Sooner rather than later you will be enjoying our hospitality. As you can tell, we have not gagged you. All the yelling and screaming will stay right here, so you can go ahead and scream as much as you want.

The three left the cell area, turned out the lights and shut the door. They retired to the office area to go over the paperwork in the envelope. They each went to the refrigerator, took a soft drink and sat in a circle. Ilsa took out the paper and started to read them to the group.

Helma, this is the first steep in the processing of a prisoner. We have a very strict list of requirements for the inflection of pain. Wither he is just a prisoner here to be punished or interrogated for information.

We have a 36 year old man around 168 pounds. He was accused of being a dissident and causing riots. He has already been interrogated for any information on his cell and gave up the remaining members. We are to make his life, what is left of it a pure "HELL". There are no limits as to what we can do to him, only that it is to last as long as possible.

Ilsa placed the report in the office safe and locked it up. Helma, I believe that this will be a great teaching session for you. We will be able to teach you different methods to both inflect pain and some interrogation techniques. Remember, you must place your Doctor's Creed aside and not worry over him. He is not human anymore. The three departed the lower dungeon and went to their room.

Day One

The three women returned to their room from breakfast. Ilsa had them seated in their living room to prepare for their first day of work on the new prisoner. She turned to Helma and asked her if she had done any of the planning for the days work. She said that several thoughts had come to mind.

I think I want to start by doing a good whipping on his back and ass. Frieda said that this would be a good start. We do not want him to get too hurt as the punishment phase was to last for several days. Next and for maybe the remainder of the day, I want to stretch him in two different directions at the same time. The strain on him should turn him into a slobbering pile of slime.

The exchange of ideas continued for the next hour. When a firm plan was organized, they departed for the lower dungeon. Helma was told to go first and start the prep of the prisoner.

She entered the cells area. Turned on the lights and went to the table with tools on it. She picked up the cattle prod and shoved it into his balls. He tried to rip himself from his bonds without any luck. Helma stood by the head end of the cell and told him that he had better do as told or the prod would be used on his eyeballs. Also, while we move you, one of us will have a stun gun ready and apply it where it will really sting.

Both Frieda and Helma raised the top of the cage. To make you better understand just how much worse it can get. Frieda started by kicking his balls. They began to release the ties from his ankles. He tried to bend his legs to relieve the stiffness from being tightly secured overnight. Ilsa moved over to him and reminded him what would happen if he moved again. He took a position of not moving again.

The rest of the restraints were removed, leaving him totally loose. Now stand up, hands behind your head. As he tried to stand, his motions were a little slow for Frieda. She used the cattle prod to encourage his movement. Now step out of the cage and start moving to the other room. His steps were slow, but steady. He turned the corner and into the dungeon area and he tried to stop. Keep moving toward the far walls and stand looking the wall in your face.

At this point, Frieda and Helma used chains from his wrist shackles and stretched his arms wide, securing them to rings high up on the wall. He was standing on his tip toes at this point. Chains were now attached to the ankle shackles and his legs were yanked out from under him. This left him hanging by his wrists and in pain.

Helma went up to his head and whispered that from now on, his pain would be far worse than anything the secret police had done to him. She stood behind him, grabbed his balls and yanked on them. He let out a scream which reverberated through out the dungeon.

Ilsa and Frieda went to the wall and each picked out their favorite bull whips. Standing on either side of him, they let loose on his back with their whips. Twisting and turning, he tried to move out the way. The tail or each found a different spot, bring up welts and even a little blood showed.

After at least twenty strikes each on his back, the two stood back. Helma stepped forward with her riding crop and began work on his balls. The sound of a wounded animal was leaving his mouth. The whipping and beating continued on and off for hours, with several breaks to allow the women to get a cool drink and rest their arms.

It was approaching the dinner hour for the woman. Ilsa turned to Helma and asked what she wanted to do to bed him down for the night. She answered that she thought he should be placed down on the floor and his arms and legs be spread tight.

They released the chains from his ankles and than wrists. He fell to the floor into a limp pile. They grabbed him under the shoulders and dragged him to the center of the room. The control box was tapped, releasing the four corner winches. The hooks and cables were brought over to him and attached to his wrists and ankles. Another tap of the control box buttons took all the slack from his body.

Ilsa handed the box to Helma, telling her to place him in as much stretch as she wished. She remembered how it felt for her spreading and said that she wanted him even more open. The processed for what must have felt like hours, but in reality was only a minute or two. Helma went over to a hip, kicked it to see how much he could move. He wasn't even able to get a quarter inch of relief. I think this should start to make him a little uncomfortable over night.

I want to give him a little more to think about tonight. She took the box and brought a cable and hook down from an overhead winch. Helma now went to a box on the table and selected a dozen 1/0 fishing hooks with leaders. Now let me see where I will set them.

She dropped to her knees and one by one pushed them through his ball sack. You could hear the popping sound as it penetrated in one side and out the other. The levels of the screams increased till he had no voice left. This looks very pretty, but lacks a little something else. She gathered up the ends of the leaders and hooked each one over the hook coming down from the ceiling.

Turning to both Ilsa and Frieda, she offered the control box to them. They both shook their heads and told her to have fun. Helma went over to his head and asked him to let her know when it hurts. With a flick of her finger, the cable began to be taken in and took the slack out of the leaders. A little at a time, slack was taken out of his ball sack. She flicked at the leaders to test how tight they were.

He was now trashing his head around, begging her to stop. She turned to him and said how sorry she was, but than took another half inch of slack out. A little at a time, he tried to raise hip hips off the ground to relieve the pain. This is exactly what she was going for.

When he was an inch off the ground, she stepped back and said what a beautiful piece of art she had formed. Ilsa turned to Frieda and said, this will be fun to see how much meat from his sack will be torn off his ball by the morning. With that, they turned the lights out and locked the door.

They returned to their room and discussed the day's events. Helma sat by listening to the critique from the other two. You did wonderful for your first day. The position you left him in for the evening was great. He will have a great deal of trouble moving in the morning.

They each went and had a hot bath and dressed for a nights fun. They went to the dining room and took in many wonderful items. Wining and Dancing finished off the evening. They returned to the room and sat to go over the next day. Helma turned to the others and asked, were we supposed to feed and water hi tonight. A loud "NO" came back from the two. Just as if you were going to operate on a patient, you don't want anything in their system. You don't want them to pee or drop a load when working on them. Good night and try to get some sleep.

Day Two

The door to the lower dungeon was very quietly opened as to not alert the prisoner. He lay on the floor in a semi trance. There were small streams of blood coming from the area of his ball sack. The fish hooks had done there jobs in tenderizing his man hood. Helma walked over to the cable holding the fish hook leaders and gave it a swat. The reactions to this action were immediate. His head trashed and his bottom bounced off the ground as much as possible.

I think he is enjoying himself way too much. I need to settle him down so we can play more. Helma went to the wall and removed the carbon dioxide, CO_2, fire extinguisher. She spun the plastic cone from the end of the hose so the hose could be used in a limited area. I think we should cool him down.

She walked over to just between his legs and placed the hose tip up against his anal opening. With a push, the tip entered the rose bud opening. Even though he tried using the mussels closing the opening, she roughly worked the tip of the hose into the opening. I think this will cool him off and she gave the handles a quick squeeze.

Again, he tried to jump and dislodge the nozzle. Ilsa said that she hadn't thought of this action before. Frieda walked over to Helma and asked if she could give it a squeeze. I would love to share the fun with you. Frieda gave the handles several squeezes, sending him into begging as well as screaming rages. Wonderful, he is very much awake.

Frieda removed the tip of the hose from his anal opening. As she removed it, she gave it a brief burst of the icy cold air over his inflamed balls. If by now he wasn't going insane, he was approaching it quickly. Ilsa looked at Helma and told her that she was in charge of the remaining session. You lead and we will do as you want.

Helma look a little surprised as this was her first session doing Sisterhood work. Before we release his legs, we need to approach his fish hook problem. I know we could just cut the hooks in half and remove both halves, but what fun would this be. Helma went to the tool table and selected a set of heavy duty linesman's pliers. Next, she released the hook leaders from the hook which drew them to the ceiling.

His balls with hooks now lay on the floor. His face showed a little relief, but it was shorted lived. Helma looked carefully at the tip of the hooks. There was a barb on the end, preventing the hook from slipping off. Wow, I wonder how much meat I can rip apart yanking them out. She took the pliers and grabbed the hook. She withdrew the hook taking it back out the way she had put them in. As the barb reached the opening, it tore the skin, causing it to rip flesh wide open.

His reactions were instant. He screamed himself almost horse and begged to have them left in. Ilsa placed her hand over his mouth to muffle his feeble attempt to cry out. Helma told him to not let out any more cries or she would take a scalpel and cut them out. Believe me; this will hurt much less than that move. He settled down and Helma went about finishing the task.

As the last hook was removed, Helma called for a bottle of 70% alcohol and poured the solution over his open wounds. Ilsa had to hold her hand tighter over his mouth to silence him. Great reaction to making sure infection would not invade his ball sack. Frieda spoke up that they should cover them.

She went to the table and brought back two different bowls. The first one contained cut up pieces of Habanero hot peppers. Several pieces were rubbed into the open bleeding openings. We now need to set the wounds and a handful of salt was used to coat the balls. You would have thought that a blow torch was brought up and jammed into the flesh.

By this point, he had passed out. Ilsa said that this was a good time to remove him from his position and reposition him. The tension of the cables spreading his arms and legs was released. His body instantly dropped to the floor. The hooks were released, leaving him limp.

Where do we go next Helma? I want to his wrists to a wide spreader bar and hook the bar to a ceiling winch. His arms were pulled behind him and than hooked to the bar. The ceiling winch was attached and the slack was removed. He was slowly being lifted off the floor when the pain of having his shoulders wrenched from behind brought life back into his semi broken body.

Helma took the slack out till he was now on his tip toes. She noted that he was not in as much discomfort as she thought he should be. She looked a Frieda and suggested that she might install one of the sharp needle pin point parachutes around his balls. With a big smile on her face, she snapped it in place. Now, let us hook it to one of the other winches from the ceiling.

Next to come was a pair of 35 pound weights hooked to his ankles. That should just about make his next few hour of paradise. Helma took the winch control box and pressed the button to the winch connected to his balls. A reaction was instant to come. Wither it was the maddening strain on his shoulder being yanked backwards or the needles inserting themselves into the tender skin of his ball sack. Either or both brought incredible pain to his soon to be broken body. Freda went to his head and whispered that the more he kept from struggling, the better he would feel.

I guess that he got the message. He tried to stop flailing after several minutes and a slight relief showed on his face. Still even the slightest movement sent him into a screaming session. Helma now told him he was going to have to endure this for several hours. Don't bother to beg for relief as it was not to come.

Ilsa's phone rang at that moment. She answered it and it was Wolfgang. Ilsa, I want you to come to my office as soon as you can. She answered the she was on the way. She turned to the other two and told them of the call. Just carry on and I should be back in and hour.

Frieda decided that the man was becoming too relaxed for his own good. She took a red felt tip marker and drew bull's eyes on each of the exposed ball within the parachuted and an "X" on the tip of his cock. She exclaimed that it was time to practice their skills with the BB gun. We should have a contest to see how accurate we are. The first one to hit both bull's eyes and the X will win.

Helma asked what the prize was going to be. Frieda chose a sharp scalpel from the table. The winner will have the privilege of digging the BBs from he cock and balls. WOW, that will be great fun. I wonder how far they will penetrate the skin. Don't know as this is the first time we have done it this way. You came up with some great fun games.

Each took turns firing three times each. The first several shots didn't even come close. The either bounced off his ass or legs. The actions instantly got him trashing again. After maybe the fifth or sixth round, Frieda got the first bull's eye. It stuck in his left ball. The second shot hit his cock on the X. Small drips of bright red blood were now starting to stain the floor. Helma was luckier that she got both his balls, but not the cock. Frieda put all three of her shots in the crack between his ass checks.

Helma turned and took the rifle and the next three shots met the mark. The tip of his cock was now bleeding quite profusely. The balls just dripped steadily. I won was shouted from Helma. Frieda just turned to her and said that this was the most fun she had had in some time.

Helma started to work on her prize for winning. She dug the copper BBs out, one by one. The prisoner no longer had the life left in his voice to scream, only in little whimpers. The bleeding was now flowing from every cut Helma made to dig the round balls out. Frieda brought over the container of salt and spread it over the area to crust over the wounds.

Helma told Frieda that if the bleeding didn't stop soon, that she would have to cauterize the wound. She went to the table and picked up the plumbers torch. A little crude, but this should work. Before I start, Frieda, I want you to cover his mouth. I think this will be the loudest scream so far. Frieda took an old set of her panties and peed on them. She fully soaked them and jammed them down his throat.

I think he is sound proofed. Helma held the torch, opened the valve and clicked the igniter. She adjusted the size of the flame and moved toward the cock. She started at his pee hole and flicked the flame over it. The skin sizzled and bubbled. He would no longer to be able to get anything out of it anymore.

She slowly worked the tip up to the exposed, bloody ball sacks. What wonderful little targets they are. She just let the tip of the flame touch a little spot at the time. The smell of singed hair filled the air. She traced the bull's eyes with the thin pencil tip of the flame till all the skin was blackened. Frieda looked into his eyes and told Helma that he was on his way out.

Helma turned and said that she wasn't done having fun. Frieda said that all fun has to come to an end at sometime. She walked to his front and began working on his nipples with the flame. She went around the coronas and than to the tip of his nipples. By this time he didn't even move any more. Frieda checked his breathing and eye movement and declared him dead.

With their prisoner gone, they started the cleanup before Ilsa came back down. The winch released the pull on his balls. Helma took the parachute off and placed it in a bucket to be cleaned. Next the weights on his ankles were released and placed in their storage place. Frieda looked at Helma and said I will teach you a trick so you don't have to work so much.

Go and get the laundry cart. Frieda took the winch control box and raised his body to almost five feet off the ground. As the wench ground to raise the body, you could hear the shoulders crack and pull from their joints. Now bring the cart and place it under his body. Helma did and saw why she was doing this. She lowered the body into the cart. You see, no heavy lifting and all we have to do is remove the spreader bar and shackles.

The covers were placed over the body. The cart was now pushed up the ramp to the dock door. Stay here Helma and I will get the truck. She backed the truck up to the dock. Both women pushed the cart into the back of the truck and each got into the cab for the drive. Helma, was carefully watching as we go to the way back of the property.

After maybe a fifteen minute drive they arrived at a non-descript building. Helma, this is the crematorium. This is where we get rid of all the bodies from the dungeon. Did you ever wonder where we took the "TOY or Party Favor' from the fun? They rolled the cart inside the building. Frieda showed her how the trap door opened and they slid the body inside. Frieda closed the door and went to the control box.

We first turn on the blower. This will make it clear for a clean burn. With the air passing around the body, she set the controls and the ignition process began. A loud roar like a jet engine was heard. A quick look into the inspection window made sure that the fire was roaring. From this time till five hours from now, the automatic controls will ensure the body will be nothing but ash. They closed up the door and reentered the truck.

The short drive back to the truck parking area was short. They walked the rest of the way to the dungeon entrance. They finished cleaning the tool of their trade and pressured washed the floor to remove any blood and pieces of flesh left. They both put on their "Chalet Proper" clothes and returned to their room.

When they returned to the room, Ilsa was sitting there waiting for their return. I went to the dungeon and saw laundry cart missing. I figured that the fun was over so I came back here. Let us all go and get a long, hot bubble bath, put on some light, fun dresses and get dinner. Later when we get back, we can cuddle some and get good nights sleep.

The next morning, they dressed and went to breakfast. They sat down to eat and were met by Wolfgang. I see you did a good job with him. As is tradition, Helma I want to debrief you when you get done with breakfast. She said that she would join him in an Hour. Wolfgang departed for his morning walk around the Chalet. They finished their meal and the two returned to their room and Helma went to Wolfgang's office.

Helma entered the office and was greeted by the secretary. She said that he was waiting for her and to go right in. Helma knocked and heard, come in. She entered the office and was told to have a seat. She did and was offered a sipping mug of very old brandy. She accepted the mug and sat back in the chair.

Helma, as with the other dungeon, there are cameras all around to watch and record the work being done. Both Carl and I watched how you did with your first event. We were very pleased at both how you responded to what was going on as well as how you got into the action. We both believe that you were a very good choice to join the sisterhood. Thank you sir, I very much enjoyed the challenge.

Helma, how are you feeling now that you have the first one behind you? Are you having any problems both being a doctor as well as an interrogator? To answer both questions, I feel like I have never been in the past. As for the doctor, I am sure that I can still separate the two. That is good as we just took a contract for two more prisoners.

I spoke to Ilsa yesterday and she will brief you later today. Now go out and do some sunning on the sixth floor and relax. Thank you sir and I hope I can meet your standards in the future. With that she went to her room, changed into her bathing suit and blow off the rest of the afternoon.

The Briefing

The three women departed the dining room after breakfast to work on their new project. Helma, I think you should secure some of those great pastries and a large pot of coffee. Maybe you should make those two pots as we may be downstairs a while. Down they went to the lower dungeon.

Ilsa took the package given to her by Wolfgang. Ladies, we have a paid interrogation. Helma, I am sorry that you haven't had time to digest the prisoner we just worked on, but this is how it is sometimes. Unlike yesterday, this will be two females, a mother and daughter combination.

This is a paid job. Carl is doing this for a fee of $100,000, unlike the man we just did which was a favor. The two are 22 and 47 years old. Helma, do you think you will have a problem with a family affair? Helma answered that she didn't think so.

They will be arriving in the morning. Besides several very armed guards, a fellow sister, Jane will be with them. She has been apart of the sisterhood for several years. She is almost a cruel as you are. I want you to play off of her and the both of you can learn each others tricks.

This will be your first actual interrogation and you will be going off and doing them for others at their location.

Wolfgang described the younger one as having the information. She is either a drug Kingpin or the girlfriend of one. It seems that a rival gang didn't like the way their group was cutting in. We are to find out all the information from her as possible. The entire process will be recorded so the group that is paying can see how we handle it.

Helma asked if she is the one with the information, than why the mother? They feel we can use her for leverage. In other words, we torture the mother to get what we need from the daughter. Either way, neither of them will be leaving. According to the paperwork, both are very pretty and we should be able to use this to our advantage. Are there any questions from you right now?

Helma started by asking how much difference there was between this and what we normally do. The ones you have worked on prior have not been rush jobs. The request is that we make this as quickly as possible to get the information need. After the information is confirmed, we can "Play" as much and hard as we want.

Helma, I know this is your first true interrogation, so I want you to take the lead. We will be here if you have any questions. Remember that your Sister is also here and will most likely jump in. Both Frieda and I have the fullest confidence in your skills and zeal to get the job done.

Your interaction with Jane will get around fast and you will most likely be requested often. Some jobs, it will just be you and some of their guards to assist, so go into it and do your very best. Helma turned to them and said I will not let you down. We know that you won't.

Suddenly they heard someone coming into the dungeon. Peering out of the office, Wolfgang was rounding the corner and heading to the office. I just received an up date on this job. Instead of being here in the morning, they should be arriving in several hours. I suggest that you go get lunch and change into your work apparel.

The group went to the dining room and made their selections. Helma, I need to ask, do you have any problems so far. She answered no and she was anticipating the start of the job. Great, have you thought of what you will be wearing? I have thought about it lately. I think I want to be known as the butcher Doctor. I will down scrubs for my work uniform. With a surgical mask on, I should look very scary.

Ilsa received a call from Wolfgang saying they had an hour to arrival. The three went to the loading dock. Just as they opened the door, a truck with four heavily armed guards was backing up to deposit their cargo.

Frieda went to get the laundry cart and joined them. The side door of the truck opened and out jumped Sister Jane. She walked over to Ilsa and they joined in a passionate hug and kiss. She next went to Frieda and the greetings were the same.

As she walked in to the corridor, Ilsa introduced Helma. Jane, this is Helma. She is the newest of the Sisterhood. I think you will get along with her just fine. The two exchanged pleasantries.

The next thing that Jane did surprised Helma. She ran her hand around her breasts and than let it drop down inside the waste band of her scrub pants. She is every bit as lovely as I have heard. I do hope that we can jump into bed when we are done. Helma was only too happy to oblige.

Ilsa butted in and said should we get started. Jane shock her head yes and the cart was rolled onto the back of the truck. The four of soldiers there shouldered their weapons and picked up the limp bodies of the two women. Without any care, each body hit the bottom of the cart and a sheet was place over the pair.

Jane turned to Helma and handed her the antidote. Once we have them secure, five cc's each will awaken them from their sleep. I know you are a doctor and understand what we gave them. By the way, I love the Doctor idea and know it will bring praise from her employers.

The four guards did all the heavy lifting of shuffling the cart down the ramp. Frieda was there waiting for them and opened the door. Helma instructed them to roll it next to the one wall with many rings in the wall. Frieda, could you get me two sets of old rusty shackles and connecting chains. I want to start them stretched tight on the wall spread eagle. Make sure they are facing out as I want the other to see the pain we are going to use.

The limp pair of women were shackled and than chained tight to the wall. They were left with only being able to touch the floor tip toe. Helma approached the pair and ran her gloved hand around all the crevices and up to the large breasts. I do believe it will be a waste to destroy this beautiful woman flesh, but so what.

Helma asked Jane if she know much about the women. I have a little information. They are very close and should be very interested in not letting the other suffer too much. I think we should be able to use this against them. Do you think the younger one is the leader? Yes we do as she has been observed holding the meetings with the local pushers.

What about the mother? Is she involved in the drug trade? Jane answered that most likely she knows nothing about it. Just by being the mother, she lost. I think I want them both gagged for the warm up I have planned. Also, I will need one of the one foot by three feet benches. Frieda answered right away and took one of the guards to the upper dungeon storage rooms.

When everything was ready to Helma's requirements, she took the syringes and gave each woman their shot to awaken them. With her surgical mask on and her hands gloved she waited for movement. Slowly both women arose from the drugged sleep. Good, I see that you are with us now.

Standing between them, she spoke in the meanest voice she had. Welcome to my operating room. I am the butcher Doctor and will be working on you. As I am sure you know well why you are here, I advise you to give us the information quickly.

The look on the mother's face told the whole story. From behind the gag she pleaded to know why she was there with her daughter. She than looked down and found herself naked. Well I will tell you. Your daughter is a big drug dealer and has stepped on others turf. She doesn't want to tell us much about her dealings. So your body will be used to get her to talk.

Your stay here will neither be pleasant or painless. I am a real surgeon and know the ins and outs of your body. With that, Helma took a closed fist and planted into the stomach of each woman. The mother doubled up as much as she could in agony. The daughter was more defiant. She tried to spit on Helma and brought two more slugs to each breast. OH, I can see I will be having fun with you when we finish with your mother troubles.

Turning to Jane, she asked if the guards could be trusted. She said that they were the personnel enforcement squad for the main dealer. Do they want to remain or do we need to find a spot for you to kill time.

No that won't be necessary they have been instructed to watch and report back to their leader. Great, but I want them to place their weapons in our room. They will find several chairs there to watch from over there on the opposite wall.

When all was readied, Helma asked Jane if she wanted to help in the whipping of the pair. Helma went to the wall and selected an eight foot bull whip. Jane just reached into her toy bag and removed a heavy leather flogger with knots on the tip of the twenty tails. Jane turned to Helma and said, let us begin.

Jane started on the breasts of the younger woman. At first she didn't even make a sound, not even a twitch of pain. I guess that she is the hard ass. Several more strikes and she could not hold it in anymore. Even though she tried to muffle her screams, they along with some tears came. Her breasts and nipples started to show lots of red strips.

It was now time for Helma to begin on the mother. I love the tender area of the thighs and the womanhood. The first strike caught her on the upper half of her right leg. A quick response of great pain came from behind the gag. I think we should match the stripe on the left legs. She drew back and let the whip fly. The older woman was now begging for all it was worth not to hurt her anymore. Helma just laughed and coiled the whip for its path to the area between her legs.

The woman was now in uncontrolled fear. Begging and pleading to know why she was to suffer. You are a dumb person. Like I said before, your daughter is the why you are here. This is only he beginning of your suffering. I hope you enjoy the pain as much as all the things your daughter bought for you. The whipping continued for fifteen minutes.

Helma and Jane changed sides and began the working over of the other. As with before, the daughter defied the feel of the whip as long as she could. After several well placed tips of the whip on her pussy lips, she was just about in tears.

Helma said; let me see if this is getting to her. She handed the whip to Jane and preceded to the patch of skin between the daughters legs. At first, she gently rolled the thin lips between her finger, Just as the play was about to bring her to orgasm, Helma grabbed the tender flesh and twisted and yanked on it. This brought the effect she was looking for.

Let me see if your mother is doing as well. Helma again grabbed the mother's lips, bringing wild screams. How about the nipples? With a nipple in each hand, she did the lets tune the radio routine. Back and forth Helma twisted the rosy nipples. You know for an old woman, you still have nicely shaped tips. It sure will be a shame when I have to cut them off and place them in a jar to carry them back to the head man.

She turned to her daughter and tried to ask why she was I this spot. Ilsa stepped up to the mother and back handed her in the mouth. You are here to encourage your daughter to give all the information we need. Only when the warlord is satisfied, will the pain stop. Until than, we have control of your body and its pain. She was now crying and begging again not to hurt her anymore.

Ilsa said to Helma that it was time to kick into high gear. Helma turned and said she wanted the wooden block table moved to the center of the room. Frieda moved it there and secured it in place. The drawer from under the table top was opened and the quantity of wide leather belts was removed. Prepare the two large ones to strap to the top.

Helma motioned to the four guards that their services were needed. I want her taken down from the wall and placed on top of the bench. They approached the older woman, first struck her in the stomach and unchained her from the wall. She cried as she was released and than showed fear in her eyes. Place her on the bench, face up with her head facing this way.

Each of the men took hold of either a wrist or an ankle. They held her down and two wide leather belts were placed over her. One strap went just over her belly button and the other one below her breasts. Once they had her cinched down tightly, Helma pressed the button on the winches, releasing the four cables. The hooks were now hooked to the shackles on her wrists and ankles.

Helma said to stand back. With a touch of the button, the winches took in the slack. The woman's limbs now were pulled outward creating an "X" pattern. In addition to the spread eagle pattern, they were drawn down placing undue pressure on her shoulders and hip. She continues to remove slack, a half inch at a time.

Jane walked over to the woman and felt the pressure on her limbs. She turned to the others and said how great it was. The four women moved in and each caressed a portion of the body. It seems that she was straight only and had never been touched by a female. Helma looked at her in the eyes and said how pretty she was.

Your breasts are so full and soft. It will be such a shame to destroy them a little at a time. Also you pussy will be made into a bloody mess. This can be all over and your soul saved from my vengeance. I have no problem making the pain so intense that you will be begging me to end it.

The woman began crying and begging her daughter to tell them what they needed to know. The daughter just looked at her mother and tried to spit on her. Shut up mother, there is nothing to tell. Ilsa went to the daughter and said that if she didn't talk, she would be replacing her mother in pain. Again, no response was given.

I think it is time to warm her up so we can play. Frieda went to the table and picked up a four foot snake whip. We will start by tenderizing your pussy. The lips are so large and make a delicious target.

The tip met the outer lips and blood curdling screams came from her gagged mouth. Strike after strike was turning the woman into a babbling mess. Several strikes later, Jane went to the lips and pinched the skin up and twisted them. She attempted to shake her fingers loose, only causing Jane to pinch and twist more.

Helma stood over her face and asked if she enjoyed it. She pleaded to not hurt her anymore as she was not involved in her daughters work. I would love to do that, but your daughter isn't interested in relieving you pain. Helma went to the table and picked up a set of linesman's pliers. I bet you nursed your daughter when she was a new born. The tips of the pliers were placed on her left nipple and closed a tight as was possible.

Let me try twisting them back and forth. Her head thrashed back and for, crying at the peak of her lungs. Wow that was fun, let's try the other one. This time, besides twisting, she pulled the tip of her nipple out and away from the breast. Seepage of droops of blood now was coming from the tips. The woman passed out from the pain.

Ilsa went to the daughter and grabbed her face and asked how much pain she was going to put her mother in? The only words to come from her were, piss on my mother. With that comment, Ilsa took out a pair of pliers and repeated the process on her. The tuff daughter just bit her lip and said nothing. I guess that we need to work harder on your mother.

We need to bring the mother around again. Jane took the adjustable cattle prod up from the table. She dialed in the highest setting and stuck the two tips up inside the woman. Jane pressed the button setting the woman into spasms. I see you have joined us again. All laughed and than went over to her. Helma, where do you want to go from here?

Helma went to the table and retrieved the "Pear of Agony". This item is meant to bring out the most in a person. Frieda stood on one side and Ilsa on the other side of her hips. Ladies, please open the cannel so I can insert it deep. She first went to the daughter, showing her the toy. She spun it open and closed. With the four leaves in their open position and pointed to the four points.

Here, I want you to feel how sharp they are. Helma turned the points toward her stomach and pressed them into her flesh. You could see the expression change on her face. I want you to think of how the points will feel as they are plunged deep into your mother's womb. The girl didn't even flinch or show any expression.

She walked over to a position between the mother's wide spread legs. With the pear closed, the tips with its sharp points were started up inside her. The tender flesh up inside of her was heard tearing. Small amounts of blood were seen coming from inside her. Helma pushed harder until it hit bottom.

With the pear fully seated, Helma started the process of spreading its leaves. I want to do this very slowly and bring as much pain to her as possible. Small pieces of each turn were expanding the birth cannel. Helma turned to the daughter and asked, do you think she had to expand it this far delivering you. I will bet that you didn't even cause her anywhere near the pain.

As each full turn of the handle, she looked as if she was pregnant again. Ilsa and Frieda released the lips and began to knead her belly. The pain was extreme and she begged for its removal. Lady, I am sorry, but your daughter has condemned you to the max. I am an OB Surgeon and I can tell you that you are not in extreme pain yet.

Helma pushed the button releasing the cable and it was brought to the handle of the pear. I want to do one more thing prior to hooking her up. I need an electrode to insert in her real hole. Taking the electrode in her left hand, she raised the pear up ward so she could insert it item. The item was pushed deep into her anal passage all the way as far as possible. She let the wire running from its end drop on the floor. When the time is right, I will put it to use.

Jane, would you like to hook up the hook from the cable to the handle of the pear. She took the hook and placed it to the handle. Here, take the box and take out the slack. As the winch ground out the slack, pressure was now being within her. With only several clicks of the button, extreme pressure was being exerted on the opening. With the pear fully expanded, there was little chance of it being pulled out, except if it was ripped out.

The screams coming from the mouth of the woman were those of a wounded animal. Lady, we have only started to inflect pain on you. What you have gotten so far is child's play. They looked at the daughter and asked if she wanted to tell them what they need to know. I will never and I don't care what you do to that bitch. Very well, let's continue.

Helma went to the table and picked up four strips of ten needles each. She handled a strip to each of the four women. Let me show you how I want you to insert them. She removed the cover from the inch and half long syringe needle. She went to the left breast and grabbed the nipple. She grabbed the nipple and inserted the needle in the lower portion of the breast. I love the feel of the popping skin as it enters. If you twist and corkscrew it in, the pain is music to your ears.

One by one the forty needles were inserted, twenty in each breast causing small rivers of blood to surface. I think that this is so much fun. Now rub you hands over the hub of the needles and increase the pain.

Don't worry; this is only the destruction of your breasts. Just think of how much fun it will be to pull them out.

While I start another procedure, I want you to take a wide tip crop and give them a good tap. Jane. I want you to take more slack from the pear. As she placed more pressure on her pelvic area, Helma was hooking up the leads from an electric magneto. To start the games going, she turned the handle on the generator. Shocks of searing pain were sent deep up inside of her. It will take away the attention of the needle work.

I just love doing this to a female. The more I turn the crank, the more she will orgasm. As she turned the handle, the woman began biting her lip, bring tickles of blood. Any information spoke from the daughter yet. The answer was "NO" so let us continue.

First, I need the needles removed. Each woman removed their ten and placed them in a container. I do want to say that what I am about to do to you will totally mess up you very beautiful breasts. Helma selected a pair of thick knitting needles from the table. Holding the nipple out, she inserted the tip of the needle at the base of her breast.

It took a good deal of force to get them totally through. As it exited the other side, screams came at a high volume. Wonderful, it looks so pretty. She went and inserted one on the other side. Now, I want the hook brought down from the ceiling. She hooked a rope around the ends of the knitting needles and than to the hook.

She took up the slack stretching them upward. The pain was now getting so bad, that it was hard to tell when it started or stopped. Helma stepped up to her head and said she was sorry for what was coming. She than turned to Jane and asked if she wanted to do a bar-b-q. I think that will be a great idea. How do you want to start?

By now, I think the charcoal in the brazier should be red hot. Jane took a lump of the fiery coal. You could see he waves of heat coming from the lump. Little streams of smoke rose as she brought it over. Jane asked where she should start. Helma said, it's your call, just make it good.

Jane with the lump in the tongs placed it on the top of her breast. Smoke curled up from the point of contact. The skin started to sizzle and the smell of roasting meat was taken in. Several more pieces were places, causing intense pain.

It is taking a long time to get the answers. Bring me the plumber's torch. Helma lit the torch and brought its blue tip close to the brass leaves of the pear. She flicked the torch back and forth, causing the leaves to heat and turn red. She added several turns of the generator to increase the action.

A shrill voice from the wall was heard. The daughter said that she would talk. I just can't take watching my mother suffer anymore. I will tell you all of the information you want to know. Over the next half hour, she gave them the dates and locations of incoming shipments of drugs. The head guard started to pass on the information to his superiors.

All actives stopped for almost an hour till conformation was received. It checked out and all is good. I am glad to hear this. Jane, what is the next direction you want to do. Since we have the information, it is a full go. The guards went back to their truck and were escorted off the grounds to return home.

Ilsa turned to the others and suggested that they change into some better clothes and take in a good dinner. They returned to their room, quickly showered and dressed. Jane was the same size as Frieda, so she provided a nice set of pants and a top. They went to the staff dining room.

As the four ordered their meal, Wolfgang pulled up a chair and seated himself. Jane, it is nice to see you again. It has been awhile since you were at the Chalet. It is always great to return home for a visit. Helma, she is a sister from many years ago. I forget, were you number eight or number nine? Actually Wolfgang, I was number ten, but who is counting.

So Jane, how do you like your new sister. I think she is a great addition to the sisterhood. I was very impressed with her skills. I had better watch out or she will be replacing me in the history of the sisterhood. Helma, up to you, she was one of our most vicious interrogators in our line up, besides Ilsa and Frieda.

I received a call from our client stating his full appreciation for your fast work. His losses were more in a day than what it cost him to send the pair here. Helma, I trust that you had a good time with them. Yes sir and I intend to finish playing more in the morning. As for tonight, Jane has asked me to spend some quality time in our living room. Gee, can't think of anything to do with her, but I bet we will find something.

They finished their dinner and raised a glass of champagne to toast Helma's first time in charge. Jane added that it was an inspiration to have worked with her. All clanked their glasses together and took in the sweet bubbles. Wolfgang left for his office and the four departed for their room.

Once they arrived, all retreated to their rooms for a hot bath. Helma returned to the living room first. Being totally naked, she took up her place in the center of the stack of pillows. One by one, each of the others entered and took up placed on either side of Helma. Jane turned to Helma and whispered that she liked her better without the scrubs. She ran her fingers thru Helma's silky hair and than they embraced in a very sensual and long kiss. Helma, you are better than even Frieda told me of you.

The rest of the evening was spent in each others arms. The long embraces were mixed with much kissing as well as oral sex. Somewhere in the second hour, Jane took out one of the strap on harness with a twelve inch dildo. She rolled Helma over and began to insert as much as she could into Helma's rear. This brought the reaction she wanted. Helma's breathing went wild as did her panting. Before they all collapsed for the night, the smell of sweet orgasms filled the entire living room.

Day two with the Mother and Daughter

As the sun rose, the women took their showers and departed for the dining room. Jane was first in line saying, I don't normally get this kind of cosine where I am stationed. Just the thought of having real bacon instead of boar hog makes me hunger for the good times. Don't get me wrong, I love the perks where I am stationed.

They ate while having some good girl talk. There time on the on the stacks of pillows was far beyond what she normally got. Jane said it just wasn't the same using a slave girl. They just didn't move or suck as good as the sisterhood women.

As they finished their breakfast, Wolfgang seated himself at the table. Ilsa, I hope that you remember that you have an intense slaved training package next week. Yes sir I do and we have already gone over the applications. Good, no what about our guests downstairs? Now that they have given us as much information as they can, we will start to just have fun with them. I can ensure you that they won't last more than a day or two.

Well, than I will leave your four to your morning coffee. Have a great day of play and just be finished by tomorrow night. Will do and thank you for your gracious hospitality. He asked Jane is she missed being at the Chalet. I do miss it some, but the challenge outside is great.

Frieda, get some of those pastries and a pot of coffee to go. Sure, but why? The two have not eaten or drank anything in several days and the smell should be an additional torture in itself. I will add a plate of bacon to the favorites; anyway, I know how much Jane loves to snack on it.

Frieda retrieved the goodies and the four departed for the lower dungeon. As they went thru the upper dungeon, Helma said she wanted to go to the storage area and retrieve several pieces of equipment to play with. Let me see, there is the electric stimulation fucking machine. She went to the storage cabinet and selected a three inch in diameter by twelve inch long dildo with all the electric strips to shock the inside of the victim. The dildo also was covered in half inch long stainless steel bristles which when used would rip the inside of the female.

This will be a great start, but I will have to come up again to draw more items. She loaded the items on a cart and proceeded down to the lower dungeon. Once down in the main torture room, she went over to the mother on the table and grabbed her extended belly. Looks like you are still pregnant with the "The Pear" inside of you. The woman instantly came alive and Helma gave the cable pulling it from within her a yank. Even though she was exhausted and in pain from the strain on her arms and legs from being pulled all night, she let out loud yelps of pain.

Glad to see you are still with us this morning. For you, I don't anticipate that you will be with us all day. Helma than walked over to the daughter stretched wide spread eagle against the wall. I hope that you were able to watch your mother suffer so badly over night. You are one hell of a daughter to have put her through it.

Never mind, it means nothing to me. What I hope is that you see her go today, your imagination should be thinking of how you will join her. With that, Helma stood back and laid a closed fist directly to her pussy. Cherish the feeling as before I am done with you, there will not be any thing left to feel.

I need to set up your mother for some pleasure. She started by releasing the tension on the line from the winch attached to the pear. A little at a time was slowly loosened and the hook was allowed to be released from the pear. The area where the pear held the skin and organs away from her crouch started to retract. Wonderful, but you still look nine months. I can fix that now.

She turned the screw to slowly relieve the pressure up inside of her. The leaves slowly came back together. First, I want you to feel the points from the ends of the leaves once more. With an open hand, she gave the pear a good hard hit imbedding them in as far as she could. A feeble scream erupted fro the mother's mouth. Good, you still have some feeling in your pussy.

The pear was withdrawn in one quick pull. It was covered with bits and pieces of skin and a slow dribble of blood. For now, I am going to give you a thrill of many orgasms and than will deal with the internal damage. Jane will you assist me? Sure, what do you want me to do.?

Help me roll the fucking machine over and set it up. I need you to screw the dildo attachment on the end of the arm. Helma, I think you selected the right item. I did and can hardly wait to see the effects. Watch as you handle it as the points are sharp and I don't want to repair you also.

The tip was inserted into the already damaged birthing cannel. I think that maybe three inches in will be good to start. Jane made sure that the electric wires from the shocking unit were firmly attached. I think we should start slow and the controls were switched on. The three inch diameter spiked dildo started its journey in and out. Once on every entry as with withdrawal, a hefty shock was given.

Take a good look at your mother expression. She is going to have some of the best orgasms she has ever had. She won't be enjoying them very much, but oh well. Within minutes, little trickles of blood were escaping the vaginal opening. I will tell you that she is loosing a lot of blood, just as you will be shortly.

I think the last thing I want to do to her is introduce her to two of my hunger friends. Helma produced a two part cage in front of the daughter. I call them Chip and George. They are from the stable out back. These large rats are very hungry and haven't eaten in a few days. I wonder where I can find something for them to snack on. Jane, where do you think we should fine them a snack.

Jane pointed to the large breast of the mother. Great idea, they should be a nice meaty snack. As you can see, the cage has a wooden door which slides open to let my friends to their meal. Helma with Jane's help placed the age over the breasts. A large leather strap went over the cage and will hold it firmly on.

Ilsa and Frieda, I want you to count down from ten so I will know when to slide the door open. The count went down till 3, 2, and 1. Helma slowly slid the wooden door open and the eating frenzy started. Inhuman screams were coming from the woman. The long, sharp teeth ripped pieces of the large breast. They even used their sharp claws to assist in the ripping.

Pure hysteria was enveloping her. Blood now spurted from her damaged flesh. Her show was entertaining for the group. I think that this should keep your mother busy for a while. Helma went to the corner and with the help of the others, brought an "X" frame out to the main floor.

Since your mother is kind of having a tea party with her new friends, let us concentrate on you. The younger woman was now punched several times and shot with a stun gun to disable her for several minutes. She was taken down from the wall and placed on the "X" frame.

Her arms and legs were spread wide and four leather belts were placed around each of them. A two inch wide belt held her I place at the middle of the X. I think that this should hold her in place for now. Jane looked at Helma and said that they might need more help to hold her in place. Good idea, what did you have in mind. Jane went to the corner where the X was stored and brought back four heavy and large diameter spikes and a mallet.

Where do you want to start? I think her ankles. She took the first spike, placed on her ankle and drove it through it and into the frame. She handed the mallet to Helma and she did the other ankle. This time it was the daughter instead of the mother that was screaming.

Ilsa and Frieda stepped up and demanded it was their turn to have fun. Ilsa started on the left wrist and drove the spike into the soft flesh and into the wood. Frieda got the privilege of finishing the right wrist. They all stepped back and took in the sight in. Wonderful job was said by all.

I think we should let her take in the pain for a few minutes. There is some unfinished business on the table to tend too. Helma took a look at the minced meat of the woman's breasts. They were mutilated beyond recognition. The rats had long since finished their feast and were in a semi trance. Helma sled the board back across the breasts trapping them in the cage again. She removed the cage and set it aside.

Next to come was the bloody and dripping pussy opening. I guess that I need to do something about that. Jane will you help me remove the dildo from her. They slid the machine away and placed a plastic bag over the blood and skin covered dildo. There was a good deal of blood coming from the opening. I think I will need to suture it up.

Helma selected a curved sewing needle used to repair chair cushions. I think maybe eighteen inch of that twine should do the job.

With the skill of the surgeon she was, Helma began the process of pushing the needle in one side and out of the other pussy lip. A little slip of the cord up and over and she had a nice little knot tying it closed. After ten of these beautiful large sutures, the opening was closed up.

She stood back and said that it was a pretty good job if she did say so. I think your mother is all finished up. The only thing left is to clean up the shredded meat that you most likely sucked on when you were young. Frieda would like the opportunity. She reached for the bottle of 100% pure alcohol and began to pour it over the bloody stumps of her breasts. The woman gave out her final scream and the body went limp. She was finally not feeling any more pain.

Over the next several minutes, the Mothers body was released from the winches and placed in the laundry cart. Helma looked over at the daughter and said that she would be joining her sometime tomorrow. The cart was covered and pushed away to the corner. The wooden block table was also removed, clearing way for the further work on the daughter.

The Daughter's play

The four women each took one of the corners of the X frame. They carried it to the center of the dungeon floor. A section of chain was attached to the frame where her hands had been nailed. Next the cable from the winch from the ceiling brought the cable down and the hook was attached to the chain. Jane took the control box and started to lift her arms off the floor.

As she was raised up, her weight started to fall onto the nailed hands and ankles. The belts which were around her limbs still held her somewhat snug to the frame. Her body was raised to about three feet off the floor.

Ilsa brought over a steel piece of pipe attached to a base plate. She was screwing the same dildo with the stainless steel brush bristles onto the pipe. As she finished installing the tip, she looked up to the daughter and spoke to her. I though we should let you feel the same fun your mother did.

Ilsa positioned the dildo head under the daughter's pussy opening. Jane let her down to just when the tip of the dildo was touching the opening. Wow, this will be a tight squeeze and maybe a little hard to insert. Helma looked the daughter in the eyes and said it will fit, a little at a time.

Frieda and Jane spread her lips as far as possible while Helma made sure the tip impacted into the opening was lined up. The tip sunk into the opening just an inch. Well girl, how does this feel? Your mother at least had the advantage of the Pear of Anguish in her over night. It had expanded the opening to better accept it. Don't worry; you will love it the further down you go.

You will be allowed to settle onto it around one half inch per hour. This will allow you to better know how your mother felt. Meanwhile, we have so many items that you will enjoy. We need to start on your nipples and breasts. Helma placed a step ladder in front of her and was soon at the same level as the breasts. They sure are beautiful and I am truly sorry that I have to destroy them. The daughter began to cry and beg to let her go.

That is impossible you young slug. You made the decision when you decided to try to steal your compactions business for your self. The man you tried to screw is the one that paid for your pain. He even wanted a copy of the tape of your end. So far, he is thrilled with what happened to you and your mother. He has requested that your end be very slow and extremely painful. We always complete the requests we get.

I need to sew a set of rings onto your nipples. She took the same heavy duty needle that was used to close your mother's pussy up. Helma started by pinching the nipple between the fingernails and pulling it tight and away from the breast. Don't scream yet as the needle as not hurt yet. Helma took the tip of the curved needle and punctured the skin behind the nipple and went through the skin and exited the other side. The girl was thrashing her head to and fro trying not to look down.

As she brought the needle around, a two inch in diameter stainless ring had the twine placed through it. This procedure was repeated several times till there was a good attachment. A ring was also sewed to the other nipple having the two rings lying on her chest. Helma turned to Frieda and asked for a two foot piece of the heavy chain to be used to bind the bodies. She attached the ends to the two rings.

Helma let the chain drop allowing the three pounds to drag the breasts and nipples to be stretched. This action got her screaming and wanting mercy. Helma turned to her and in a loud and demanding voice said; your mother asked for mercy many times, but you just kept you mouth closed. You could have kept her from all the pain by just answering the questions. Now it is you turn to experience what she went through.

It is time to drop you down again. The control box button was pushed lowering her down causing the dildo to enter to the point the stainless steel points now were cutting into the soft skin lining of her canal. Does that hurt slut? Before she could answer, Jane started to message the pubic mound, causing the bristles to start to embed themselves.

Wonderful, I am glad to get her stimulated. Ilsa reached up and grabbed the chain and dragged her nipples down more. I think we need some weight for them. Frieda walked up and attached a five pound weight. Helma, with a smirk on her face, placed the cattle prod to her pubic mound and pulled the trigger. The resulting movement caused her to try to jump off the X frame.

We need to add another type of pain. Ilsa retrieved the telephone magneto and cables. The two alligator clips were placed on each pussy lip. While down there, she took hold of the pipe holding the dildo and gave it a shake. Helma turned and told the other three; I just love playing this way. All agreed and began to talk about the ways of increasing all the pain.

We need to start to remove the straps holding her arms and legs against the frame. I think we should start at the ankles. The lowest belts were removed causing more pressure to be applied to the nailed joints. Her shoulders started to shake causing more pressure. This is wonderful, I love it was heard from Jane.

OK, who wants to start with the turning of the magneto handle? We will start with Jane, than Ilsa and finally Frieda. I just want to message the needles inside her opening. The shocks started, in between each shock, Helma took her hand and struck the tender area. The pain increased as they played.

Helma again stood up on the ladder, next to the chained nipples. Frieda, will you let the other cable down from the ceiling. The cable made its way down as Helma made a grab for it. She removed the five pound weight and replaced it with the hook.

Take the slack out of the cable. As you heard the cable being taken up, the pain in her nipples went to its extreme. How much do you want to stretch them upward? Only enough to make them tight and with each lowering of the main winch, she will feel the pull.

I think we need to take a long break and let her hang. She will not expire for some time. I think it is supper time and we will need our strength this evening. They went to the room and changed into normal dinner clothes.

When we return, I want to have some fun in front of her. We should each take one of the large pillows from the living room with us. Helma, are you saying we should play with each other while she suffers? That is exactly what I mean. Never did that before, but it sounds wonderful.

They returned to the dungeon with their pillows. Before we start, we need to remove two more straps. The two next to her wrist are next. With the straps removed, the body was allowed to flail more. I am going to place the winch on the remote timer so it will come down on its own.

The four women got undressed and assembled on the stack on the pillows for play. They placed their arms and hands around each other. Moans could be heard as fingers entered the openings of each other. Wow, you are very sexual active Helma. Jane continued to plunge deep into Helma's love box. Helma returned the favor by using her tongue to clean the love juices out of Jane's love box.

All four women continued to trade partners. This is even better than last night; just the thought of doing it within sight of this condemned woman made it more fun. Helma heard the winch let more cable out bring more screams. The steel bristles were now imbedded firmly inside her. Helma in her naked body made her way to the prisoner.

She rubbed her body against the bear leg of the daughter. The woman was so confused with the pain; she didn't even understand what she was feeling. Instead of just pushing on her pubic mound, Helma took a fist and planted it firmly. I think she is getting used to the feeling of the points up inside of her.

Helma, as the GYN person, how much more can she take. I am

betting that with the amount of blood dripping form her love box, maybe two more hours. I think Just about enough time to do something more painful. I think she has enough strength left to realize what is happening. What do you girls suggest?

Answers came from each of them. Frieda wanted to take branding irons to her ass. Ilsa suggested spraying her with sugar water and dumping red fire ants over her breasts. Jane thought for a minute and wanted to just drop her body down and fully impales her in the dildo. Helma just want to take a scalpel and skin her alive. They all agreed that their answers brought many great ideas.

Jane said that we should just ask the woman how she wanted it to end. A quick look at her and they knew that wasn't going to work. By this time, she was a babbling idiot. I don't even think she even cares, just get it over with. Ilsa said that she most likely wished that she hadn't crossed the other drug lord.

So how do we choose? Frieda looked at each of them and suggested that they should each do a little of each to her. Ilsa agreed that this would be a way to increases her very much in pain at the end. Let us take it so she is impaled and the fire ants at the end. Helma, where do you want to start skinning her? Why don't I do her pubic mound while Frieda you work the red hot irons on her ass cheeks.

The fun started. While Frieda's irons got red hot toasty in the brazier, Helma took a magic marker and drew designs on her pubic mound. Jane come over and said what a wonderful artist Helma was. Helma said she had some art in college but never did much with it.

Frieda was playing with the irons in the fire. She was stirring the red coals, plunging the tips further into the heat. Helma selected a brand new scalpel from the table and started to trace the designs. With her precision as a surgeon, the tracing went just deep enough to break the skin without making it bleed much.

Ilsa was getting a solution of sugar water together. Make it sweet as we want the ants to feast on her as well as the sugar. Don't worry this is one of my favorite interrogation methods. Very well, I have one of the irons hot enough to play. Frieda brought the tip over to the woman's right ass cheek. She very slowly brought it to within an inch of the skin.

She was just feeling the red/white hot tip begin its trip down the firm white skin. It intimately brought swirls of black smoke, and the sound of sizzling skin, bringing the woman to screaming life. Down the tip went till it reached the top of her legs. Frieda now stated the she never got tired of seeing the skin blister up.

Your turn Helma, I need to get another hot iron. Helma stepped up and slid the knife under the corner of a square of skin. Once a corner flap was drawn up, she took a pair of tweezers and pulled the flap of skin clear of her mound. Jane checked out the work and complimented her on the precision used. Helma responded it's a piece of cake. I can do this all day.

Over the next hour or so, both Helma and Frieda continued to press the tips of the hot iron on her ass cheeks. Helma was removing thin layers of the skin and placing them in a bottle. I guess I just want a souvenir of my first time. Ilsa interrupted the fun the two were having and said it is our turn before she fades into the next life.

Very well if you must, at this point both Frieda and Helma moved back from what was left of the woman.

Ilsa got up on the ladder and whispered to the woman. I think that you learned your lesson the hard way. All you're suffering should be over in less than an hour. With that said she said this is for the suffering you put your mother through. Ilsa twisted the lid on the jar and than dumped the red fire ants over what was left of her breasts. As it was, the stress of having her nipples pulled over the last hours made her breasts stand out in large mounds.

The effect of the ants was instant. With what little was left in her, she tried to scream, but nothing cane. She was over whelmed by what was being done to her. The ants worked their way to the area stripped clean by Helma's knife. The venom from the ants entered her skin quickly and was an instant jolt to her system. Jane said; stand clear as I am going to start to drop her.

Jane over rode controls of the auto drop of a half inch an hour. She set the controls to a half inch every five minutes. Her body started to drop, causing the dildo to insert itself deeper within the womanhood. The metal bristles were raking the inner layer of tissue causing blood to flow a more rapid pace. Even the strain on the tied up nipples was ripping the flesh at an increased pace.

The pace that the body racked with the pain increased rapidly. Every bit of her was in tremendous pain. The mussels in her legs and arms twitched and the hands and feet were trying to tear themselves from their spikes. The four interrogators stood back and patted each other on the back at the show they made. The last cry of life was heard from the woman. Her head slumped back and than fell down to her chin.

There were no signs of movement over the next five minutes. Helma went to the woman and said, well, she is gone. Jane spoke up saying that she took much more than she thought she would. Ilsa took her phone and informed Wolfgang that it was over and all that was left was to take both women to the crematorium.

Wolfgang told Ilsa that he was satisfied with their work. I have been watching as was Carl. We even had a live feed going to the War Lord. He was so excited that he authorized a ten thousand bonus to split between the four of you. When you finish, both Carl and I want to meet with you. One thing first, please make sure you go to your room and clean up. Ilsa said she understood the request as they all stunk from the work.

Jane finished lowering the body to the floor. The remaining belts were removed and a crowbar was used to take the spikes from her hands and ankles. Frieda wheeled the laundry with the mother's body to the limp, very dead body of the daughter. The four of them lifted it and placed it next to the mother's body. Ilsa went and got the truck and backed it up the dock door.

With a good push, the cart with the bodies within was loaded and the tail gate was raised up. Ilsa and Frieda rode in the front seat while Jane and Helma in the back with the cart. The trip was short and the bodies disposed of in the typical manor. The trip back to the Chalet was quiet. All were tired from the long hours of work.

Per Wolfgang's instructions, all four went to their room and sunk into a hot bubble bath. Ilsa and Frieda emerged first. Helma was next and Jane said she enjoyed the bubble tub as she didn't have access to one where she was stationed. When all were dressed, Ilsa called Wolfgang and stated they were clean and smelled much better than over the last several days. He told her they could meet in an hour.

The four women arrived at his office and were told the meeting was changed to Carl's office. The four proceeded to Carl's private suite and knocked. Wolfgang opened the door and said to come in and be seated. When they were seated, he closed the sound proof door and went and told Carl all were ready. Carl entered and had a seat at his desk.

He spoke to them and said how great they worked together. They all thanked him for his comments. I can see that I have a good team of workers here. Helma, how do you feel after your first interrogation as a Sisterhood member? Helma responded that she felt good with her work and was happy she decided to join. Carl than told her that it would not be the last one and be prepared to travel all over the world and do her specialized work.

Helma's Career

The days, weeks and months passed by very fast for Helma. Her day to day actives of the programs as well as being the Chalet doctor brought her a warm feeling of closeness to the group. As her reputation as the Butcher Doctor spread, she was in great demand. She traveled the world performing the many duties given to her. On many occasions, both Carl and Wolfgang would call her into their offices and commend her on her work. Her job would go on for many years. She never once regretted leaving her practice or her private patients. Not once did she utter her favorite phrase "I hate this place".

Printed in the United States
By Bookmasters